Arthur Meeker, Jr.

The Far Away Music

Books by Arthur Meeker, Jr.

THE IVORY MISCHIEF

THE FAR AWAY MUSIC

IF *a man does not keep pace with his companions, perhaps it is because he hears a different drummer. Let him step to the music which he hears, however measured or far away.*

—Henry David Thoreau

THE

Far Away Music

ARTHUR MEEKER, JR.

HOUGHTON MIFFLIN COMPANY · BOSTON

The Riverside Press Cambridge

The Riverside Press
CAMBRIDGE · MASSACHUSETTS
PRINTED IN THE U.S.A.

࿐

This book is dedicated

To the memory of my great-grandfather

Edwin Eugene Griggs (1808 — ?)

Without whom I should have had no story to tell

And with grateful affection to my aunt

Margaret Beekman Meeker Cook

Without whom I should have been unable to tell my story.

࿐

Prefatory Note

THE AUTHOR'S RELATIVES will doubtless discover, sometimes in altered form, scraps of legend and traditional stories that are familiar to them all as parts of our ancestors' history. The author, however, would like to remind them that they are only scraps. 'The Far Away Music' may be a footnote to a family saga, but it is also a novel: none of the characters in it is intended to be a portrait of any actual person, living or dead; nor do these fictional characters' fictional actions bear more than a tenuous resemblance to their factual counterparts that are matters of record.

Contents

One Fine Sunday Morning	1
The Little White House in State Street	9
Aunt Betsy at Breakfast	21
The Bascombs at Dinner	30
The Forty-Niners	43
In My Ladies' Chamber	56
The Two Young Men from Hamilton College	67
The Closed Door	85
The Concert	98
A Week in the Country	116
Aunt Zeph	131
The North Meadow	147
The Excursion	157
The Spiritual Rappers	175
The Letter	189
The Family	203
September Afternoon	220
The Party	240
Papa's Story	262
The Wedding	284
The End	300

The Far Away Music

One Fine Sunday Morning

O NE FINE SUNDAY MORNING towards the end of June, 1856, Jonathan Trigg walked out of the Lake House at the north end of the Rush Street ferry in Chicago.

It was not long after dawn. The sky was a clear, soft blue, flecked with scraps of cloud still pink from the sunrise. A breeze blew just hard enough to flutter the flag on the cupola that crowned the hotel. The short, choppy Michigan waves, each with its diamond crest, were dancing in this same breeze; Jonathan had been watching them a few minutes ago from his bedroom window. But from here in the street they were invisible. The Lake House belied its name; it was near the lake, but not on it; the big, irregular, white-painted brick oblong even turned its back on the river. The elaborate front steps flanked by marble columns faced north, commanding nothing more picturesque than a row of small houses across the street.

Such stupidity could not help bringing its own punishment with it. It was no wonder that the hotel, once the pride of the West, had been outstripped by its competitors, the Tremont House and the Sherman, which had been clever enough to offer urban luxury and convenience in place of the profitless beauty of location they could not afford.

But many old-time travellers, untroubled by its remoteness or the shabby accommodations, still loved the Lake House. Jonathan, quite possibly, shared this affection. It had undoubtedly been his first thought on arriving in the city by steamboat the previous day. He had not heeded the stare of the cabdriver, who had volunteered the information that folks passing through town most generally didn't care about crossing the river.

'*The Lake House, please,*' Jonathan repeated, adding in his limpid, rather precise baritone: 'And you need not be all day about it; I'm in somewhat of a hurry.'

'Yes, sir; of course, sir' — and the cabby had not dared say more, though he stared harder than ever.

His curiosity would have been further aroused could he have seen his fare at this moment. Chicago of the thirties and forties had been used to the spectacle of men and women, too, in all kinds of unconventional clothes; but frontier days were past, especially since the opening of the new railway to the East; citizens and travellers alike were expected to look as civilized and well-tailored as natives of older parts of the country.

Perhaps, however, Jonathan would have attracted attention less on account of the way he was dressed than because he wore his theatrical outfit with an air of slightly swaggering assurance. He was not tall — barely five feet eight, though his high leather boots with their thick soles and heels added another inch to his height — but he carried himself as straight, if not as stiffly, as a soldier; slim yet stalwart, he had the compact strength of a man used to an outdoor life, and not an easy one.

His shirt was of bright red flannel, open at the neck; his black cloth breeches fitted neatly into the tops of his boots; a wide-brimmed hat of the style affected by gamblers was jammed, with studied carelessness, on his curly pate. Jonathan's hair, heavily grizzled at the temples, was almost as black as his hat and his breeches. It was crisp and coarse and looked sturdily independent, like its owner. His eyes were dark blue and piercing under strongly marked brows; his face was tanned, his mouth full-lipped; sharp vertical lines ran down from the corners of both nostrils, giving his expression a melancholy cast. On the whole, his appearance was unusual enough to prove arresting anywhere — but this morning there was none to observe it. Being early and a Sunday, an aspect of peace and pleasant withdrawal brooded in the summer air over the North Division.

Jonathan did not seem to be depressed by his solitary condition. Whistling cheerily, he strolled round the corner into Rush Street and covered the few remaining feet that divided him from the river.

Here an admirable panorama came into sight. Jonathan might have been recalling an old fancy that the distant prospect of Chicago bore a striking likeness to pictures of Dutch towns, their high jumble of

2

shipping etched against a background of belfries and sober brick houses. This likeness time had increased. There were more belfries, more brick houses than before; the grey-green river was even fuller of tall-masted brigs and schooners. True, there were modern paddle-wheel steamers amongst them — Jonathan could read the names of the *Lady Elgin*, the *Ontonagon*, the *Queen of the West*, as he drew near the brink. It was true, also, that the large warehouses and grain-elevators dominating the banks did not look specifically Dutch. But Fort Dearborn was still there, adjoining the south ferry landing . . . at least, on closer appraisal, *part* of Fort Dearborn. The stockade was intact, and the block-house, and the giant spreading honey-locust tree that shaded the latter — but the main buildings, the balconied officers' quarters, were gone. The little old whitewashed stone lighthouse and the stone cottage in which the lighthouse-keeper lived stood as they always had directly outside the stockade, though they were no longer in use. (That Jonathan had ascertained the night before from his hotel room, whence he had caught a glimpse of the new lighthouse flashing its beams far out at the end of the breakwater, where the river was lost in the lake.)

At the landing, it was obvious that the ferryboat lay on the opposite side — the same flat-bottomed tub that had been in service for years. Jonathan cupped his hands to his mouth and gave a shout. Immediately the ferryman appeared from behind the stockade, climbed aboard, pushed off from the muddy bank, and slowly, hand-over-hand on the rope, propelled his clumsy craft across the river.

This was old Bill, the hoary Irishman who had been running the Lake House ferry since the beginning of time. Before the boat reached the landing Jonathan pulled his wide-brimmed hat down over his eyes, as if to avoid being recognized. If that were his intention, he was successful, as the ferryman's first words made clear.

'Good day, stranger,' said Bill; 'and where might I be takin' you on this fine summer morning?'

Jonathan probably felt that this question was too silly to answer, for he gave an unintelligible grunt and sprang aboard before the boat had quite touched the pier.

'Mind what you're doin' now!' exclaimed Bill.

Plainly disappointed that his passenger was disinclined to talk, he still could not resist beguiling the brief trip with a few stereotyped

3

remarks he conceived it his privilege to utter in his well-known rôle of quaint old character.

'Are you stayin' at the Lake House, sir?' he began.

'Yes,' said Jonathan.

'And have you stayed there before?'

'Yes,' said Jonathan.

'Then you know Chicago well, I suppose?'

'You suppose right,' said Jonathan.

'Ah, but you've not been here lately, I dare say. If you had, I'd remember you. I'm a rare hand at rememberin' faces. Well, sir, what I always say is, if you've been away from the city for more than a twelvemonth, I'll warrant you'll lose yourself the first time you leave the hotel. Sure, there never was such a place for growin'! Mushrooms ain't in it. They're talkin' now of doin' away with the ferry altogether and buildin' a grand new bridge made of iron that'd swing about to let the boats through. Not that I take much stock in *that*. . . . Why, d'you know, when first I came here, thirty years ago, there was nothin' at all outside of the fort but wild painted savages and a row of log huts — and the river was bordered with trees, pretty as a picture, and the houses along the shore had gardens runnin' straight down to the water behind them, so they did. You'd never believe that now, would you?'

'Yes,' said Jonathan, 'I would.'

By this time they had reached the south bank.

He jumped ashore and turned to toss a tip to the ferryman.

'I used to live in one of those houses myself.'

Before Bill had taken this in, Mr. Trigg vanished round the corner of the lighthouse-keeper's deserted stone lodge. For a moment or two he walked fast, breathing hard; but as soon as it was certain that no one was following him, he slackened his pace and showed no desire to hurry away from the river.

If what he had told Bill the ferryman were true, there was much to ponder over, many mental reconstructions to make, before he could find traces of the primitive Chicago of long ago in the bustling, progressive Chicago of today. Gardens no longer edged the waterfront anywhere; there were no trees except the honey-locust inside the crumbling stockade of the fort. The entrance to the stockade was barred by rusty pieces of wire tacked untidily across the gap in the

4

boards, but Jonathan gazed tenderly at the drooping, feathery branches, as if this lone survivor of the past had some special significance for him. He was also, however, apparently deeply interested in what was new. The almost continuous line of docks, the tangled mass of shipping, the towering warehouses, all received keen inspection. One of the warehouses, an aggressive brick building rising abruptly from the river, with an entrance in South Water Street and a large sign in gold letters over it reading:

CHARLES BASCOMB AND COMPANY
SHIPPING AGENTS — WHOLESALE GRAIN MERCHANTS
COAL AND PIG-IRON

he examined with particular earnestness. He surveyed it from the front, from both sides, and as nearly from the back as the river permitted. Indeed, he was induced to move on only by the appearance of two men, probably labourers at the docks, who glanced at him inquisitively.

Since it was patently Jonathan's strongest wish to avoid being engaged in conversation, he marched off forthwith, humming in an off-hand manner the words of the song he'd been whistling when he came out of the Lake House:

> '*Way down in de meadow,*
> *'Twas dere I mowed de hay;*
> *I always work de harder*
> *When I think ob lubly Mae . . .*'

Still singing, he made his way south to the beginning of Michigan Avenue, nor did he pause till he had reached Randolph Street, where the lake front suddenly opened out before him.

To the right stretched the green rectangle of Dearborn Park, enclosed by railings and planted with shrubbery and young trees. Beyond that, a line of handsome private dwellings led still farther south, each with its prim iron-fenced front yard and back garden plumed with elms and maples.

To the left, on the other side of the avenue, lay another long strip of park paralleling the beach; then the narrow pale blue lagoon dotted with pleasure-craft, sailboats and rowboats tugging gently at their anchor-lines in the fresh breeze that ruffled its surface. Outside the lagoon was the stone breakwater guarding the railroad; and outside the breakwater, the deeper blue of Lake Michigan.

As Jonathan swung down the avenue a train of cars led by a gay, snorting little steam-engine rolled along the track inside the breakwater and puffed importantly to a stop, with a shriek and a grinding of brakes, not a hundred yards from where he stood. His amazement at this unprecedented occurrence gave place to nervousness as he observed the crowd of passengers alighting, the row of hacks and omnibuses awaiting them, as well as a general increase in activity owing to the advancing hour and his gradual approach to the centre of the city. Dogs barked; a boy ran past him chasing a hoop; up over the trees of Dearborn Park rattled a flock of pigeons. The sound of bells came from the distant steeple of Saint Mary's Catholic Church on Wabash Avenue. Along the lake front several couples were strolling, while a man standing on the deck of one of the little boats in the lagoon hoisted his sail to the breeze. Chicago had waked up!

Jonathan cut across the park by a diagonal path, emerging behind the big speckled Presbyterian Church, and followed the creaking wooden sidewalk into the heart of the residence section of the South Division.

Now for the first time since quitting the hotel he began to show hesitation.

He still walked, but less briskly; the song about 'Lubly Mae' was no longer even a whistle; by the time he reached leafy Wabash Avenue all his former jauntiness had left him.

Slowly he covered another block, then halted at the corner, almost colliding with a Negro youth holding a basket of cherries, who was sauntering along at a pace even more leisurely than Mr. Trigg's and with far less regard for where it might take him.

"Scuse me, boss!"

But Jonathan had not noticed: it was clear that at last he had reached the end of his pilgrimage.

Chicagoans of the fifties found it humorous to reflect that their chief north-and-south thoroughfare was called State Street. It could not be denied that its width at the northern end was twice that of its rivals; the view looking north, too, from where Jonathan was, seemed splendidly closed by Market Hall, a fine brick-and-stone building with an

6

openwork steeple supposed to be an exact copy of Faneuil Hall in Boston. But the street was unpaved and perpetually muddy, and except for the market, which stood in the middle of it at the corner of Randolph, it had no landmarks worth mention. The houses were small and straggling, for the most part one- or two-storeyed wooden cottages. South of Washington they became even smaller — rather shanties than cottages — the roadway between them full of dust and dogs and barefoot children. Lake Street was the business centre; Washington, sanctuary of God; Wabash and Michigan Avenues, the abodes of the wealthy. But State Street obviously was an humble relation, tolerated only because it led to the city's breadbasket.

After standing for several minutes on the corner, Jonathan crossed State Street, turned north towards the market, and halted once more in front of a cottage in no way distinguished from its neighbours. It was one of perhaps half-a-dozen on the west side of the street, no two precisely alike, but all bearing a depressing family resemblance. Fenced in by wooden pickets, there was a gate in the middle of the fence, and a row of honeysuckle bushes just coming into bloom behind it. A narrow bit of yard in front and a narrow bit of garden at the back were both sprinkled haphazardly with shrubs and an occasional discouraged maple tree. The house itself was narrow, two-storeyed, white-painted, with a high-pitched roof and a flight of ten steps leading to the front porch.

Jonathan did not hesitate any longer. Almost as though he preferred not to pause for fear of faltering in his purpose, he pushed the gate open, tramped up the path; then, at the very foot of the steps, changed his mind about mounting them and deflected his course across the lawn to the rear.

There had been no signs of life at the front of the house. The door was shut, the blinds were drawn. The sharpest observer could not have told whether anyone were up and about. But in the back garden a bucket half full of water stood under the dripping pump; some speckled hens were scratching in the earth beneath two of the maple trees; best of all, the back door, level with the ground, was ajar: if Jonathan had a mind to enter unannounced, nothing would hinder him.

That, it appeared, was his intention. He took off the wide-brimmed black hat, passed his hand over his curls to smooth them as best he was

7

able — as he did so it could be seen that his brow was beaded with sweat, though the day was scarcely warm enough to warrant it. After this, with a smothered exclamation, he squared his shoulders, flung up his head, and strode boldly through the doorway into the kitchen.

For a moment nothing happened. Then a long, loud shriek from within broke the Sunday hush of State Street.

The Little White House
in State Street

WHEN LOULIE TRIGG opened her round blue eyes that morning she was immediately sure she was the only person in the house who was awake.

This she could tell by various signs: the yellow slant of the sunbeams striking through the partly open window, the absence of traffic in the street that was not merely because it was Sunday, a certain mysterious quiet within, as if the house were holding its breath. . . . It was the first time Loulie could remember waking so early. Generally she slept until she was called, and often Mamma or Nancy had to pull her out of bed.

It was also the first time she had ever slept alone. Till yesterday she and Nancy had shared the big black-walnut bed in the back room that was called the Red Room, though the chintz hangings to which it owed its name had long since faded to a muddy, hesitant pink. Nor had it been intended originally for her to change now; this little corner, scarcely more than a closet, with its miniature window overlooking the garden, had been made ready for Sissy, just home after three years at boarding-school in the East. Sissy had not asked for it — Sissy never asked for anything — but it had been felt she deserved a room of her own, now that she was eighteen and engaged to be married (though Loulie could not help thinking the dignity of this crowning achievement diminished by the fact that her eldest sister's betrothed was only Aaron Miles, whom they had all known for years).

She had taken part with enthusiasm, nevertheless, in the absorbing task of transforming the old sewing-room. Mamma had bought a few

9

yards of crisp white muslin at the summer sales and, with Aunt Jane's help, made some new curtains and a bedspread. Aunt Bertha, who had more furniture stored in the attic of the big house on Michigan Avenue than she could possibly use, sent over a whole set — bedstead, chest, and chairs of pretty fawn-coloured maple. She had also given them a dressing-table with an elegant oval mirror that could be tilted as one chose. Nancy contributed a bouquet of red roses in a blue opaline jar, faintly chipped, as were all Nancy's possessions; Loulie, a satin pin-cushion with a cross-stitched cover (her own handiwork, painfully constructed in the long spring evenings under Mamma's expert eye). Aunt Betsy, who lived in the country, wrote that she was bringing her niece a china washbowl and pitcher painted — by Aunt Betsy herself, a graduate of the course of instruction in *Godey's Lady's Book* — with a design of daisies and clover.

When it was finished the room looked really charming, even without Aunt Betsy's bowl and pitcher. Sissy had swept in to inspect it as soon as she arrived, slim and stylish in her grey French barèges travelling-dress and shawl, straw bonnet with pert little clusters of plumes, and (actually!) a pair of gold hoops in her ears. It was the gold hoops that made Loulie realize that Sissy was grown-up now. The younger girls — for Nancy, too, though sixteen past, felt suddenly immature — hung back in the hall, too shy to follow, until Sissy saw what the matter was and dragged them in after her, crying out that she was the same Sissy still, even if her hair was braided up and her skirts touched the floor. She looked at everything, exclaimed aloud in admiration, thanked them all for their beautiful presents; but then she said: 'I like it so much — it's perfect — prettier far than the Turnhams' best bedroom in Utica — but would you mind a great deal if I didn't sleep here to-night? After three years away Nancy and I have so much to say to each other. You know, I've not long to be with her now, if Aaron and I get married next winter!'

Mamma, for once disposed to indulgence, had sanctioned the change. . . . 'That is, children, if you promise not to sit up till all hours talking . . .' and Sissy had said of course they would not. But, equally of course, they had. Every time Loulie waked, she saw the line of light burning steadily under her door (for the sewing-room connected with the Red Room), heard the untiring murmur of voices. . . .

10

But it wasn't that that made her restless — no, nor even the fact that Aunt Bertha's mattress was rather hard. The reason was yet another in Loulie's astonishing series of new experiences: last night was the first time in her life she had had to go to bed without her supper.

Poor Loulie! She had meant it for the best. (Nancy, to tease her, sometimes said she was too stupid to mean anything else.) She often helped Mamma when Susan was out; this time there seemed more reason than ever to make herself useful, since Mamma and Nancy were gone to the station to meet Sissy, and there had not been room in the landau for Loulie. At least, Uncle Charles and Aunt Bertha had said there was not, and it was their landau.

At eleven years old, such exclusion bordered on tragedy. It was to keep herself from crying that Loulie decided to set the table while Susan was at the market.

Rather to her own surprise, all went ominously well. The appropriate cups and saucers and plates, the right number of knives and forks and spoons, were conveyed to their places without mishap. Loulie even fetched the white china hen with the red crest that was used to cover the boiled-egg dish, and arranged a few pansies she found in the garden in the best cut-glass bowl for a centrepiece. Then, alas! as Susan was still out, she began thinking how nice it would be if some of the food were brought in, too. . . . The first thing she spied on the larder shelf was a large cherry-pie, juicy and flushed with crimson triumph. Mamma had taken it out of the oven just before leaving for the station; in fact, the crust was still warm, Loulie discovered, as she nibbled a loose crumb. . . . This pie was intended to serve as the climax of the supper-party in honour of Sissy's return — well blanketed, of course, with sour-cream sauce, as the Bascombs preferred it. Uncle Caleb and Uncle Charles, Aunt Jane and Aunt Bertha (who had been wives of Bascombs long enough to have 'learned how to live,' as Uncle Charles put it), as well as Mamma and Aunt Betsy, born Bascombs both, though they'd married a Trigg and a Walworth, respectively, and survived them, all maintained that cherry-pie *without* sour-cream sauce was not fit to eat.

Loulie, too, was fond of cherry-pie. Wistfully she eyed its sticky splendours, scarcely dared stretch out her hand to lift the plate off the shelf. . . . Better if she'd never tried; for Susan's slamming the kitchen door, her loud voice calling out as she crossed the threshold, startled the child into dropping the treasure face down — of course, it *would* have to be face down! — on the larder floor.

When Mamma came back from the station, she found Loulie in floods of repentant tears. There was no disguising the enormity of her sin. Mamma was very angry, and she had a right to be. The pie was quite spoilt. Fortunately, there was another in reserve — an apple-pie, left from yesterday's dinner. It was a good pie, too, with a brown flaky crust and spicily seasoned fruit; but it wasn't what Mamma had wanted for her party. She talked about it all evening, lamenting the lost cherries and exclaiming what a pity it was to waste so much sauce — for naturally sour cream was unthinkable with apples!

The Uncles and Aunts lamented, too, when they arrived for supper full of happy anticipation and learned of the catastrophe. For they had been told beforehand what they were to enjoy; Mamma had promised them a treat, as soon as Aunt Betsy had stripped her trees out on the farm. The combination would have been ideal, for Betsy's trees were the best in the county, but Betsy's crusts were unreliable; whereas Julia (who was Mamma) was an unexcelled baker. . . . 'I ate no sweet at noon on purpose,' mournfully announced Uncle Caleb; while Aunt Jane, who suffered from a weak stomach, remarked, also in a minor key, that she really need not have bothered to bring that bottle of Perry Davis's Pain Killer, for apples agreed with her perfectly.

Little else but the pie was discussed during supper; it seemed as though its loss had overshadowed their pleasure at Sissy's return.

Loulie, however, heard only distant echoes of these elegies. She was upstairs in Aunt Bertha's maple bed, dismissed in disgrace. Mamma had been sorry, but firm about it. She would not listen even to Sissy's coaxing. . . . 'Oh, please, ma'am, on my first night home . . .'

Some time later, after Loulie had already dozed off several times in spite of her hunger, Sissy tiptoed into the darkened room with a slice of the despised apple-pie on a saucer. . . . 'There, dearie, can you see to eat it? I daren't light the candle.' And she kissed the round, tear-stained face tenderly before slipping out again.

Loulie found no fault with the apple-pie. She gobbled it up in a trice and went to sleep comforted . . . but that had been hours ago. Now she was hungry all over again!

She sat up in bed and wrinkled her snub freckled nose as a delicious fragrance stole up the stairs. Susan must have come in without making her usual clatter and started frying crullers in the kitchen. The smell was almost too good to bear! Breakfast would not be for an hour yet; Loulie did not see how she could possibly wait until then. She had never got dressed before without Nancy's help, but it did not take long to wash her hands and face and twist her long, straight hair into two molasses-brown braids. After her underclothes came her lace-embroidered pantalettes. Then her Sunday frock, a pink muslin. The rows of buttons in the back she managed to fasten pretty well except for a few in the middle her short plump arms could not reach; but the sash was another matter. If she couldn't see it, she couldn't knot it; and strain and stretch as she would . . . Oh, dear! Nancy had told her, only yesterday, that without a sash she looked like a parcel that needed tying.

Outside the Red Room she stopped and listened, but all was quiet. The older girls, worn out by their conversational night, must still be sleeping. And the door to Mamma's room was open, but Mamma was not there. Loulie had forgotten till that moment that Aunt Betsy was expected by the early train; no doubt Mamma had gone to the Galena and Chicago Union depot to meet her. Aunt Betsy was apt to be hurt if she weren't met; besides, no matter how short her visit, there were sure to be numbers of boxes. She always said she could take the Parmelee omnibus, but she never did; and since it was unlikely that Uncle Charles should have offered the landau this early, Mamma had probably ordered a cab. Well, there was no help for it: Susan would have to lend a hand.

On the top step Loulie was halted by a cry from below — a very loud cry indeed, for it came all the way from the cellar, where the kitchen was. Yet it was certain who had cried. Susan might be a small person, but her voice was exceedingly resonant.

'Help!' shouted Susan. 'Murder! Murder! Help!'

She continued her racket while Loulie, still clutching her sash, sped valiantly to the rescue. Afterwards, Sissy had kissed her and told her how brave she had been, though Nancy had laughed and said: 'Brave? Pshaw! She's not clever enough to know when she ought to be afraid!' But that was not true: Loulie was very much afraid. She ran down only

13

because she felt she'd rather see the worst for herself than stay upstairs and not be sure what was happening.

'A burglar! It must be a burglar!' she thought.

When she got as far as the front hall there were sounds of commotion as well as Susan's screams, and as she opened the door that led to the kitchen stairs there was a heavy crash, as of something falling. (What if it were the kettle of crullers? Or, worse still, Susan herself?)

In the kitchen Loulie found the situation less alarming than she had feared. Susan was neither dead nor dying: she had backed into the space behind the larder door and was trying to shut herself up in it; her familiar florid countenance under the mop of sandy hair seemed reassuringly much as usual. It was only a pile of plates that had fallen, tin ones, which accounted for the clatter. The kettle was still on the stove, the crullers still frying merrily in their sea of fat — but there was a strange man standing beside them. As Loulie appeared he reached in a long fork, speared a cruller, held it smoking in the air until it had partly cooled, and then took a bite out of it.

'Excellent!' said the man. 'I haven't tasted anything like that in seven years!'

Loulie paused in the doorway gaping, because she was out of breath after her wild descent, and also because she could not think of anything to say. She was vaguely conscious that she had torn the lace on one of her pantalettes. . . .

On second thoughts, she had not finished being frightened, either.

If the man were not a burglar, he looked exactly as Loulie supposed burglars must look. He wore no cravat, his shirt was bright red, his boots were tall and black and sinister; his face, too, was as dark as a gypsy's.

At least, as far as she could tell, he had no gun.

As he stood there munching the cruller he nodded and smiled at Loulie — but his smile was the most startling thing about him: a sudden white flash in that gypsy-face.

'How do you do?' said the man. 'Let me see, now — who are you? I believe — bless my soul! Is it possible? — Yes — *you* must be Louise.'

'They call me Loulie,' said that young person automatically.

'They *would*,' said the man. 'Never mind — Loulie be it, then.'

14

'But,' said Loulie, after turning this over, 'how do you know my name? And who are *you?*'

'Who is he? A housebreaker, no more nor less!' exclaimed Susan, who by this time had recovered her courage and advanced from behind the door, holding a cooking-spoon like a bayonet. 'A common thief, that's what he is! Why, he wa'n't in the kitchen more'n a minute before he had that there fork out o' my hand. Don't you pay him no notice, Loulie dear — the hull thing's a trick to git you distracted while his pardner robs the house. Murder! Help!'

'Partner!' said Loulie, to whom this was a new thought. 'Where's his partner, Susan?'

'I ha'n't seen him yet,' replied Susan. 'That's what makes it all the worser. Don't I tell you it's a trick?'

'I'm quite alone, really,' said the man. 'And I haven't a gun, I assure you. I'm sorry for that, in a way — I meant to bring one — it only needed that . . . but I'm afraid I forgot it. Have a cruller?'

He speared another cake from the cauldron and extended it with a friendly smile — but Susan shrieked again.

'I'll send for the police!' she declared, belying her words by retreating once more towards her corner.

'Loulie will, then. Won't you, Loulie?'

Loulie accepted the proffered cruller before she knew what she was doing, and bit into it: it was very hot. Her mouth was too full for her to try to speak, but Susan more than made up for that.

'Git away from here, do!' cried Susan. 'Git off o' these premises this minute, or I'll send for the police, I tell you! Ain't you ashamed o' yourself stealin' honest folks' food an' frightenin' innocent children out o' their wits?'

'Why, you're not frightened, Loulie, are you?' said the man pleasantly.

Loulie shook her head. It was odd, but she really was not afraid any more. She was still, however, unable to speak, having taken a second bite of her cruller.

Susan meanwhile had evolved another idea.

'Oh,' said she, in a gusty stage-whisper that could have been heard, Loulie thought, from one end of Market Hall to the other, 'Mr. Aaron's in the garden next door. I seen him there weedin' when I come in, not

15

half an hour ago. Why didn't I think o' him before? Run, Loulie, there's a good girl, an' tell him to fetch his pa's shotgun an' come over as fast as he can, if he don't want to see the lot o' us dead as so many door-nails!'

Loulie did not run. Seldom inclined to rapid motion (her flight downstairs had surprised her almost as much as it had Susan and the stranger), she was likewise of the opinion that Aaron Miles would be useless in an emergency. Moreover, was this dark man in the red shirt — now blamelessly occupied in skimming the crullers out of the smoking fat by means of a small wire basket — actually so dangerous?

Susan, thwarted, cast away her spoon and wrung her hands.

'Lord save us!' she cried. 'What will Mrs. Trigg say when she gits hum an' finds us all lyin' murdered in our beds? (No, *not* on the plate, for pity's sake — there's a strip o' brown paper beside o' the stove!)'

The stranger looked interested.

'Thank you, Susan,' he said; 'the brown paper, of course; how forgetful of me! Then this *is* Mrs. Trigg's house? I thought it must be, but I wanted to make sure. One kitchen looks very like another, and there might be a number of girls named Louise living in State Street, you know.'

Susan stared suspiciously.

'What's it to you whose house it is?'

'A good deal,' replied the stranger. 'In a way, it's really *my* house, too. I beg your pardon for speaking in riddles. I should have explained before. You see, Mrs. Trigg is my wife. I am Mr. Trigg.'

At that, even Loulie stopped eating her cruller. Nancy might say she was dull, but she could add two and two as well as anyone else.

'Then *you*,' said Loulie slowly, as though to savour the full significance of the tremendous discovery, 'must be my *father!*'

The stranger nodded.

'Precisely, my dear. I'd hoped you might recognize me, but it's been a very long time, and you were hardly more than a baby when I last saw you. However, all things considered, I think you might give me a kiss, don't you? Since we've had time to grow a bit more accustomed to each other, if you see what I mean.'

This was more than Susan could stand.

'Now I'm *sure* you're a burglar!' she asserted. 'For don't we all know

16

the poor child's pa is dead an' buried in a gold-mine out in Californy? Git out o' my way! If you ain't goin' to call Mr. Aaron, Loulie, I'll do it myself!'

A curious shadow came over the face of Jonathan Trigg.

'Is that what they've told . . . well, after all, why not? They had to say something, I suppose.'

Loulie continued to meditate for some moments in silence. She looked first at the man in the red shirt and high boots, then at what was left of her cruller, then at the man again. How could she be sure whether he were telling the truth? He might be her father, and he might not. He did, she thought, look a little like the picture in the gilt lacquer frame that stood on Mamma's dressing-table — but not very much. The man in the picture was younger and somehow softer in outline. Moreover, he wore a beard, which concealed most of the lower part of his face; whereas the stranger was clean-shaven except for a small black moustache. (Was it waxed a trifle?) Loulie had no recollection of her father, who had left home when she was not quite four. She knew only that he had gone West to look for gold; he had never come back; and later, when she was old enough to ask questions, Mamma had told her to pray for dear Papa, who was in Heaven.

At this point there was a sound of running feet on the stairs, and Sissy and Nancy burst into the kitchen.

Come to think of it, it was queer they had not appeared before, but Loulie soon saw what had delayed them: they were fully, if somewhat hastily, dressed, though they still wore nightcaps and their hair streamed over their shoulders — Sissy's, a cloud of chestnut-brown silk; Nancy's, an unruly tangle of jet-black curls. The latter carried a poker.

'You trip him up, Sis, and I'll hit him over the head,' she was saying bloodthirstily as they came in. 'Quick! Before he can . . .'

Then she stopped short where she was, and stared and stared, her mouth left open in the middle of her sentence (which was something Loulie had never seen, although she had read about it in books). The poker went crashing to the floor — What a lot of things are getting dropped this morning! thought Loulie — but Nancy had nothing to say. It was Sissy who flushed all over her pretty face, clasped her hands, and settled Loulie's doubts, once and forever, by whispering, as if she herself could scarcely believe it: *'Papa!'*

17

Afterwards Loulie was not quite sure what happened next.

There was an interval of screams and exclamations punctuated by kisses. Papa had to embrace each of his daughters in turn. Good-natured Susan, bewailing her doubts of the master's identity, was clapped on the shoulder and told not to mind. . . . 'My dear woman,' said Papa magnanimously, 'you did perfectly right. What else could you have thought? It was my own fault. If I'd knocked at the front door as I ought to have done . . .'

This brought Sissy to her senses: leaving the chastened Susan to finish preparations for breakfast, she headed the procession upstairs.

Here Papa surprised them by displaying signs of extreme interest and affectionate delight.

'The same, everything is exactly the same!' he murmured, gazing enraptured at the worn matting on the hall floor, the brown landscape paper (so dingy that its pattern could barely be discerned), the framed colour prints of the Swiss waterfall and the two little girls in mauve dresses looking over a fence at a dejected donkey. And he was even more charmed when Sissy flung open the door and ushered him into the parlour.

Now that, thought Loulie, was absurd, for there was nothing remarkable about the parlour at Number Eighty, State Street. Home, of course, was home, to be accepted without question and cherished for its familiarity; but it could not be compared to Uncle Charles's and Aunt Bertha's sumptuous house on Michigan Avenue, with its Blue Room and its Yellow Room, its lofty ceilings and tall gilt mirrors and marble mantels and fringed brocade curtains and carved rosewood and black-walnut furniture. . . . The parlour at Number Eighty was narrow and ill-proportioned, like all the rooms in the white cottage. It was of no particular colour, or, rather, it was a mixture of a good many different colours, faded by time to an undistinguished greenish drab. The mantel was not marble at all, but plain painted wood. The old plush sofa by the fire had been repaired so often that it had a permanent sag in the middle, like a swaybacked horse. And the furniture was a haphazard collection of shabby utilities, varied by chairs the Charles Bascombs had tired of, a table or two the Caleb Bascombs had not found room for when they broke up housekeeping and went to live at the Tremont House.

18

Loulie and her sisters knew why this was so. Mamma had often told them that Grandpa had had to leave almost everything behind when the family came West from New York State in '45. There were no railroads in those days; it was as much as they could do to move themselves, let alone their belongings. A few household treasures only had been kept — Loulie saw that Papa paid particular attention to them, pausing bemused before Grandpa's walnut desk, with its worn leather top and the purple ink-stains that would not come out; then beneath the portraits of Grandpa and Grandma Bascomb in pearwood frames hanging on either side of the mantel: Grandpa Caleb, dour and disapproving in side-whiskers and a fearsome high linen stock; Grandma Rhoda (for whom Sissy had been named), vaguely benign in plum bombazine with lace ruffles, by her side a small almond-eyed doll with corkscrew curls and a stiff white frock, who clutched a rose with determination and (incredibly) was Mamma as a Little Girl.

'The same — all the same!' murmured Papa once more. 'Forgive me, my dears; for a moment I fancied . . . but you're all standing. Won't you please sit down?'

'Oh, Papa, won't *you?*' they chorused politely.

Everybody sat down at once, only to make the discovery, simultaneously, that this did not help matters, for they had little to say to one another. Loulie looked at Nancy, Nancy at Loulie; then they both looked at Sissy, who was still flushed a beautiful pink and whose eyes had never left Papa's face. But even Sissy would not speak. Papa, too, kept silent, though his eyes were smiling the kind messages he dared not put into words. Why . . . Papa was shy! As shy as his daughters! . . . This was a revelation: it had never occurred to Loulie that grown-up people *could* be shy.

In the quiet room the sound of a cab drawing up at the door could be heard very plainly. There was the cabman's voice, and Aunt Betsy's, the latter's sing-song soprano pitched uncomfortably high as she superintended the removal of her luggage. There were steps on the stairs leading to the front porch — Aunt Betsy's firm and thumping, Mamma's light and quick yet decisive. Mamma opened the door and entered, saying: 'You know the way to your room, Betsy. Tell the driver to set the bags down inside the vestibule, but on the matting, not on the door-rug. And, whatever you do, don't give him more than a tencent tip; he wasn't at all a pleasant man! I'll just go see if Susan . . . Sissy! Nancy! Where *is* everybody?'

Loulie suddenly caught Papa's eye. He was smiling still, but he looked shyer than ever, and as Mamma came in he sprang up from his seat and flattened himself against the wall on the same side as the door, so that at first she did not see him.

Mamma was wearing her camel's-hair shawl and her best summer straw bonnet, the one trimmed with bunches of white poppies. She looked very pretty, her eyes shining, her cheeks rosy from the drive. Loulie had time to marvel, as always, how her mother managed to keep her back as straight as she did without seeming to think about it. She stood so erect that she looked several inches taller than she was; no one ever called Julia Trigg a little woman.

'Girls, Aunt Betsy has come! Why, what's the meaning of this? Loulie half dressed, and Sissy and Nancy in nightcaps with their hair all unbound! What *has* got into everybody? Even Susan . . . Past eight o'clock and breakfast not on the table. How many times have I told her . . .'

Here she caught sight of Papa and froze to the floor in the middle of the parlour. It was the most awful thing her children had ever seen. Mamma turned to stone in front of their eyes: she grew as white as a statue in the exhibit of Living Waxworks Loulie had been taken to last winter at the Mechanics' Institute Fair. There was no colour left in her cheeks or her lips; only her eyes were still blue, staring and terrible, devoid of expression. Her lips were moving, but no words came out.

After a moment Loulie remembered her father. He looked, she thought, almost as stricken as poor Mamma. But at least he had not lost the powers of motion and speech. As she watched him he hurried forward, stretched out both hands, and said just four words — but Loulie would never forget the tone in which he spoke them:

'Julia, are you sorry?'

Then Mamma did something none of her children had ever seen her do. She collapsed on the old plush sofa, leaned forward, buried her face in her little gloved hands, and began to cry, not silent, ordinary tears, but wild, half-strangled sobs that shook her frame and sounded as painful to hear as they must have been to give.

20

Aunt Betsy at Breakfast

By THE TIME Aunt Betsy had come downstairs, Mamma had succeeded in calming her emotion. Alarming as her outburst had sounded, it had been a nervous convulsion rather than a real fit of weeping: she shed almost no tears. Still deathly pale, she took off her bonnet, put on her cap, tied Loulie's sash, dispatched the elder girls to dress their hair, scolded Susan (who had appeared, flushed and flurried, to set the table) for her slovenly ways, and at the same time managed to pay some attention to Papa. . . . Yes, decidedly, Mamma was becoming herself again.

Aunt Betsy, on the other hand, gave full rein to her feelings; she was so much excited that she forgot to be elegant. This could be told by her choice of voices — for Aunt Betsy had two: one, reserved for formal occasions, high, sugared, and affectedly lilting; the other, loud, cheerful, unmannered, and interested. She usually, Loulie noticed, began with the first, and then relapsed by degrees, as she grew more engrossed in what she was saying, into the second. But, in this case, 'Well, I never!' said Aunt Betsy at once, in her everyday Bascomb tones. And, 'Did you ever!' And, 'La, who'd have thought . . .?' And, 'Dear heart, after all these years!' And, 'Lord, Thy ways are not our ways! And, 'Lazarus from the dead . . .' And even, 'Julia, don't mention food — I couldn't touch a morsel!'

That, of course, as Loulie well knew, was not to be taken literally.

Mamma, overwrought as she was, knew it, too: as soon as Susan opened the double doors that divided the parlour from the dining-room, she led the way to the breakfast-table.

Sissy and Nancy tripped in, rosy with haste and giggling over nothing at all. Correct and composed, Mamma took her seat behind

21

the coffee-tray and motioned Aunt Betsy to the place of honour at her right.

'Mr. Trigg,' she said, waving Papa to the other end of the table, 'will you take your usual seat?'

'With pleasure, my love,' replied Papa.

He smiled with his lips, but not with his eyes. Mamma did not smile; but then, she was busy pouring out coffee with hands that were strangely steady. Susan brought in the crullers. She brought in, also, a number of other things: a basket of ripe strawberries; bowls of porridge and rich Jersey cream; a platter of scrambled eggs and bacon; another of grilled chops; cold ham; fried potatoes; toast, muffins, mounds of sweet butter; buckwheat-cakes and maple syrup . . . very nearly everything, thought Loulie happily, she liked best to eat.

'I do hope you're getting enough,' said Mamma, in a worried way.

She always said that, Loulie reflected, no matter how much had been laid on the board; always peered anxiously up and down, as if she were sure that in spite of her efforts someone had been slighted. (Nancy had once remarked that when Gabriel blew his trumpet, Mamma would arise with a frown and a plate of hot biscuits, and beg him please to wait just a minute, a fresh batch was coming in directly!) Yet Mamma herself cared little for food.

'The cakes are delicious, dear,' said Aunt Betsy encouragingly. 'That Susan of yours is a treasure. And to think you trained her in three months' time! I only wish my poor Maria had some of her dispositions: fry she can, but bake she can *not*, and she don't seem to want in the least to learn.'

'You can't imagine how good everything tastes to me,' said Sissy, smiling, 'after the bill-of-fare at the Academy. We had hash for dinner five days a week.'

'You *did?*' cried Mamma and Aunt Betsy together; and the latter added: 'That's nothing in the world but bad management, child. I'm surprised to hear it. I thought Miss Crandall knew how to live. Most folks in the East set a very good table.'

'I'm only sorry it's not winter time,' said Nancy, 'for Papa's sake. In winter we always have salt mackerel and potatoes in their jackets for Sunday breakfast.'

'Your father,' said Mamma bleakly, almost as if she were speaking without thinking, 'does not care for salt mackerel.'

Nancy looked aghast.

'But, *Papa!* Everyone knows . . . why, what else can you eat on Sunday?'

'Ah, Nancy, my dear,' said Papa quickly, 'when you know me a little better, I fear you will find my vagaries of taste are the least of my sins. But let's not talk of the few things I don't like that aren't here, when so many I do are set before me. Mrs. Trigg, my best compliments, ma'am; I've not sat down to such a feast since I left your home and board.'

Mamma bowed her thanks. She even smiled a little, for the first time that morning. But there was no mirth in her smile; she looked at Papa without seeing him, just as he looked at her without seeing her. And, in spite of his words, Loulie could tell he wasn't enjoying his breakfast — he was only pretending to enjoy it. Oh, what was the matter with them both?

Aunt Betsy, however, ate something of everything, chewing slowly so as to savour each mouthful. But that did not stop her from talking. She talked before eating, she talked after eating, she even talked a good deal of the time while she *was* eating (which Loulie had always been cautioned not to do). Meanwhile, she turned her prominent light hazel eyes first up the table, then down, as if she could not decide whether to watch Julia or Jonathan Trigg.

No one else, it soon appeared, was going to be able to talk at all.

To be sure, Aunt Betsy started in by exclaiming eagerly: 'Brother Jonathan, tell us your story straight from the very beginning: we're all ears, my dear man, we're all ears!' But whenever Papa cleared his throat for a trial opening, she brashly interrupted him with her 'La, Julia, I declare . . .' or, 'Mr. Trigg, you're as brown as an Indian!' or, 'Children, aren't you thankful your father . . .' So that, in the end, Loulie felt, they did not really know what to think. Papa was well, Papa was ill; he had written to them constantly, but his letters had gone astray; he had *not* written, for fear of alarming his family; he had been living in Placerville, Sutter's Fort, Sacramento, San Francisco, some towns in the South with odd-sounding Spanish names nobody contrived to catch.

23

Nothing was definite, because poor Papa was never allowed to finish a sentence.

And before he had got well launched on even such fragmentary explanations as he was allowed to present, Aunt Betsy remembered that *he* must be pining for tidings of the Bascombs and began a series of news bulletins of her own. . . .

Brother Charles, of course, was monstrously rich. All his ventures had prospered amazingly well. At first he had feared when railroads came in that the shipping business would suffer, but so far it had not. He had some boats, too, on the canals running south and west of the city; the trade in grain doubled every six months. And now that he was interested in these new iron deposits up North, there was talk of starting a regular line to the mines before the end of the summer. Oh, Charles had his finger in everything going round about Chicago, you could depend upon that! He had built himself a palace over on Michigan Avenue . . . four storeys . . . five parlours . . . six servants (two of them men!). There was an elegant iron fence all round the property . . . a grape arbour . . . conservatory . . . smokehouse and buttery . . . and every stick of furniture had been bought in New York. That, naturally, was just Bertha's way. She could have done as well here in town, but she liked to pretend life in the West was still crude. Bertha never would forget that her father had been mayor of Albany for two terms, and her grandfather, old Judge Curtis, a distinguished patriot in Revolutionary times; she hadn't stopped thinking she had done young Charles Bascomb, the son of an innkeeper in Hebron Springs, an honour by marrying him. . . . Charles and Bertha had a son now themselves . . . yes, after all these years . . . 'Let me see, Joshua's nearly seven, so he must have been born right after you left for California. Of course, it's nice they have him as long as they wanted him so much, but I must say, of all spoilt children . . . the worst I ever! . . . Why, he's not even allowed to go to school; they pretend his stomach's weak (though you should see him stuff himself!) and have a tutor to teach him at home. Did you ever hear such nonsense?'

Caleb and Jane were rich, too. Caleb was one of the best lawyers in Chicago. Everyone said so. He had a handsome office all paneled in oak in Dearborn Street across from the post-office, and a suite of rooms at the Tremont House. No, they didn't keep house any more. Jane

24

said she wasn't strong enough. It was true she looked rather peaked —
no constitution *at all!* — 'but you can't tell me Jane don't eat a sight
more than she lets on. If only she'd stop doctoring herself with those
physics! . . . You ought to see the new Tremont, Jonathan. They say
it's the best hotel in America west of New York, and I shouldn't wonder if it was. Hot and cold water on every floor, shower-baths in the
bathrooms, and it's heated with those new-fangled steam-pipes you've
heard about. Fancy that! Jane don't have to light a fire in the fireplace
the whole winter through; she's got a paper frill in the grate and there
it stays from one year's end to the next.'

From her brothers' prosperities Aunt Betsy turned suddenly to the
mournful recital of her own brief marital bliss. It was a story Loulie
had heard often, always in the same words: the hero of it seemed like
a character in a book, yet somehow more real than the shadowy figure
of the Uncle Walworth she had known.

'He was the Baptist minister from Geneva,' said Aunt Betsy. 'I met
him at prayer meeting, and he proposed the third time we met. We
were walking across Court House Square, I remember; he offered me
his cape to wear, for it was raining, and I hadn't an umbrella. It was
the fall after you went West, Jonathan: I remember that, too, for we
were in mourning for Pa, and there wasn't much we could do except
go to church. . . . Well, we were married at Christmas. There didn't
seem to be any reason to wait: I was thirty-two past and Doctor Walworth wouldn't see sixty again. But he was a fine-looking man —
wasn't he, Julia? — as handsome as you generally see, was my Phineas
— you'd not have taken him for a day over forty — and he made me a
good, kind husband. We were happy as could be for three years; we'd
have been that way yet but for Doctor Walworth's devotion to duty.
Geneva's a country kind of place; some of the parishioners live miles
out of town. One cold winter's night Doctor Walworth was called
to attend a dying woman who lived on a farm near Sugar Grove, clear
over on the other side of the county. It was snowing real hard, and I
begged him not to go. But he would do it: he took cold on his chest,
it turned to inflammation of the lungs, and he didn't live a week,
cheerful and pious to the last. "I've been blessed a-plenty, Betsy," he
said, "if it's God's will I should leave you now, I want you to know
how happy I've been, and I'll watch over you till we meet again." I

25

buried him in the churchyard by the river, not a mile from the house we bought with my share of Pa's estate, and there I've stayed ever since — it seemed like a comfort being so close to him.'

Aunt Betsy paused to dab at her eyes with her handkerchief, and then resumed in a brighter key:

'I've plenty of friends in Geneva, and Sister Julia always has a bed to spare when I want to come into the city. That's only once in a while, though I can manage it better than I used, now that the railroad goes out to Wheaton. But the farm keeps me pretty busy, 'specially this time of year. I've three hundred hens laying — Plymouth Rocks and Rhode Island Reds, mostly — Caleb and Charles set me up last year in the poultry business — Oh, and Julia, that reminds me: whatever you do, don't let me forget to ask Charles what he thinks of those new self-raking reapers that are on the market. My neighbour 'cross the road, Si Tompkins, bought one and says he wouldn't take twice the money he gave for it. I've a notion to get one, too, if Charles approves — I like to keep up to date, and it'd certainly be a help when haying time comes. . . . Brother Jonathan, aren't you proud of your daughters? You ought to be, for they do Julia credit; she's trained them up in the way they should go. Sissy's her grandmother over again — you must have known she was going to be, when you named her for Ma. She got home only yesterday, if you please, with a diploma in her pocket from the Utica Female Academy. Julia always wanted to send her East to school, but she didn't see how she could do it, with you disappeared off the face of the earth and nothing coming in except the bit of money she had from Pa — and that mostly went for the rent of this house and food and clothes for the children and such. Well, if Charles and Bertha didn't offer to pay her expenses for three whole years! It was the best thing for everybody, and Sissy's been boarding with Bertha's sister, Anna Turnham, that's married and living in Utica. You remember Anna, Jonathan? She had russety hair and front teeth like a rabbit and used to come over to the Springs every summer with her mother and their pug dog that had gout. . . . Well, it's all worked out fine, except I expect Julia's missed Sissy a good deal, as handy as she is in the house, though she won't say she did — you know Julia — same old sixpence as ever — all for others and nothing for herself. And now Sissy's back, as fine a young lady as you'd wish to meet — but

26

mercy on us! Just as we're all so pleased to see her home again, if she isn't thinking of leaving us for good and getting married in the fall!'

Aunt Betsy, finally out of breath, wound up her speech with a triumphant wag of the head, pleased that she had saved her most startling nugget of information for the last.

Papa appeared to be quite as deeply impressed by it as she could have hoped. He had not so far, Loulie thought, paid much attention; but now he straightened up in his chair, looked at Sissy as if he had never looked at her before, and rapped out: 'Married? *Sissy?*'

Sissy blushed and glanced down at her plate.

'Yes, Papa.'

'Who's the man?'

As Sissy could not, or would not, speak, Nancy said officiously: 'Oh, it's only Aaron Miles. *I* don't see anything exciting in being engaged to Aaron Miles!'

'Aaron Miles?' said Papa. 'I don't recall . . . yet stay, now it comes back to me . . . a thin small face with a drooping mouth . . . silent, solemn . . . why, it must be the little boy next door!'

'Just so!' said Aunt Betsy. 'He's still silent and solemn sometimes, but you couldn't call him small or thin any more: he's grown to a good six feet! You needn't ask for a better son-in-law, Jonathan. Aaron's an exemplary young man. He didn't care about going to college, so when he graduated from the Seminary Charles gave him a chance in his office, and he's done real well there. Charles thinks the world of him; he says he never saw any young fellow so downright industrious — and he's smart for his age, too. You'd never take him for just twenty-one. Charles has sent him East several times on business for the company — that's how he got to see Sissy so often in Utica and persuade her to wait for him — and this summer he's going north to the iron mines to take charge of the Bascomb interests. Oh, I tell you, Sissy's a lucky girl! Now, what are you blushing for, Sissy? I declare, the child's nothing but a sensitive plant!'

Sissy seemed powerless to utter a word. She sat quietly with her eyes cast down in her place at table between her two sisters, until Papa sprang up to embrace her.

'My dear little girl,' said Papa, 'my own good daughter, I wish you all joy!'

'Thank you, Papa,' said Sissy—and now at last she looked up to smile at him as she returned his kiss. 'I know I shall be happy.'

But she still did not act like herself. There was a mild distress in her eyes, a faint flutter of uncertainty in her manner, as if she were not perfectly sure she meant what she said. Getting married, thought Loulie, must be a very grave and important thing: Sissy had behaved precisely like this every time her engagement was mentioned.

Mamma roused herself from her preoccupied mood to take part in the discussion.

'I'm glad you approve, Jonathan. I couldn't ask your permission, not knowing where you were. And since Caleb and Charles thought well of the match, and we've known Aaron so long ourselves, I saw nothing for it but to say yes. They're both young to be married, Sissy especially so, and I don't know how I'll manage without her; but she's been a good and obedient daughter since the day she was born; I couldn't refuse the first thing she asked me.'

'Dear Mamma,' said Sissy, on the verge of tears, 'you know, I don't want to leave you at all!'

The ebony grandfather clock in the hall gave a warning whirr and then struck nine.

'Run, Loulie,' cried Nancy, 'or you'll be late for Sunday School!'

Loulie knew it only too well. She ought really to have left ten minutes ago, but she had sat tight, hoping the family might forget for once. . . .

Of course, it would have to be Nancy who reminded them!

'Oh,' said Loulie, getting down from her chair with deliberation (for she had eaten almost as much as Aunt Betsy), 'do I have to go to Sunday School this morning, Mamma? Can't I wait and go to church instead with you and Papa?'

Mamma shook her head.

'Nonsense, child! Be off with you! Quick! You'll be tardy enough as it is. What makes you think your father is going to church? He hasn't said he was.'

'Oh, but Papa!' gasped Loulie; for everybody knew that everybody had to go to church on Sunday.

Sissy and Nancy looked their astonishment: this was a far more serious matter even than not liking salt mackerel.

28

'Children,' said Mamma dryly, as she rose from the table, 'when you're as old as I am, you'll learn not to take too much for granted. In the twenty years I've been married to your father I've never been sure, ten minutes ahead, what he would do.'

'Julia, my dear, what a character to give me before my children!' Papa murmured, rising, too. 'Of course, I am going to church. But I hardly consider — do you? — this costume I am wearing is suitable. Have I time to return to the hotel and change?'

Mamma coloured slightly and looked at Papa for the first time as if she were seeing him, all of him, right there, close to her, as someone who mattered. But her voice was as prim and prosaic as always as she replied: 'That won't be necessary. Your clothes are upstairs, just where you left them seven years ago.'

The Bascombs at Dinner

LOULIE was very late to Sunday School, but she had too much to think about this morning to worry about it. Moreover, Mrs. Miles, Aaron's mother, who taught the older girls' class, was both short-sighted and absent-minded, and seldom was sure whether her full complement of scholars were present.

Mrs. Miles was a North Carolinian, with a drawling, melancholy voice that matched her long, lean, melancholy face. (Loulie never saw her without recalling Nancy's naughty comparison of Aaron's mamma to Dolly, Uncle Charles's favourite bay filly.) Like most Southerners, she was chronically homesick for the country she had left. Chicago seemed to her ugly and uncivilized; when she enlarged, as she did to-day, on the delights of the Land of Canaan which the Lord promised Abraham, it sounded as if she were extolling the regretted richness of Beaufort County, where she was born.

But Loulie had no time to spare now for Mrs. Miles and her nostalgia. Although she kept her eyes fixed placidly on the branch of the elm tree waving against the sky, glimpsed through the window just above her teacher's head, her mind was not placid at all. Directly class was dismissed, she hurried out to the front steps of the church, which commanded a view of Court House Square, to take up her vigil. Bella Nixon and Clara Wall, her bosom companions, approached her at once to ask her to go for a walk; but their invitation was coldly refused. Instinctively Loulie felt that only a member of The Family would appreciate the tremendous importance of what had happened.

The first Bascomb she found proved disappointing. This was her cousin Joshua, who was a member of the Junior class, a fat little tow-headed boy with a small mouth puckered as though for a perpetual

30

whistle. With profound detachment he listened to her emphatic announcement that Papa had come home at last.

'Oh,' said Joshua; 'has he?' And he departed with some of his cronies to skip stones in the basin of one of the fountains that stood in the four corners of the park round the Court House.

By this time Washington Street was full of ringing bells and people in their best clothes on their way to church. Some were Methodists, some Presbyterians, some Universalists, some Unitarians, and some Baptists — for these five churches stood close together. All the people Loulie knew were Baptists, headed for the fine red-brick building with its soaring steeple, on the steps of which she was standing. That is, all the people but one. . . . It was very sad about Aunt Bertha. Mamma had explained it all years ago, when Loulie had demanded to know why the phaeton was ordered every Sunday to drive Mrs. Charles Bascomb, in solitary splendour, across the river to Saint James's in the North Division. Poor Aunt Bertha! It was not really her fault that she had been born an Episcopalian. Mamma had explained that, too; she had said that they must never question their uncle about his 'great cross.' They might pray for their aunt if they liked; pray that she be shown the light and led at last into the true fold. . . . 'But, Mamma, then Aunt Bertha isn't a *Christian!*' said Loulie, shocked and sorrowing. 'Hush, dear, you mustn't say so,' replied Mamma quietly. . . .

Yes, it was a pity, in more ways than one, about Aunt Bertha. Loulie realized, as she spied her relatives crossing the square and waved to them vigorously, that she was somehow missing the cream of the occasion. It was going to be fun to break the news to Aunt Jane and Uncle Caleb and Uncle Charles, but she could tell pretty well in advance what they were likely to say. Their responses would be good, thoroughgoing Bascomb responses (for Aunt Jane, whose mother had been a Seeley from Stephentown, was partly a Bascomb herself). No one, however, could predict how Aunt Bertha might act. Who could forget the scene she had made, screaming and stamping her foot because Abel, the gardener, had planted red geraniums instead of pink in the round bed by the summer-house? Or the dreadful time she had turned green and fainted dead away in the street, when the circus was in town and Joshua was lost and the Town Crier had rung his bell on the corner and said . . . Ah, but it was really too bad! Loulie bit her

31

lip, almost crying at the trick ill luck had played her. Her aunt and her uncles were now within hailing distance — but so were the Triggs. It was clear that the two family parties would meet at the church door.

First in the procession walked Sissy, composed and charming, in her rosebud bonnet and prettiest dress, carrying her new French parasol; Aaron Miles was, as usual, her faithful attendant. Then came Aunt Betsy with Nancy; the latter, heedless of the companion allotted her, kept tossing her curls as she turned back to point out the grey marble magnificence of the Court House to her father. Last of all were Papa and Mamma. Papa had changed his clothes; he was dressed like anybody else in a dark suit and a tall hat — but he still did not *look* like anybody else. As for Mamma, it was not her clothes that were changed. The colour had come back to her cheeks; her eyes had never been so blue, her head held so high, as this moment; she smiled proudly as she strolled along Washington Street in the bright June sunshine on her husband's arm.

Loulie forgot her own disappointment in her surprise at the transformation. Mamma looked young, Mamma looked pretty; but that was not the whole of it. What was the difference? What was it about her expression that had not been there before? Why — but of course — Mamma looked *happy!*

As Loulie had foreseen, all the family arrived in front of the church at precisely the same time — but just then, before a word could be said, the bells stopped ringing, the doors began to shut, and everybody had to go inside and sit down and pretend, for the next two hours, that nothing out of the ordinary had occurred.

Some of them pretended better than others.

Mamma, for instance, thought Loulie, was wonderful. Throughout the sermon she sat quite still beside Papa, glancing neither to the right nor to the left, her eyes fixed on Doctor Travers, as if every word he uttered were precious to her.

But it was doubtful whether she really were listening.

There was no doubt about the rest of the family: they were suffering a trial the like of which they had never known. In a crisis like this, to be a Bascomb and not allowed to talk out loud! What could be more terrible? . . . Aunt Jane leaned back, crying softly, one hand holding her handkerchief to her eyes, the other clutching a flask of smelling-

32

salts. Aunt Betsy leaned forward, smiling and whispering with the Uncles, whose pew was just in front of the Triggs'. Sissy sat very close to Aaron, finishing in a soft murmur the explanation she had begun on the way to church. Nancy flashed mischievous smiles at each of her relatives in turn; when she thought no one was looking she made faces at Joshua, who at last had begun to realize that Uncle Trigg's arrival was something important and stared owlishly at the dark curly head behind him.

Poor Doctor Travers, who had just come to the pastorate from Boston and could not possibly guess the cause of the excitement, began to grow bewildered. He was an eloquent preacher and had been famous for years in the East, but never before had he so stirred his auditors. As it happened, his sermon was based on the fifteenth chapter of Luke: *But the father said to his servants, Bring forth the best robe and put it on him; and put a ring on his hand, and shoes on his feet: And bring hither the fatted calf, and kill it; and let us eat and be merry; for this my son was dead, and is alive again; he was lost, and is found.*

When he gave out the text there was a stir amongst the congregation. And as he enlarged upon it the stir increased: heads were craned curiously from every corner, meaning glances were exchanged, and from mouth to mouth in a subdued hum the word passed along: 'Brother Trigg has come home — Brother Trigg is returned from California!'

It was no better when they got up to sing:

> *'Tis a point I long to know, —*
> *Oft it causes anxious thought, —*
> *Do I love the Lord, or no?*
> *Am I His, or am I not?'*

This morning nobody, alas! was thinking very hard about the Lord. The question really agitating the First Baptist Church was, Where had Brother Trigg been these last seven years? . . . And the second verse was quite as bad:

> *'If I love, why am I thus?*
> *Why this dull and lifeless frame?*
> *Hardly, sure, they can be worse,*
> *Who have never heard His name!'*

33

Even Loulie perceived that lifeless and dull were by no means appropriate adjectives to describe the general ferment produced by Papa. It was not only her own family that was affected: if the Bascombs fidgeted, so did their friends. It seemed almost silly to go on:

> '*When I turn my eyes within*
> *All is dark, and vain, and wild;*
> *Filled with unbelief and sin,*
> *Can I deem myself a child?*'

For anyone could see that not a single pair of eyes was turned anywhere except on the centre pew where Mr. and Mrs. Jonathan Trigg sat with their children. Mamma began to look uncomfortable now; she stopped singing, and so did Sissy, whose flute-like voice was one of the best in church. Nancy's warm, velvety alto continued bravely for a little; then she, too, relapsed into self-conscious silence. Neither Loulie — who knew it — nor Aunt Betsy — who didn't — could carry a tune; so presently Papa was left alone to persist undaunted to the end.

Uncle Caleb and Uncle Charles relieved their feelings by passing the plates for the collection. Then, almost before Loulie realized it, came the final prayer (was it shorter than usual?), Doctor Travers dismissed his flock, and the unnatural strain was over at last.

Outside the door the Aunts and Uncles pounced upon Papa; but they were not able to monopolize him as they'd have liked, since everyone wanted to shake Brother Trigg's hand: without knowing how it happened, the Bascombs found themselves holding a kind of triumphal reception on the steps of the church. Papa, thought Loulie, must be growing quite tired of having his fingers squeezed and his back slapped and of saying, again and again: 'Thank you, thank you — yes, it *is* wonderful — yes, I am glad to be home once more!' He smiled a good deal, but they were not the same smiles he'd given his wife and his daughters. . . . Were they smiles at all? Loulie speculated. His face was so dark and his teeth were so white that all he had to do was open his mouth. . . .

Then, just as there seemed to be a prospect of breaking away, Doctor Travers, who had finally got wind of this miraculous addition to his fold, bore down on them with a benevolent 'My son, my son, I spake better than I knew! Sister Trigg, this is in truth a joyful day for you and yours. Dear friend, I know not how it was, but when I first met you I gained a distinct impression that you were a widow!'

Mamma blushed and murmured something noncommittal; it was Aunt Betsy who pursed her lips archly as she replied: 'Indeed, sir, for all she knew, she might have been!'

Papa grasped the minister's hand, showed his teeth once more, and said: 'Glad to have met you, sir. We'll see you later, I hope. Now, Mrs. Trigg, if you're quite ready . . .?' Whereupon Mamma laid her hand on Papa's arm and said: 'Doctor Travers is dining with us, my dear.'

'Of course,' said Papa. 'Of course, of course!'

His teeth made a final appearance: this time nobody could have taken it for a smile! Loulie thought — but perhaps she was mistaken — that she heard him saying under his breath something that sounded like 'I might have known it!'

When they reached the little white house in State Street, there was Aunt Bertha, superb in a leaf-brown taffeta that just matched her hair, and a blond lace shawl, stepping out of the phaeton.

She opened her eyes very wide when she caught sight of Papa, threw up her hands, and then clapped one of them to her mouth, as if to stifle a scream. But she did not scream. Neither did she turn green, nor faint, as she had done when Joshua was lost at the circus. Instead, she gave a high ripple of laughter and flung both arms round Papa's neck in a hearty embrace.

'The prodigal brother-in-law!' cried Aunt Bertha — although she could not have known about Doctor Travers's sermon.

She turned and led the way into the house. That was like Aunt Bertha; she seemed to feel it her duty as the wife of the richest, if not the eldest, Bascomb to assume an air of command in emergencies. She never said so, but her manner implied that she was sustained by the aristocratic tradition of the Governor's Mansion in Albany; whereas Sister Jane had not the least notion how things were done in the great world. How could she have, poor thing! when all her early life had been passed in a rustic retreat like Hebron Springs?

However, it soon became clear that today, for once, Aunt Bertha was not going to be able to hold the centre of the stage. The Family,

as a whole, were conscious of two persons only — and those persons were Doctor Travers and Papa. Doctor Travers, of course, was a hindrance. He kept them from talking to Papa and cross-examining him, as Loulie knew they must be aching to do. But Papa himself held their tongues in check: not that they wished him away (perish the thought!), still if he had not been there, they might at least have talked *about* him. . . .

It was a relief to everyone when Susan announced that dinner was ready.

Mamma asked Doctor Travers to say grace, a duty he performed with gratifying dispatch. (Loulie remembered that his wife was an invalid and that Mamma and Aunt Jane had heard she was a very poor housekeeper.) The minister was placed at his hostess's right, Uncle Caleb at her left, with Uncle Charles next his brother. (They always preferred being near each other, so that they might at intervals discuss those mysterious matters known as Business Prospects.) Aunt Betsy, clearly the most eminent Baptist of the party, sat on the other side of Doctor Travers; Papa divided Aunt Jane and Aunt Bertha, the latter, with a pretty, tinkling laugh, deftly pre-empting the post of honour; the young people were distributed at random towards the middle of the table.

Susan carried in and out dozens of dishes, beginning with Grandma Bascomb's cold potato purée, progressing through roast prairie chickens with stuffing and gravy to a fabulous strawberry shortcake. Mamma never once relaxed during this series of culinary triumphs, keeping up a constant twitter of whispered instructions to the 'girl,' varied by candid criticisms, not at all in a whisper — 'Susan, those scalloped tomatoes were miserable! Did you forget the brown sugar *again?*' — and warm entreaties to her guests to help themselves liberally to the fare provided, 'for that's all you're going to get.'

The Family were served twice to everything; Uncle Charles and Aunt Betsy were sometimes served three times. Aunt Jane, who was subject to strawberry poisoning, groaned softly when the shortcake appeared — but she took just as much of it as anybody else. . . .

Doctor Travers, too, was a most appreciative guest. He ate as heartily as a Bascomb — almost as heartily as a missionary, decided Loulie,

36

whose experience of that class was vast and detailed — and was profuse in his compliments to the mistress of the house.

In reply to his questions Mamma told him how she had learned to cook — how all the Bascombs had learned — from Monsieur Alphonse, the French chef, in the great kitchens of Chancellor Hall, their father's hotel in Hebron Springs, high in the Taconic Hills of eastern New York State. And Uncle Charles added the story, familiar as a nursery rhyme to the children, of how Grandpa came to move to the West.

'Yes, sir,' said Uncle Charles, smoothing his plum-coloured waistcoat over his comfortably rounded stomach, 'that was a portrait of our honoured father you saw in the parlour — Mrs. Trigg was his eldest daughter, he died in her house — and there's a picture of the Hall hanging over the sideboard, though it don't do it justice, according to my opinion. It was painted by a Spaniard who was spending a season at the Springs — there were always lots of foreigners there, the same as at Saratoga and Richfield — but if you ask me, those artist fellows have too much imagination. Yes, sir, that's what's the trouble with 'em: a good daguerreotype would have pleased me better. . . . Captain Bascomb owned and ran the Hall for more than forty years, and there wasn't a finer watering-place in the whole United States, if I say it myself. Famous men and women came there every year from far and wide . . . Daniel Webster and John Quincy Adams and President Van Buren . . . and none of us Bascombs will ever forget, though we were children then, the reception given for Lafayette. There were so many guests in the Hall that night that they were afraid the floor'd give way! . . . No, sir, the Captain wasn't a member of the military, though he was a militiaman and raised a company at the time of the last war with England — in the year 'thirteen that was. He was set to go then, if his country needed him. There wasn't a smarter man in Columbia County, nor a finer gentleman. The people in Hebron Springs were mighty sorry to see him leave. I reckon he was sorry himself in some ways; he was getting along in years then, and sometimes it's crossed my mind since that maybe he knew he wasn't going to live so very much longer and he'd as soon have spent his last days in his boyhood home, where his wife was buried, and three of his children, too. But he cast in his lot with us when the time came to move. I guess, if the truth were told, what decided him was Julia's wanting to go. Mrs. Trigg was always the apple of his eye, and when she figured to follow her husband West, Pa pulled up his stakes and came, too.'

Doctor Travers, who had apparently forgotten his host, peered down the table at Papa and observed, with mild surprise: 'Then you, sir, were the original pioneer?'

Papa nodded, but it was Uncle Charles who replied: 'Brother Trigg came to Chicago in '44, on business for me. I'd bought a share in a shipping firm operating on the lakes and needed a man to look out for my interests, for I was fully occupied then in the East. So my brother-in-law took my place — temporarily only, of course — liked it here, and made up his mind to stay.'

'Brother Trigg was always one for changes,' said Uncle Caleb, scraping his throat very slightly, as though to indicate that *he* was not.

'He came back to Hebron in the spring and persuaded us all to go to Chicago,' Aunt Betsy took up the tale. 'La! What a trip that was! I often wonder how we survived it.'

Loulie had heard it over and over, but she enjoyed hearing again how Papa and Mamma and their three little girls, Grandpa, and Aunt Betsy rode by coach from Hebron Springs to Albany, by railway car from Albany to Schenectady — just think! that was all the railroad there was in those days! — by coach again from Schenectady to Syracuse, and by packet boat on the Erie Canal from Syracuse to Buffalo. The canal trip took a whole week, and it took another week after that on the lake steamer (one of Uncle Charles's steamers) from Buffalo to Chicago. . . . 'Oh, that trip on the lakes! I never was so sick in my life! Do you remember, Julia, how rough it was? I didn't get out of bed for three days and nights, and you wouldn't have either, if you hadn't been afraid that Sissy or Nancy'd tumble overboard. You were a babe in arms, then, Loulie — you knew nothing about it.'

Loulie realized this was true, but she wished Aunt Betsy had not mentioned it. It made her feel out of things, not to recall The Family's pilgrimage. But at least she'd been there, though she couldn't remember, which was better than Joshua, who hadn't even been born.

'Pa was on deck every morning,' continued Aunt Betsy, 'whatever the weather. I can see him now, with his old blue cap pulled back on his head, leaning on the railing and gazing over all that wild grey water. . . . We landed at the dock at the head of State Street and spent

38

the night at the old Lake House. When I opened my eyes the first morning and looked out across the city — you could see all of it then, it was so small and there were so few tall buildings — it seemed to me we'd got to the ends of the earth. But it wasn't a week before we'd found a nice house in Lake Street, with a garden running down to the river; and it wasn't a month before Caleb and Charles and Jane and Bertha arrived, and we began to feel we'd lived in Chicago most of our lives.'

Doctor Travers expressed polite interest in this narrative, although not so much as Loulie felt it deserved. Chicago was so new that almost everybody in it — even the children, unless they were as young as Joshua Bascomb — had come from somewhere else. Then the conversation passed to matters of more general concern. The men talked about the schooner that had gone aground on a sandbank outside the mouth of the river, and about the drought that was said to be bad for the corn crop. They talked, also, about the Anti-Slavery meeting the Baptists had held at the Tabernacle Church, and the 'Bleeding Kansas' riots, and the coming presidential election. Uncle Caleb and Uncle Charles were Democrats; their ideas on politics were definite. . . . Buchanan was 'safe'; Colonel Frémont was an 'adventurer' — who knew what he had been up to, all those years in the West? . . . 'I hope, Brother Trigg, you're not going to be a Republican; it was bad enough in the old days having a Whig in the family!'

The Uncles laughed a good deal at this, Uncle Caleb decorously, through his teeth; Uncle Charles uproariously, as he slapped his plum-coloured waistcoat. Meanwhile, Mamma went on saying things about food — wouldn't *anyone* have some more shortcake? —; Aunt Jane about medicine — she had given up Iodine and Sarsaparilla and for a change was trying Doctor Hayden's Improved Family Pills —; Aunt Bertha about clothes — French barèges were twenty cents a yard at Potter Palmer's and she had heard that drop earrings were coming back into fashion. . . . Aunt Betsy then introduced the question of the self-raking reaper, only to be squelched thoroughly by her brothers. Uncle Charles said: 'Who told you it would pay for itself in two years' time? That's foolishness, Betsy; that don't make sense.' And Uncle Caleb said, with an air of finality: 'You've not enough land, girl, to warrant the investment.' Aunt Betsy bridled and blushed, but stuck to her guns. . . . Sissy and Aaron conversed in undertones. Nancy made Loulie choke over her shortcake by whispering that Doctor Travers looked like Petruchio, the mangy lion in Herr Driesbach's Menagerie. Joshua ate his way perseveringly through every course. Neither he nor his cousin Loulie troubled themselves to take part in what was going on round them — but they *were* part of it, all the same.

Only Papa, though he carved the game skilfully and waited on his sisters-in-law with gallant good manners, appeared out of things. Why this was, it was hard to tell. It was true that he did not resemble The Family. He was dark and spare and angular, while the Bascombs were pink and plump. It wasn't, however, merely a matter of looks. Aaron Miles was just as dark as Papa, and even thinner. Aunt Jane had auburn hair and hatchet features; Aunt Bertha had small, snapping black eyes, a delicate nose, and a damask complexion. But there was nothing aloof or mysterious about them. The Aunts were Bascombs made, if not born; Aaron seemed completely accounted for as Sissy's betrothed, Uncle Charles's chief clerk, or even as the little boy next door, son of Mr. Miles who worked in the bank and Mrs. Miles who taught in the Sunday School.

On the other hand, what was Papa? Yes, and *where* was he? . . . It was the strangest thing, thought Loulie: it was almost as if he weren't with them; as if the man at the end of the table were a kind of dummy, while the real Papa was miles away. That was rather frightening, wasn't it? How could a person be there and *not* there, at the same time?

The Family were there, no mistake about that. The Bascombs were ready, their smiles seemed to say, to forgive the past and make a fresh start. The lost had been found, yes — and with him, doubtless, a suitable treasure to explain and atone for the seven lean years of his absence. No one quite dared let drop the word 'gold,' but even Loulie knew why people went to California: the magic monosyllable vibrated unspoken all the way round the dinner-table.

Curiosity about Papa and his mining experiences rose so high that it was barely kept from boiling over till dinner was finished. Then, when Mamma got up, expecting to retire with the ladies to the parlour, leaving the gentlemen to their cigars and a leisurely discussion of church business, there took place instead a general stampede towards

the front of the house. On the crest of it Doctor Travers, to his bewilderment, found himself swept through the door to the porch, down
the steps, along the path, out the gate, and into the street. He hardly
had time to thank Sister Trigg for her hospitality. Not that he hadn't
been heartily welcome. Ministers were welcome at any Bascomb board,
deferred to and treated with all possible honour. But now at last The
Family wanted — nay, it were better to say that it *had* — to be alone.

The final problem remained of what to do with Aaron: was he one
of them yet, or was he not?

Aunt Bertha thought not. She said as much to her eldest niece, in
an audible whisper that provoked the usually gentle Sissy to defiance.

'Aaron,' said Sissy, 'has as much right to be here as any of us. If
he leaves, Aunt Bertha, then so do I.'

And Aunt Bertha said nothing more. That was not like her. Perhaps, thought Loulie, it's just that she can't bear waiting another
minute to hear . . .

The Family returned to the parlour and began finding their places,
as if to witness a play.

The Uncles sat, as they often did, on either side of the old plush
sofa. They were enough alike to be taken for twins, blond and bland,
growing bald the same way up the centre of their foreheads. Only
Uncle Charles looked like a gilt-edged edition of Uncle Caleb: his boots
were shinier, his flowered silk cravat wider, than his brother's; the
watch-chain he twirled in his short, blunt fingers was a little too heavy
and handsome.

Mamma sat between them, as *she* often did, too. It was the spot
where Loulie knew the springs had been broken, but that made no
difference to Mamma, who never bent her back like other people. The
Aunts disposed themselves on the other side of the fireplace. Aunt
Jane and Aunt Betsy took the Shaker rocking-chairs; Aunt Bertha
settled, with much rustling and twitching of her taffeta skirts, on a
high-backed, uncomfortable throne she trusted because it had once
been hers. Their hands were idle, for it was Sunday and sewing would
have been sinful.

Aaron and Sissy occupied the centre, side by side on the long, low
bench in front of the hearth. Nancy and Loulie repaired to the win-

dow ledge, where behind the curtains they found Joshua, overcome by his industry at table, curled up asleep.

This left Papa alone in the middle of the room, opposing the circle of waiting faces. Grandpa and Grandma Bascomb, in their carved pearwood frames, seemed to be waiting, too. . . .

Papa must have been conscious of their expectations, for he did not sit down, but stood with his feet well apart, his hands in his pockets, and his head slightly lowered as he considered his relatives. He was not really smiling — Loulie had decided by now that Papa seldom smiled: you could not call showing your teeth smiling — but he looked as though he might be *thinking* about it.

There was a short silence, more urgent than any words could have been. Then Uncle Caleb, as the eldest, the head of The Family, cleared his throat, thrust his thumb in the open buttonhole at the top of his waistcoat (which was not plum-coloured, like Uncle Charles's, but sober steel-grey), and said: 'Well, Brother Trigg, we've waited as long as we can. Tell us your tale. Did you find gold?'

Papa shook his head. His eyes were dancing; the smile was coming closer.

'No, sir — but I didn't look for it! That is, I didn't look long. I soon saw there were thousands of poor devils in the same boat with me, who'd risked all they had for a will-o'-the-wisp. There was gold enough to go round, but it took too confounded long to get it. I talked to men who'd been slaving away for months, and all they had to show for their pains was a miserable handful of dust that'd hardly pay their expenses home. No, Brother Caleb, I wasn't made to be a miner.'

Uncle Caleb's pink face began to turn purple.

'But then, sir, what *did* you do? Good God, man, where have you been all these years, when we thought you were dead and buried in the wilderness?'

This time Papa's smile broke clear through the clouds; it was so gay, so charming, that Loulie forgot to be horrified by Uncle Caleb's language.

'Why,' said Papa, 'bless your hearts, I'm afraid you'll be very much disappointed when you hear . . . To tell the truth, I started a bookshop in Sacramento.'

42

The Forty-Niners

AFTER Papa had made his confession there was a long pause. During it the Bascombs seemed to be busy changing their minds about him. But even after they had finished changing they were not able to speak directly. The shock was too great: it was nearly a minute before Aunt Jane fetched an 'Oh!'; Aunt Betsy, a 'La!'; Aunt Bertha, a 'Pshaw!'; and Uncle Charles, most regrettably, a 'Hell's fire and damnation!'

Mamma, more grievously stricken than any of them, remained silent. She kept looking at Papa, as if she hoped he might say something further. Uncle Caleb, too, was beyond words; he did, however, manage to utter his famous noise. . . . His nieces all knew that noise very well and were duly afraid of it. Between a grunt and a groan, not 'faugh,' nor 'phew,' nor 'pfui,' though partaking something of the character of each, it expressed the extremes of indignation and disgust and was reserved for situations of the gravest import.

That such a situation had arrived was now painfully clear. However deep the Bascombs' distrust of their brother-in-law, however dark their flights of fancy concerning his past, they could never have pictured so dismal an anticlimax as this. . . . *A bookshop!* Merciful Heavens! What would Grandpa Bascomb have said to that?

Even Loulie was old enough to know what The Family thought about books. Books were all very well in their way and at the proper time. The proper time was youth, and the proper way was for educational purposes. Education was an excellent thing; the Bascombs thoroughly believed in it. They had all gone to school in Hebron Springs; Mamma and Aunt Betsy had had a year besides at the Schenectady Seminary for Young Ladies; while Uncle Caleb had graduated with honours from Hamilton College as well as from Law School in Albany.

Later in life, too, it was not wrong to *own* books. Uncle Caleb's

43

legal library was one of the finest in Illinois; Uncle Charles had shelves upon shelves, in the house on Michigan Avenue, filled with handsome morocco-bound sets of the best authors. Loulie supposed that these volumes were part of the decoration of the Yellow Room, and were meant to be looked at but not moved from their places. At all events, no one did move them. Uncle Charles never read anything out of business hours except the *Daily Democrat* and *Putnam's Magazine;* Aunt Bertha's sole connection with literature was the fact that she had once, years ago, met Mr. Dickens at an evening party in Boston.

Aunt Betsy, younger and more frivolous, sometimes bought novels, especially since Uncle Walworth, who hadn't approved of them, was no longer there to discourage her levity. She liked Dickens and Thackeray and Miss Edgeworth, and even less classical fare. On her bedside table that minute, awaiting a surreptitious inspection by her nieces, were two bright-hued trifles: *The Creole Orphans; or, Lights and Shadows of Southern Life,* and *The Three Marriages; or, Life at a Watering Place,* by Mrs. Hubbock, authoress of *The Wife's Sister, May and December,* etc.

Mamma herself, whose own reading was confined to cookery books, the *Christian Times,* and the Scriptures, kept illustrated editions of *William Tell* and *Hermann and Dorothea,* in quarto form, on one end of the long parlour table, balanced on the other by the portly family Bible — red velvet with heavy brass clasps, the names of six generations of Bascombs living and Bascombs dead carefully copied in violet ink on the fly-leaf in Grandpa's spidery hand. These, with *Pilgrim's Progress, The History of the Fairchild Family,* and lives of several celebrated female missionaries to the heathen, were the only books on display at the Triggs'. There was, however, an old case in the upstairs hall, its sagging shelves fairly bursting with poets from Shakespeare to Shelley, fiction from *Don Quixote* to Scott, and a random collection of essays, travels, memoirs, and plays.

The girls were allowed, within limits, to help themselves from this case. Sissy and Nancy had read most of its contents; even Loulie had made her way laboriously through some, without realizing until this moment, when it burst on her with sudden conviction: 'Why — those books must belong to Papa!'

While she was still struggling with this troubling idea, Nancy ex-

44

claimed, with an air of triumph, as if she had discovered a missing clue to the puzzle: 'But, Papa, your *clothes!* You must have gone mining in them!'

And Papa, whose smile had grown broader, though he looked a little embarrassed all the same, folded his arms as he faced them and replied: 'A harmless deception, my dear. Or — I don't know — perhaps it wasn't harmless, after all.'

'Do you mean to tell me,' demanded Aunt Betsy resentfully, 'that that suit wasn't genuine?'

'Oh,' said Papa, 'it's genuine enough. Only I'd never worn it before. As a matter of fact, I bought it yesterday at a tailor's in Lake Street. My daughters, you know . . . I thought they'd expect . . . and I couldn't bear to disappoint them. No doubt it was foolish.'

'Foolish!' said Uncle Caleb. 'It was criminal! Good Heavens! Trigg, you don't seem in the least to realize what this means to us.'

'No,' said Papa, with spirit; 'but I'm trying to. At least give me credit for that. And hear me out, Caleb, before you judge me. That's the only fair thing to do.'

Uncle Caleb set his lips in a firm, thin line.

'We'll hear you out,' he said grimly. 'It's our right to be told as well as it's yours to tell.'

Papa glanced from one face to another, as if wondering which to choose for his audience. Loulie observed that he looked first at Mamma, and sighed as he saw that her expression was blank and flint-like. Finally he fixed his gaze upon Sissy, whose soft grey-blue eyes were wide with excitement. Her lips were parted, a spot of bright colour burned high in each cheek, as she sat beside Aaron on the bench in front of the fireplace.

'Well,' said Papa quietly, in a different voice, 'these things seem very far away and long ago to me now, but it all really began when I quarrelled with Eben Jenkins.'

Uncle Caleb made his noise again; he could not help it. Uncle Charles, exasperated, snapped his fingers loudly.

'Eben Jenkins! . . . That rascal!'

'I never,' said Aunt Bertha judicially, 'trusted Eben Jenkins.'

'No,' said Papa, 'you never did, did you? None of you liked him. I haven't forgotten that. And maybe you were right. He was no one

45

in particular, was he? Just a poor devil of a carpenter, who had to work with his hands for a living and kept a little shop over in Hardscrabble, where other poor devils like him lived, too. But if you remember him, you must remember, too, that I'd not have got to California if it hadn't been for Eben. It was always his dream to go West. He scrimped and saved every penny he could for years; two-thirds of our outfit was his. We had four stout wagons and a whole string of oxen and mules. I still can recall how proud I felt the day I met him in Independence — that was the town in Missouri, you know, just this side of the Blue River, where most of the trains started out. . . . It was the last week in April, rather early to go. Eben was wild to be off; he said we'd better get a head start if we could, for there was sure to be a crowd on their way to the mines that year. . . . As I say, it all seems a long time ago. . . . For the first month everything went pretty well. The weather was good; we were lucky there. I heard afterwards none of the men who came later found it so. It wasn't too hot, and there'd been enough rain to make pasturage for the animals. We were lucky, too, in avoiding trouble with the Indians.'

'Indians, Papa?' cried Loulie, in a fright. 'Were they dangerous?'

Nancy, who had a taste for gore and had read the tales of Fenimore Cooper, asked cheerfully: 'Might you have been scalped?'

Sissy said nothing, but her eyes grew rounder than ever. Loulie saw Aaron press her hand sympathetically, and then blush, for fear he had been observed.

'Scalped?' said Papa. 'No, I hardly think that — though a few of the parties had some fairly hard fights before the summer was over. Indians, you know, are no nobler than white men; they'd rather take what they want without working for it, if they can. Besides, could you blame them? What would you think if you saw the land you lived in invaded by a horde of men and women and children and beasts of burden and wagons — thousands upon thousands of them — all travelling in one direction — the beasts and the wagons laden with stores of bacon and salt beef and flour and sugar and coffee and rice and clothing and bedding and furniture and firearms — enough for everyone, and a hundred times over? For that was the trouble with most of us: we had more than we needed or could comfortably carry. Can you wonder the savages thought we were mad? — or that they felt they had

46

a right to levy duty on our belongings, and take their share of the overflowing abundance? . . . No: the marvel to me is, that they stole so little. . . . We were happy enough, Eben and I, in those early days along the Kaw and the Sweetwater. It was like an army on the march: there were folks from every part of the States — yes, and from nearly every country in the world you ever heard of, too. The work was hard by day, but at night round the campfires of greasewood and prairie grass there were singing and dancing and card-playing and tale-telling, till we stumbled off to bed with our heads in a whirl. It was all new to us, you see, a surpassing adventure; and no one was sure what lay ahead. If we had known, perhaps we shouldn't have been so merry.'

'So you encountered hardships later?' inquired Uncle Caleb, who had averted his head — as had Aunt Jane and Aunt Betsy — during the latter part of Papa's deplorable recital. 'The whole of your journey wasn't, I take it, a party of pleasure?'

'No, indeed, sir — far from it! I don't wish to give you a false impression. As soon as we left Fort Laramie, we plunged into an absolute wilderness. It's what they call the Black Hills country — mountains covered with scrub pine trees and parched rocky land where nothing much would grow. There weren't any roads — we had to break our own trail all the way — and the worst of it was, we broke our wagons, too. They were pounded to pieces going up hill and down dale through those rough stones. Two of them were so badly damaged that they weren't worth repairing — we had to let them go. That meant letting some of our stores go, also. Eben took it mighty hard — he'd saved so long to have money enough to buy them. . . . Then, near Soda Springs, we ran into a train of Mormons heading south towards their new settlement in the valley.'

'Mormons!' gasped Aunt Jane. 'Mercy on us! Brother Trigg, you don't mean to tell me you made friends with those heathens?'

'Well,' said Papa, 'they seemed pleasant enough. They gave us all kinds of good advice, information about water-holes and the like. We stopped several days in Soda Springs, patching up the carts we had left as best we were able — and they helped with that, too. Oh, they were very agreeable fellows — or so we thought. But when they pulled out one morning a good third of our mules went with them.'

'Ah,' said Uncle Charles, 'I fancied as much. I've heard tell of the Mormons' tricks and manners.'

'But we didn't know what trouble was till we started crossing the great desert,' said Papa. 'Nothing we'd met before was as bad as that. I wonder if you'd understand . . . no, there's no use: if you haven't seen it yourself, you can't possibly imagine what it's like. That desert's not brown or yellow, nor even reddish, like some of the mountain country — it's a kind of no-colour, dirty light grey, with patches of white like salt here and there. No living thing grows on it. It's without exception the worst bit of the earth's surface I ever beheld. I couldn't help thinking sometimes, the moon must look rather like this. . . . It's a dead world, empty, played-out, good for nothing. . . . How can I tell you what we went through in the Humboldt Valley? How can I make you feel the heat, the dust, the utter desolation? — share the worries that oppressed us? There was no water for the animals; the little that was left we had to keep for ourselves; and when we did come across a pool now and then, it was one of those bad alkali holes — you know they're bad before you touch them — there's something mean about the way they look. The beasts that drank there never rose again. . . . We lost more than half our oxen that week on the Humboldt, and almost as many mules. The desert was littered with dying cattle, and with the carcases of those that had died before we got there. Even now I don't like to recall that stench. . . . The last day of all, crossing what they call the Sink to the Carson River, at the foot of the Sierras, Eben began acting mighty queer. Poor fellow! He'd lost 'most everything he had, and he was alone in the world — he hadn't a wife and children like me — there was nothing to keep his mind straight. . . . We were trudging along under that awful sun, with old Cato behind us. Do you remember Cato, Sissy?'

'Oh, yes, Papa,' said Sissy. 'Your pointer with the yellow ears, you loved so much. But — didn't you give him to Mr. Jenkins?'

'Yes,' said Papa; 'that's right; I did. Your mother said he was too big to keep in the house, and no doubt that was true. But Cato never agreed with her: he felt he still belonged to me. He used to wag his tail half off if I stopped in at the carpenter shop with a bit of meat for him, and when I joined the outfit at Independence he almost went crazy with joy. A good watch-dog was Cato, wise as the man I named him for. He slept by the campfire every night, with his head folded on his paws like a lion: but his eyes were never tight shut. Many a time he warned us when there were cattle-thieves about—wolves or Indians—he wasn't afraid of any of them. Cato was old, but he earned his keep and shared the luck of the road with Eben and me just like one of the family. . . . Well, as I told you, that last day crossing the Sink of the Humboldt was the worst we'd had. It was all sand and heat and blinding light—and we were forty miles from the nearest water at Carson River. The cattle were so nervous from hunger and thirst and plain fatigue that they jumped at the merest sound. All of a sudden a dog barked, somewhere down the line. It wasn't Cato—that I could swear to—it must have been a terrier belonging to one of the outfits in the rear. Men didn't like to cross the Sink alone; they generally joined up with anyone they met for protection's sake, in case they broke down in the middle of the desert; and we had four or five trains directly behind us. . . . Well, our cattle couldn't stand the noise. There was an old brindled ox with a crumpled horn—I never liked the beast anyhow—threw up his head and bellowed as loud as a foghorn. Then he bolted like a jack-rabbit, with all the other oxen that weren't in the wagon-shafts after him, and those that were, kicking and plunging like mad. Some of the mules bolted, too. I was scared to death for a minute. There was so much dust in the air that at first I couldn't even see what was happening. One of the men in the outfit next ours was riding a pony, and he dashed out on the desert to try to head off our stock. We couldn't have stopped to round up those that ran too far, or we'd never have got through the Sink before nightfall. . . . Well, then and there Eben kind of went crazy. He'd been talking to himself all morning, mumbling away with a strange set look in his eyes. I'd thought nothing of it, because so many of the men were the same. Things had gone pretty hard with most of us: I guess nobody had realized beforehand how much it was going to cost to get to California. . . . Anyway, Eben yelled: "That damned dog of yours!", whipped out his gun, and shot Cato dead in his tracks. I hadn't time to raise my hand to stop him: he gave him a bullet straight between the eyes—the poor old fellow was done for before he knew what had got him.'

'Oh, Papa! Poor Cato!' cried Nancy. Two great tears rolled down Sissy's cheeks.

'So that was the end between Eben and me,' Papa pursued sorrowfully. 'I'd put up with a lot from him, first and last. He was a quick-tempered, fidgety fellow, but I knew he'd made a great sacrifice to go West — and I owed him my chance of making the trip. I didn't mind what he did till he killed Cato. After that, something happened — perhaps the heat had a bit to do with it, or the lack of food and rest — I can't tell now what it was — but suddenly I felt I was through with him. Through for good. I didn't care if I had to walk all the way back to Independence by myself, I wasn't going on with Eben.'

There was a murmur of sympathy amongst the ladies, in the midst of which Aunt Bertha's knife-like tones could be heard clearly reiterating: 'I never trusted Eben Jenkins.' Uncle Caleb and Uncle Charles, whose masculine nerves were steeled to sustain the shock of the tragedy, were obviously on the point of protesting; but Papa held up his hand as a token that he had not finished his story.

'I couldn't leave straight off. I helped him recover as many of the cattle as I could — and that took some time. It was close on midnight before we got through to the river. I think I never was so glad in my life to see anything as that clean, shining water. There's a regular oasis on the other side of the Sink, underneath the high Sierras — groves of cottonwood trees and alders, and a fine lot of streams running ice-cold down from the mountains to feed the river. The grass was long and green. . . . It looked like Heaven after what we'd been through, I can tell you. We were too tired that night to do more than throw ourselves down where we were and fall asleep; but in the morning I woke Eben and told him I was going on alone. I took my pack from the wagon — we had only one wagon left by then — filled it with as many clothes as I could carry, and some bread and cheese and salt beef to eat on the journey. Then I buried Cato under a cottonwood tree by the river and started off on foot over the mountains. I never saw Eben Jenkins again.'

A collective sigh escaped the Bascombs. Its meaning was plain: How like Jonathan Trigg to go off in a huff, abandoning all he had, all he hoped to gain, for the sake of a sentimental whim!

Uncle Charles, who loved to ask questions almost as much as to answer them, could contain himself no longer. 'But, sir, then what? How did you fare? What did you do? Surely it was madness to — '

Papa shook his head and looked irritatingly pleased with himself.

50

'No; I was all right after that,' he replied. 'I managed better on my own than ever I had with Eben. I reckon it may be I'm not made to work well in harness. I got across the mountains quite safely. It was only the middle of September — the snows hadn't started. Of course, it was a long climb, but by that time I was used to a hard outdoor life. It took me just eight days to reach Placerville, where I struck the first of the gold mines — but the rest of my story you know, or at least as much of it as concerns you.'

At this there was a general cry: 'But, Brother Trigg, we *don't* know — you've not told the half — what happened at the mines? — really, sir, of all irresponsible . . .'

Papa held up his hand again.

'Very well, then: I'll continue. Forgive me: I see I have made a mistake. I thought I had gathered from your attitude that, as long as I didn't find gold, you didn't care what else I did find.'

The outcry redoubled in fury. How dared he assume — of course they cared — in Heaven's name, man, what did you next? . . . Loulie saw, however, that Papa was right: though the Uncles and Aunts were curious, his fate did not matter to them any more — it was only Mamma to whom it still mattered.

After a few weeks' inspection of operations round Placerville, and as far north as the Feather River country, the winter rains set in and Papa made his way to Sutter's Fort, intending to return to the mines in the spring. But somehow during the long wet season his enthusiasm melted away. It wasn't the hard life he objected to — though that was primitive beyond anything he'd ever experienced — nor the danger of being robbed or even murdered for his gold (that rather appealed to him). But he was appalled by the monotony of the daily digging and washing, digging and washing, for such small gain. Stories he heard at the Fort were by no means encouraging: it seemed it would take a man ten years at least to make a fortune, and Papa was too old to be patient. At length he decided that prospects were too risky, competition too keen. When the rains stopped, instead of retracing his steps, he used what money he had left to take passage on a boat down the American River to the little city of San Francisco. He stayed there a while, but the place was a bedlam; eventually he travelled along the coast to the beautiful southern part of the new State of California.

Papa had spent months wandering in this land of flowers and vine-yards, soft purple mountains, and hospitable Spanish folk; always expecting to settle, but still driven on from one town to the next by some impulse he could not explain. He'd worked in a dozen different places at as many different jobs in the next four years, trying everything from ranching to roadbuilding, from clerking in a store to running the post-office in some back-country hamlet. Several times he'd been on the verge of sending for his family, but his financial position had never quite justified it. Besides, he remembered how definitely Julia had said she wanted security, a permanent home — things he wasn't able to promise her. . . .

In the fall of '54, without planning it, he'd arrived a second time at Sutter's Fort, where by now the flourishing new town of Sacramento had sprung up. Settlers were swarming thither, attracted as much by the richness of the soil as the nearness to the mines. Money was plentiful; the bookshop idea seemed a good one. There was literally no place to buy stationery and periodicals; one step led to the next; presently Papa found himself part-proprietor of a small business. He and his associates published a paper on the side. Their quarters became a meeting-ground, a kind of haven for the dawning intellectual interests of the community. Things were really beginning to do well — and again Papa thought of his family. His first idea had been to send for them, but then he recalled the hardships of the journey and realized that the only way to manage it was to fetch them himself. He could explain it all, anyhow, better in person than by letter. . . . He hadn't the courage to face the terrible trip overland (though by that time it was nothing compared to what it had been in '49); fortunately he'd been able to arrange passage in a trading vessel bound round the Horn for Boston. Another four months were consumed by the voyage; then, directly after landing, he had fallen ill and lain near death for many weeks, unable to communicate with anyone. At last, however, he was at home in Chicago, ready to make amends for the past. And if Julia were willing to trust him once more . . .

Towards the end of his speech Papa paid no attention to the Bascombs. He even stopped looking at Sissy; more and more directly he addressed himself to Mamma. He appeared conscious of nobody else; he spoke exactly as if the two of them had been alone together. It seemed wrong, thought Loulie, for The Family to be there — they had no right to hear what her father could have meant for her mother's ear only.

'Oh, my Julia,' said Papa, 'I've no doubt in the world I've been a bad husband. I've no doubt you've every right to be angry with me. But I love you as much as ever, and if you can forgive me, I don't see why we should not make a fresh start together. It's not too late for that, is it? My dear little wife, don't say it's too late!'

As he finished his plea he dropped to his knees, as easily as if he'd done the same thing a hundred times before, and stretched out both hands in a gesture half humble, half passionately appealing.

As if in a daze, Mamma gave him hers: before everyone he kissed them, while Loulie felt, still more uncomfortably, that The Family ought not to be in the room.

The next moment Julia Trigg recovered herself with a brisk 'Jonathan, don't be absurd! Such play-acting! Get up from the floor and behave yourself! . . . There! You may sit on the stool at my feet, if you will. . . . Of course, I'll forgive you, if that's what you want. But I still don't believe you appreciate my position. Why did you never write? *Why?* What was I to think? What could I say to our children? I feared you were dead. I might as well have been a widow. I was *worse* than a widow. Not one word from you in seven years!'

Papa had seated himself on the footstool; he tried to take Mamma's hand again — but this time she drew it away.

'Oh, well, my dear,' said Papa, 'as to writing, I do think you might have pretended to hear from me, at least once or twice. You could even have made up a letter. . . . I'd have done it for you, if I'd been in your place.'

Mamma drew her lips tight together, as she did when one of the children displeased her.

'That would have been a lie,' she said coldly. 'Mr. Trigg, you forget yourself. Besides, what would have been the use in pretending? What could I suppose but that you'd forgotten us? Why, we might have starved, for all you knew or cared to know!'

'Ah, no!' said Papa. 'I did not leave you alone, my dear. How could I ever have left you, if I hadn't been sure you'd be safe with your own people? Caleb and Charles have always, worse luck! been able to do more for you than I. And you'd Jane and Bertha and Betsy, too. . . . One thing's certain: in an emergency, there are always plenty of Bascombs!'

'But, Jonathan,' cried Mamma, 'that's not the point! The point is, I was *your* wife — *your* responsibility — not Charles's and Caleb's. I am as grateful to my brothers as I can possibly be, but it was your duty to provide for me and the children — and you failed in your duty. Oh, I don't know what to say to you! You're as wild and heartless as you've always been. Pa was right: I should not have married you. I can never hold up my head again!'

She buried her face in her hands and burst into tears, for the second time that day. But these were real tears: salty, stinging, pitiably abundant. Her eyes grew red, her cheeks flushed and swollen; yet she could not stop. . . . It was as if she were weeping enough to make up for the many years when she had not wept at all.

Loulie looked at her sisters; Sissy and Nancy looked back at her; none of the three had a word to say.

The Uncles and Aunts, on the contrary, all began talking at once in different keys. In the loud and vigorous chorus of abuse, Loulie could make out only a phrase here and there . . . 'Damn it all, man! . . . An outrage, an outrage, I say! . . . served you right if she'd married again . . . always said the Trigg blood was no good. . . . Oh, and with *three* little children . . . the pity of it . . . wasted years . . . repentance . . . how you can ever atone . . .'

As the tumult was reaching its height, Loulie was startled to see Papa jump to his feet, bend over Mamma to kiss her on both cheeks, and start for the door.

Mamma was still crying too hard to speak. Sissy looked helpless and frightened. Loulie seemed tongue-tied. As usual, Nancy was the first to regain her self-control.

'Papa,' cried Nancy, at the top of her voice, 'where are you going?'

'To the Lake House, my dear,' replied Papa. 'I think — don't you? — we've all had enough for one day!'

'But, Papa,' said Sissy, coming to life unexpectedly, 'how *can* you . . . This is your *home!*'

Jonathan Trigg paused in the doorway, came back for a moment, and laid his hand very gently on the shoulder of his eldest daughter.

'I know that, Sissy. It was, once — and I hope, with all my heart, it may be again, some day. But now your uncles and aunts and — yes, your mother, too — seem to feel I've forfeited my right to its possession. That's, I surmise, as it may be. I don't admit it! But for the present I think it best — you all agree, don't you, that it will be best? — for me to remain where I am.'

He swept the assembled family a splendid bow.

'So that, if you see what I mean,' he added, 'I may be near you — but not *too* near!'

The door opened and shut, there were steps on the stairs, the gate to the garden closed with a click — and Papa was gone.

In My Ladies' Chamber

WHEN Nancy was dressed for the evening in her yellow dress, with the gold beads clasped round her neck, she placed all the candles there were on the dressing-table, and then retreated three paces so that she could see her image full length in the glass.

In the soft radiance her eyes sparkled, her cheeks glowed; the gold beads caught the gleam of the candles only to give it back again. Nancy herself was a source of light. . . . She smiled and nodded and kissed her hand.

'I look like a Trigg!' said Nancy aloud to the young girl in the mirror, who smiled and nodded and kissed her hand, too.

It was true, she was no Bascomb. She had often wondered where her features came from: the coarse curly black hair, wide mouth and determined chin — Bascomb chins all receded a trifle — above everything, her eyes, dark blue, slightly slanting, which were not in the least like her sisters' eyes. Now she knew: they were Papa's.

'Papa,' thought Nancy, fastening a rosebud in the ribbon that bound her curls, 'doesn't look like anybody else I ever saw — except me. And he doesn't act like anybody else, either.'

That she was sure of: there had been ample time to study her parent's behaviour in the week since his return. . . . Was it really only a week? she wondered. During it more had happened to make her think than in all the rest of her life up to now. . . . The rosebud, from a bush in the garden, became her, though it was not exactly the right shade of yellow. (Lucky Sissy, with a young man to send her the flowers she wanted!) Nancy frowned, then smiled, then — as there were no further touches to be made to her toilet — plumped herself down on the bench before the glass, leaned her chin on her hands, and gazed enraptured at her shining reflection while she considered at length the problem of Papa.

Papa . . . Papa . . . Papa! What had they thought of before he came? Had they not missed him without even knowing it? Yes, but — and this was even more important — what did Papa feel for his family? Did he love them? If so, why had he left them? If not, what had made him return? Oh, how could one be sure of *anything,* with a man like Papa?

Towards his daughters, Nancy admitted, his conduct had, so far, been exemplary. He had called to see them every day: twice he had stayed to tea, once to dinner. He had taken them for walks in the park, asked them to supper in the great dining-room at the Lake House, made them presents of cakes and sweetmeats as well as some keepsakes brought back from the West. For Loulie there had been a black-haired, barbaric Mexican doll in robes of magenta and orange; for Sissy and Nancy, strings of turquoises set in heavy hand-wrought Indian silver. Best of all, he treated them precisely as if they were grown-up — not only Sissy, which was to have been expected, but the younger ones, too. He acted as though they interested him — that was it, Nancy decided, tossing a scrap of gauze over her head and simpering delightedly at the effect thus produced. (Didn't she look like Lalla Rookh?) It was very flattering and agreeable, to be sure.

On the other hand, why was Papa still at the Lake House? It put the whole family in a most embarrassing position. Had Mamma a husband, or hadn't she? Had Sissy and Nancy and Loulie a father? . . . Sometimes it seemed as if he were merely a distinguished and charming acquaintance, pausing briefly to renew an old tie of friendship with Mrs. Trigg and her children, before moving on about his real business in life. When was he coming home to settle down? And how could *they* settle down until he did?

None of the girls had any idea of his plans. And Mamma knew, if possible, less than they.

Poor Mamma! This week had been hardest on her. Nancy, who loved her mother, but often disagreed with her privately and seldom admired her, felt compelled to applaud her behaviour now. For Mamma, wisely, had chosen to act as if Papa were not there. . . . Not that she ignored him. She was perfectly polite to him when they met, but perfectly

57

calm when they didn't; showed neither impatience nor bewilderment over his unpredictable comings and goings; was, in fact, so completely her old active, impersonal self that it was easy to forget that, inside, she could not be the same. If she no longer looked happy, as on that memorable Sunday morning at church, neither did she look sad. The brightness was brushed from her face, but it had bloomed there so briefly that few noticed its absence. And she never cried again.

This, thought Nancy, was the more remarkable because Mamma, for once, was deprived of her usual comfort of Talking Things Over with The Family. Her pride, very properly, forbade it. There, seething with excitement and curiosity, was Aunt Betsy, whose oblique overtures were checked by a nipping 'Mr. Trigg knows what he wants to do, sister. I presume when his mind is made up he'll say so. Now tell me, would you scallop these edges or hemstitch 'em to match the napkins?' (They were sewing in the parlour at the time on linens for Sissy's hope chest.)

Faced by this stately indifference, Aunt Betsy could only choke and hold her tongue as best she was able.

But of course *she* could relieve herself by running round to her brothers and sisters to discuss every phase of Julia's predicament. This had happened so often in the last few days that she had grown quite breathless scurrying between the Tremont House and Michigan Avenue (with side-stops at home on her way, to make sure that there had been no developments during her absence).

There was nothing any Bascomb enjoyed more thoroughly than exploring, with a second Bascomb, the affairs of a third. Certain subjects seemed perennially attractive: Aunt Jane's Constitution, Aunt Betsy's Chicken Farm, Uncle Charles's and Aunt Bertha's Terrible Extravagance (which could only lead to Ruin). These were frequently enlivened by a new variation on an old theme — for instance, the Self-Raking Reaper (should Betsy buy one? Was it Feckless Folly or True Economy in the end?), or even, occasionally, by something entirely fresh like Sissy's Engagement (were the young people *too* young? What was Aaron Miles's salary? Did Charles really think his prospects were brilliant?).

However, never within Nancy's memory had The Family stumbled upon such a rich, rare, and altogether appetizing topic as the Case of

Julia and Jonathan Trigg. They hashed it over so hard that they tired themselves out: Aunt Betsy returned from her daily excursions hoarse from fatigue — which did not keep her from trying, directly Mamma had left the room, to draw out her nieces' opinions.

Sissy, moved by loyalty to her mother, had refused every bait. So had Nancy, out of simple unconcern. To the latter the question appeared theoretical: with each day it became increasingly clear that what The Family thought Mamma ought to do about Papa, or even what Mamma herself thought, could not affect the outcome. The decision was not theirs to make.

All that mattered was what Papa would (*not* ought to) do about Mamma.

So far, he had given them no clue.

On the contrary, there was no doubt about his intentions regarding The Family. He was not going to see them. Aunt Betsy he spoke to politely whenever they met, which was as seldom as Papa could manage it. The others he frankly avoided. He took no issue, made no scene: simply when they were there, he was not. If he knew they were coming, he stopped at home at the hotel; if an Uncle or Aunt appeared while he was with his wife and children, he excused himself and left, unobtrusively but firmly, by the back door into the alley. (Nancy chuckled aloud as she recalled the first time she had shown him the way to escape.)

Nor did he emerge in public where two or three Bascombs were gathered together. He had not been to church since the first fatal Sunday. No one was surprised when he missed the Young Men's Christian Union on Monday evening: Papa was a man, but no longer young, and by no means so Christian as could have been wished. Fears arose when he stayed away from the Wednesday Lecture and the Friday Prayer Meeting as well. They became certainties as he declined each successive invitation from his relatives.

The Caleb Bascombs nobly asked all the Triggs to dinner at the Tremont — but Papa regretted, with implacable courtesy, that he was already engaged to dine with his old friend Jake Ralston, who wrote editorials for the *Times* (the Uncles read the *Democrat*).

A day or two later Uncle Charles, overlooking this slight with singular magnanimity, suggested assembling some of his business associates for a friendly conference at the Washington Coffee House. Brother Trigg's views on Life in the West, if unconventional, were entertaining: as Uncle Charles said, it took all sorts to make a world. Besides, who knew what avenues might be opened for Jonathan through meeting the leaders of the community? 'A word from me, you know, Julia . . .'

This time Papa had a sick headache.

Unluckily, Uncle Charles, driving home from his office that very afternoon, had passed the alleged invalid, looking the picture of health, out for a stroll in Dearborn Park. It was later reported that Papa had been discovered feeding crumbs to the pigeons — two of which were perched on his shoulders — and engaged in lively conversation with the coloured Town Crier and a disreputable old woman who sold newspapers on the corner by the Presbyterian Church.

Uncle Charles, quite naturally, had looked away to conceal his displeasure; so had his wife, who was with him in the phaeton. But Papa had smiled and waved his hand cheerfully to his brother-in-law, swept off his hat in a splendid salute to Aunt Bertha. . . . What, Nancy reflected, could you do with a man like that?

Since then The Family had made no further gestures. It could only be conjectured what Papa's life was in his hours away from the house in State Street. He was rumoured to have attended, with the renegade Ralston (whose habits were as lax as his politics were dubious), a reception at Market Hall for General Tom Thumb, the celebrated midget. He was also said to have gone several times to the play: that week a troupe of Swiss Bell Ringers were in town, and there had been a performance of *The Merchant of Venice,* after which Papa had been seen by reliable witnesses supping at the Sherman House with Mr. MacFarland, the manager of the theatre, and his pretty wife, who played Portia. . . .

The grandfather clock in the hall downstairs began striking eight. Nancy, who had grown tired of posing in the glass and pretending to be Lalla Rookh, jumped up and began drifting about the bedroom, humming softly to herself. What to do till it was time to go to the party? She might look for Loulie, though there was little point in that, since Loulie was too young to be interested in clothes: her one concern in the evening's festivities would be the hope that her sisters might fetch her a handful of sugarplums. Then there was Aunt Betsy, who was far too apt to want to be waited on: if Susan were not available, Nancy would be sure to be pressed into service to help knot a ribbon or pin on a lace collar. . . . Oh, why didn't Sissy come? From the moment the Charles Bascombs' invitation arrived Nancy had looked forward to discussing in detail every possibility it suggested with her sister as they dressed.

For it was a very special occasion. A family party at the big house on Michigan Avenue would have been delightful enough, but this was to be something quite different, a formal reception for the purpose of introducing to Chicago society Aunt Bertha's cousin, Mr. Wilfred Morgan, of New York City. Mr. Morgan, a graduate of Hamilton College near Utica, had come all the way from the East only yesterday to study law in Uncle Caleb's office. Meanwhile he was stopping at Uncle Charles's with his friend and classmate, Theodore Amberley, who had been engaged to tutor Joshua Bascomb.

It was almost too exciting to be borne! Fancy *two* strange young men appearing at once — strange, that was, to Nancy; for Sissy had met them both in Utica. This gave the latter, her sister considered, an unfair advantage. Ever since she'd heard of their arrival Nancy had tried to make up for it by extracting as much information about them as possible. Sissy had had disappointingly little to say. But Nancy, undismayed, returned to the charge again and again. She had meant to make one more attempt this evening. . . . Where, oh, *where* was Sissy? Past eight o'clock . . . They both ought to be dressed and ready to leave in a minute.

Nancy danced round in circles, so that her saffron skirts took the air. As she danced she sang aloud: 'Oh, the two young men — the two young men — I'm going to meet two young men from Hamilton College!'

Just when she felt she must surely burst if something didn't happen directly, there was a light step in the hall, the door opened, and Sissy came in.

Nancy paused tiptoe in her whirling.

'Sis, I thought you would never get here! What was the matter? Did Mamma keep you?'

'Yes,' replied Sissy calmly. 'About six o'clock she started making

61

cherry jam, and I couldn't get away till the fruit was pitted and ready to boil.'

'Oh, dear, what a bother! Wouldn't you know Mamma'd make jam tonight of all nights? Loulie saw the basket in the kitchen before dinner — we kept out of sight all afternoon on purpose,' declared Nancy, with candour. 'Sis, you're too good. Why should you always be the one to help?'

Sissy smiled her slow, serious smile.

'Well,' she said, 'if I didn't, I wonder who would?'

'But you're grown-up now!'

'What difference does that make? Besides, I like helping — truly, I do. I've done so little these last three years. I'm late, though, ain't I? You'll give me a hand, won't you, dear? I see you're quite dressed — and very sweet you look.'

'Do you really think so?' Nancy spun round on her toes once more. 'This is the first time I've worn my new dress. Aunt Jane made the bodice and sleeves; I just cut out the skirt from the pattern in *Godey's*. Mamma doesn't like it. She says yellow's not a suitable colour for young girls. I *hate* suitable colours, don't you?'

Sissy smiled again.

'Well, no,' she said, 'I can't say I do. But I think, for once, Mamma's wrong. You've done your hair very well, too. I shan't have half enough time to fix mine. Now tell me, Nancy, would you wear the pink tarletan or the white silk?'

'What flowers is Aaron bringing you?'

'Pink roses. I told him what I wanted. If I didn't, I'd never be sure — Men have no taste, have they?'

'Then either will do. Choose the white, so you'll look all right with me, if we're asked to sing. Pink and yellow are horrid together. There, dear, just let me know how I can best be useful . . . Oh, Sissy, have you heard — *is* Papa going to take us?'

'I haven't the slightest notion.' Sissy, at the washbowl, was scrubbing her hands and face briskly. 'And neither, I'm sure, has Mamma. I was there in the hall with them both when she asked him. He wouldn't say he'd go, and he didn't say he wouldn't! All she could get out of him was, "It all depends, my dear." Poor Mamma! Isn't it dreadful? No wonder she wanted to make jam! You know, it helps to

62

be *doing* something —' Sissy wielded her towel with vigour, as if to prove the truth of her words. 'Oh, I did hope, when Papa came home, things would be again as they used to be! But perhaps they can't, ever . . .'

'How did they use to be?' said Nancy. 'I don't seem to remember. And why shouldn't Papa want to go to Uncle Charles's and Aunt Bertha's party? Why shouldn't *anyone?* I don't understand. They give regularly splendid parties.'

'Oh, child, can't you see? That's just the reason —' Sissy began. Then she broke off short, shook her head, as if Nancy were too young to follow her — which was extremely irritating! — and gave a little scream as she looked at her watch. 'Dear me! Twenty minutes past eight — I *shall* have to hurry!'

Nancy, in her efforts to be helpful, upset a tray of pins, dropped her lace handkerchief and then stepped on it, and bumped into the furniture so frequently that she decided at length it was wiser to retire to the bed, from which vantage-point she surveyed admiringly her sister's orderly preparations.

Sissy knew where everything was, wasted no energy, proceeded to shake out and don the white silk, brush and braid her hair, as if she had the whole evening at her disposal. Her eyes in the mirror, as she sat twisting the chestnut-brown satin loops into place, were as grave and tranquil as ever. . . . Or were they?

One could not be sure about that. In the last week Nancy had felt sometimes — this was one of the times — that she did not know Sissy any more. True, they had been separated almost three years — but that was not what had made the difference. During those years Sissy had twice come home for the summer holidays; once all the Triggs had spent August together as Uncle Charles's guests at the Profile House in the White Mountains. And always before the girls had been children together, ready to laugh and play and share a thousand trivial, terribly important secrets.

Now Sissy, though no less dear and loving, seemed suddenly many years older. She was not consciously patronizing, but her demure air of assurance marked a subtle withdrawal from the old intimacy. Could being engaged have changed her so much? . . . Nancy felt it could, if the man had been anyone except Aaron Miles. But *Aaron!* whom

63

they'd played tag with, and hide-and-seek and blindman's buff, ever since they'd lived in the little white house in State Street! Aaron, who was honest and good and simple and stupid about everything outside his old business. . . . Whenever she thought of her future brother-in-law Nancy recalled how she once had slapped his face hard in a childish rage, and Aaron, instead of retaliating in kind, had stared at her with big, black, reproachful eyes and said virtuously: 'I mustn't hit you, Nancy, because you're a girl and don't know any better' — which, of course, had redoubled her fury and made her slap him again. . . . No, it *couldn't* be Aaron, could it? Then *who* — ? Nancy thought she might have a clue, but it was best to proceed with caution.

'Aaron will be here directly,' said Nancy meditatively. 'He's never by any chance a minute late, is he? That's why Uncle Charles says he can be counted on. I expect it's a very good thing, really, but it seems so dull always to be sure of a person, don't you think? . . . But of course you *don't* think, or you wouldn't . . . He'll have to wait till you're quite dressed, and he won't like that one bit. However, I'm thankful he's coming, for now, if Papa doesn't call for us, we'll not be left to go to the party alone. I must say, it's too bad of Papa! Men are trying, aren't they, Sissy?'

Sissy smiled, though her eyes still looked grave. She was busy binding her hair with a rose-coloured ribbon.

'Some men,' she said. 'Not all. Aaron isn't, for instance.'

'Oh, *Aaron!*' said Nancy, with scorn. 'You can't tell me anything about *him.* He's not the only man in the world, though. What about Mr. Morgan and Mr. Amberley?'

'What's *what* about them?' obtusely asked Sissy, engrossed now in polishing her already smooth shining nails. 'I know them both so slightly.'

Nancy pouted.

'That's what you always say.'

'Well' — Sissy's brown head remained bent — 'it happens to be true.'

'But, Sissy, how can you? They called on you at school at least seven times. Minnie Miles told me so. She counted each time. Yes, and she told me you'd dined with them twice at the Turnhams' besides, and been sleighing and skating together in the Christmas holidays — she didn't know how often, because she was home in Chicago then. Yes,

64

and she said — Minnie said that when Mrs. Turnham had your daguerreotype taken Mr. Morgan borrowed the one you gave her — Minnie,
I mean — and he kept it a whole week, and then gave it to Mr. Amberley — and all the boys at Hamilton saw it, I guess, for they didn't
return it for 'most a month — and when Minnie wrote Aaron about
it he was as mad as could be. Yes, and *then* . . . ouch! Rhoda Clemen-
tina Trigg, stop pinching me!'

'Very well!' Sissy relaxed her hold and turned back towards the
glass, her face suddenly flaming with colour. 'But don't you dare repeat that story to a soul! So that's what you and Minnie were giggling
about together this morning in the garden! I might have guessed it.
Minnie Miles is a horrid tattle-tale: you can tell her I said so, if you
like. . . . Anyhow, it wasn't my fault. I couldn't help it if she lent my
picture without asking my permission, could I? I thought she'd sent
it to the shop to have the frame repaired — she said she had dropped
it in the yard. But the minute I found out the truth I got it back. I
explained the whole thing at once to Aaron; he understood perfectly.
Minnie has no right to say he was angry. She's jealous, that's all, because nobody wanted *her* old daguerreotype, though she left it about
in the parlour for days and hinted ever so. No wonder she said . . .
well, come, now confess, what else did Minnie say? I might as well
hear the worst.'

Nancy opened her eyes very wide and looked childishly innocent.
She had accomplished her purpose; there was no point in prolonging
the comedy.

'That's all,' she declared. 'Cross my heart, truly! I'd not have said a
word if I'd guessed it would upset you. I only wanted to see if Minnie
were telling a fib. Now let's forget the whole silly business and talk
about the party instead. I wonder whom Aunt Bertha has asked to
come to it. Who do you suppose she thinks is good enough for her
elegant cousin from New York City? Oh, Sis, just imagine! I'm going
to meet two young men I've never seen before, and I don't know a
thing about them. Not one single thing. You've never described them
at all.'

Sissy arched her eyebrows with a splendid show of indifference.

'Have I not? Dear me! What would you like to hear?'

'Oh,' said Nancy, 'dozens of things! Are they handsome? Are they rich? Shall I like them? Will they like me? Which one do *you* like best?'

Sissy held her slim hands to the light and considered them attentively.

'Handsome?' she said. 'No; I shouldn't say they were particularly handsome. Neither is half so good-looking as Aaron, if you want to know.'

'Oh, you and your Aaron! Well, then?'

'As to their fortunes, I can tell you little. I think I've heard Aunt Bertha say the Morgans were very well-off. Cousin Wilfred, as I believe we are supposed to call him, kept his own carriage and horses at college; he wore a fine fur-trimmed coat when we went sleighing together. Mr. Amberley is an orphan; I know nothing about his people. But if he were rich, do you suppose he would have come to Chicago to tutor Joshua? As to your liking them, I hope very much that you will. As to their liking you, I shall be keenly disappointed if they are not charmed by my little sister. But as to which one *I* liked, there, my dear, you must excuse me. I couldn't possibly tell you. Really I never thought about either seriously enough to have formed an opinion. And I certainly don't expect to devote much time to the matter tonight. Aaron is leaving tomorrow for the Michigan mines. It is my duty — and not only that, but my pleasure . . . Yes, Mamma, we're coming!'

Sissy sprang to her feet, slender and graceful in her white frock, caught up her gloves and her handkerchief, and rustled to the door, where a loud double-knock had just sounded. She flung it open on Papa, in full evening dress, bowing before her.

'My dears,' said Papa, 'will you do me the honour . . .?'

The Two Young Men from Hamilton College

IT HAD BEEN a very hot day. Now, though the sun was gone, the rosy dusk kept some of its heat. There was no wind: the young elms lining the street stood still in their fresh lace dresses. They showed bright green where the gaslight struck them; green, too, were the May flies, clustered thick about each lamp. Nancy exclaimed at their numbers and would have tarried to watch their airy dancing; but Mamma bade her hurry. They were late; there was no time to lose, said Mamma, looking coldly at Papa as she pattered along the wooden sidewalk as fast as her little feet and the uneven pavement permitted.

Papa seemed unconscious of her annoyance. And, after all, did it matter so much? thought Nancy. It was only three blocks to Uncle Charles's; they would be there soon enough. . . . On the avenue a faint breeze was stirring. It blew in from the lake with a warm, minnowy fresh-water smell.

The Bascombs' house was lighted extravagantly from top to bottom. Golden shafts streamed from the windows between tall Doric pillars and fell in bars across the tidy velvet lawn. Mamma and Aunt Betsy remarked them disparagingly as they unlatched the gate and slackened their pace to march, dignified in their best shawls and bonnets, up the path to the door.

'Shocking waste of candles!' said Mamma, with a toss of her head; and Aunt Betsy nodded mournful agreement, pausing to point out the latest addition to the group of iron statues scattered at intervals amongst flower-beds on the grass.

'From New York — arrived yesterday — Charles gave one hundred dollars for it!' moaned Aunt Betsy.

Nancy knew that, keenly as they had looked forward to the party, they were already anticipating, even more keenly, that supremely satisfying moment when they would find themselves once more at home, free to criticize the proceedings to their hearts' content. For there was always, alas! a great deal to criticize at Uncle Charles's and Aunt Bertha's. It seemed sometimes as if Mamma and Aunt Betsy, Uncle Caleb and Aunt Jane, could not call too often to spy out and sigh over each fresh evidence of their rich relatives' ruinous tastes.

The house itself was much too big for them. Its severe classical style, the height of fashion six years ago when it was new, now looked plain compared to the rows of stone dwellings that had begun to spring up along the lake front, flaunting their proud front steps and peaked French roofs and fretted ironwork. (Uncle Charles still thought his home the handsomest in town, but Aunt Bertha no longer cared for the neighbourhood. She disliked the noise and smoke of the railroad and had lately been hinting, heretically, that they might be forced to move to the North Division.)

But it was not the house The Family most seriously objected to, nor even what was in it — though that was bad enough — : it was the use its owners made of it that excited the deepest resentment. Uncle Charles and Aunt Bertha were the only Bascombs who appeared to enjoy entertaining outsiders. Not that they failed to do their share for their own at least once a week, to say nothing of Thanksgiving and Christmas and other appropriate feasts, when they frequently emerged victors from the amiable strife to play host on the incontestable grounds that they had more room at their board than anyone else. Recently, however, their hospitality had become rather dangerously general. They often gave parties for cousins only distantly connected, and once in a while even offered dinners to people who were *no relations at all.* On such occasions The Family were not always included: dismal speculations as to what went on in their absence could not conceal an uneasy suspicion that Charles and Bertha considered these their most elegant routs.

This evening when the Triggs arrived the Blue Room was already quite full. It was apt to appear so even when empty, for it was crowded with chairs and tables and settees and whatnots, statues on pedestals and flowering plants in tubs. Moreover, the rows of portraits on the

brocaded walls seemed like guests come to call. Aunt Bertha, in turquoise taffeta with touches of rust-coloured velvet and a bouquet of
rust-coloured plumes on her head, was so busy weaving about amongst
the furniture and giving arch little cries as she greeted her friends that
at first she did not notice Papa and Mamma.

Nancy saw her father stop on the threshold and stiffen, a trifle awkwardly. (Perhaps he was shy.) Her mother and Aunt Betsy stopped
and stiffened, too — but that was not from shyness. Diminished
though they might feel by the Charles Bascombs' grandeur, they would
never admit it. No, the trouble tonight, Nancy realized with a guilty
thrill, was that they had fallen by chance upon a distinctly *Episcopalian* party.

Mr. and Mrs. Miles were there, of course; but they were the only
Baptists outside The Family — and would one not count them almost
inside it now? . . . The Leslies, the Wheelwrights, the Huntingtons,
were all from the North Division, couples of high fashion, and members of Aunt Bertha's church, Saint James's. Nancy knew them well by
sight: white-haired, benign Mr. Leslie owned the bank where Mr.
Miles worked; jolly Mr. Wheelwright was an associate of Uncle Charles
in the lumber business; sober Mr. Huntington's law firm had its offices
in the same building as Uncle Caleb's. The stately wives of these gentlemen the Trigg girls sometimes met and curtsied to in the Lake
Street shops — but that did not make them really *friends*. . . .

Now Uncle Charles, florid and cheerful, was taking his sisters and
brother-in-law in charge.

'Come in! Come in! Delighted to see you!' said Uncle Charles, who
was so pleased to play host that he did not care to whom: actually he
had forgotten that he was supposed to be angry with Papa and clapped
him cordially on the back.

Aunt Bertha, meanwhile, recalled to her duty, had caught sight at
last of her nieces and Aaron Miles. She smiled at them graciously, precisely as though she had never seen them before in her life, and exclaimed: 'Welcome, my dears!' Then she began steering them towards
a group of young people in the embrasure of the bow window overlooking the garden. 'Here,' continued Aunt Bertha, in her most re-
fined 'New York' voice, 'are two gentlemen who are most anxious to
make your acquaintance. But dear me! How silly of me! Of course,

you've met Sissy already. Wilfred, let me present you to my younger niece, Miss Nancy Trigg. Nancy dear, this is your cousin, Wilfred Morgan, and Mr. Theodore Amberley.'

Minnie Miles, who looked as much like her brother as a plain young woman can look like a personable young man, glanced up relieved to see re-enforcements arriving. (Poor Minnie, long and limp as the white muslin she wore, never knew how to talk to boys.) She blushed now, unbecomingly, all over her thin sallow face, and said 'Oh, Mrs. Bascomb!' with a meaningless giggle.

Nancy blushed, too, but dropped a competent curtsy. The shorter of the gentlemen (why had Nancy counted on Cousin Wilfred's being tall?) bowed elegantly from the waist and murmured, in accents quite as Eastern as Aunt Bertha's, something indistinct about being 'most happy.' If short, he was also far the handsomer of the pair, very fair, with yellow hair rising in waves so orderly as to appear artificial, and thick blond eyelashes he had a trick of dropping over his sleepy, good-humoured eyes.

The other young man was not, Nancy considered, really handsome at all. He was so tall, and had such long arms and legs, that he seemed ill at ease in the Bascombs' drawing-room. His red hair was straight and abundant, brushed back anyhow from a high forehead. He had a pale face and large light green eyes — remarkable eyes, thought Nancy: they looked straight through you and beyond, as if fixed on some distant horizon. Where had she seen another look that recalled . . .? Nancy pondered a moment, then said suddenly to herself: 'Why, of course — it's like Papa, when he was telling us about California!'

Tall Mr. Amberley bowed with less grace than his companion. He also followed Cousin Wilfred's suit in shaking hands with Aaron, whom they had both met in Utica. Cousin Wilfred smiled pleasantly, but Mr. Amberley looked serious: as for Aaron, he positively glowered: probably he was in one of his tiresome sulky tempers, which were apt to last the whole evening.

Mr. Amberley did not seem to notice anything amiss. Having discharged his duty, he approached Sissy, who stood a little apart from the others, and said surprisingly, in a low tone that yet all could hear: 'You see, I came, after all. I told you I would, and I did.'

Sissy's behaviour was still more surprising. She turned pale, but made no reply. Instead she drew herself up, pursed her lips together, and began laughing and waving her little white fan.

'Oh, Cousin Wilfred,' said Sissy, not even looking at Mr. Amberley, 'what a pleasure it is to welcome you to Chicago! Now tell me, what do you think of our city?'

'My dear child,' said Cousin Wilfred languidly, 'how can I possibly have an opinion so soon? All I've seen of it as yet are the railway station and Cousin Bertha's house and garden. I don't mind admitting, however, that my estimate of your society has recently risen much higher than I'd expected it to on my first evening!'

Minnie Miles gave another wild giggle and hung her head. But Cousin Wilfred was as completely unconscious of her as Sissy seemed to be of Mr. Amberley. He glanced at Nancy with intention and began at once: 'You must forgive me for staring, cousin. I was not prepared, you see — Rhoda hadn't told me what a charming little sister she had at home! I vow, if all the ladies of Chicago are as pretty . . . Tell me, do, why they've kept you hidden till now?'

Nancy tossed her curls — how delightful it was to be called a lady, when The Family still considered you a little girl! She thought it unnecessary to explain that she was attending her first grown-up party; it was much more fetching to sigh pensively as she answered: 'Oh, I'm nobody in particular — just the useful one in the house who runs errands for the rest.' (This, of course, was not true — Sissy was ten times more useful any day in the week — but it *sounded* true. For the moment Nancy almost believed it; she saw herself briefly as the family Cinderella.) 'Uncle Charles and Aunt Bertha sent Sissy East to boarding-school, but somebody had to stop at home with Mamma. Besides, she couldn't afford to send me anywhere. I only go to Sawyer's Seminary in West Madison Street!'

That was a terrible admission, but Nancy knew it was best to be frank. After all, Cousin Wilfred was sure to find out sooner or later where she went to school. It appeared that she was right: he sighed in his turn, put his head to one side, and murmured: 'Happy Sawyer's Seminary!'

Then he guided her politely to a seat against the wall, took the chair next hers, and leaned forward in an attitude of flattering deference.

'Dear Miss Nancy,' said Cousin Wilfred, 'will you be kind enough

71

to inform me who all these good people may be? Cousin Bertha introduced me to so many in a row that I couldn't manage to keep them straight, and Miss Rhoda, I'm sure, is too much excited at seeing her faithful swain Ted again to have a thought to spare for a mere cousin.'

Nancy opened her eyes very wide.

'What do you mean? Sis is engaged, you know — to Aaron Miles.'

Cousin Wilfred laughed on a lazy tenor note.

'I know. But look about you a bit, my dear, and you'll see I'm not far wrong.'

It was true — though Nancy could scarcely believe it! Minnie Miles and her brother were left alone in the window, standing disconsolate, not even pretending to talk to each other. Mr. Amberley had drawn Sissy towards the door that gave on the front porch. It was ajar in this warm June weather; their figures were silhouetted against the blue night. They were conversing earnestly. Nancy could not see Mr. Amberley's face, but Sissy faced the room, her head very high, her eyes very bright, her cheeks as red as they had been pale before. She went on waving the little white fan. . . . Nancy was just too far away to hear what they said, which was infuriating. Oh, to be in two places at once! — for it was unthinkable to desert her present post.

Nancy was enjoying herself immensely. She had expected to do so, and so far her expectations had not been disappointed. After that one doubtful moment at the start — rather like pausing to summon one's courage before plunging into a pool of cold water — all had gone perfectly well. Here she was, Nancy Trigg, the youngest person in the room, not ten minutes after her arrival in full possession of the attentions of the principal lion of the evening. Cousin Wilfred seemed to find her artless prattle interesting. (By instinct Nancy had divined that the more artless it was, the better.) He leaned still farther forward, smiling with his eyes as well as his lips, and swore, when she asked him to guess her age, that she must be quite nineteen. . . .

Aunt Betsy, passing on Mr. Wheelwright's arm, shook a roguish finger towards the young people in general, and cooed: 'Oh, what a happy little group!' It was typical of her not to have noticed that both Mileses were miserable, and Sissy and Mr. Amberley as good as quarrelling.

'That's my Aunt Betsy Walworth,' said Nancy. 'I don't like her very well; she has a chicken-farm in Geneva.'

'Is that,' inquired Cousin Wilfred, with deceptive innocence, 'why she wears so many feathers on her head?'

A comfortable buzz of conversation came from the centre of the Blue Room, where Aunt Bertha, enthroned on the tapestry sofa between stout old Mr. Leslie and little leathery Mr. Miles, presided over a circle of the middle-aged and frankly elderly. Uncle Caleb, unaccompanied by Aunt Jane (who was at home in bed, as he explained to all who would listen, suffering from an acute attack of dyspepsia caused by unripe tomatoes), was contributing actively to the buzz. So was Mamma, poised, erect and eager, on the edge of her chair. Only Papa once again, as so often, looked out of place. Flanked by two plump, proper matrons, he appeared a trifle depressed. Poor Papa! He didn't belong with those old people, did he? Not that he wasn't as old as they were — but they were so settled, while Papa was somehow not settled at all. As Nancy regarded him he caught her eye, without warning, over the head of one of the matrons, and gave her a solemn, speculative wink.

Uncle Charles, she observed, did not seem to be settled either. Uncle Charles, for once, was not enjoying his own party. Nancy knew why: it was because, so far, he hadn't been able to show anything off. For this purpose midday dinners were what he preferred, followed by tours of the parlours, the conservatories, the gardens and stables, while he pointed out his books and his ornaments, his plants and his animals; told how much he had paid for them and how much better they were than anyone else's. Deprived of this pleasure, there was nothing for him to do but wander uneasily about the room until it was time for supper, meanwhile disappearing occasionally with some of the gentlemen in the direction of the library, where, judging by the sparkling eyes and heightened colour they displayed on returning, unorthodox liquid refreshments were being served. (Mamma and Aunt Betsy were sure to bewail this, later.)

After a number of these disappearances Uncle Charles plucked up spirit enough to marshal a troop of his weaker-willed guests for an inspection of the ancestral portraits. They were Aunt Bertha's ancestors, but he had lived with them so long that he had virtually adopted them

73

and discoursed with reminiscent ardour of the Washington Allston of his father-in-law, the Mayor; the Gilbert Stuarts of Grandfather and Grandmother Curtis, the Benjamin West of Uncle This, the Trumbull of Aunt That, the Copley of Cousin the Other. . . . Relentlessly down the line he went, describing the history of each relative, as well as the artist who had painted him, at such cheerful length that his audience began to grow restive and perfunctory in their praise. Aunt Bertha, basking in reflected glory on her sofa, called out an infrequent correction of some biographical fact or date.

At last, with the air of reaching a climax, Uncle Charles halted before a picture of his own father, on the wall above the chairs occupied by Nancy and Cousin Wilfred. This was not the stern, starched personage of the portrait at Mamma's, but a much earlier edition: as though in tribute to the clear-eyed, smiling youth, Uncle Charles went far back of the final years in Chicago, back even of the successful career of the master of Chancellor Hall. . . . Half pleased (because she loved it herself), half embarrassed (for what would Cousin Wilfred think?), Nancy realized that Uncle Charles was going to tell what all the children called the 'Indian Story.'

When Grandpa Bascomb was a baby, in the days just before the Revolutionary War, there had been many troubles with the natives in the remote mountain valleys. One day a band of Iroquois had attacked the Bascomb farm, a lonely one on the outskirts of the village. Great-Grandmamma Bascomb was alone with her five children; her husband had driven into Pittsfield early that morning. The four children old enough to walk she bade run and hide themselves in a disused well behind the barn. But what to do with Baby Caleb, who had just been fed and was asleep in his trundle-bed? If she picked him up, he surely would wake and cry! Breathing a prayer, his mother barely had time to push his trundle-bed under the big family bedstead and then rush to join the others, before the Indians, uttering horrible warwhoops, bore down on the farm. . . . Picture the poor woman's cruel anxiety, said Uncle Charles, as she cowered in her damp, musty refuge, cautioning her children neither to move nor to speak as they valued their lives. She knew full well that if her baby made the least sound, he would be found and scalped by the savages. . . . The Iroquois searched the premises, as they thought, thoroughly; helped themselves to food from the larder, stole some clothes from the cupboard; and finally drove two cows and the horse that was left at home out of the barn, after setting fire to it. Then they rode off. Hours later, when Great-Grandmamma Bascomb, half dead with fright, dragged herself up out of the well and ran to the house, there in his trundle-bed, still sweetly sleeping, lay Baby Caleb. . . . 'And do you know,' Uncle Charles ended, glancing around with a happy smile, 'we all owe a debt to that baby; for if he'd cried while the Indians were there, where would the Bascombs be today?'

Mamma and Aunt Betsy and Uncle Caleb nodded agreement: they, too, were smiling. Nancy gave a sigh: she did love the Indian Story, and hoped only that Cousin Wilfred would not think it silly. The guests, most of whom had heard it before, said: 'Oh, indeed!' and 'How interesting!' and 'That's a fact, sir!'

Then, as they had got to the end of the portraits, old Mr. Leslie ventured to change the subject.

'Speaking of Indians,' said old Mr. Leslie, 'it occurs to me that amongst the guests in this house tonight is one who, I dare say, has had all manner of exciting adventures. Mr. Trigg, sir, if I may make so bold as to suggest it, would you be kind enough to favour us with a sketch of your trip to California? I am sure I speak for everyone present when I state that we should be most happy to hear an informal account of your life and discoveries in the Far West of our great country.'

There was a general murmur of approval; Nancy flashed a pleased glance at her father; at last, she thought, someone's taking notice of him.

But Uncle Charles evidently thought otherwise.

'Oh, Brother Trigg had no adventures worth speaking of,' he said, waving his hand impatiently, as though to brush away Jonathan's doubtful claims to the attention of the company. 'He saw nothing remarkable that I can remember — scarce had a glimpse of the gold mines — and ended up in a small town running a stationer's shop.'

Nancy's face fell. Papa's did not; but then, he had probably expected no less from Uncle Charles, who had much to forgive him. Papa, according to The Family, had had his chance and had failed to take it: henceforth he would be only 'poor Julia's husband, who turned out badly.' He looked supremely unconcerned as he shrugged his shoulders, saying quietly: 'Brother Charles is correct, sir. I doubt whether you'd find my story either informative or rewarding.'

Old Mr. Leslie seemed bewildered. He hemmed and ha'd several times, but obviously did not feel like pressing the point under his neighbour's roof. Uncle Caleb thereupon seized the opportunity — for he was a Bascomb, too, and, host or not, Charles had monopolized the conversation long enough — to embark on a monologue about the political situation. 'Slavery ... Anti-Slavery ... Buchanan ... Frémont ... do the Douglasites think? ... fundamentally unsound ... what would the Founding Fathers? ... ruin of the country, sir! ...'

Soon no one else could be heard at all.

After the blazing heat of the Blue Room's wax candles it felt agreeably cool on the porch. The breeze from the lake had freshened; the row of little boats on the lagoon rocked gently at anchor; it was too dark to see them distinctly, but their lanterns bobbed up and down. Nancy and Wilfred almost stumbled over Minnie and Aaron Miles, seated at the top of the steps. As they stopped to speak to them Sissy and Mr. Amberley came into view, having evidently just returned from a stroll in the garden. The six young people found themselves forming a group without having planned it. They were strangely ill at ease. They had nothing to say to one another. It was odd, thought Nancy: only a moment before she had felt like a young lady, capable of commanding any situation. Now, although she could not tell what had happened, she knew suddenly she was a little girl, with no idea what to do. Minnie was angry with her for capturing Cousin Wilfred; Aaron was angry with Sissy for disappearing with Mr. Amberley; and Mr. Amberley, if not angry, was upset for some reason of his own. Even in the half-light Nancy was impressed by his stiffness. ... 'Shall we go in?' said Sissy. 'We've just come out,' said Nancy. Nobody knew what to say next. Oh, it was all a horrid muddle!

A man's figure appeared in the doorway, dark and definite against the hot brightness inside.

'Damned nonsense if ever I heard it!' said the man, in the peculiarly distinct undertone that could belong to one person only.

'Papa!' cried Nancy.

Everything was all right again.

The six young people who had been unhappy were happy once more. The Bascombs' front steps seemed to be the place of all places where they wanted to be. They formed a circle upon them, Papa between his two daughters in the middle, hugging his knees, throwing his head back to drink in deep draughts of the soft night air.

'That's good,' said Papa. 'That's very much better. Charles's houses were always too hot. Feels like rain, though. There's one thing that never happens in California in summer.'

Ted Amberley, on the step below, turned round to look at Papa. As he did so a candle-beam from within struck across his pale brow and large, cold, shining eyes.

'I've been wanting to speak to you, sir, all evening,' he began, with an air of barely suppressed excitement. 'It's the dream of my life to go West. I'm determined to get there as soon as I can save enough money for the trip, so naturally I'm anxious to glean as much information as possible. Anything you can tell me, and care to, will be most gratefully received.'

Papa bowed.

'Why, of course, young man, I'm yours to command, though I fear you may find my tale as deadly uninteresting as my wife's family do. But first I've something to ask *you*. Can you tell me — the moment I heard your name I thought of it — are you by any chance a relative of the Amberley I knew in California? His name was James, and I remember he came from Illinois. The name was unusual; so were the circumstances of our meeting. I wonder . . . perhaps . . .'

Ted Amberley's face lighted up. When he smiled, Nancy thought, he was not so plain, after all.

'That must have been my Uncle Jim. He died out there, but his home was in Naperville, about thirty miles west of Chicago. Did you meet his wife, too?'

'She was a Frenchwoman, I think,' said Papa, 'with an odd-sounding name . . . Zoë . . . Zélie . . . Zéphirine, that was it!'

'My Aunt Zeph, sir!' exclaimed Ted. 'Fancy your knowing Aunt Zeph!'

'It's been a long time since I've seen her,' Papa continued, 'but I am sure that no one who'd once laid eyes on Mrs. Amberley could fail to remember her. A very charming and unusual woman she was and, I doubt not, still is. I came across her and her husband near Placerville. As I recall it, they'd been married only a few months before. Your uncle had been mining up country and had struck it rich. But he'd fallen ill of a fever there in the mountains and was lying at death's door in a miserable log hut. Your aunt was an admirable nurse, but she was at her wits' end what to do. No doctors, no medicines to be had in the wilderness — not even a proper glass window to keep the wind out of the house — and there were plenty of rough fellows about only too ready to take advantage of her trouble to make off with their gold. I was glad to be able to help her get Mr. Amberley to Sutter's Fort and on board the boat down river to the coast. I never heard what became of them after that. It was my own fault, though — she'd promised to write — but a rolling stone like me has no address. . . . Your uncle died out there, you say?'

'Yes, sir: about six years ago. It must have been just after you saw them. They were in San Francisco, waiting to take passage home round the Horn. Aunt Zeph came back alone, and she's been living on the old Amberley farm at Naperville ever since. That was one of the reasons I was so much pleased to accept Mr. Bascomb's offer to come to Chicago. I'm an orphan, you know — Aunt Zeph's all the family I've got, and I'm all *she's* got — so we hope now to be able to see more of each other.'

'A charming woman,' said Papa again. 'I beg you will give her my best compliments and tell her that Jonathan Trigg has never forgotten her.'

'Why, Papa,' said Nancy, 'how romantic! It's just like a story-book, isn't it? — your meeting again after all these years.'

'We've not met yet, my dear,' Papa reminded her, 'though I sincerely hope we may. And I'm afraid there wasn't much romance about those days. Most of the time it was just dirt and discomfort and plain hard work. That was why I admired Mrs. Amberley: she couldn't have expected — no woman of her sort could have been brought up to cope with such terrible conditions. Yet she stayed as cool and serene in that wretched hovel, surrounded by cutthroats and thieves, as if she had been in her own Paris drawing-room.'

'That's Aunt Zeph for you!' said Ted. 'Look at the way she runs

78

her big farm with no help except one half-grown boy and an Indian girl she brought home from the West. She lives there alone all the year round; plants her gardens, tills the land, harvests the crops — and she writes me she ends each season with money to put in the bank.'

'Three cheers for Aunt Zeph!' cried Wilfred. 'Take me out with you some time to see her, will you, Ted? I'd like to meet a woman like that. She must have the regular pioneer spirit. I tell you, no country on earth can beat America!'

'Only Aunt Zeph is French,' said Ted, smiling.

'Well, after all,' said Papa, 'if you go far enough back, all of us came from somewhere else. Maybe there's something in the American air that tends to turn us into explorers. How otherwise can you account for men like Daniel Boone and Kit Carson, who've spent their lives pushing back the frontiers of civilization, pressing on ever farther into the unknown till through their efforts it becomes the known?'

Ted's green eyes flashed fire.

'Oh, that's what I'd like to do, sir — that's how I want to spend *my* life! And that's why I'd count it a privilege to talk with you, to learn all you're able and willing to tell me. Mr. Trigg, you don't know how much this means to me.'

'Perhaps I do know,' said Papa. 'I was young once myself, not so many years ago. I was on fire to make discoveries, too.'

He spoke in his usual level voice, but there was a note in it of underlying longing Nancy had never heard before. And although he went on clasping his knees and gazing tranquilly straight ahead, his eyes were no longer fixed on the bobbing lanterns in the lagoon, but beyond them, where a line of lights showed a steamboat making its way out of the harbour into the black boundless lake.

'Well, sir, you had luck: you were born at the right time,' said Ted. 'Our generation's too late. There are no frontiers any more. Everything exciting is over, it seems to me, that's going to happen to this country. I see nothing ahead but dull commercial development, with every day like every other.'

'There's a place for development, too, isn't there?' said Aaron, speaking for the first time, though Nancy had seen he had been listening closely to the conversation from the beginning. 'We can't all be pioneers. Some must come later to make use of the discoveries, or they

79

might as well not have been made. The man *I* admire is a leader like Mr. Bascomb, who builds on the foundation he's given a fine strong structure with room and opportunities for all.'

'Yes, and good Heavens! Ted,' said Wilfred, in his indolent, amiable way, 'what a world it would be if we all insisted on rushing West! Why, the desert itself wouldn't have space enough to hold us! I speak for the ladies, at least, I am sure, when I say it's a good thing the day of the prairie schooner is passing, if not yet quite past.'

'Mercy, yes!' said Minnie Miles. 'It's no better than being gypsies with no proper homes and out in all kinds of weather. Mamma says she and Papa came all the way from Beaufort County in a coach-and-four, stopping at inns for the night; but even so she wonders how she ever had the courage to leave North Carolina.'

'I remember, don't you, Nancy?' said Sissy, in her soft voice, 'when we first came to Chicago and lived down by the river, there was an empty field next our place where travellers put up their wagons for the night. I used to love to hang on the fence watching them cook dinner over the campfires. I was sorry for the women; they often looked anxious and tired, poor things! Some of them had babies, too.'

'Personally,' said Wilfred, 'I never could see how anyone would care to live anywhere but New York. I mean to say, it's the only place for a gentleman. Even Chicago . . . well, of course, it's all right for a visit and I expect I'll enjoy my year here enormously — but to *live* in, you know, it really won't do. I mean to say, a fellow wants to go to his clubs and the play, and keep up with the opera and all that. I wish I might take you to the Academy of Music, Miss Nancy, to hear Madame de Lagrange in *Norma.* That's what I call music, if you like.'

It was Nancy's turn to be enthusiastic.

'Oh,' said she, 'how I'd love it! I've never been to an opera, nor even a first-rate concert. Mamma said I might hear Jenny Lind if she came to Chicago, but she didn't come, nor Grisi either. That's *my* dream — to wear pearls and diamonds and beautiful gowns and be the greatest singer in the world, with kings and princes at my feet!'

Everybody laughed; and Wilfred made her a little bow as he said: 'I can believe your dream will come true, cousin, when your eyes sparkle so dangerously. Ted and I may be neither princes nor kings, but such as we are, Miss Nancy, we are ready to lay our homage before you. If I mistake not, here comes our hostess in search of you: I was told beforehand we might expect a musical treat this evening.'

Aunt Bertha, a preoccupied frown on her brow, swept out on the porch.

'Oh, there you are, girls!' she exclaimed, in what her nieces secretly called her 'curdled company' voice. 'I could not imagine *where* . . . Brother Jonathan, you have charmed all our young people, have you not? I am sorry to interrupt this delightful little party, but, Nancy, my love, have you brought your music? I've been telling Mrs. Leslie what progress you've made under Signor Tonetti, and she's *most* anxious to hear . . . Sissy dear, you'll accompany your sister? That's a good child! Now come, everybody . . .'

Nancy went willingly to the piano. Singing was as natural to her as breathing; she was humming to herself half the time she was awake; even when silent, scraps of melody chased one another through her curly head. An audience pleased and excited but did not frighten her. She stood very straight in the curve of the Bascombs' big shiny brown mahogany grand piano — an agreeable contrast to the little old upright at home that never stayed in tune — and breathed deeply several times before beginning to sing.

Her contralto voice was warm and rich, and surprisingly dramatic. Nancy listened to it happily yet critically, almost as if it belonged to somebody else.

She sang some Scotch ballads her aunt asked for — *John Anderson* and *Jock o' Hazeldean* — as well as various more modern fashionable fragments Signor Tonetti had chosen as suitable for the young ladies of Sawyer's Seminary. These involved the vegetable rather than the animal world, flowers being the favoured theme, with an occasional bird or busy bee thrown in for good measure, but seldom, if ever, a handsome young man. . . . Sissy dutifully tinkled out the innocuous accompaniments, her slim fingers not missing a note, bending her head a trifle as she peered at the music in the wavering candlelight; while Cousin Wilfred turned the pages with a devoted air.

Nancy was conscious of his admiration, but it did not matter to her so much as she had thought it might. Cousin Wilfred, in spite of his killing glances, did not really care for music. That was something you could tell about people at once. Aunt Bertha did not care either, though she drooped with a far-away listening look on the sofa, sighed at the end of each song, and murmured, 'Quite charming, my dear!' Nor did Mamma, tense with anxiety, as always when her children were performing in public. It was Papa who cared; Papa, who had followed his daughters back into the Blue Room and sat by himself in a corner, hunched up in his chair, apparently heedless of everything but his own thoughts. If Nancy sang better than ever before, it was to win her father's praise.

The climax of the programme was the Grand Duet from *Norma*, which Sissy and Nancy had practised all week so assiduously that they were certain Lagrange and Alboni could scarcely be finer. Signor Tonetti had flung up his hands in unfeigned admiration; he had taught them, too, how to stand half turned towards each other, their feet at 'ten minutes to two,' their hands clasped genteelly, Sissy's on her fan, Nancy's on a lace-bordered handkerchief.

Sissy's soprano was high and clear. It was neither so loud nor so expressive a voice as her sister's. Nancy felt, also, that Sissy lacked the true operatic temperament; more than once she'd regretted not being able to sing both parts herself!

That, however, was impossible. It was likewise impossible for Sissy to play if she were to sing, and a dispute arose as to who should provide the accompaniment. Mamma, the logical choice, had left her spectacles at home; Aunt Betsy did not read fast enough; none of the rest of The Family was musical. A movement was started to draft the wretched Minnie, who protested, giggling and wriggling with mock modesty, that really she couldn't . . . she'd much rather not . . . well, maybe she'd *think* of it, if they'd just give her time. . . .

Finally Papa solved the dilemma by jumping up from his corner, seating himself on the bench, and saying gently: 'My dears, shall I try it for you?'

It became clear immediately that Papa was a musician as well as a music-lover. Never at rehearsals had the Grand Duet gone so well. Nancy, delighted, for a moment almost forgot to sing her first phrase; but then she put forth her best efforts, determined to outdo herself so as not to disappoint Papa.

'*Mira, o Norma, a tuoi ginocchi questi cari tuoi pargoletti,*' warbled Nancy, in the parrot-Italian she had learned from Signor Tonetti.

Sissy came in correctly on '*Ah, perchè, perchè la mia costanza,*' betraying more feeling than she had done at home, and ceasing, moreover, to look quite so placidly cheerful at the prospect of murdering her children.

The number came to an end with a creditable cadenza; Papa improvised some grand thumping chords that produced a storm of applause; and the blushing prima donnas retired in high feather.

So far, so good. Papa had won unexpected esteem by saving the concert. Mamma's back relaxed, slightly but significantly; her brothers broke into smiles: Uncle Charles readily, Uncle Caleb with a kind of grudging geniality. The Bascombs' guests crowded round the piano with compliments. Stately Mrs. Leslie rustled up in her high flowered cap, like a schooner making port under full sail, to inquire if Mr. Trigg knew any Spanish songs.

Papa replied that he did, and obliged with a brief ballad in a soft minor key. It was very pretty, though no one quite knew what it was about: the one word plainly understood by all was *amor.* . . . But Papa's voice, if light, was limpid and well trained; it had, also, a certain wistful appeal that caused Aunt Bertha not only to put on her listening face again, but even to go so far as to support her chin on one hand. The young people made a circle about the singer: Mr. Trigg was well on the way to becoming the success of the evening.

When the Spanish song was finished, Papa swept his audience with a curious questioning glance, smiled impishly (as if somehow he had answered his own question), and then said: 'I can't tell you much about my adventures out West, but perhaps you'd like to hear one of the songs we used to sing? This is it!

> '*I am a happy miner,*
> *I love to sing and dance;*
> *I wonder what my love would say*
> *If she could see my pants.*
> *With canvas patches on the knee*
> *And one upon the stern;*
> *I'll wear them while I'm digging here,*
> *And home when I return.*

'My love writes 'bout her poodle dog,
  But never thinks to say:
"Oh, do come home, my honey, dear,
  I'm pining all away."
I'll write her half a letter,
  Then give the ink a tip;
If that don't bring her to her milk,
  I'll coolly let her rip.

'Oh, I get in a jovial way,
  I spend my money free;
And I have got a-plenty,
  So come drink lager beer **with me!**"

The Closed Door

It was so late when the Triggs got home from the party that even if nothing upsetting had happened, Papa would probably have hesitated to come in. He had escorted his womenfolk alone, for Aaron had left with his own family directly after supper. (This was odd, thought Nancy — but then, so was everything else tonight!)

At the gate Papa kissed his daughters, bared his head courteously before Aunt Betsy, and then turned to his wife . . . 'My dear, I suppose . . . I mean, I hope you don't think . . .'

There he stopped. It would have been no good going on: Aunt Betsy had already stamped off without waiting for his salute, and Mamma, sweeping him scornfully from head to foot, shrugged her shoulders, gave a small exasperated sigh, and followed her sister into the house.

'*Well!*' said Nancy, as soon as she and Sissy were in their bedroom. 'Sis, did you *ever* . . .?'

By this time fairly simmering, she was quite prepared to spend another hour discussing the events of the evening from every conceivable angle. Sissy, however, disappointingly laid a finger on her lips with a virtuous whisper of 'Ssh, dear! You forget Loulie is sleeping next door.' (What nonsense! As if they all didn't know that slugabed would not have wakened though the house were on fire!)

For some reason Sissy did not want to talk. She undressed with tiresome haste, made the briefest possible responses to Nancy's lively questioning. . . . Yes, it had been a lovely party. . . . No, she had not noticed anything amiss with Aaron. . . . Yes, it was a pity the family was angry with Papa. . . . Finally, smiling a little (though her eyes were sober), she blew out the candle, murmuring evasively: 'I'm tired, dear. To-morrow, perhaps . . .'

In a very few minutes her slow, even breathing showed that she was sleeping as deeply as Loulie.

But Nancy did not feel sleepy at all. She lay propped high on her pillows, her eyes sparkling, her cheeks burning, as she reviewed each detail of what she told herself had been the most important night in her life. It was hard to know where to begin, still harder to concentrate on one thing at a time; for Cousin Wilfred's pretty speeches were mixed up with Minnie's giggles, Sissy's peculiar behaviour led (one couldn't figure how) to speculations about Ted Amberley's mysterious Aunt Zeph, and the Grand Duet from *Norma* seemed linked forever to the lively strains of *The Happy Miner*.

Nancy shivered as she recalled the sensation Papa's song had made. The pert little tune had set the young people nodding their heads and tapping their feet, but their elders' faces — particularly Bascomb elders' — had darkened as they listened to the words, every syllable of which, owing to Papa's crystalline diction, had been audible to the guests in Aunt Bertha's Blue Room. Moreover, *The Happy Miner* was mild compared to its successors — for Papa, alas! knew a great many other songs, and he did not leave the piano until he'd sung at least a dozen of them.

Some were only vulgar, but some were worse than that. One in waltz-time, about gay *señoritas* who smoked *cigarritos,* enchanted Nancy until she caught her mother's eye; another, dealing unabashedly with Brigham Young and his half a hundred wives, caused Uncle Caleb to rise from his chair and quit the room.

How long it might have continued no one could tell, if Aunt Bertha had not jumped up, just as Papa was informing the company that

> 'Hangtown gals are plump and rosy,
> Hair in ringlets mighty cosy;
> Painted cheeks and gassy bonnets,
> Touch them and they'll sting like hornets!'

and announced, in a tone so thoroughly curdled it was scarcely fit for company, that supper was served.

Uncle Caleb, it transpired, had been so much shocked that he had gone home without waiting to eat. Aunt Betsy had stayed, but she had

86

markedly shown her disgust by not once speaking to Papa in the dining-room. Uncle Charles and Aunt Bertha could not exactly ignore a guest under their own chandelier; their frozen manner, however, made it plain what they thought of Brother Trigg's disgraceful performance. While poor Mamma . . . Oh, *what* would happen tomorrow?

Nancy was beginning to grow drowsy at last. The various pictures in her mind started revolving more rapidly: Aunt Bertha, chin in hand, wearing her listening look during the Spanish ballad; Uncle Charles's cherubic smile as he told the Indian Story; the blaze in Ted's eyes when he talked to Papa; Sissy waving her little white fan; Cousin Wilfred laughing and saying, in his light tenor voice, 'You must forgive me for staring, cousin. Tell me, do, why they've kept you hidden till now.' . . . Clearest of all, and the last thing she saw before drifting off, was Papa again — not Papa being snubbed by the Uncles, nor paying them back for that snubbing at the piano in the only way he knew; but Papa on the steps in the dark, his head lifted, his eyes solemn and shining, as he watched the little steamboat setting forth on its lonely voyage.

The next day, as Papa had predicted, it rained.

Nancy woke to hear the first drops pattering against the glass. She had overslept; Sissy was shaking her hard to rouse her.

At breakfast the whole family seemed to be in a bad temper to match the weather. Coffee tasted bitter; the toast was soggy; Loulie had a head cold and was snuffling unattractively; Sissy looked pale and distrait; Aunt Betsy refused pancakes and sausages with an air of austerity — Bertha's galantine of chicken had upset her digestion. ('Such extravagant fixings! A good plain cold fowl would have filled the bill much better.' And there was twice too much of everything — did you notice, Julia?')

Yes, Mamma had noticed. High-coloured and cheerful behind the coffee urn, she alone appeared quite as usual. If her blue eyes betrayed signs of recent tears, no one would have dared mention it.

As soon as breakfast was over she declared her intention, Sabbath or no, of potting her cherry jam — 'I know it's not right, but 'twon't be safe to wait till morning' — and, summoning Sissy to help her, descended to the kitchen.

Aunt Betsy went upstairs to pack; she was returning to Geneva on the early Monday train.

Nancy knew she ought to offer her services, but she did not; and Aunt Betsy was too much out of spirits to insist on it. The younger girls were left by themselves in the parlour. Loulie sat on the sofa with her favourite doll Jerusha, a battered one-eyed wax maiden for whom she was making a dress.... 'You mustn't sew on Sunday,' Nancy reproved her. But Loulie said stolidly, as she paused to wipe her nose, that she wasn't sewing, she was only *trying on*.

Tossing her head, Nancy flounced over to the window. Sheets of rain were slanting from a dull grey sky. So much water had fallen that State Street, already a mud-hole, was speedily turning into a brown boiling lake. It was the kind of day on which one could not imagine anything interesting happening.

Nancy stared at the street because there was nothing else to look at. It was quite empty. Up to that moment she had hoped against every probability that Cousin Wilfred might be coming to call, but now she stopped hoping: nobody would be out today who could stay at home.

Suddenly her restless eye was caught by the figure of a man under a huge dark green umbrella. He was wearing a long cloak; the umbrella hid his face; the wooden sidewalk was slippery, so that he could not swing along it with his accustomed impetuous stride — but no one else in Chicago had a walk like Papa's.

Nancy met her father at the door before he had time to knock. He stood in the vestibule shaking his dripping umbrella and smiling a little shamefacedly.

'My dear, is your mother at home?'

Nancy nodded and bade him come in. Papa looked doubtful.

'I don't know, child. Perhaps I'm not welcome.'

'Of course you are!' said Nancy, with vigour.

That much she was sure of. Whatever sins Papa had committed, the white house in State Street would always be open for him. She helped him doff his cloak, took his arm and led him into the parlour, dispatched the wondering Loulie to the kitchen to fetch Mamma. As soon as Loulie was gone Papa ran his fingers through his hair and began striding nervously up and down in front of the fireplace.

88

'Nancy, Nancy, what have I done?' said Papa.

His face was not really pale — no emotion could rob him of what seemed an ingrained sun-tan — but it looked drawn and unhappy, and suggested a sleepless night.

Nancy could not think what to say. There was no use in pretending not to understand what he meant. But Papa was too much distracted to take heed of her embarrassed silence.

Still striding up and down, and as though talking to himself, he cried out: 'I should never have come home! I don't deserve a home. It would have been better had I died in the West —'

'Oh, no, Papa!'

'— than to return only to bring shame and misery on my loved ones. . . .'

To Nancy's relief Mamma arrived. She was flushed from her work and was wearing a long white apron stained with cherry-juice.

'Good morning, Jonathan,' said Mamma, in a voice as brittle as glass. 'I am surprised to see you up and about so early. Have you come to take me and the girls to church?'

'Church?' said Papa, as if he'd never heard the word before. '*Church?* Yes — no — I don't know. Julia, I wish —'

Mamma removed her apron, shook it out and carefully hung it over one arm.

'I'd ask you to dinner afterwards, but we're all dining at the Tremont House with Caleb and Jane. However, I presume they'd be pleased to include you, if you cared to join us. 'Twon't matter your being unexpected, at an hotel. Will you go, Jonathan?'

'Good God, no!' said Papa, looking wild. 'I mean, certainly, dear, if you think . . . do they want . . . after all . . . I mean . . . I mean . . . Look here, Julia, may I see you alone?'

'Yes,' said Mamma composedly.

She beckoned Papa to follow her into the dining-room. As she was shutting the folding doors between it and the parlour Nancy thought she detected — though she could not be sure — the faint beginnings of a smile round her mother's primly folded lips.

Nancy and Loulie were left gazing blankly at the closed door, behind which could be heard a steady murmur of voices.

'What's the matter?' asked Loulie. 'Papa looks queer — and so does Mamma.'

'Oh,' said Nancy, 'you'd not understand if I told you. Isn't it time you were off to Sunday School?'

'Not for nearly half an hour,' replied Loulie comfortably.

'Wouldn't you like to start early this morning? I'll give you five cents to buy limedrops with, if you will.'

Loulie considered the offer, then slowly shook her head.

'I'll give you *ten* cents!'

'No,' said Loulie. 'It's raining too hard. Besides' — as an afterthought — 'I'm not going to Sunday School this morning. Mamma said I didn't have to, 'cause of my cold.'

'Well, then,' said Nancy impatiently, for the voices on the other side of the door were beginning to rise, 'say something, why don't you?'

'What shall I say?' Loulie looked puzzled.

'How should I know? It don't make any difference — just talk, that's all!'

'But,' Loulie objected, 'I've nothing to talk about.'

'Oh,' cried Nancy, 'I could shake you, that I could! You're the very stupidest girl in the whole world!'

The voices were getting louder and louder. It seemed wrong to listen, yet how could they help it? . . . 'Disgraced before all my family,' Mamma was saying, in a thin, angry tone. 'I'd never have believed . . .'

Nancy wrung her hands. She did not dare to leave the room, for fear of someone's interrupting. It was the first time Papa and Mamma had been alone together since Papa had come home. Surely they *ought* to be alone; for how could they be happy if they did not understand each other? — and how could they hope to reach an understanding if they were not left to themselves to talk things out?

Bascombs were never left to themselves . . . 'But it's high time they began,' thought Nancy grimly, taking her post as guard just as Aunt Betsy, her arms full of silk scarves and ribbons she had been about to pack in her trunk, came bustling downstairs.

'Your father's here, isn't he?' said Aunt Betsy. 'I saw him from my window walking in the street. I wonder he has the impudence . . .'

'He's with Mamma in the dining-room,' said Nancy superfluously

90

— since the sounds at the back were no longer a conversation so much as a commotion. 'I guess he wants to explain . . .'

'Merciful Heavens! I should just think he would,' said Aunt Betsy. 'I should think he'd do it now if never before. Though what he can say to make amends for his brazen behaviour last night . . . Of all the barefaced exhibitions . . .! I'm only thankful your poor Uncle Phineas wasn't alive to hear it. If he had been, the shock would've killed him on the spot.'

'Mamma's crying,' said Loulie, round-eyed and worried. 'Papa's making her cry. He must be a bad man.'

'Of course he is, Loulie!' said Aunt Betsy. 'I've known Jonathan Trigg for thirty years — he's as bold and bad as they make 'em! Nancy, why are you standing in front of the door? I'm going to join your mother; she needs me.'

Nancy shook her head.

'No, Aunt Betsy; she doesn't. We'd better leave them alone.'

'Stuff and nonsense! What for, may I ask? Your parents were never alone since the day they were married; they can have nothing to say to each other the rest of us shouldn't hear. Besides, your father owes *me* an apology, too. He's insulted the whole family. The least he can do is say that he's sorry and beg our pardons. Stand back, child, I'm going straight in!'

'No, Aunt Betsy, you're not!' Nancy shook her head even more positively, wondering meanwhile how she found the courage to do it.

Aunt Betsy's pink face began to turn mauve; her armful of silks and ribbons fluttered unheeded to the floor.

'No impertinence, miss! Out of my way, if you please! I'm going in, I tell you!'

Flushed and formidable she advanced. Nancy stood firm, flinging her arms out defensively, as if she were flying. It was unfair — it was cruel — they were all against Papa! Desperately she glanced about in search of help. Where on earth was Sissy? Loulie, gaping on the sofa with Jerusha in her lap, was no good at all. . . . Just then the doors swung open behind her, causing her almost to lose her balance, and Mamma and Papa appeared framed in the opening. Mamma's eyes were like dew-drenched cornflowers. Papa was smiling and holding her hand.

91

'Good day, Sister Betsy,' said Papa. 'I've come to take Julia and the children to church. Dare I hope for the honour of escorting you, too?'

For the rest of the day everything seemed very cheerful. Nancy was so much encouraged that she forgot the pelting rain; she was only slightly disappointed not to see Cousin Wilfred in church. (Of course, he would be at Saint James's with Aunt Bertha.) The sight of Ted Amberley's red head in the Bascomb pew between Uncle Charles and Joshua was novelty enough; he turned quickly when the Triggs came in, and then turned back again, blushing hard.

Papa was docility itself. He sat next Mamma, listened devoutly to Doctor Travers's sermon on 'The Missionary Spirit at Home and Abroad,' joined with lusty fervour in the hymns. When they sang

> *'How beautiful the sight*
> *Of brethren who agree*
> *In friendship to unite*
> *And bonds of charity!'*

he gave Aunt Betsy, on his other side, a humorous look, which she quite failed to return. However, she never stayed angry long: by the time they had reached the Tremont House, though it was raining harder than ever, the domestic atmosphere was clearing.

Uncle Caleb, dourly disapproving at first, and Aunt Jane, who dutifully presented a weaker copy of her husband's attitude, soon found their hearts melting in the warmth of Papa's evident intention to please. He clasped his host's hand with a cordial 'It's mighty good of you, sir, to welcome the unbidden guest!'; inquired with solicitous detail into the state of his hostess's stomach; ploughed his way through a series of overpowering courses almost as enthusiastically as a Bascomb born.

Nancy did not enjoy dining with Uncle Caleb and Aunt Jane. The Tremont House, with its fine marble entrance, its sumptuous parlours, its miles of Turkey-carpeted corridors, was both elegant and exciting; but the young Triggs were always whisked through the crowd and upstairs before they could catch more than a passing glimpse of the lively grandeur below. Uncle Caleb thought it vulgar to be seen in the public dining-hall, so meals were served in their private suite, an oppressive apartment cast in a hushed, perpetual gloom by six pairs of heavy magenta damask curtains lined with china silk of an even deeper hue. The furniture, dark, tortured mahogany, was their own, but it had somehow acquired through transplanting an impersonal look. Nothing suggested human occupancy save a large carved wood Swiss music-box the children were seldom allowed to hear (never to play), and miniatures of the Caleb Bascombs' three little sons who had died in infancy, which stood in funereal state on the blood-red Egyptian marble mantel.

Here in a kind of splendid twilight inertia Aunt Jane passed her days. Uncle Caleb left early for his office, and returned late; with no household tasks to occupy her, much of her time was spent sewing. Sheets and napkins were hemmed and hemstitched by the dozen, handkerchiefs by the score: like a frail, industrious spider she wove miracles of airy embroidery destined for her own and her family's adornment. If she grew hungry, she had but to transmit her order through a magical speaking-tube on the wall to some unseen minion in the kitchen: presently a tray would appear carried by James, a stout greypolled Negro of immense dignity, who wore white cotton gloves and displayed each dish before serving it with a triumphant flourish.

Today, as there was company, James had an assistant, Zeke, also black, also stout (though much younger), also white-cotton-gloved.

The food, Nancy thought, looked heavy and dark like the furniture. Uncle Caleb was heavy, too: he presided at his end of the table with stately solemnity, carved the roast as if he were performing a religious rite, and never laughed out loud or told funny stories like Uncle Charles. Instead he said 'Um' or 'Hum' deep down in his throat, announced how much he had paid for each item on the bill-of-fare, and was dangerously apt, as a deacon of the church, to make embarrassingly intimate researches into his nieces' spiritual welfare, or to catechize them concerning their knowledge of Barnes's *Notes on the Gospels*. Opposite him Aunt Jane, her thin features emerging pallidly from a cloud of Mechlin lace, seemed torn between a hospitable desire to press viands on her guests and dismal forebodings lest indulgence should prove harmful.

Conversation, naturally, centred about Uncle Charles's and Aunt Bertha's party. It could not be thoroughly satisfying, as by tacit consent the principal scandal of the evening was avoided. Aunt Jane, who had already received a detailed account of the guests, menu, and entertainment from her husband, now extracted two more from her sisters-in-law. Aunt Betsy revived her grievance against the galantine of chicken; Mamma deplored Mrs. Leslie's sadly frivolous coiffure; Uncle Caleb wondered dejectedly whether Episcopalians in general were not wanting in sobriety of taste. . . . To Nancy's delight, the two young men from Hamilton College were also discussed. Mamma reported what she had learned from Papa about Ted Amberley's family. Aunt Betsy was positive nobody who was anybody lived in Naperville; Aunt Jane feared the French were even less desirable as a home influence than the Episcopalians. Still it was agreed that Ted was a likely young fellow, sure to prosper if he didn't get what Uncle Caleb called 'ideas.'

Regarding Cousin Wilfred the elders went into an excess of rather dull genealogical details. They had known his mother, a Parker from Pittsfield — not the John Parkers, the Edwards (Mrs. Edward Parker had been a Curtis) — and it wasn't Caroline, the carrot-haired elder daughter (*her* husband was a farmer in upstate Vermont), but Clara, the blond second one, who'd married a Morgan from Rhinebeck and gone to live in New York City. Wilfred's father was an East India merchant, said to be very rich: Bertha had seen their town house in Gramercy Park, and there was supposed to be a big country estate near Rhinebeck as well. . . . When the others had got through with Clara and her houses Aunt Jane rolled up her eyes and declared, with a superior air, that she knew something 'terrible' about young Morgan she wasn't at liberty to tell: had Julia and Betsy any idea why he had been sent so suddenly to Chicago by his family? . . . Uncle Caleb made his celebrated noise and bade his wife be still; there were some subjects, he said, glancing severely at his nieces, altogether unsuited to present company. . . . Aunt Jane looked frightened and subsided. Mamma and Aunt Betsy exclaimed hastily: 'Oh, we're not curious!' (though of course they were bursting! What could it be? Nancy felt certain there was no use in trying to find out now. Later, perhaps, if one could manage to get a grown-up alone . . . for it was just as certain none of The Family would be able to keep a secret more than a few minutes.)

Meanwhile Papa was steering a dazzlingly diplomatic course amongst the conflicting whims of his relatives. He spoke little, but what he said was pleasant and to the point. He agreed with the rest whenever he could; when he could not agree he kept silent. And he refused to lose his temper on any pretext: he went on smiling agreeably even while Uncle Caleb insisted on telling him about life in California. (Uncle Caleb said he knew all about it, having read Buffum's *Six Months in the Gold Mines* and talked besides to a number of really intelligent men who'd spent years in the West.)

When at last James and Zeke had carried away the remains of the pudding and deposited in its place a great platter of fruit (peaches were five cents apiece—highway robbery!—but how about a few cherries?—that is, if one did not find them too acid?), the head of the House of Bascomb rose ceremoniously from his seat, laid one hand on his brother-in-law's shoulder with unwonted affability, and said, in his deepest 'Prayer Meeting' voice: 'Well, well, my boy, God's will be done! He's led you home again by the path He chose, nor should we question His Infinite Wisdom. Now that you've had a full week to recover from the fatigues of your journey I imagine you are beginning to take thought for the future. Brother Charles and I have discussed your prospects—Charles, as you know, frequently comes to me for advice and, I may say, we pretty generally see eye to eye on matters of business. Therefore I feel confident in predicting that he will be willing to take you back into his office. In fact, sir, I am authorized to inform you your old position is waiting for you. Charles wants to let bygones be bygones. He thinks—we *both* think—there may have been some little misunderstandings in the past on our part as well as on yours, but perhaps after your years of wandering you will be more disposed to appreciate the advantages of a safe berth. A safe berth, Brother Trigg—that's what Bascomb and Company offers you. Say the word, and it's yours.'

Papa hesitated for a moment. But it was plain to Nancy that whatever he said would not be the word.

'Why,' replied Papa smoothly, but in a tone that showed he was not untouched by emotion, 'that's very kind of Charles, and kind of you, too, Caleb. I am more grateful than I can tell you. Very likely some day I shall take you up on your offer. But I am sure you won't misunderstand if I say it seems to me altogether too soon to make plans for the future, except the most immediate future. That reminds me, my dear Julia—this Friday's the Fourth of July: I am told Ole Bull, the great Norse violinist, and little Adelina Patti, the child prodigy singer, are to give a concert that evening at Metropolitan Hall. I know you don't as a rule approve of the theatre — I respect your prejudice and was once inclined to share it' — echoes of the Swiss Bell Ringers were here clearly heard, to say nothing of Papa's unorthodox supper at the Sherman — 'but I thought maybe you might be persuaded to make an exception for once and honour me with your company. We could make it a gala occasion and dine out beforehand. I dare say Sissy and Nancy would be happy to go, too, if we asked their Cousin Wilfred and young Amberley to squire them. What say you? Shall the Triggs celebrate Independence Day *en famille?*'

Nancy gasped with delight, too much excited even to notice Uncle Caleb's majestic return to his chair. She had known about the concert for days, ever since reading the first announcements in the paper. How wonderful to hear Patti and Ole Bull, and to dine with Papa at a restaurant first! Think, too, of seeing Wilfred and Ted again, in such thrilling circumstances! . . . But alas! it was all too good to be true. Of course Mamma would say no — she always did.

Mamma, however, was not herself today. There had been something slightly odd about her ever since the scene with Papa behind the closed door. She gave him now a glance that was demure without being cool, and said: 'Thank you, Jonathan, I don't know but what I'd enjoy it very much. It's been a long time since I've heard a good concert. We had thought some of going to the country: Sister Betsy was kind enough to ask us all out for the day to the farm — but I guess she might be as glad of our room as of our company.'

'Oh, don't mention it!' said Aunt Betsy. 'Don't think of me for a moment! Of course, I *had* counted on Julia and the girls for the Fourth — and you, too, Jonathan, if you cared to make the trip — but that don't make any difference. Maybe I can prevail on Caleb and Jane to come out instead, so that I need not be alone. Holidays are sad days to me since poor Phineas left me. But it is a long way to Geneva and when you get there I can't offer you any elegant entertainment — just the widow's mite and a hearty welcome, my dears! You can come to me later, you know — one time's as good as another to me!'

This was exactly how Nancy had expected Aunt Betsy to behave. She knew well enough, too, from experience what would happen next: Aunt Betsy would go on protesting that she was not to be thought

96

of, all the while screwing up her face as if she were going to burst into tears — and then Mamma would say that there was nothing more to be said — naturally, they would all go to Geneva! And that would be the end of the beautiful plan for the concert.

But, to everyone's surprise, Mamma did nothing of the sort. She looked across the table at her sister, with a deceptive mildness that could not conceal the resolution in her eye.

'Very well, then, Betsy,' said Mamma, 'if you really don't mind, dear. It is a long way to Geneva and it's perfectly true — one time *is* as good as another to you. So, Jonathan, if you'll speak for the tickets, we'll consider the matter settled. Jane, I don't like to break up your party, but it's past four o'clock and I'm anxious to get back to Loulie. Her cough was very troublesome this morning and I want her to take cherry pectoral every hour till it shows some signs of improvement. I'll see you all tonight at church. Mr. Trigg, are you coming?'

The Concert

NANCY TROD ON AIR as they left the Tremont House. She was in a fever to rush over to Uncle Charles's and deliver Papa's invitation in person to Cousin Wilfred and Ted Amberley. It seemed most important that they should be told as soon as possible of the treat in store for them. What if they had already made plans for the Fourth and could not 'squire' (oh, delightful word!) Sissy and Nancy to the concert?

But it was still raining too hard, Mamma thought, for the girls to venture so far. And later, when it began to clear, there was just time before evening church to see Aaron off on his journey to Michigan.

The *Northern Belle* would not leave until midnight, but Aaron — it was so like him! — had decided to go on board early and unpack at his leisure, in case it should prove rough outside the harbour. Mr. Miles had hired a hackney coach with two horses to drive to the dock, so there was ample room for Sissy and, at the last moment, for Nancy also, as Minnie, her mother reported, had been suddenly stricken by 'one of her headaches.'

The *Northern Belle* lay in the river at the head of State Street. She was a small white steamboat — too small, the ladies feared, for safety on so long a journey over restless lake waters — but Aaron told them proudly his ship was quite new and had a screw propeller of the latest type.

The dock was deserted, for the cargo had been taken on Saturday and none of the other passengers had appeared yet. Mr. Miles at once sought the bridge to engage the captain, a friend of his, in a conversation — diligent and drawling, like all Mr. Miles's conversations — concerning the navigation prospects for the season. Mrs. Miles bustled about, superintending the unloading and loading of Aaron's luggage;

much to his embarrassment she insisted on interviewing the steward, whom she entreated, with a series of lavish southern smiles, to be sure to take care of her son (only, in her Carolina accent, it sounded more like 'kyar'!).

As Aaron refused to go aboard till his mother returned, the three young people were left by themselves on the dock. Beneath their feet the planks were still wet and shiny, but it had stopped raining: the sky was full of tumbled clouds pierced by an occasional beam from the late afternoon sun. The river looked purple-grey in the shade and green where the sun touched it. White lake-gulls were wheeling and dipping in the warm damp wind.

The little group stood forlorn, the Trigg girls brave in their Sunday bonnets and shawls, Aaron pale and serious, dutifully wearing the navy-blue scarf Sissy had knitted for him (though the weather was much too mild for wool).

Nancy felt strongly that the lovers must want to be alone. After all, they were going to be separated for the whole summer — until just a few weeks before the wedding, in fact. But when she offered to leave them Aaron demurred.

'I have nothing to say to Sissy,' he declared. 'That is, nothing, Sister Nancy, you too shouldn't hear. Sissy knows how much I shall miss her this summer. She knows I wish her the best of health and happiness during my absence. And I *hope* she knows she is sure to have both in full measure as long as her conscience stays clear and she does her duty at home as well as I expect to do mine in Michigan.'

'Oh,' said Sissy meekly, 'that's true, Aaron. I'll do the best I can, my dear. And of course I'll miss you, too. You'll take care of yourself, won't you? Don't work too hard, and don't forget to wear your warm overcoat if it turns chilly — and write to me every day!'

'Well,' said Aaron, 'I can't promise *every* day, for I shall be very busy, you know. But I'll write as often as I can — that's as much as you've a right to look for, I think.'

'Yes, Aaron,' replied Sissy, even more meekly.

She did not speak again till Mr. and Mrs. Miles came back and it was time to leave. Then, suddenly, she flung her arms round Aaron's neck and buried her face on his shoulder.

'Oh, Aaron, Aaron,' cried Sissy, 'I can't bear to have you go!'

Aaron disengaged himself gently and pressed a solemn kiss on each of her cheeks, while Mrs. Miles clucked her sympathy.

'There, there, dearie,' said Mrs. Miles, 'I know just how it is!'

But as they drove away in the hackney coach, with Sissy leaning out of the window and waving her handkerchief to the lonely figure on the dock, Nancy reflected that, really, she didn't know at all. Old people *couldn't* know, especially old people like Mrs. Miles, who was far too dull to see that Sissy's tears were for herself rather than for Aaron. Sissy, Nancy was sure, was sorry to have Aaron go, not because she would miss him so much as because she feared, now that Ted Amberley had come, she might not miss him enough.

Monday was fair. As soon as breakfast was over Nancy proposed once more that they walk to the Bascombs' on Michigan Avenue, but Mamma, who was just leaving to take Aunt Betsy to the station, had other ideas. There was a bouquet of roses fresh-cut from the garden she intended to send to Aunt Jane; besides, she had written a note to Uncle Charles about her investments that ought to reach him directly. The note was important; it would not do to leave it with Aunt Bertha; nothing would answer but for Sissy and Nancy to take it at once to the office of Bascomb and Company.

'But Mamma,' said Nancy, crestfallen, 'then what about Papa's invitation? You know we promised —'

'You can leave word with your uncle,' said Mamma. 'He'll tell the boys when he goes home to supper. That'll be time enough for them.'

There was no disputing their mother's decision. The girls started forth on their errand. Sissy lent Nancy her sunshade and carried the roses instead — for fear Nancy would drop them! She also insisted on taking charge of the note, which was placed for safety in her purse.

It was a beautiful summer day. The sky was turquoise blue, streaked with torn silver fragments of cloud racing before a strong wind. Out on the prairie west of the river Nancy knew thousands of flowers must have come into bloom after the rain. The sun was so warm and the wind so lively that the sidewalks were quite dry. The street, however, was still very muddy. Directly in front of the Triggs' house two carts were mired deep in the yellow slime, and when the State Street omnibus clattered by it raised such a wash of coffee-coloured slop that pedestrians fled at its approach.

100

Sissy and Nancy walked sedately side by side, holding their dove-grey dimity skirts with one hand to avoid soiling them as they crossed corners. They passed the small carriage factory and the business college at Randolph and State (whose recent erection caused Mamma to lament often that the neighbourhood was going down hill); then Market Hall, with its noisy crowds and prevailing smell of cabbages; then the City Hotel on the corner of Lake, where the omnibus started. A row of loungers always stood in front of the City Hotel: Sissy cautioned her sister to walk very fast and be sure not to catch any glances from roving eyes. . . .

It was not till they had got to the end of the row that the last lounger of all stepped forward, hat in hand, and accosted them with a smiling 'Good morning, cousins — well met, indeed! And where are you going, my two pretty maids?'

Cousin Wilfred himself did not seem to be in a particular hurry. He was dressed as if for a party, with cream-coloured gloves, a fresh daisy in his buttonhole; the hat he'd doffed and was carrying with elegant ease under one arm was a tall pearl-grey felt.

Nancy was pleased to see him. She smiled, too, and blushed, and echoed his greeting with great good humour. Sissy, however, looked cross. She straightened her bonnet, patted her hair, gave her bodice a little self-conscious shake — as though she realized it was essential to appear at one's best before such a critical dandy — but her eyes were cold and she curtly refused his amiable offer to accompany them. The girls should have taken the roses first to Aunt Jane — 'Sweets *from* the sweet, is that it?' exclaimed Cousin Wilfred, when he learned their destination — but Sissy decided, suddenly and illogically, that she preferred to make straight for Bascomb and Company. . . . No, they didn't need an escort: if Wilfred were bound (as he ought to be) for Uncle Caleb's office, he might help by delivering the flowers on his way. . . . On second thoughts, though, that would not do. What if he dropped them? Men were so careless! . . . Perhaps they'd see him later.

With a brisk little nod over her shoulder she pulled the laggard Nancy away.

Sissy was in an unaccountable fidget this morning. She would not linger to gaze in the windows of the Lake Street shops — usually one of their most dependable pastimes — and paid no attention to Nancy's protesting wail that they had not had time even to tell Cousin Wilfred about the concert.

'Uncle Charles can tell him tonight,' said Sissy annoyingly, just as Mamma had done. 'I dare say it won't hurt him to wait until then.'

'Sissy,' said Nancy, 'why don't you like Cousin Wilfred?'

'I don't either like him or dislike him,' replied Sissy. 'If you must know, I disapprove of him.'

'Oh, why? Is it because of what Aunt Jane said? Do you know what she meant? Have you heard why his family sent him to Chicago?'

Sissy nodded importantly.

'Oh, what is it? Do tell me! Has he done something dreadful?'

'Not dreadful, exactly. He wanted to marry somebody.'

'Oh! Is that all?'

'Somebody unsuitable,' Sissy qualified her statement.

'Unsuitable! What do you mean? Did Aunt Jane say —'

Sissy hesitated; then candour conquered her desire to appear mysterious.

'Aunt Jane didn't say a word, really. But yesterday after evening church I heard Aunt Betsy trying to get it out of Uncle Charles. He whispered something about "Niblo's Garden" — that's the name of a theatre in New York — and "pretty as a picture," and "named her own price" — so I'm sure it must have been that Wilfred was in love with an *actress*.'

'Oh!' said Nancy; and this gave her so much to think over that she was silent all the rest of the way to South Water Street.

The Trigg girls always enjoyed an excursion to Uncle Charles's office. South Water Street and River Street, headquarters of the wholesale merchants, were narrow and crowded with market wagons; parts of them smelled deliciously of coffee and spices. The lower regions of Bascomb and Company were rather bewildering, full of bales and boxes and shirt-sleeved men, who shouted and stared and spat on the floury floor. But if, instead of entering the warehouse, you opened a green-painted door to the left and mounted the stairs, you came upon the cubbyhole belonging to Mr. Stebbins, the grizzled guardian of the gate. Here he sat all day in a leather chair before a little table, on which stood a smoking oil-lamp. The cubbyhole was so dark that the lamp was lighted summer and winter: it had been there as long as Nancy could remember, and so had Mr. Stebbins. Beyond the door he watched was the big outer office, where the clerks worked in rows at their brown-baize-covered desks; and, beyond that, the small inner one paneled in walnut, where Uncle Charles sat enthroned, puffing cigars, issuing orders, dictating letters, and smiling cheerily as he meditated on the mounting successes of Bascomb and Company. On the wall behind him was a copy of Mamma's painting of Chancellor Hall, flanked by illuminated mottoes in frames: *Honesty is the Best Policy,* said one, and *The Race is Not to the Swift,* the other. Both offices, as well as Mr. Stebbins's cubbyhole, were pervaded by the clean, dusty smell of grain from the warehouse below. But it was the view of the river from their uncle's room that most charmed Sissy and Nancy. They never tired of watching the ships coming up to the dock or leaving it, being loaded and unloaded. It was fun, too, to follow the course of the Lake House ferry, and to pick out the spires of the churches and other tall buildings in the North Division.

Today, however, Mr. Stebbins, greeting them with his squirrel-smile, announced that Mr. Bascomb was out. He'd gone down the street to attend a meeting of the Board of Trade; he might, or might not, be back before midday dinner. If the young ladies cared to wait . . .

'No, no,' said Nancy, who was in haste to be off. 'We'll just leave Mamma's note in his office.'

Mr. Stebbins opened the door to the outer room. As he did so the clerks at their desks raised their heads, then lowered them discreetly as the Misses Trigg passed by. Sissy opened the door to the inner room. As she did so she started, then stopped in her tracks so suddenly that Nancy almost ran into her. At the table in the window that had been Aaron's sat Ted Amberley.

He sprang up when he saw who it was, blushing even more furiously than he had done yesterday at church. (Poor young man! Could he never hide his feelings?) For a moment he was not able to speak, but just stared at Sissy standing in the doorway, Sissy in her grey dimity dress with her hands full of roses. (Nancy, one pace behind, felt that he did not see *her* at all.)

Sissy did not speak either. Nor did she pat her hair and twitch at her bodice, as she had upon meeting Cousin Wilfred. She simply

walked forward holding out the roses. Ted took them from her, his
eyes never leaving her face. It was, thought Nancy, like a scene in a
play. Then, with a start, both actors came to themselves.

'What am I doing?' laughed Ted, giving the bouquet back to Sissy.
'You startled me for a minute — I couldn't believe you were real!'

He went on to explain that he was taking Aaron's place for a few
days, helping out in an emergency. It was holiday time for Joshua
now; lessons would not begin in earnest till September; so Ted was
glad to make himself useful in another way.

Sissy said primly she was sure that was very nice. . . . She explained
in her turn about the note, and Ted promised to see that his employer
received it as soon as possible.

Sissy seemed somehow, Nancy decided, a little confused. She stam-
mered for no good reason, kept saying, 'We must go, we must go!', although they'd just come; and when Ted inquired, rather wistfully, if
there were nothing more he could do, she answered at once: 'Oh, no,
thank you! Just give Uncle Charles our love and tell him we were
sorry to miss him.'

She turned to leave: it was Nancy who cried: 'But, Sis, you haven't
asked him to the concert!'

Sissy looked surprised.

'Why, no more I have!' she said. 'How forgetful of me!'

Ted was delighted to hear of Papa's invitation. . . . How very kind
of Mr. Trigg! He himself was only too happy to accept. It would be
a pleasure to relay the good news to Wilfred. As a matter of fact, he
felt perfectly safe in accepting on his friend's behalf as well. They
had planned to go to the country — Aunt Zeph was expecting her
nephew at the farm, and Wilfred was included in the family party at
Geneva — but Ted was sure no one would want them to miss such a
treat. Besides, their trips need not be unduly postponed, since the
Fourth was a Friday and they were both free for the whole of the
week-end.

Ted conducted his visitors back through the outer office — once
more every head was lifted momentarily — and left them only at the
top of the stairs leading down from Mr. Stebbins's cubbyhole to the
street.

'Good-bye,' said Ted.

'Oh, good-bye,' said Nancy.

Sissy said nothing, though she smiled pleasantly.

It was not until they were quite at the bottom of the steps that she fumbled in her bag and then exclaimed in dismay.

'What a stupid I am! I've still got Mamma's note!'

Nancy felt, when it was over, that she would never forget her sixteenth Fourth of July. It was utterly unlike any other she had known. To begin with, it seemed very strange to have nothing to do. Generally Mamma had the whole family to dinner, but this time Aunt Betsy had invited the Charles Bascombs as well as the Calebs out to Geneva, one could only surmise on purpose to punish the Triggs for their treason. Susan asked for, and was given, the day off: shortly after twelve o'clock she flounced down the sun-baked street under a hat trimmed with unnaturally crimson daisies; but it was so hot that nobody cared about cooking. Instead of the conventional feast the girls ate a cold lunch of bread, tongue, and pickles.

After helping clear away the dishes Mamma shut herself up in her room, saying she intended to take a nap — and that was strange, too, for she never lay down in the daytime. Loulie, who had been appeased for her exclusion from the concert party by Papa's promise to take her next week to the circus, walked with some of her little friends to the lake front to watch the Dragoons parade. There were to be patriotic speeches in Dearborn Park, followed by fireworks in the evening. Nancy could picture from past experience the heat, the crowds, the litter of paper on crumpled grass, the fitful popping of torpedoes exploded by small boys along the pavement. Proud of her newly donned dignity as a young lady, she preferred to sit with Sissy in the shuttered and stifling parlour, wondering what Papa and the 'boys' were doing, and waiting with as much patience as possible for the brassy sun to sink in the pallid and vaporous sky. A storm blew up from the west, then blew away again without dropping its load, though dust rose in little ominous eddies and thunder went on muttering at intervals over the prairie.

Towards evening, however, the wind shifted to the southeast and brought them a puff of fresh-water coolness.

The girls were ready in their best rose-sprigged muslins a good quarter of an hour before it was time to go. They heard the cab drive up to the house, steps ascending, an eager knock on the door, before Mamma came out of the room where she had remained in seclusion all afternoon and appeared at the head of the stairs.

It was not until later that Nancy remembered she ought to have been surprised to see her mother in white — Mamma, who wore sober shades from preference, brown or Quaker-grey during the week and black or dark purple on Sunday. This dress must have been new, for Nancy had not seen it before, though she did recognize the shawl that went with it, the fine soft cloud of blond lace Uncle Charles had brought from New York several Christmases ago (only to be told by his uncompromising sister that it was far too flimsy and she would much rather have had a plain Paisley!). But it was Mamma's bonnet that made Sissy and Nancy both gasp in amazement — or, rather, the ribbon that trimmed her bonnet, tied under her chin in a big bow and fell down beneath it in two long satin streamers. The ribbon was blue, azure-blue, just the colour of Mamma's eyes. If Aunt Bertha or Aunt Betsy had worn it, no one would have thought twice of the matter; but for Mamma to make so deliberately coquettish a gesture caused her daughters' world to rock on its hitherto solid foundations. The blue of that ribbon seemed to light up the hall, and more than the hall. . . . Nancy stopped staring at it only when she saw that Papa had come in and begun staring, too: it needed no mirror to show her that her wondering look was a pale copy of his.

The Restaurant de Paris was in Clark Street. Cousin Wilfred and Ted Amberley, in neat dark suits and very white shirts and collars, their hair watered and plastered painstakingly smooth, met them at the door, and Papa led the way inside. The tiny vestibule was crowded. So was the big bare main dining-room, from which issued a distracting odour of good things to eat. Mamma peered with frank distaste at the rows of happy diners enjoying their soup, and at the perspiring waiters in aprons running to and fro with untidy trays balanced at perilous angles. Nobody seemed to care that the Triggs had arrived. Sissy and Nancy, neither of whom had eaten in a restaurant before, began to worry over what to do next. Just then a plump Frenchman who had no apron, but whose tight red cheeks were spanned by the black parenthesis of a magnificent moustache, hurried forward, rubbing his hands . . . *'Ah, Monsieur Treeg! Bonsoir, monsieur: bonsoir, madame!* Zis way, if you please . . .' (So Papa had been there before!)

Up a spiral staircase that creaked they trooped to the *premier* (at least, that was what the proprietor called it, and Nancy's school-French was equal to the translation — but surely they were on the *second* floor?).

Here a row of small private apartments overlooked the street. As they passed down the hall the girls peeped into one of them and beheld, in a cloud of thick blue smoke, two stout men with napkins tucked under their chins and two equally stout dark-haired women who wore bonnets gay with a great many flowers. Both the men and the women were laughing and talking loudly and drinking a pale yellow liquid with bubbles all through it that Sissy whispered to Nancy must be *champagne*.

'Oh, Jonathan,' Mamma murmured, 'do you think we ought —'

'Par ici, messieurs — dames!' shouted the proprietor, in a jolly voice.

He flung open the door to another little room — this one was empty — ushered them in, and then shut the door again, shutting out as well the noise and confusion and funny smells. Papa and his party found themselves in a square red-brocaded box. A very tall gold mirror took up most of the space on one of the walls, so that there seemed to be *two* dinner-tables — and such pretty little round tables, too! The snowy cloth fell clear to the floor; four scarlet-shaded candles surrounded a centrepiece of fat fragrant red roses; best of all, the napkins, all six of them, were folded elaborately like pigeons' tails.

'Voilà, monsieur!' said the proprietor proudly.

He lighted the candles and, at Papa's request, pulled back the heavy rep curtains to raise the window, so that the breeze from the lake could blow in. . . . 'The French dread fresh air,' said Papa, 'but I think, my dear, we shall be more comfortable like this, don't you?'

'Much more,' said Mamma, smiling now.

'Oh, Papa,' said Nancy, 'what a lovely surprise!'

'It couldn't be prettier,' said Sissy.

'Mr. Trigg's a magician,' said Ted.

Even Cousin Wilfred felt obliged to admit that it was 'well done, really very well done indeed, sir.'

Papa seemed pleased. He seated Mamma ceremoniously at his right hand, as if she were an honoured guest instead of his wife. Nancy stole a glance at the menu, written in a pointed foreign hand in blurred lavender ink: from *consommé clair aux tortues* to *bombe américaine* it was a mystery. . . . Afterwards, queerly enough, she could not remember much about what they ate, except that it tasted good and nothing seemed so odd as its name. (It did come back to her, though, that Cousin Wilfred had said the other night the best test of a gentleman was whether he knew how to order a dinner.)

What impressed her most was the fact that there was wine on the table. The proprietor fetched the bottle himself; it was dusty with age and lay on its side in a basket, but when the cork was pulled — a breathless operation — and Papa poured some of the contents into a glass and held it up to the light, it burned fiery-red like rubies.

'*Château Lafite dix-huit-cent-trente,*' said the proprietor reverently.

Mamma frowned, as Sissy and Nancy had expected. (What else could she do, when she'd told them a hundred times there was no greater sin than drunkenness? A Christian who loved the Lord truly would never so much as moisten his mouth . . .) It was, therefore, surprising to see her take the glass Papa offered her and hold it to her lips before setting it down untouched.

'Not for me,' said Mamma, shaking her head.

But she made no objection when Papa, after serving Wilfred and Ted, wanted his daughters to have some, too.

Nancy was slightly disappointed in the wine. It tasted strong and sour. She could not help making a little face; across the table Sissy was making one, also. That started the boys laughing — but no matter! It was so stylish to drink claret. . . . After two or three sips she liked it better. She began to feel warm and cheerful and talkative. So, apparently, did the others, even Mamma, who was not drinking at all.

Mamma, in fact, was the gayest of the party. Nancy had never seen her so merry. It was as if the blue bow had changed her into a different person. She sat there in her festive gown and her frivolous bonnet, her cheeks rosy, her eyes mischievous, smiling at everything Papa said. She looked and acted like a pretty young girl with her first admirer . . . Nancy could scarcely take her eyes off her mother. Papa, for once, seemed of less importance, though as a host he was incomparable: his easy air of a man-of-the-world reduced Ted, and Cousin

Wilfred too, to the rank of good little simple boys. Even the charms of the *bombe américaine,* all artfulness and spun sugar, could not wholly distract her attention from Mamma.

Papa, also, looked at her most of the time, with a kind of happy bewilderment, as if he could not believe what he saw. But he did not remark on her appearance till the ice was very nearly finished — and then all he said was: 'Mrs. Trigg, ma'am, that's an uncommonly taking bonnet you're wearing tonight!'

Mamma returned his glance with frank satisfaction.

'Do you think so?' she said. ''Tis an old thing, really, but I trimmed it afresh this afternoon.' (So *that* was what she had been up to, while she was shut in her room pretending to nap!)

'I wonder,' said Papa, 'if you can guess what it reminds me of?'

Mamma smiled, but did not answer.

'It takes me back,' Papa continued — 'oh, a long way back, to a girl I used to know, who had a bonnet with a blue bow very like yours. Do you recall the girl and the bonnet I mean?'

'Yes,' replied Mamma. 'But that bow was made of velvet — have you forgotten?'

'Velvet, of course,' said Papa, 'and the bonnet was beaver, because it was wintertime. I'll always remember the first day you wore it. I took you out driving in the old cutter with Rufus . . .'

'Oh, tell us about it!' urged Nancy. 'It sounds like a story.'

'There was no story at all,' said Mamma severely. 'We went to Pitts-field to see Uncle Charles and Aunt Bertha, who had just been married and had a house there that year. It was in the Christmas holidays and snow was thick all over the land.'

'I can see you now,' said Papa, 'tripping down the steps of your house with your hands tucked into your big fur muff. I lifted you over the side of the sleigh. . . . I doubt if you weighed a hundred pounds then, and you haven't changed much since. . . . But I thought while you were in my arms you were the prettiest sight I'd ever seen, in your white woollen cape with the blue bonnet on your dear little golden head. Yes — and I said to myself: "That's the girl I am going to marry — Julia Bascomb's the only one in the world for me!"'

'Nonsense!' said Mamma, bridling. 'I'm certain you thought nothing of the kind. *I* did not, anyway. You were Charles's friend, five years

109

older than I, and I hadn't seen you to speak to since you'd been away at school in Albany. I was frightened to death to take that long ride with you; I couldn't imagine what we'd ever find to talk about.'

'But we got on famously together, didn't we?' said Papa. 'And it didn't seem like such a long ride, after all. On the way back it started to snow — snowed so hard that we couldn't see where we were going. It was growing dark, and the flakes came so fast they looked like swarms of white bees. I lighted the lamps on the sleigh, but they didn't help much. After a while when we got up on Hebron Mountain I began to be afraid of losing the road. It'd have been bad enough if I'd been by myself, but I had you to worry about. I didn't want to *say* I was worried . . . And you were making such a pother about getting your bonnet wet . . .'

'That was because I didn't want you to know *I* was worried, too,' said Mamma, in a soft voice that was new to Nancy.

'Finally it got so bad I didn't dare go on. We stopped just over the crest of the mountain at that farmhouse above the Shaker village — d'you remember? I beat on the door till the farmer's wife heard me, and I asked her to let us come in and wait for the storm to stop. She was a big rawboned woman, but she had a kind face: there was a fine fire blazing in her kitchen. I put Rufus up in the stable and fetched him some oats, and then went to join you. You were sitting by the stove with your bonnet in your lap, your cheeks like roses, and your pretty curls streaming over your shoulders. Girls wore their hair in soft ringlets then, not parted and pomaded down so soberly as they do nowadays; to my mind it was far more becoming. The farmer's wife came in with a pot of hot coffee, and she said to me: "Your wife's frettin' because her bunnit is spoilt. I told her you'd buy her a new one, most likely, next market day." Then she gave a loud laugh, and I blushed, and you blushed; and neither of us had the courage to tell her we weren't man and wife!'

'I was so cold that my teeth were chattering,' said Mamma. 'You made me drink a glass of wine to ward off a chill. I didn't want to do it; I thought it was sinful; but you made me. 'Twas some sort of homemade elderberry stuff. . . . Do you recollect how thick the elderberries grew on the east slope of Hebron? . . . So we sat in that good warm kitchen till it was clear again, and you hitched up Rufus and we drove home in the starlight over the fresh crackling carpet of snow. Pa and Betsy were wild with anxiety, but the bonnet wasn't ruined, after all! The velvet dried out as nicely as you please and I wore it on Sundays two winters running.'

'Oh, that's a lovely story!' said Nancy.

Papa reached for the second bottle of wine, refilled his own glass and the glasses of the young people, and then turned to his wife.

'Mrs. Trigg, here's your very good health!' he said. 'I drink to you. And, my dear, if you love me, I beg you'll return the compliment — just this once, to revive an old memory!'

Mamma said nothing for a moment. Then, to her children's astonishment, she picked up her glass and raised it briefly to her lips.

'Just this once, Jonathan,' said Mamma, still in her soft new voice.

The next minute, in her sharp old one, she was exclaiming: 'Good gracious! Do you know it's a quarter to eight? Settle the bill, there's a good man, and let's be off, or we'll never get to the concert on time.'

Nancy had been to the play only once in her life, to see *Uncle Tom's Cabin* at Rice's Theatre; and she had never heard a professional concert. It was all new and delightful: the posters at the Randolph Street entrance to Metropolitan Hall; the throng on the stairs going up; the flaring lights of the immense gas chandelier that swung from the ceiling; the potted palms flanking the stage, empty except for a big black grand piano — bigger even than Uncle Charles's —; the sound of a fiddle being tuned behind the scenes (that was Ole Bull, surely!). . . . Mamma busied herself seeking out friends in the audience. It was a satisfaction to note that a number of Doctor Travers's congregation had, like the Triggs, forgone prayer meeting tonight. . . . Papa waved across the hall to a shabby, sandy-haired little man with long drooping moustaches, who he said was his friend Mr. Ralston. Mr. Ralston waved back at him; so did his companion, a pretty young lady with very red cheeks and sparkling hoops in her ears. (Nancy thought it might be Mrs. Ralston, but when Mamma asked if it were Papa said: 'No; on the contrary, my dear!' — whatever that meant — and Mamma pinched her lips together.)

Sissy sat gracefully back in her chair, fanning herself (for the hall was stuffy) and listening with an absent-minded smile to Ted Amberley.

111

Nancy was far too much excited to sit back. Neither did she bestow much attention on Cousin Wilfred, who spent one half of his time paying her a string of uncousinly compliments and the other half dropping bits of biographical data concerning the star of the evening. Nancy did not care in the least, just then, whether she looked like a moss-rose in her sprigged muslin. And it was a matter of only mild interest that little Miss Patti, billed as the 'child Malibran' of eleven, was generally reckoned to be several years older. Who minded what her age was, as long as she could *sing?* . . . Well, said Cousin Wilfred tolerantly, of course she had a charming voice; he himself, however, preferred something a little riper and more finished — Madame de Lagrange, or perhaps Louisa Pyne.

Nevertheless, he craned forward as eagerly as his companion when the members of the troupe filed on the stage for the opening number, which, as a concession to the day, was a concerted version of the national anthem. Nancy had no eyes for the assisting artists: Signor Morino, a swarthy young baritone, and the Messrs. Schreiber and Roth, whose presence was required to perform inconspicuous duties on the cornet and piano, respectively. Even Ole Bull, tall and impressive, with his kindly blue eyes and noble crown of grey-blond locks, seemed of secondary importance. All her curiosity was centred on the quaint and elegant little figure in the gay scarlet silk gown. . . . Adelina's raven hair was parted in the middle and arranged in a coronet of braids so tightly moulded that it made her tiny head look even smaller than it was. She was as brown as a gypsy — darker than Papa — and not so tall as Loulie — 'Why, she's no more than a *baby!*' thought Nancy. — But her preliminary curtsy was nonchalance itself. She flashed a white smile and nodded composedly, causing the garnets in her gold earrings to catch the light; and during the instrumental introduction to *The Star-Spangled Banner* she stood absolutely still, only her big black impertinent eyes roving inquisitively round the hall. Then she began to sing. . . .

Nancy was sure she had never heard or dreamed of such a beautiful voice. It was as sweet as clover-honey, as darkly glowing as the wine Papa had given them; so ideally placed that it seemed to come from the singer's lips instead of her throat. Ole Bull's numbers — the *Carnival of Venice with Variations,* the *Witch Dance,* and his own *Mother's*

Prayer—were dazzling enough; but little Miss Patti did more than dazzle—she subjugated her audience completely. Like an exuberant thrush she warbled the *cavatina* from *Linda di Chamounix,* the *rondo-finale* from *La Sonnambula*—every scale, every trill delivered with careless perfection. It was the most natural singing imaginable, yet the most insolently professional. 'Young as I am,' she seemed to be saying, 'I've been able to do this for years. Yes, and I'm going to go on for years doing it, too! Don't you wish you could guess my secret?' ('And *I* wanted to be an artist!' thought Nancy contritely.)

After her share of the concert was finished the 'child Malibran' curtsied twice, smiled brilliantly, and then tripped away, only to be recalled again and again by her enraptured listeners. In response to their cheers she consented to give a few encores, but with decreasing affability. The last time she did not want to come out at all. The Triggs were sitting so close to the stage that they could hear the echoes of a lively dispute in the wings. A man's voice said, *'Ma che? Ma che?'* besides a great many other words they did not understand. And a high, thin, clear treble that must have been Adelina's reiterated with equal persistence: *'Io non voglio—ti dico, non voglio!'*

Those in the front rows smiled, but everyone went on applauding; and presently Miss Patti returned to the platform, followed by her accompanist. She did not look tired by her exertions, nor hot, nor in the least ruffled: her face was no more flushed than at the beginning of the evening; not a strand of the glossy blue-black coronet had fallen out of place. But she was palpably cross. She made a moue, shrugged her shoulders, rolled her expressive eyes heavenward, before signalling to the complaisant Roth at the piano....

> *"Mid pleasures and palaces though we may roam,*
> *Be it ever so humble ...'*

The exotic doll-like little creature, who, presumably, had no home but the series of hotels and railway carriages her wandering existence condemned her to endure, sang the simple air with as much tender feeling as if it had sprung from a lifetime's experience. The whole hall was breathless. Sissy's eyes filled with tears; Mamma glanced affectionately at Papa; Nancy did not draw away her hand when Cousin

Wilfred gave it a fugitive pressure. . . . After the last lovely whisper had died into silence the audience heaved a collective sigh and burst into frantic demonstrations of approval.

Miss Patti curtsied and smiled and rolled her eyes many times more; blew kisses to her friends; clasped to her bosom in ecstasy a bouquet of roses someone had thrown her; and finally scampered off with a parting *'Basta! Basta, Dio mio! Non posso cantare tutta la notte!'*

The lights were dimmed; people began to file out; the concert, so long looked forward to, was over.

Cousin Wilfred and Ted took their leave of the Triggs at the theatre door: as it was a fine summer night, they intended to stroll home together. Ted thanked Papa for a 'capital evening'; Wilfred approached the flowery with his 'I am indebted to you, my dear sir, a thousandfold for a truly memorable experience!' (He pressed Nancy's hand once more at parting, gave her a meaning look, and whispered: 'Don't forget what I told you!' 'I won't!' said Nancy, though she had no idea to which of his pretty inconsequential speeches he was referring.)

Papa drove his ladies home in a cab. Nobody spoke very much: they were still under the spell of the music. At the gate he alighted with them and paid off the driver. . . . 'I need a little exercise, too,' said Papa.

It was so late that the street was deserted except for a few revellers straggling back from the fireworks in the park. The breeze had freshened considerably: it fluttered the leaves of the trees and the long filmy ends of Mamma's lace shawl. In the gaslight the bow on her bonnet looked bluer than ever.

'Good night, Jonathan,' said Mamma quietly. 'The girls and I want to thank you . . .'

'The pleasure was mine,' interrupted Papa. 'It's been a happy evening, hasn't it? I don't know when I've enjoyed anything . . .'

His voice trembled uncertainly. He lingered a moment, as if loath to go. . . . 'And why *should* he go?' thought Nancy, with quick vehemence. 'Why shouldn't he come into the house, and shut the door, and stay at home with us where he belongs forever and ever?'

114

If only Mamma would say the word! But she said nothing at all; so what could he do except bid them good night and raise his hat and walk slowly away down the street through the wavering shadows made by the leaves and the lamplight? . . . Tip-tap, tip-tap, went his heels on the high wooden sidewalk.

It was not till Papa was out of sight that Nancy saw her mother's face had turned suddenly grey.

A Week in the Country

THE LETTER on top of the pile looked different from those underneath it. Sissy took it from the post-office clerk and glanced at it curiously: it was a square of thin bluish paper, not encased in an envelope, but folded in twelve and sealed with wax in the old-fashioned way. The writing was different, too, sharp and slanting and almost illegibly small. Sissy guessed at once who had penned it; she needed no postmark for that.

On the steps of the post office she paused, so absorbed by her thoughts that she paid little heed to Wilfred, who, as usual, was watching from the front window of Uncle Caleb's office (had he nothing more important to do?) and kissed his hand enthusiastically to his cousin. For form's sake she exclaimed 'Popinjay!' with a toss of her silky chestnut curls, which relieved her feelings and did not hurt his, as he was out of earshot. But all the way back from Dearborn Street, walking as fast as she could in spite of the sultry sun, she went on revolving the problem of the letter. It filled her mind to the exclusion of everything else; she even forgot her irritation with Nancy, whose day it had been to fetch the post, but who had gone gaily off after dinner with Aunt Bertha in the carriage to pay calls north of the river. . . . What if their mother were out also? Sissy felt she could not bear that; she could not wait a single unnecessary instant to find out what was inside the thin bluish square.

Fortunately the whole family was at home. Mamma was on the front porch entertaining Aunt Jane, who had 'brought her work' and come to spend the afternoon. Loulie had just come out of the house with a pitcher of lemonade and a plate of sugar cookies; and as Sissy approached the Charles Bascombs' carriage drew up to deposit Aunt

Bertha and the renegade Nancy, fine in their festal plumage, at the door.

Mamma was very good about letters. As a rule she opened them at once and read them aloud to anyone who cared to listen, realizing that nothing was more intolerable to a true Bascomb than a veil of secrecy cast across matters of general concern. Today, though, she was disconcertingly slow in getting down to business. In the first place, hot as it was, there was a certain amount of kissing to be done. (Sissy, unlike Nancy, never objected to this, but it took a good deal of time.) Then Mamma had to make sure that everyone had her share of lemonade and cookies (taking care, also, that Loulie should not have *more* than her share!). After that, Aunt Bertha and Nancy were pressed to describe their itinerary; for it was a cardinal point in the family creed that no excursion, however trifling, should remain unaccounted for. The Huntingtons' new hall carpet, the Wheelwrights' troubles with their cook, the beautiful gilt basket of pine cones and acorns sent Mrs. Leslie by her sister in Baltimore, had to be discussed in detail: Mamma was too busy, and Aunt Jane too indolent, to pay calls themselves, but that did not mean that they were uninterested in their neighbours' affairs.

It seemed an eternity before Mamma, becoming finally conscious of the letters in her lap, picked up the top one and said: 'Naperville! Now whom do I know in Naperville?'

Sissy had trouble in suppressing a gasp, but she sat back in her chair with all the composure she could muster, while Mamma broke the seal, unfolded the sheet, adjusted her spectacles, and then read as follows:

Monday, July 7

Dear Mrs. Trigg:

I am writing to ask if you and your husband and your three daughters would give me the pleasure of coming to stop with me for a week in the country.

Will you forgive that I send you this invitation so abruptly, without having had the honour to meet you? For a long time now I have been hoping to get to Chicago and call upon you, in order to make

117

your acquaintance and renew that of Mr. Trigg, formed many years ago in California. I have also wished to thank you for your kindness to my nephew.

Theodore is staying with me now. It is his presence that emboldens me to waive formality — since at this season I am very much occupied with my duties here — and dare hope that you may be willing to do the same.

I need not say how happy I should be to welcome you all at the farm.

Trusting that I may be so fortunate as to receive a favourable reply, and with sincere assurances of my personal esteem, I beg to remain, dear madam,

> *Yours most truly,*
> *Zéphirine Amberley.*

The thin blue sheet fluttered to the floor.

Sissy and Nancy caught each other's eyes, but neither dared speak: they knew well enough that Mamma would want to hear first from her sisters-in-law. Aunt Jane gaped with surprise and dropped her embroidery hoop; Aunt Bertha, sitting a little apart from the rest, very smart in her apricot-silk afternoon gown, nodded her head several times with an inscrutable air. Loulie, taking advantage of her seniors' preoccupation, unobtrusively finished the sugar cookies.

'Upon my word!' said Mamma at last. 'Now what do you make of that?'

Aunt Jane glanced at Aunt Bertha, as if in search of a lead, and then temporized feebly: 'Zéphirine! What an odd name, to be sure! Where can she have got it?'

'Why, she's French,' said Mamma. 'Have you forgotten that, Jane?'

'Dear me!' said Aunt Jane. 'French — of course, so she is. Well, I suppose that explains it. Otherwise it seems almost forward, don't you think? — approaching you so boldly without having met you, as she says herself. Still I dare say it's meant kindly.'

'Forward!' sniffed Aunt Bertha. 'Brazen's the word *I* should use. The woman's determined to know you, whether you will or not. Of course, Julia, you intend to decline?'

Sissy held her breath: life itself depended on her mother's reply.

118

For once, it appeared, Mamma found herself in a state of indecision.
'Well,' she began hesitatingly, 'I'm not sure what to say. I can't
figure out why she wants to ask the lot of us, when she's never met
any of the family except Mr. Trigg—and not even him for years and
years. Perhaps Ted got her to do it. *I'm* much too busy this month
with my canning and preserving to go anywhere at all, but I don't like
to deprive the girls of a healthful holiday. The city's very stuffy this
weather; a bit of fresh air wouldn't do them a mite of harm. No, and
I doubt if Mrs. Amberley would, either. That's a real pleasant letter
she's written me.'

'Very sly and deceitful, I call it,' said Aunt Bertha. 'Pretending she
hasn't time to pay calls! A woman with any sort of position in the
community can always *make* time for her social obligations. Look at
me! With all that your brother expects of me—and Heaven knows
many a stronger woman would have been under the sod years ago!—
do *I* neglect my duty towards my neighbours?'

'Well, but Mrs. Amberley isn't a neighbour,' objected Aunt Jane.
'She lives thirty miles away.'

'All the more reason, then, for taking care to keep up appearances.'

'And I can't see that she *has* any duty towards Julia, particularly.
Maybe it's just as she says—she means to be kind . . .'

Aunt Bertha tossed her head.

'Stuff and nonsense! No Frenchwoman I ever heard of means to be
kind—unless she expects to be paid for it.'

Mamma—on whom, Sissy saw, Aunt Bertha's worldly suspicions
were having their customary effect—observed mildly: 'Your Joshua's
out at the Amberley farm now, I think you said, dear?'

'Certainly,' replied Aunt Bertha unblushingly. 'I sent him there Saturday. Chicago's no place for a growing boy in summer. Besides, Ted
seems to be able to manage him in a really remarkable way. I can't
think how he does it: the dear little fellow follows him round all
day like Mary's lamb and is so good and amenable it's a positive delight to see them together. But that's a *business* arrangement. I am sure
Mrs. Amberley's a perfectly respectable person; her charges for board
are most reasonable. Naturally, if Julia wanted to send the girls out
en pension, I'd not have a word to say against it. But to put things on
an ordinary social footing—oh, impossible! Why, before you knew

it Mrs. A.'d be getting notions about . . . Well, the French are all artful and designing by nature, and we realize when it comes to young people they've just one idea . . .'

'Oh, Bertha,' said Aunt Jane, who had been nibbling the end of her thread like a nervous rabbit, 'surely you don't think—'

Mamma began to look angry.

'My patience! I see nothing whatever in the letter to suggest—'

'Ah,' said Aunt Bertha, narrowing her eyes, 'you wouldn't, my dear! The creature's too clever to show her hand. Go ahead, Julia, if you insist—disregard my advice! After all, I'm not a Bascomb: I only married a Bascomb! But don't say later I didn't warn you what would probably happen. Mark my words, you'll rue the day you let Jonathan take your daughters to Naperville!'

Mamma's blue eyes sparkled dangerously.

'*You'd* never run such chances yourself, Bertha, would you? You'd never risk an unpremeditated romance in your own family circle, I'll be bound! Very well, my dear: I quite approve of your prudence, with your "Cousin Wilfred" here and your "Cousin Wilfred" there! Only let me tell you this: Ted Amberley's a good young man and an honourable young man. He knows perfectly well that Sissy's an affianced bride and Nancy's far too young for sentimental nonsense. There'll be no such ideas in his head, or his aunt's head, I warrant you, unless *you* put 'em there. As for "letting" my husband do this or that, I have no control over his actions. I presume you're aware that Mr. Trigg goes where he likes and does what he likes; always has and always will! To tell the truth, I'm not sure it wouldn't be an excellent thing for him to get out of the city for a little, while he's in this unsettled state. I know he wishes to think over Charles's offer in peace and quiet—and how can he, when you're all after him every day, wanting to know what he's doing and criticizing him when he's done it? I intend to show Jonathan Mrs. Amberley's letter tonight, and if he thinks as well of the plan as I do myself, I'll pack the whole family off to Naperville next week. Now there's an end to the matter! Who's ready for some more lemonade?'

Sissy stared through the window of the railway carriage at the green meadows and dark patches of woodland flying past her, scarcely able to realize that they were on their way to the Amberley farm. She thought, with a smile, that if she were a young lady in a novel, she would have pinched herself to make it seem true. In the last three days nothing else had been talked of but their week in the country: so much had been said by so many, both for and against it, that it often seemed they would never get off. For, of course, Mamma's bravely decisive speech had *not* been an end to the matter. No one, not even Mamma herself, had supposed it would be. Uncle Caleb and Uncle Charles had had to discuss the plan, first with their respective wives, then together. After that, each Uncle approached Mamma individually. Aunt Bertha, also, returned to the charge several times. Even Aunt Betsy, apprised of the rumour in the midst of the haying season, laid agricultural problems aside long enough to write to her sister to say she was not seriously hurt, but exceedingly surprised and, yes, a little disappointed, too, to think that her nieces were contemplating a sojourn in the immediate neighbourhood of, yet not actually with, a near and dear relative.

Mamma had listened patiently to everybody. She did not get angry; on the other hand, neither was she moved an inch from her original position. She merely repeated, over and over, that (a) Mrs. Amberley had written a very kind letter; (b) the girls ought to benefit by a change of air; and (c) Mr. Trigg went where he liked and did what he liked — always had and always would.

So here, incredibly, they were, puffing over the prairies at the dizzy rate of twenty miles an hour, in the precise train they'd have taken had they been bound for Aunt Betsy's! Nothing, felt Sissy, more strongly emphasized the extraordinary difference in their present situation. Everything was the same — yet nothing was, really. How strange, for instance, it seemed to be travelling anywhere with a man! — or, rather, *two* men; for when they had got to the station that afternoon Cousin Wilfred had been waiting on the platform beside Papa. . . . Mamma, thought Sissy, might well have wavered at the last moment if she had known about Wilfred; but no one had known. That, at least, was what one must hope: it was not easy to tell whether Nancy's loud exclamations of surprise were entirely sincere. She was sitting with him now in the front compartment of the carriage, laughing at everything she saw (though it were only a red-painted barn or a drove of pigs in a field) and everything Wilfred said. . . . Nancy, it was only too obvious, had got to the giggling stage.

Sissy drew herself up in a superior manner: *she* hadn't giggled for two years or more. Indeed, she had never had time for fun, except in Utica with the girls at Miss Crandall's. Life at Number Eighty, State Street, was not exactly conducive to merriment. Besides, Mamma told her, she was the eldest and must set an example to the others.

Mindful now of her responsibilities, she looked down at Loulie, who was next her. Loulie's fat legs were too short to reach the floor; she sat clutching in one hand a new purse Mamma had given her and, with the other, smoothing down her plum-blue valencia skirts to prevent her pantalettes from showing unduly. The effort kept her solemn and pre-occupied; today she did not even tease, whenever the train slowed down near a station, with her usual cuckoo-cry of 'Sis, are we there?' — to which Sissy, sweetly indulgent, would reply: 'No, dear; it's only Cottage Hill' (or 'Babcock's Grove,' or 'Danby,' as the case might be). 'I'll let you know when it's time to get out.'

On the opposite bench Papa was reading the *Times*. He glanced up, as he felt his daughter's eyes upon him, and gave her a smile. Sissy smiled back, happy because he seemed to be. Papa, after all, was also one of her responsibilities — indeed, on this trip the chief of them. She was glad, for his sake, they were going to Naperville. The last few days had been very hard. His return to the family favour had been painfully brief: ever since his evasion of the Uncles' offer the atmosphere had grown colder and colder. Surely, then, it would be best for everybody that he be removed for a time from his relatives' reach — perhaps from his wife's reach as well! If Papa and Mamma were not to live together like a proper married couple, why, they had better be quite apart, at least until they made up their minds what they *were* going to do.

Nancy, Sissy knew, did not agree with her; she wanted to throw their parents continually together, hoping that with repeated exposure they might grow used to each other again. And Nancy blamed their mother for the separation; she could not see why Mamma did not just say the word and call Papa back. . . . What a child she was still! As though it were as easy as that! For what *was* the word? And supposing Mamma could find it — supposing she did decide to hold up her hand

122

and give the signal — who could guarantee that Papa would heed? Or even, if he did, that he would be willing to return on her basis — on a sensible Bascomb basis, that was — and not on some wildly extravagant terms of his own? (For though Sissy loved Papa dearly, she could not pretend *he* was sensible.)

No! Mamma was right. She would not stoop to entreat; she would not force herself on Papa. She waited with patience, with dignity, for him to come to his choice. If he chose her and the children, they would receive him. If he chose freedom instead, she would accept her fate proudly. So much was clear. . . . Sissy applauded this strength of character. She would have acted the same way herself. She had not dared say anything to her mother, but she knew, without being told, that the latter was grateful for her unspoken approval.

'I understand Mamma because I am like her,' said Sissy to herself. 'And Nancy understands Papa, perhaps better than I do, because *she's* like *him*. Both of us understand both of them pretty well, though, because there's some of each of them in each of us. But *who* is going to make them understand each other?'

Then, as there was still a long way to go, she began thinking about herself, which was something she really had not had time to do lately. Or perhaps — Sissy puckered her brow while she forced herself to consider — she had deliberately avoided the topic. For to think about herself *by* herself, as a separate person, strangely did not seem to be possible any more. She could no longer restrict her reflections to 'My velvet snood's becoming,' or, 'Shall I get the drawing-prize?' or, 'I wonder if Miss Crandall's having blackberry jam to tea.' She was a woman now, with a woman's problems. (Miss Crandall had said that to the graduating class at the Academy: Sissy found it was only too true.) And the principal problem a woman had, it seemed clear, was Other People. Once you were an adult there was always some person — some *man*, to be specific — thrusting himself on your notice, pushing his way into your life, wanting to be with you, to influence you, to *own* you, till you felt distracted enough to scream.

'Take me, for instance,' thought Sissy mournfully, 'I'm in a worse position than *anybody*, because there's not one person wants me, but *two!*' . . . Aaron and Ted — Ted and Aaron! If either were out of the picture, would it be easier to come to terms with the other?

Of course, Aaron *was* away for a while. Although she did miss him, Sissy could not help being glad of that. But he would come back. In September he'd come, and then they'd be married. There was her future, happy and definite, lying straight ahead. She had known Aaron so long and so intimately that she could not imagine life without him. He had been part of it almost ever since she had come to Chicago. The grave, quiet little boy, sharing her games and Nancy's; the grave, quiet youth, carrying her books with his to school; the grave, quiet young man, choosing her as his partner at dances or singling her out, with steady persistence, to sit next to at the weekly church suppers after sewing circle — why, she could scarcely recall a time when he'd not been there, firmly attached, no less surely her slave because she was too gentle to play the part of tyrant. (It was Nancy who had ordered him about.) Sissy had taken his devotion so much for granted that there had been little need of words to define it; now, on her conscience, she could not say when he had proposed or if, indeed, he had ever formally asked her to marry him. Neither, assuredly, had she asked herself whether or not she loved Aaron Miles. . . . She *liked* him very much; she admired his honesty, his dependability, his sturdy capacity for work. It would have been pleasant if he had had a sense of humour, too; but humour wasn't essential. (In many ways it was easier to love people who never made you laugh. Fancy feeling sentimental about a mounte-bank like Cousin Wilfred!) And there was no question that Aaron cared for her; she was fond of Mr. and Mrs. Miles and, of course, of Minnie (poor Minnie!). . . . The Mileses were fond of her, too, and Mamma and Uncle Charles and all the rest of The Family thought the world of Aaron. So why need she worry for even a moment . . . ?

Naturally, she did not need to. There was no doubt about anything. Aaron was her betrothed. He would be her husband. He was in love with her — so she *must* be in love with him — that was all there was to it!

Why, Sissy wondered, was she obliged to think about Ted Amberley at all? Why should a boy she had seen scarce a dozen times have so quickly assumed the power to excite and upset her? Seven months ago she hadn't even known he existed. . . . They had first met at the skating-rink in Utica, one December afternoon. It had been a very cold day, bitter and biting as it was in central New York. They had marked each other at once, for it was late and the rink was almost deserted; but they might not have spoken, if one of Sissy's skate-straps had not come loose. Ted had briefly offered his services; Sissy had accepted them, equally briefly; after thanking him she had skated away in the gathering dusk, with her muff held to her face. . . . And that night (how they'd laughed about it later!) he'd appeared at the Turnhams' with Wilfred Morgan (for whom, of course, Mrs. Turnham was Cousin Anna). After that, they had seen each other fairly frequently at skating and sleighing parties. The Hamilton College boys were often in Utica. In the spring they'd gone berrying together on picnics. But that was all, really: both young people had been hard at work preparing for their respective graduations.

Now since Ted's coming to Chicago they had met very seldom. Four times all told: at Aunt Bertha's party, in Uncle Charles's office, the night of the Patti concert, and once when he'd come to call after prayer meeting and Mamma had asked him to stay to tea. Sissy had never seen him alone.

Then why — she was back where she'd started from — did young Mr. Amberley take it for granted their lives had crossed for a purpose? Why had he seemed to feel he must be important to her, because he said she was important to him? Why had he vowed, in Utica, he was coming to Chicago by hook or by crook, and that when he came the first thing he'd do would be to present himself at the Triggs' door? Why had he swept aside as irrelevant her earnest disclaimers, her firm declarations that she was betrothed and therefore she couldn't . . . she *mustn't* . . . ? Why had he persuaded his aunt to invite the whole family to Naperville? (For that was *his* doing, surely!) Why, ever since coming home, had Sissy expressly avoided all opportunities for intimate talks with Nancy, her time-honoured confidante? Why for weeks had her dreams been haunted by visions of tall young men with red hair and cold flashing green eyes? Why was her heart beating higher and higher, with every mile that the train sped westward?

'Come, now,' Sissy told herself resolutely, 'this is nonsense, you know! I've nothing to conceal, nothing to be ashamed of. I'm engaged to Aaron — and Ted knows it — and I'm going to marry Aaron — and Ted knows that, too! (And Aaron's in Michigan, and Ted's in Naperville — and who can tell what may happen during our week in the country?)' . . .

'Sis! Sis!' (Loulie was tugging at her sleeve.) 'Wake up! We're getting into Wheaton, and I've lost my gloves I don't know where. Do you s'pose I could've dropped 'em under the seat?'

It was very hot at Wheaton. The four-o'clock sun beating down on the boards of the platform was so glaring that Sissy at first could hardly see. How queer it was not to find Aunt Betsy's plump pink face smiling a welcome from the surrey behind the strawberry roans! Could there be a mistake? Had they not been met, after all?

There was no carriage in sight but a big, rough-looking, three-benched farmer's cart drawn up in the shade of a row of box elders. A tall fellow wearing overalls and a wide-brimmed straw hat was just getting out of the driver's seat, followed by a small tow-headed boy also in overalls.

Sissy then saw that the tow-headed boy was Joshua Bascomb and the tall fellow, who doffed his hat and strode across the platform to salute Papa, was Ted Amberley himself. How bright his hair shone! How sunburnt he was! Smiling, he explained that he had only just arrived — he'd been awfully afraid he was late, but luckily the train was a little late, too. They were haying in the north meadow. . . . He hadn't even had time to change his clothes; would the ladies forgive him? And he was extremely sorry — so was Aunt Zeph, who sent her deepest apologies to her guests — but for such a large party no decent carriage was roomy enough. Would they mind very much? The farm was only four miles away, and really the springs were better than they looked.

'Capital!' said Papa, who appeared in high spirits. 'Mind? Why should we mind? That's a fine pair of horses you have there, my boy.'

'They're not proper carriage horses,' said Ted. 'They're part Irish and part I-don't-know-what. Aunt Zeph uses them round the farm, but I think you'll find they go pretty well. Her own riding-horse and mine are broken to harness, but they've never been driven together. I mean to try them out this summer some day when I have time.'

Meanwhile, Joshua was shrilly explaining to Loulie that the horses' names were Damon and Pythias, their manes were buff and their coats were chestnut, and Mr. Amberley had promised he should ride one round the yard next week, just as soon as he'd learned to sit in the saddle without holding on to the pommel. . . . 'Yes,' added Joshua, still at the top of his voice, 'an' I've been here only five days, but my nose has peeled twice already — an' Mr. Amberley's aunt has three cows called Star and Bess and May Lily, an' a dog called Tartoof an' a cat called Minet, an' ducks an' geese an' pigeons an' turkeys an' 'most a hundred chickens, I guess — not ugly speckled ones like Aunt Betsy's, but all pretty snow whites. Mrs. Amberley lets me collect the eggs for her every day, an' gives me a slice of bread-an'-honey afterwards — they have their own bees, an' it's awful good honey! Maybe she'll let you help me, Loulie — an' then you can have a slice of bread-an'-honey, too. But mine must be the biggest, 'cause I'm a man an' men work harder than women.'

'Little pig!' said Nancy; and they all laughed.

'Now, then,' said Ted, 'if everybody's ready . . .? Will, how are you, lad? Mr. Trigg, have we all the luggage aboard? Joshua, help the ladies into the carriage. Three to a bench'll just make it, with one next the driver. Sir, where will you find yourself most comfortable?'

'Up front with you!' replied Papa promptly. 'I wonder if you've any objections to my holding the reins for a little? It's a long time since I've had an opportunity of driving; it would be a great pleasure to me.'

'Certainly, sir.' Ted's face fell a trifle; Sissy supposed he had been about to ask her to share the driver's seat with him.

It might have been that Papa noticed this — what did Papa *not* notice? — for he continued at once: 'But why shouldn't we have the pleasure of a lady's company as well? The front bench is quite as wide as the others, I think. How about it, Sis? Could you manage to slip in between us?'

Ted looked at Sissy for the first time since their hasty greeting.

'Will you come, Rhoda?' (He was the only one of her friends who never made use of her nickname.)

Sissy nodded. Ted and Papa between them swung her up over the wheel, Papa grasped the reins and chirruped to Damon and Pythias, and they were off.

Wheaton was such a small town — a mere huddle of white-painted houses round the church and the inn and the railway station — that they were soon in the open country. It was still hot, but now a pleasant breeze blew over meadows and cornfields. The road was yellow with dust; grasshoppers shrilled in the flowering weeds that edged it. The weeds were purple and white, with here and there the bright pink of a late-blossoming wild rose. A bobolink poised on the topmost strand of a wire fence to tinkle its rollicking song before plunging into the deep green grass.

Sissy felt unaccountably cheerful. At the beginning she had sat very straight, watching tensely to see how Papa would drive. But he handled the horses with the skill of a veteran; she soon saw Ted was admiring him, too; so she relaxed in her seat, enjoying the soft fresh air on her face, glancing at her companions occasionally with a smile. For some reason she was disinclined to talk; it seemed more restful to listen to the others. Papa was asking about the prospects for the corn crop, and Ted was telling him that the weather had lately been rather too dry, just a few scattered thundershowers, not enough to do much good. On the other hand, for the sake of the hay, he did hope the rain might hold off at least till the end of the week. They were behind schedule this year, it seemed. It was hard to get help; and Lem, Aunt Zeph's one regular hand, was laid up just now with a lame shoulder, owing to a fall in the loft.

'It's jolly good luck my holiday came when it did,' he concluded, 'or my aunt would be losing most of her hay.'

'Well, now you'll have helpers a-plenty,' declared Papa. 'You'll find me not too bad a hand — I've had a bit of experience in the West — and Morgan here, too, I'm sure won't want to do less than his share. How about it, young Wilfred? It's no eight-hour day, you know — up at dawn and work till dusk — but your room and board's included. And if I know Mrs. Amberley, the board will be bountiful indeed. What say you? Shall we meet tomorrow at five in the north meadow?'

An appalled silence in the rear greeted this sally. Then Nancy said, with a laugh: 'Papa, you're joking!'

'Not the least in the world,' said Papa. 'My dear, I was never more serious. And you girls will have to pick currants, you know, or gooseberries, or whatever's in season, and make yourselves useful about the house. A farm's no place for idlers.'

But he smiled as he spoke, so that Sissy could not help thinking it

128

might be a joke, after all. That was the worst of Papa: you never could really be sure . . .

Presently the road crossed a rattling plank bridge over a stream, and Damon and Pythias slackened their pace to a walk as they began climbing a little hill.

'At least, it's what they call a hill hereabouts,' laughed Ted. 'Back in York State 'twould be a hummock if we chose to notice it.'

At the crest of the slope Ted said 'Right!' and Papa turned the horses — which probably would have turned by themselves, anyhow — between two round brown wood gateposts surmounted by brown carved wood pineapples.

'This is the beginning of the Amberley farm,' said Ted. 'Aunt Zeph owns two hundred acres here, and another forty down by the river. That's mostly swamp land and pasture, though.'

The drive led for perhaps half a mile past cornfields — the corn, about three feet high, fluttered its glossy pennants in the breeze — and then sank into a hollow. There was a round pond at the bottom, fringed by big old willow trees, some of which had crumbled to the point of blowing over, but, prone as they were, went on sending out sprays of new shoots as is the way of willows.

A flock of white ducks with yellow bills and beady, impertinent eyes quacked loudly as the carriage passed by; two mud-turtles that had been sunning themselves on a log plopped into the water and disappeared. . . . Sissy began to have a strange feeling of having seen all this before. The feeling grew stronger as the road rose once more through an apple orchard and Ted pointed ahead with his whip: 'There it is.'

The Amberleys' house stood halfway up the second rise of ground. It could be seen from some distance, long and low and rambling, of unpainted wood weathered to a soft, indescribable grey. The farm buildings, grey also, were inconspicuously placed to one side, partly hidden in a clump of box elders. The house itself was bowered in lilac and mock-orange bushes; two fine elms stood guard in front; a grove of tall, feathery larches — rare in Illinois — trooped up the hill in the rear and gave the view its particular stamp.

'How pretty! How peaceful!' said Sissy, in a whisper.

Papa with a flourish brought the horses to rest. A fat woolly sheep dog came gambolling round the corner of the house, barking a furious greeting. Ted sprang from his seat with a cheery 'Here we are!', held out his hand to help Sissy alight, and said to Papa: 'Just drop the reins, sir — they'll stand — and Lem'll be here directly.'

The front door flew open, and a thin, small woman wearing a checked gingham dress and a white sunbonnet appeared on the threshold. She smiled when she saw her guests and flung up both hands in a funny, abrupt little gesture — which was, Sissy remembered long afterwards, the only really French thing they ever saw her do. Then she said, without accent, in a thin, small voice that just matched her person: 'With all my heart I bid you welcome!'

Aunt Zeph

IF AUNT ZEPH were embarrassed at being surprised in her working clothes, unlike her nephew she did not say so. With perfect self-possession she ushered the party inside, and then calmly removed her sunbonnet, as though it were the most conventional headgear imaginable. Without it she looked smaller than ever: her pale, pointed face, thickly powdered with freckles, appeared a mere frame for her eyes, which were large and peculiarly brilliant, fringed by heavy black lashes. (Sissy noticed that they were the same shade as her hair, a lively hazel.)

Altogether, she did not look in the least like anybody else; and as was Aunt Zeph, so was her house. Once she had stepped within-doors Sissy lost the curious feeling that had haunted her of having passed this way before: where were the familiar front and back parlours, divided by portières or wide sliding partitions? Aunt Zeph had instead a series of little rooms connecting with one another, each provided with doors that could be shut as tight as a box. . . . As they were led through the rooms Sissy caught a prevailing impression of greyness. The walls were painted grey, and the ceilings; so were the chairs and tables and sofas, with their straight, delicately fluted legs. Then she remarked a few unobtrusive touches of colour. The pretty marble clock on the mantelpiece in the largest room repeated the saffron note in the pattern of the Aubusson rug. The Chinese jars flanking the clock were partly saffron, too; they were also rose and blue and faded green to match the floral pattern in the antique chintz curtains. Even the books in the library (Sissy supposed it must be the library, for there were more books there than anywhere else, reaching on open shelves to the ceilings) glowed discreetly in the background with their worn browns and golds and lacquer-reds.

131

Here Aunt Zeph bade her guests be seated. The library was cool and dim; a profusion of ferns in pots filled the windows; the light filtering through the larches cast a green shadow over all. Aunt Zeph took her position in the middle of the sofa by the fireplace, folded her hands in her lap, and smiled. (Her smile was not an embellishment; thin lips and teeth slanting slightly inward gave it a melancholy quality.)

'You must, I fear, be very tired and hot after your journey from the city,' she said. 'Will you have some currant wine?'

Sissy glanced at Nancy in bewilderment: of course, French people drank wine like water, but she knew that Mamma would not approve. On the other hand, would it be rude to decline? The tray was there before them — and they *were* very thirsty. . . . Aunt Zeph, without waiting for an answer, poured out the contents of the pitcher, and Ted handed the glasses round. Sissy was glad then she had made no objection, for the drink proved to be nothing but pure currant juice, iced and very refreshing.

'It's a *sirop de groseilles*, really,' said Aunt Zeph. 'You have no word that describes it in English.'

She spoke without a trace of an accent; still her speech had a faintly foreign sound — was it because each word dropped out by itself, quite separate from its neighbours?

The young people sipped their wine. Nancy observed politely that it was very good. Loulie, who, as usual, had gulped hers much too fast, inquired whether she might have some more, ma'am? Sissy frowned a warning signal — for Mamma had expressly instructed them never to ask for second helpings — but Aunt Zeph replied: 'More? Of course you may, my little dear! Simple though it be, there is always plenty of everything.'

She swept the circle again with an encouraging smile, and then seemed to wait for someone else to break the silence.

Sissy felt exceedingly shy; she thought the others were feeling shy, too — even Wilfred, who had made his hostess a magnificent bow upon entering and pressed his lips to her hand. It was hard to tell why. Aunt Zeph appeared to be a very kind person, not even formal, only perhaps a little remote.

The woolly sheep dog had come into the room and stretched himself out panting at his mistress's feet. Sissy demanded his name, only to be abashed by Joshua's 'I *tole* you, Sissy — he's called Tartoof!'

'Tartuffe, yes, from the play, you know,' said Aunt Zeph. 'Or perhaps you don't: Molière's not acted often in this country, I fancy. Well, Tartuffe, you see, was a great hypocrite — he pretends to be good, and he's really very bad. It is just the same with my puppy, only the other way round: he pretends to be bad — barks like mad and frightens everyone who comes to the house half out of his wits — while all the time he's quite gentle and harmless — aren't you, my silly one?'

'Oh!' said Sissy.

'Won't he bite, really?' asked Nancy. 'May I pat him?'

'Indeed you may. He likes it, of all things. Scratch behind his ears — see how pleased he looks!'

There was silence once more, during which Sissy tried with all her might to think of something to say. She looked at Papa in search of help — but Papa would not help: he contented himself with beaming, as if the situation pleased him far too much for words.

Aunt Zeph finally, seeing that her visitors were at a loss, began plying them with questions about their trip in the train and the drive from the station. She questioned them also about their mother — how had they left her? ('In good health, I trust? Oh, I cannot tell you how sorry I am that Mrs. Trigg could not have come with you, too!') — and about their school: what classes were they in, what lessons did they study, and how did they like living in Chicago? In fact, it was just the sort of kindly catechism they had often submitted to at the hands of members of outlying branches of The Family, or friends of Mamma's; but somehow Aunt Zeph seemed to *care* what you said. At any rate, she listened as if she cared, keeping her large, bright eyes fixed upon you. It might be a trick (Sissy could almost hear Aunt Bertha's dark hiss of 'French insincerity!'); but, if so, it was an agreeable trick.

After disposing of the younger ones Aunt Zeph turned to Sissy: 'You, I believe, are no more at school. Theodore told me you were graduating and that you were engaged to be married. My felicitations! Ah, Mr. Trigg, I do not extend them to *you*. You cannot be congratulated upon losing a daughter. I know how much it must mean to you to find yourself once again with your children, after the long years of absence. And I have not forgotten, in the old days it was chiefly of the little Sissy you talked.'

'That would have been because I'm the eldest,' said Sissy quickly. 'The others were only little things, Loulie scarcely more than a baby, when Papa left home.'

'Ah,' said Aunt Zeph mildly, as if only partly agreeing, 'it may have been that, of course. But come, I am forgetting my manners: you will want now to see your rooms and to rest after your journey. With such a large party a few small adjustments are necessary, I hope not seriously to your inconvenience. Joshua I keep with me in the house; it seems wisest so; then at least at night I may know where he is! There will be room upstairs also for the three young ladies, and Theodore has moved out to the barn to give his room to Mr. Trigg. . . . Oh, please, do not forbid it! He has wanted to so much. He often sleeps there from choice at this time of year, and indeed it is no hardship. We have arranged most comfortable quarters, so high, so light, so airy, with a view far more extensive than one gets from the house. And the hay-beds are soft and fragrant. No, my nephew will be most happily installed. It is only — ' She paused, frowning a little, to consider the case of her remaining guest. 'I am not sure . . . Mr. Morgan, you see, Theodore did not prepare me as he should — I was not expecting quite such an elegant young gentleman! Would you, I wonder . . . ? But of course I know that a man of the world can accommodate himself to any contingency.'

Now that, thought Sissy, was clever of Aunt Zeph, for it left Wilfred no choice except to fall in with her plans. He *had* been standing diffidently enough, twiddling his fingers as much as to say: 'Plaguey awkward fix for a fellow like me!' But there was no gainsaying this smiling assurance that his sophistication must make amends for her insufficiencies as a hostess, especially as Ted flung an arm round his former schoolmate with a cajoling 'Come, old chap, you won't find it half bad! 'Twill be something new for you, and the view's all my aunt claims for it.'

Here they were reckoning without Papa.

'If you boys can sleep in the barn,' said Papa, 'then so can I. In short, I *insist* upon it. Dear Mrs. Amberley, I've just this one favour to beg of you during our visit — I know I shall not speak in vain. Let us

134

leave the house to the ladies, and my graceless young nephew here, and keep Bachelor Hall over yonder.'

Aunt Zeph hesitated. It did not seem quite right to her. Still, if he would have it so — Oh, he *would!* Papa interjected — there was nothing to be done but accede to his wishes. Then Theodore's room would be free for the little *fiancée* and only the two younger sisters must share their apartment.

Papa's action made the barn unexpectedly fashionable. Joshua teased — though fruitlessly — to be allowed to sleep there, too; while Nancy lamented aloud that her sex debarred her from making a similar plea. Of them all, Sissy was most pleased by the turn of events. For some time she had wished a room of her own, but had not known how to get it: to express a desire for the closet that had been prepared for her, now that Loulie was established there, would have been upsetting to everybody and might very possibly have wounded Nancy's feelings.

Upstairs the farmhouse was painted soft ivory-white instead of grey. The curtains everywhere were of chintz, like those in the living-rooms (not a single damask or satin brocade — one could imagine Aunt Bertha's contemptuous sniff!). Sissy hung back in the hall outside Ted's bedroom, a little bashful about going in.

'It's a man's room, I'm afraid,' said Aunt Zeph. 'I can give you a dressing-table with muslin flounces and a low looking-glass, if you prefer; else I don't quite see how you are to do your hair.' But Sissy said no, often she stood before the mirror; she liked everything just as it was. And indeed it was a charming room, with the same view of the larch grove as the library had directly beneath it. Its cool green-and-white-striped simplicity was enhanced by the huge mahogany 'Napoleon' bed and the fine Empire chest of drawers that went with it. One ornament stood on the chest, a vase full of yellow roses.

Sissy examined the vase with interest: it was a tall cornucopia of shiny gold oak leaves that sheltered a white china nest containing three eggs. A pair of china doves hovered anxiously over the nest, but it was the picture painted on the vase itself, and partly screened by the leaves, that caught Sissy's fancy — a romantic background of dusky blue mountains, in the middle a high, spiky mediaeval castle perched on a hill so steep that it was hard to imagine how one could ever hope to scale it.

Aunt Zeph was amused by Sissy's enthusiasm.

'Theodore loves that vase, too,' she said; 'it's here by his special request; and when I was a little girl it was my dearest possession. My grandmother gave it me. I was very fond of my grandmother: she was the sweetest, gentlest old lady and she really did live in a castle on a hill — in the Haute Savoie it was, not far from Annecy. This vase stood in the room I had there and when I arrived each year for my summer holiday it was always full of roses, just as you see it now. I used to lie in bed, when I was very small, and look at it and look at it, and wonder if the birds got tired of fluttering over their nest, and try to figure to myself how it could be done, to climb that little hill. *Le château impossible,* I called it.'

'Yes,' said Sissy; 'I think that would have bothered me, too. And if you couldn't see any way — if you were never able to get there at all — '

Aunt Zeph smiled her pensive smile once more as she prepared to depart.

'Ah,' she said, 'but when you reach my age you realize that an impossible castle is perhaps the best kind. It's well to have something to look at, you cannot expect to attain, do you not think so? But no, how silly of me! At *your* age, my dear, there should be no impossible castles.'

As soon as Sissy had washed her face and hands, and exchanged her travelling dress for a comfortable gingham, she hurried downstairs to join the others in a tour of the farm.

Farms were no novelty to the Triggs. They had see Aunt Betsy's often enough to know what to expect. Besides, thought Sissy, cows were cows and chickens were chickens, the world over.

Aunt Zeph's, of course, was quite small. The long, low buildings, of the same unpainted wood as the house, were grouped informally round a courtyard shaded by box elders and sugar maples. There were no proud, square red barns like Aunt Betsy's; no doors marked KEEP OUT; no cross superintendent or dairymen to shoo them away and tell them not to do this or that. (Lem, the sole hired hand, was a quiet boy of eighteen, with a shock of white-blond hair and gentle,

not-too-intelligent eyes, who was glad to answer the visitors' questions.) Aunt Betsy had twelve cows, Aunt Zeph only three; but the
stately Jerseys Star and Bess and May Lily each had a roomy stall with
her name over it; and Lem opened the gate to the calves' pen, so that
the girls might pat the fawn-brown, frolicking occupants.

The spring-house, too, could be freely inspected. They tasted the
milk set to separate in round copper pans on the mossy stones, and
marvelled at the great mounds of butter kept in crockery jars in the
trickling waters of the spring itself.

When they came to the horse barn, where Damon and Pythias
were contentedly munching their evening oats, Ted bade Lem lead
out Aunt Zeph's own mount, a graceful grey mare named Priscilla,
and asked Sissy if she would care to go for a ride in the morning.

Sissy's eyes sparkled. 'I'd like it more than anything. But what will
you ride?'

Ted pointed to the next stall, inhabited by a cheerful calico pony
with a roving eye.

'He's mine — his name's Toby — nothing much to look at — but
he can go like the wind! Hey, there, boy, leave my fingers alone!' —
as Toby, in search of sugar, began nibbling at his master.

Joshua, crushingly superior on the strength of his five days' residence, helped his tutor do the honours and insisted on ushering his
cousins through the piggery and the poultry-house, the fields of his
own special interests.

'They haven't no names, the pigs 'n' chickens 'n' things,' explained
Joshua. 'I asked Mrs. Amberley why; I thought maybe there was
too many of 'em; but she said no, it was 'cause sometimes they get
eaten, an' she didn't like eating animals with names.'

Meanwhile Wilfred and Nancy were amusing themselves by finding resemblances between some of the livestock and their acquaintances in Chicago. Wilfred, thought Sissy scornfully, had got to the
point where he deemed it exquisitely humorous to declare that the
big white rooster was the image of old Mr. Leslie, or that pig in the
corner — the runty one with the spots — really looked — sh! don't
tell Sissy! — but he did, didn't he? exactly like Aaron's father. And
Nancy, alas! was just at the age to feel this extraordinarily witty: the
pair were in fits of laughter half the time.

It took so long to see everything that when Ted led the party again up the hill red shafts of sunlight slanted through the trunks of the larches and Sissy exclaimed in dismay: 'We must be terribly late to supper! What will your aunt think?'

'There's nothing to worry about,' said Ted easily. 'We don't have supper at the farm.'

'No supper *at all?*' cried Nancy with horror. Loulie turned pale; even Sissy mournfully measured the time elapsed since the scanty early lunch they'd eaten at home and recalled with regret her refusal (for fear of spoiling the next meal) of the sweet biscuits that had lain on the tray with the currant wine.

'We have dinner instead,' Ted continued, 'at eight o'clock, as they do in Paris. And we dress for it, too, you know — Aunt Zeph's particular about that.'

Loulie's colour returned. 'Dinner at eight — how queer!' said Nancy; but Wilfred checked her criticism by commenting approvingly: 'Of course, quite the proper thing, my boy! I'm not surprised to hear it — I could see at a glance that your aunt was accustomed to the ways of the *beau monde*. We have dinner at night in New York, too — at least in the circles that lead the fashion. At seven in winter, on account of the play; but my mother often sets it as late as half-past the hour in the summer at Rhinebeck.'

The gathering round the Amberleys' oval table seemed more like a party, thought Sissy, than a good many actual parties she had attended. This was partly because the scene was lighted by wax candles, always, at home, a sign of festivity, oil-lamps being good enough for ordinary use and few people having as yet gone to the expense of installing the luxurious new gas chandeliers.

As they took their places Aunt Zeph lamented that there were too many insects in Illinois for it ever to be safe to eat outdoors; but Sissy admired the dark-paneled dining-room, with the family portraits in peeling gold frames, the graceful nut-and-fruitwood furniture, the fine old silver and glittering crystal candelabra: it had a kind of faded elegance and was obviously the one room the Charles Bascombs might have considered not wholly unworthy of the mansion on Michigan Avenue.

Aunt Zeph, too, looked elegant — and not at all faded — in apple-green taffeta with black lace at the neck and sleeves. She wore a chain of big, round amber beads and, in her ears, amber pendants, which beat against her thin cheeks whenever she turned her sleek head in one of her quick, birdlike movements.

The hostess took the centre of the table (was that the French custom?), with Papa on her right; Ted, in a dark suit and a white collar, sat across from her, with Sissy on *his* right. At his aunt's request he said grace; the meal was then served by Marie-Claire, Aunt Zeph's Indian maid.

The children were rather afraid of Marie-Claire. Sissy heard Joshua whisper to Loulie that he was not sure, but he *thought* she might be a witch. ('There ain't any witches,' said Loulie at once, with the superiority of eleven over seven's credulity; but she looked uneasy just the same and shrank back a trifle when the maid proffered a platter.) Sissy, who as a child had been accustomed to seeing scores of Indians in the Chicago streets, glanced curiously at the tall young squaw: Marie-Claire had the slant eyes and impassive expression of her race; her dark skin looked even darker in contrast to the conventional white of her uniform.

She performed her duties in the dining-room with unhurried ease, speaking only when necessary and confining her remarks, in a deep, calm voice, to the barest *oui, madame,* and *non, madame, bien, madame,* and *j'y verrai, madame.*

Sissy wanted to ask why she spoke French, but did not quite dare; fortunately, Papa also wanted to know; and Aunt Zeph told them that, though she had engaged Marie-Claire in California, the girl had been born on Mackinac Island and educated at the Ursuline convent in Quebec. She was an excellent servant, strong and willing, always contented, and perfectly devoted to her mistress's interests. 'And then, she knows no English whatever, which is very convenient; there is no way for her to get into trouble.' (Sissy rather wondered what trouble Marie-Claire could possibly manage to find, on a lonely farm with no society but the Amberleys' and that of the gentle, slightly daft Lem.)

The dinner was very good, and quite as abundant as even Loulie could have hoped. If there did not seem to be so much as at home, that was because it was served in the French fashion. Instead of loading the table with an array of dishes, as Susan would have done,

Marie-Claire fetched only one thing at a time — first the soup, then the chicken *en casserole*; even a bowl of green beans from the garden appeared, disconcertingly, by themselves.

Another strange thing was that Aunt Zeph never mentioned the food. At any Bascomb board each of The Family would remark upon every dish as it arrived, shrewdly appraise its superior qualities, and consume it to the last mouthful with a sober, triumphant relish. At the Amberleys', on the contrary, conversation not only had nothing to do with the menu, but moved at a tempo directly opposed to it: the courses might be spaced, but the talk was crowded. Instead of engaging first your right-hand, then your left-hand neighbour, you were allowed — nay, even expected — to speak all at once. Even Loulie and Joshua were encouraged to voice their views. Aunt Zeph never said: 'Silence is golden'; or, 'Children should be seen and not heard.' She seemed, in fact, to regard a dinner-party as a kind of symphony; her mission it was to give each guest a part to play, acting herself as a general harmonizing influence.

Moreover, she did not care — that much was clear — to dwell upon her own affairs. She accepted compliments on the pretty table, the glass, the china, the flower arrangements, with a sidewise smile and a deprecating 'Ah, you like my old things? They are just bits and pieces saved from the shipwreck. When I settled in Naperville I sent to France for them.'

Her principal attentions were devoted to Papa — not unnaturally: his age might be said to demand them. But Aunt Zeph — it was very odd — insisted on treating him with deference as well as indulgence. She inquired his opinion about business conditions in Chicago and California, or the American political situation, exactly as if she had been talking to Uncle Charles or Uncle Caleb. And Papa, to Sissy's intense surprise, had ideas worth hearing. He spoke entertainingly yet seriously, seeming to expand in the warmth of his hostess's interest.

'Why,' thought Sissy, amazed, 'Papa's a very intelligent man!'

No Bascomb had ever called him intelligent; and Sissy now saw she had, doubtless unconsciously, accepted her father at The Family's valuation. (Nancy, although so much younger, had been wiser there; *she* had always maintained that The Family were too dull to see Papa was clever. Of course, that was nonsense; no one could be cleverer than Uncle Charles, for instance; but perhaps there were different kinds of cleverness?)

Sissy had not guessed before that Papa was a passionate advocate of Abolition. So was Aunt Zeph, who hoped Frémont and the new Republican Party would take a strong stand against slavery. Papa told her she ought to be in Chicago on the nineteenth of July to hear a speech in Dearborn Park by Mr. Abraham Lincoln, a lawyer from Springfield, who was beginning to be known as a powerful orator for their cause.

Aunt Zeph said she would try to come. She remarked, further, that here in the country they were all Abolitionists, but were too lazy to do anything about it. 'You know what farmers are! The prices they get for their corn and their cattle are more important to them than the traffic in human flesh and blood. It seems to me there must be men in Chicago who feel strongly enough to fight for what they believe to be right. Oh, I should like to meet those men!'

'So should I,' said Papa. 'I haven't, yet.'

'But surely you must, if you decide to settle here. Of course, Illinois is so new that it is still in some ways a primitive community.'

'I so agree with you, dear Mrs. Amberley!' cried Wilfred, who for some time had been fidgeting about waiting, as Sissy uncharitably put it, for a chance to shove in his oar. 'With all due respect to my cousins and their family, there is a general lack of gentility in the Middle West. Why, you can almost count on the fingers of both hands the number of families that keep their own carriage! And I fear you could never boast of Michigan Avenue as I have heard New Yorkers boast of Broadway, that it is possible to walk the whole length of the street and not meet so much as one gentleman without a top hat.'

Aunt Zeph smiled and said gently that that was not precisely what she meant by primitive. 'What I have missed — and what I think Mr. Trigg misses, too — is the society of artists — writers, painters, musicians, men of that stamp. Chicago hasn't had time to feel the need of them yet, but we who were born in older communities must always be conscious of their absence.'

To this Wilfred could only reply, as he thoughtfully stroked his upper lip (where a blond moustache was just starting to grow), that he believed he knew a man who knew a cousin of Mr. Washington Irving — deuced fine fellow and all that, you know!

As soon as dinner was over Aunt Zeph sent the youngsters, who were dropping with sleep, off to bed, and led the rest of the party outside. Some rustic benches had been placed under the larches; it was cool there, although the breeze had dropped. Swallows still skimmed against the glowing western sky; fireflies were beginning to gleam intermittently round the base of the shrubbery. In spite of the lack of wind the sweet, clean smell of the hayfields reached them, borne on a breath of air so faint as to be scarcely perceptible.

It was so pleasant to sit there that Papa remarked at once on the advantage of having a fine grove of trees near the house.

Aunt Zeph agreed; they had been planted, she said, by her husband and his brother — Theodore's father — almost twenty-five years ago, when they first came to Naperville. 'They are rare hereabouts; the farmers don't care for them because they're not evergreens. This country was settled mostly by New Englanders and I am told that in New England every house has its firs or its spruces close by. It is true the larch loses its needles in winter — but oh, they are lovely and light in the spring, like a troop of dryads floating up the hill! I think that larches are my favourite trees. Perhaps it's because I remember them when I was a very small girl — there were so many at my grandmother's place in Savoy — the place I told you of, Rhoda.'

'Oh, yes,' said Sissy; 'where the castle stood on a hill.'

'It was quite by itself in the mountains, five miles at least from the nearest village — but it was very beautiful, like a house in a fairy-tale, you know. And the air! How can I tell you young people what *that* was like, since there's nothing here to compare it to? A dry still wine, perhaps.'

'My children,' said Papa, 'have never tasted wine. Didn't you notice they refused it at dinner? The Bascombs are all teetotallers.'

'Oh, Papa, you forget the Fourth of July!' cried Nancy. 'And we have been to the mountains, too. Uncle Charles took us to stay at the Profile House in New Hampshire, two years ago. Is that like Savoy, Mrs. Amberley?'

Aunt Zeph replied that very likely it was; she could not be sure, never having been in New Hampshire.

'How you must pine for your cool native breezes!' sighed Wilfred.

'Well, of course, sometimes I do,' admitted Aunt Zeph. 'But it is many years since I was last at Valombre. It is many years, also, since my grandmother died. Strangers live now in the house I knew, distant cousins I've never met. And then, you know, Savoy is not my native air — I am a Tourangelle — I was born and brought up near Chinon — and Touraine is a very hot country, too, quite as hot as Illinois. Besides, to leave a place one loves is not always to lose it. I guard it closely in my memory; I can see it all just as clearly as if I were there — perhaps *more* clearly — for there must have been changes made since my time, and those I do not see. Does it matter much where the body is?'

This was a new thought to Sissy, and rather an oppressive one. She could not agree with Aunt Zeph: it seemed to *her* that it mattered a good deal! Only last night, for instance, in Chicago, she had been hot and uncomfortable, and depressed by the imminence of her various emotional problems. Now, in this restful, agreeable atmosphere, she felt cool and relaxed; and her problems had obligingly moved some distance away to a pale, indeterminate horizon. . . . Ted, too, all angles and restless impatience, had achieved, apparently, a measure of poise. Even Papa, so moody, so mettlesome before, was a different creature. Sissy grew aware of that gradually through the calmer rhythms of his speech, his very breathing, though it was too dark to see his face.

For the light was fading fast. (That, said Aunt Zeph, she did find a pity: night came too soon in America!) And as it faded the figures in the little group under the larches faded, too — the men first, then Aunt Zeph's green dress, till finally only Sissy's and Nancy's white muslins made two blobs of grey against the dusk. The swallows had gone, making way for their nocturnal counterparts, the little brown bats. The fireflies, whose sparkling manoeuvres scarcely outlasted the twilight, had likewise disappeared, though here and there a straggler shone as it were impaled on the topmost twigs of the apple-trees down the slope of the hill. They had been replaced by the steadier glow of Wilfred's pipe and Papa's cigar.

After a pause Aunt Zeph called for music. The night was too fine to go indoors, but Ted, who was not smoking, was despatched to the house to fetch the banjo. Aunt Zeph herself did not sing; she had, she

143

said, a mere thread of a voice. She could play a little, and so could Ted; but that would not be necessary tonight. Surely the Triggs must know that their father was a remarkable musician!

Sissy and Nancy murmured something politely evasive; the former's cheeks burned as she recalled the last time she had heard Papa sing.

'My wife's family, ma'am,' said Papa, as he took the banjo from Ted and struck a few chords to see how much tuning it needed, 'do not agree with your estimate of my musical powers. (No, that's all right, boy; I shan't need a light.) In fact, I scarcely know whether I dare render a good part of my repertory in present company. In Chicago my mining ballads are not considered at all the thing.'

'Are they not? *Parbleu!*' Aunt Zeph's surprise led her to lapse for the first time into her mother tongue. 'But they are some of them so funny and you sing them all so well. Not the thing! *Tenez,* one would have thought them sure to appeal to people who not long ago were pioneers themselves!'

'Oh, Papa, please do sing!' said Nancy; and Sissy added: 'Yes, Papa, please.'

So Papa sang. He gave them all the songs about *The Happy Miner,* and the gay *señoritas* who smoked *cigarritos,* and Brigham Young and his half a hundred wives, and the rest — and somehow tonight they did not sound bad. Was it because the rollicking banjo accompaniment suited them better than the Bascombs' grand piano? Or that the larch grove was undeniably a more appropriate background than Aunt Bertha's gilt and flower-bedecked drawing-room? Was it the absence of disapproving elements in the audience that made the difference? Or simply that the songs themselves were really quite innocent, after all?

Sissy was not prepared to say. She knew only she enjoyed them with a clear conscience. And Aunt Zeph was right: they *were* funny. All the young people were chuckling; Aunt Zeph herself joined in the merriment. Her laugh was surprising — they had not known before that she *could* laugh: she had seemed, though so kind and quite ready to talk, a sober, sedate little person. But now it rang out again and again, as gay and unforced as a child's.

From the miners' ballads Papa drifted to old songs everyone knew:

144

Annie Laurie, Comin' thro' the Rye, The Last Rose of Summer, and many another. He urged the others to sing, too. Nancy and Wilfred took part with a will, the latter in a melting tenor that was just right for Beau Morgan (as Papa called him behind his back). Ted contributed an occasional obbligato with his pleasant boyish bass, but Sissy sat silent: it was so beautiful to listen to music in the dark.

In the intervals between songs Aunt Zeph praised Nancy's performance. A real contralto was very rare, she said; she had not heard one of the first quality since Pauline Viardot's début in Paris, many years ago. 'And *la Viardot* is more noted as an all-round artist than for sheer voice. They tell me now that Alboni . . . No, Mr. Morgan, I have not heard her. No, I never go to concerts any more. It's been a long time . . .'

Sissy wondered, as she had already done more than once that evening, how their hostess managed to be content in what was really a wilderness, cut off from everything ordinarily supposed to make life worth living. Only a great mission, it would appear, might compensate for all she had missed and was missing—but surely running her farm, and providing a periodic home for her late husband's nephew, were hardly to be looked upon in that light! . . . 'And even *I* have heard Alboni,' thought Sissy.

Aunt Zeph, however, did not seem to pity herself, nor to wish to be pitied by others. There was no regret in her manner, although in her enthusiasm over Nancy's prowess she grew almost as much excited as a young girl. Nancy, who'd begun by protesting loyally her sister's voice was much finer, really—Mrs. Amberley would think nothing at all of *her,* once she'd listened to Sissy—ended by singing everything she knew that Papa could possibly improvise an accompaniment for.

It was not till she had run through her whole list that a light appeared through the trees towards the house. A tall figure in white approached, bearing a lamp in one hand and a tray in the other.

'*La tisane, madame,*' announced Marie-Claire's deep voice.

Sissy sat up and rubbed her eyes. It was like waking from a dream suddenly to see all the faces again.

The *tisane* turned out to be a kind of tea, which Aunt Zeph made every summer out of dried mint-leaves. It was strongly aromatic and tasted rather good; after drinking it, said Aunt Zeph, they would sleep soundly. . . . 'And that reminds me, it's high time I sent you off to bed—you especially, Rhoda, if you are really rising at five for your horseback ride.'

Sissy's last thought that night, as she snuggled comfortably between lavender-scented sheets in Ted's Napoleon bed, was for the little castle painted on Aunt Zeph's grandmother's vase. How would one ever be able to climb it? . . . 'Perhaps, if one went round *behind*,' she told herself drowsily. 'Perhaps, you know, it isn't so steep at the back—and then—'

Before she had even finished her sentence she was asleep.

The North Meadow

S ISSY WAS WAKENED next morning, as Ted had promised, by a shower of gravel against the windowpane. It was a beautiful day, the light softened by a touch of pearl-mist to betoken the heat to come; already the sun was laying long golden fingers upon the dew-drenched lawn, where robins and flickers were seeking their breakfast. . . . She put on her riding-habit as quickly as possible. Downstairs Ted was waiting to lead her to the kitchen for coffee, with new bread and a bowl of cream and raspberries fresh from the garden. They talked in whispers so as not to disturb the others — even Marie-Claire had not yet made her appearance — but while they were eating they heard the sound of voices outside; and when they followed the sound there were Papa and Aunt Zeph strolling together in the slanting sunshine.

Aunt Zeph was wearing gingham again, but she had exchanged her sunbonnet for a gay flowered handkerchief tied peasant fashion round her head. Papa was bareheaded; he had donned the scarlet shirt and black cloth breeches Sissy had not seen since the Sunday of his return. The place where they were was a kind of kitchen garden at the back of the house, scooped out of the hillside and buttressed by stones, against which espaliered dwarf apple and pear trees were growing. It was a maze of neat gravelled paths and geometrical beds filled with flowers and vegetables and herbs; larkspurs and hollyhocks, lettuce and leeks, rosemary and sweet marjoram flourished companionably in the practical French way.

Aunt Zeph had plucked a handful of mignonette from one of the borders; she gave it to Sissy, saying with a smile: 'So you did get up for your ride, after all! Last night you looked so sleepy I had half a mind to tell Theodore not to call you.'

'Good morning, my eldest daughter,' said Papa. 'You seem surprised to see me.'

'I *am* surprised,' replied Sissy frankly. 'In Chicago we'd never a glimpse of you before noon.'

'Ah, but today I'm going to pitch hay! Did you think that was only a joke? Mrs. Amberley has just engaged a new field hand. She might have had two, but Ted and I concluded to leave Beau Morgan to his beauty sleep.'

Aunt Zeph frowned. 'I don't know what to say. Indeed, my dear sir, I had not expected . . . there was no thought . . .'

'Of course you hadn't! Of course there wasn't! But believe me, ma'am, you will be doing me a service. I've had nothing to do for weeks. I'm fairly spoiling for exercise, after so much city life. Then I've looked at Lem's shoulder myself; 'twon't be fit for him to work for another three days at least; and your hay ought to be fetched in before that. It's so warm the weather may break at any moment.'

'I feel like a shirker going for a ride,' said Ted. 'Aunt Zeph, don't you want me to —'

'No,' said Aunt Zeph, very positively. 'You've done your share already. This is your holiday time, my dear; I want you to enjoy it. Your first duty is to your guest. Besides, I shan't need you. I am going with Mr. Trigg myself.'

Sissy gasped. 'Do you mean you'll work in the fields like a man?'

'Surely — why not?'

'I should think, if you needed help so bad, that Marie-Claire . . . She looks so strong . . .'

'She *is* strong. And she'd gladly do whatever I asked her. But I prefer her to stay in the kitchen. You see, if she weren't there, I should have to be — and I'd much rather pitch hay with the men than cook your dinner! No, no, children, don't worry about us. We may call on you later. Meanwhile, Theodore, if you want me, you know where to find me, in the north meadow. I hear Lem bringing your horses to the front door. Be off with you, and amuse yourselves well!'

Sissy greatly enjoyed her ride. Like most Chicago girls, she had been accustomed to horses since childhood, when carriages were not common in the city. Luckily, too, the Turnhams in Utica had been able to mount her whenever she wished, so that she was not out of prac-

148

tice. Priscilla was a well-mannered mare, as gentle and coy as the
Puritan maid she'd been named for. And the weather was glorious!
The grass still glistened with dew; in the fields it was starred thickly
with Queen Anne's lace. Meadowlarks whistled; the clover-sweet air
was soft to the cheek. . . . Moreover, Ted was excellent company.

Sissy reflected, as she had already done several times since coming
to Naperville, how much more fun he was in the country than in
town. Even here, he appeared infinitely less constrained outdoors than
indoors: there was something rangy and rough-hewn about his looks;
in formal clothes he seemed to be all arms and legs, never could manage to make himself comfortable in a chair! Now, on the contrary, in
his old blue shirt and worn corduroys, leaning easily back in the saddle
astride Toby, the calico pony, he was quite in the picture. . . . He felt
happier, too. His diffidence, his reserve, were gone. They laughed
and chatted together as if they had been friends for years.

Ted knew the countryside well, from other summers. He was able
to lead his companion along the prettiest and least frequented roads.
After a brisk canter they descended to the bottom-lands and walked
the horses beside the river. Here were more matters of interest:
beds of emerald-green watercress, kingfishers perched on a dead treetop,
a muskrat's sleek head disappearing downstream, the flash of dragon-
flies' wings over the clear brown waters. . . . Sissy marvelled at the
silence of the current moving slowly between its willow-fringed banks
— so different from the tinkling mountain brooks of her childhood in
the Taconics. . . . Yes, said Ted, it was quiet all right, and a slowpoke,
too — but it knew well enough where it was going and went about its
business with the least possible fuss, just like everything else in this
workaday Illinois!

Climbing again, they reached an open prairie, covered with long
waving grasses and myriad bright-coloured flowers. They were back
on the Amberley property, Ted told Sissy. This prairie was one of the
few remaining in the county. Aunt Zeph *would* keep it in its primitive state, though her neighbours thought her mad; for the land was
as rich as all prairie land. 'That's why there's so little of it left, I suppose. These plaguey farmers! They'd rather an acre of corn than the
loveliest scenery in the world; a stable full of fat cattle appeals to
them more than a fine herd of bison thundering over the plains. This

country's too civilized for me. Not *all* America's like that, thank God! Just wait till I have my independence and get to go West!'

'Oh, you and your independence!' cried Sissy, in derision. 'I never saw such a man — you've just one idea in your head!'

'Yes,' Ted flung over his shoulder, 'and there's just one woman I'd care to take with me!'

'Your aunt, of course,' said Sissy demurely.

He flashed her a look that made her catch her breath. 'My heart! What a thundercloud! Come, I'll race you to the gate on the other side of the field!'

Priscilla and Toby finished at a dead heat, their riders laughing and breathless, peace quite restored between them.

Beyond the gate there was a lane leading between a wood, of oaks and hickories and a few feathery ashes, and a little hill crowned by a tangle of unpruned shrubbery. No buildings were in sight except one old barn, very dilapidated and obviously no longer in use, that stood at the edge of the wood; but a stone well, now planked over, and the remains of a garden showed that the place had been inhabited.

'Why,' said Sissy, 'it looks as though there ought to be a house up there.'

'There was, once,' said Ted. 'I brought you here on purpose to show you. Let's leave the horses in the lane. They know where they are; they won't try to bolt; however, just to be on the safe side, here's a hitching-post I can tie them to. Do you want a hand down?'

For answer Sissy leaped lightly out of the saddle — '*You're* independent, too, miss!' exclaimed Ted — and tossed him Priscilla's bridle.

Ted led her — the skirt of her habit dragging over the long grass — through thickets of lilac and bridal wreath to the top of the hill, where there was the stone foundation of a farmhouse. A few blackened bits of wood showed, even now, what had been its fate; but intervening years had covered the ruins with a mass of greenery. Daisies and clover sprinkled the space where the house had stood; a woodbine ran riot over the wall; weeds grew so high that they all but covered the stone front steps, isolated by the disappearance of the porch.

'I was born here,' said Ted. 'This was the old Amberley house.'

'Why,' said Sissy, 'I thought we were living in the old Amberley house!'

'No, indeed. Aunt Zeph built that one herself, lower down on the slope, when she came here after Uncle Jim's death. This place was burnt while he was away in California, and she didn't want to build again on the old foundation. I don't know why — she's not the sort of woman to be superstitious. Of course, my parents died while they were living here. But I don't think it was that. She wrote to me from Chicago — I was at school in the East at the time — to find out if I minded. She said she'd like to do what would please me most, but she felt it might be a good idea to start out quite fresh — and she was crazy about the larch grove from the first.'

'But didn't you mind?' asked Sissy. 'I'd have felt awful. I'd have wanted to go on living where I always had lived, and where my family'd lived, too.'

Ted shook his head. 'It was different for me. (Look, Rhoda, we can sit on the steps — I'll spread out my handkerchief so the stones won't soil your skirt.) No, you see, I never really had much of a home, even here. My father and mother both died when I was three, of cholera.'

'Grandpa Bascomb died of cholera, too,' said Sissy. 'A lot of people did in those early days, didn't they? Had your family been here long then?'

'Not more than a year or two. They came out from Utica about the beginning of the thirties, I guess — anyway, 'twas right after the end of the Indian war. My father and mother (who'd just been married) and Uncle Jim (who was a bachelor and my father's much older brother) bought this land and built this house and settled down to farm. Then I was born; then my folks died, on a visit to the city. (It was the bad water killed 'em; that's what makes cholera, you know.) I can't remember them — not either one of them — not anything at all. I wish I could. I haven't even a picture or a scrap of their writing to keep; when the house burned everything in it went, too.

'Well, Uncle Jim took charge of me, because there wasn't anybody else. He was a man, was Uncle Jim! I wish you had known him, Rhoda. He was a big fellow, with a bush of dark hair. I used to think, when I was young, he looked like a great shaggy buffalo. He was as good to me as he knew how to be; stuck to me like a trump till I was old enough to go away to school. But he didn't take to farming, though he stuck to that, too, pretty well as long as he had to. It just

151

wasn't in his blood. 'Twas my father who liked it and insisted on buying in Naperville. If Uncle Jim had had his way, he'd have gone farther west. It seems I really should have been *his* son, doesn't it? . . . Anyhow, he was away more'n half the time on trips, and when I was sixteen he came to me and said he couldn't stand it any longer — he had to go to California with the gold miners! Of course, I was wild to go, too. I begged and begged — but he wouldn't let me. It wasn't so much on account of my age, he said, as because I hadn't finished my schooling. He'd saved enough money to send me to the seminary in Utica where he and my father had gone, and he was set I should try for a scholarship at Hamilton College. Uncle Jim was a great believer in education, though he hadn't had much himself. But he did promise faithfully that when the time came, if I didn't want to go to college, I shouldn't have to. Poor old fellow! It was here on these very steps he said that and we told each other good-bye. I guess you know me well enough, Rhoda, to know what I would have done if it had been up to me. But, in the end, as things turned out I had no choice. Uncle Jim was dead — this house was gone — I hadn't a home or much money — but I *did* have my scholarship. That's all there is to the story.'

Sissy did not agree. There was a deal else she was eager to hear. In response to her questions Ted told her as much as he could about his uncle's romance with Aunt Zeph. They'd met in San Francisco, shortly after the latter's arrival by ship from France. Her father had died on the voyage over and been buried at sea. She was alone in the world: her mother had died long ago, and her grandmother, recently. . . . There'd been some trouble between the two families. The mother's people were aristocrats; the old lady, Madame de Beaubourg, was a countess, though Aunt Zeph never boasted of that — it was as much as you could do to get her to admit it! The father had been quite a different type, a commoner, a brilliant lawyer, and (Ted surmised) an adventurer at heart — else how could he, a poor man, have thrown up his practice and set sail in search of gold? — worse still, have been willing to expose his young daughter to such dangers? . . . 'Poor Aunt Zeph! All her life, it seems, she's had to do with born wanderers. . . .

'Well, there she was, in a strange country, and a pretty wild part of it, too. She knew nobody; I don't suppose she spoke much English then. Uncle Jim met her at the hotel, liked her, and wanted to be-

152

friend her; but the only way he could get a legal right to do it was to marry her. I can't figure out that it was exactly a love match. Uncle Jim was thirty years older than she; he must have seemed more like a second father. Anyhow, married they were and went to the gold fields together. She was grateful to him, stuck to him nobly through thick and thin; when he fell ill she got him safe back to the coast and nursed him till he died. Your father's told you that part of it. When there was nothing more she could do she came to Illinois. That's when she wrote to me, as I told you. You can imagine I hardly knew what to think — to find I had no uncle any more, but an aunt instead, a foreigner I'd never even heard of, a woman almost young enough to be my sister. But the moment I saw her I felt it was going to be all right. She's kept things going here ever since, made a home for me whenever I needed it; and I care for her now just as much as if we really were kin to each other.'

After Ted had finished speaking there fell a short silence, during which nothing could be heard but the soft rustle of leaves and the plaint of a mourning-dove lost in the wood. Sissy selected a grass blade with care and began meditatively to chew it (something both Mamma and Miss Crandall were agreed well-brought-up young ladies were never caught doing!). Finally she said: 'I don't wonder you care for her. She's a lovable person. I feel I could care for her myself, and I've known her less than twenty-four hours. But it's queer, isn't it, when you come to think of it, that a woman like Mrs. Amberley, who's had the best things in life, is willing to settle down in a quiet country spot and do without them all! I mean, it's queer, considering that she could go where she liked, Chicago or New York or back to France, even. She must be rich enough to be her own mistress.'

'Rich?' Ted looked surprised. 'Aunt Zeph isn't rich. What made you think so?'

'Why, I don't know,' replied Sissy, in embarrassment; 'she has such pretty clothes — and such beautiful furniture and things —'

'It's as she told you — she saved a few scraps from the family shipwreck. Of course, she inherited from Uncle Jim, too, but by the time she'd taken care of him and buried him and come to Illinois and built herself a house, there couldn't have been much left. Oh, she's comfortable enough, especially living here on our property — this place is half hers and half mine. She earns her living and a bit more besides. I don't believe she had a natural taste for farming. She does it because it's the nearest thing to hand; and then, as she says, it's in the French blood to make the most one can of the land — *faire valoir ses terres,* she calls it. Aunt Zeph is nobody's fool. I know what you mean about her missing things. I've thought of it often, and worried enough to ask her if she didn't mind, if she were really happy here. And she always makes the same answer: "I've known it better — but so much worse, too." That's all I can get her to say. No, I guess Aunt Zeph is all right, as long as I can be with her at least part of the time. I do worry sometimes about how she'll manage when I go West.'

'I don't see,' said Sissy simply, 'how you can leave her.'

'She wants me to go. She's said so, over and over. She's promised to give me my share of the profits this year to help start me off. That's why she's especially anxious for the crops to do well. And she's giving me letters to friends of hers in California. So is your father, Rhoda. I can't tell you how splendid they've both been about everything.'

'But what will happen when you get there?' asked Sissy. 'It mayn't be so easy, you know. Papa didn't find it so — and he went years ago when there weren't nearly so many people. Maybe it will be quite different from what you think. Maybe you won't like it at all. What will you do if you can't find work?'

'Do? What will I do? Rhoda Trigg, I'm twenty-three years old, and strong as Toby there. I've had a first-rate education, thanks to Uncle Jim's foresight. If I can't manage to lay my hands on a job, I'll be ashamed to live. I'm not afraid to take risks, any more than my uncle was, or your father. Aunt Zeph's not afraid for me either. She says she's only sorry she can't go with me. Someone has to stay here to run the farm. Then she thinks I'll do better without her — that a man gets along faster without a woman to hold him back. *I* think that depends on the woman. If she's the right sort, she can push him ahead. And a man knows straight off when he's found the right sort for *him.* Don't you remember that night at the concert, how your father told us about taking your mother out driving in the sleigh, the first time they met as grown-up people? He *knew* then and there she was going to be his. That's the way it always happens, I guess. That's the way it was with me, last December. I was *sure* —'

154

Sissy jumped up, startled no less by Ted's words than by a sudden scuffling in the bushes.

'Goodness me!' she cried. 'There's Tartuffe! How can he have got so far from home?'

'It's not far,' said Ted, as composedly as if he had not just been interrupted in the middle of what was as good as a declaration. 'Look, we've come round in a circle!'

He followed her down from the steps and pushed the shrubs aside to make a path through. As they emerged from the thicket Sissy saw that the hill they were standing on was the crest of the long, gentle slope, halfway up which Aunt Zeph had built her house. It nestled underneath the larches, perhaps a thousand yards below. Between them and it lay the north meadow, close-cropped and stubbly as the hay-makers had left it. At the far end of the meadow stood Damon and Pythias with the hay-wagon, now nearly loaded. Papa, in his scarlet shirt, was still pitching manfully; Aunt Zeph, on top of the pile in the wagon, received the last fragrant forkfuls and deftly made room for them where there seemed to be no more room. They were within earshot, but so deeply engrossed in their work that they failed to see the young people above them.

'Let's ride down and surprise them,' proposed Sissy, 'and see if we can help.'

'All right,' agreed Ted. 'They must be about through. But it's breakfast-time anyhow.'

As he helped Sissy into the saddle he gave her a long, serious look and said quietly: 'You stopped me then, just as I'd got to the point of what I wanted to say. I know why you did it. I know you won't let me speak now, but perhaps some day you'll change —'

'Never! Never! Oh, Ted, what's the use?'

But Ted did not turn away disconsolate. Instead he remained half-clasping her in his arms — he was so tall that, even when she was mounted, his head was not far below hers — and fixed her again with his strange, light green eyes. Sissy's glance wavered before them; yet she could not look away: she felt rather frightened, intensely conscious of Ted's nearness and of a number of feelings as new as they were disturbing.

They stayed as they were for a long moment; then Ted released her, muttering awkwardly: 'You know confounded well what's the use!'

All the way home he rode close beside her, not once taking his eyes from her face.

As they entered the meadow they passed the old barn at the edge of the wood. It was a ruin; once red, but now faded to a dull rust colour, with many cracked boards and a sagging roof, in contrast to the neat buildings of the home farm. The sole sign of life was a flock of swallows twittering about under the eaves. Ted told Sissy that it was the only part of the original homestead the flames had spared. Although it was good for nothing, Aunt Zeph still would not have it pulled down.

'Even a practical Frenchwoman has her sentimental side, you see. It used to be the cow-stable, but it's quite empty now except for a few mice and spiders, and in winter, perhaps, a hoot-owl or two.'

Sissy shuddered. 'Don't let's go in!' And Ted smiled and said she would not have to.

Midway across the meadow Sissy turned, she did not know why, to look over her shoulder—and there, in front of the barn, was Marie-Claire. How she had got where she was, was a mystery. She must either have been inside the whole time, or have been hiding in the wood and have stepped out just after they rode by. Yet the entrance had been nailed up securely—Sissy remembered that—and the trees at the edge of the wood were not at all thick. . . . There was something uncanny about the tall, white-clad figure, standing with folded arms, calm and motionless.

Shivering a little, Sissy told herself she did not wonder that Joshua had taken Aunt Zeph's Indian handmaiden for a witch.

The Excursion

Long before the week was over Sissy, Nancy, and Loulie Trigg felt the Amberley farm was home, and that they had never had another. Young people, of course, quickly grow accustomed to novelty; what was strange here, thought Sissy, was that it was the very strangeness, the complete contrast to anything they had known, that made them adjust themselves so easily. For the first time in their lives they were absolutely free.

Sissy's day began an hour or so earlier than her sisters'. She had feared at first to be selfish in monopolizing Priscilla, but Loulie did not know how to ride, Nancy frankly preferred to sleep late, and Aunt Zeph asserted she was too busy at this season of the year and was only too thankful to have the mare exercised. (This might be true, or it might be merely another example of their hostess's exquisite tact: how would one ever be able to tell?)

After a cheerful family breakfast the men went to the fields. Haying was over, but oats had to be cut. Lem was still laid up; he was hardly missed, however; for Aunt Zeph had found three itinerant farm-hands in Wheaton, Ted was strong and willing, and Papa was nearly as good as two men. Sissy marvelled at her father's capacity for work. At first she supposed he did it because he was happy and grateful to Aunt Zeph; later, she was not sure. There was something feverish in his application to the task, as though he hoped to outdistance his troubles by sheer physical effort.

In the beginning Wilfred, too, made one of the party. He had insisted upon it, and had driven all the way to the general store in Naperville to buy a wide-brimmed straw hat and a gay-checked shirt to complete an appropriate costume. (Lord! What would his mother say if she could see him? Should he not — he appealed to his cousins —

157

have his daguerreotype taken to send her?) Sissy could not imagine that Wilfred was much good at cutting oats; he must have wanted to go only because he would have been ashamed to stay home; but Ted told her privately that the poor fellow had tried desperately to do his share. One day of such unwonted labours had made his muscles so weary and so badly blistered his hands that he was forced to retire; whereupon he consoled himself by following the girls, performing occasional odd jobs to help them, but generally rather tiresomely in the way, till Aunt Zeph hit upon the happy expedient of asking him to read aloud. *John Halifax, Gentleman,* or the latest Dickens, recited in Wilfred's agreeable tenor, provided a delightful accompaniment to various household duties.

For the girls worked as well as the men. Aunt Zeph had not expected it; indeed, she had been loath to accept their repeated offers. But Mamma's instructions had been plain: they *must* make themselves useful. Besides, it was really more fun to be doing something — Aunt Zeph made it fun.

This week had been Currant Week. Currants, it appeared, went with oats as cherries had gone with hay and strawberries with rye, and as, later on, grapes would go with corn. (Could farmers never take a rest?) Baskets piled high with the round shiny fruit, some red and some white, had been picked and carried into the kitchen, there to be sorted and washed and sugared and boiled, and turned into currant jam and currant jelly and strong, sweet currant wine.

The Trigg girls, of course, were used to jelly-making. Mamma put up quarts every year. So did Aunt Betsy; so had Aunt Jane, in the days when she had had a house of her own, although preserves in any form brought on her bilious attacks. Even Aunt Bertha, in an elegant ruffled apron and with a set look of grim resignation on her handsome features, would make an annual descent to the kitchen to make sure that Deane, her very competent cook, was boiling the apricots as long as Uncle Charles said his mother had always boiled hers. . . . But in The Family it was a terrible task, involving an interruption of the normal pleasures of life. Company was banned; meals were scrappy and irregular; while the mistress of the house stood over the stove, flushed crimson and scolding sharply anyone who came near her.

At the farm more cheerful conditions prevailed. Aunt Zeph never scolded anybody, not even Marie-Claire, who, according to Bascomb ideas, was being paid to be scolded. In Mamma's house servants were neither abused nor overworked; but they were treated *as* servants — that is, as a kind of natural enemy. Relations with them at best were in a state of armed truce; at worst they degenerated into a long, exhausting duel to be ended only by the 'hired girl's' departure and the arrival of a new highly suspicious character. Mamma and the Aunts took it for granted that Susan (or Mary or Amanda) would be lazy and impertinent and would make every conceivable blunder, unless given specific instructions and then watched with fanatical perseverance to make sure they were carried out to the letter.

Aunt Zeph, on the contrary, assumed carelessly that Marie-Claire was a help, not a hindrance. She called her *ma chère* and *ma bonne,* as if she were her friend instead of her maid. And Marie-Claire requited the trust by an unhurried efficiency and a single-hearted devotion; one felt that the bond between the two was a deep one. (Sissy tried to imagine Mamma's calling Susan 'my dear' or 'my goody,' and failed utterly.)

After the midday meal Aunt Zeph insisted on everyone's stopping work for an hour to take a siesta. This, she maintained, was advisable, even necessary, on account of the heat; for each day had been hotter than the one before; the sky had grown paler and paler blue, the white clouds more puffy, edged with an ominous violet, as if presaging a storm that never came. After the siesta Papa and Ted returned to the fields, Aunt Zeph and Marie-Claire busied themselves in the buttery or the linen cupboard, and the rest of the party were at liberty to do what they liked. Loulie and Joshua took Tartuffe for a run in the woods, or wandered down to the pond to try to catch mud-turtles. The elder girls, with Wilfred in attendance, strolled round the grounds, or perhaps drove Priscilla in the pony-cart to Wheaton or Naperville. Evenings were always the same: late dinner, all dressed in their best (Sissy and Nancy had had to send post-haste home to Mamma for a more varied assortment of party frocks); followed by an hour in the larch grove, watching the sunset go and the stars come out and the fireflies flash about the lawn. Sometimes they had music, sometimes not; but there was always harmony in the atmosphere.

For that, it was evident to Sissy, Aunt Zeph was primarily responsible. She conducted her personal relations as she did the conversation at dinner: she seemed to be equally interested in every one of her guests, giving each his or her share of prominence. Her manner with Papa, for example, was perfect: perpetually conscious of the claims of past friendship, yet never presuming upon them. Even the children were regarded as reasonable beings. When Joshua, one very warm afternoon, was caught chasing the ducks till the poor things fell to earth with half-spread wings and gaping beaks, Aunt Zeph, instead of smacking him, sketched the performance, as it must have appeared from the ducks' point of view, so graphically that the culprit was reduced at once to blubbering repentance. . . . When Loulie, overzealous and ever unlucky, stubbed her toe on the kitchen threshold and let drop a whole saucepan of the precious currant juice, her hostess did not chide her, nor murmur trite maxims, such as 'The more haste, the less grace.' On the other hand, neither did she break into false smiles (because Loulie was 'company') and pretend that the loss made no matter. It *did* matter; it *was* a pity — but it hadn't been Loulie's fault (this was the burden of her philosophy), so let the accident be forgotten as quickly as possible.

With the older girls Aunt Zeph's way was no less fortunate. She seemed glad to see them when they sought her out, but left them in the main to their own devices; did not offer advice, but gave it freely if asked. She was generous, too, willing at a moment's notice to lend ribbons or handkerchiefs, a bracelet or a bodice, to complete their best toilets. Nancy was pressed to accept as hers a Roman sash that just matched her pink tarletan; and when Sissy one evening voiced dissatisfaction with the prim coiffure Mamma approved, Aunt Zeph, all-aflutter with pleasure, devised a new method of dressing her hair, making use of its natural waves, that turned out to be vastly becoming.

Moreover, her duties as a chaperon were discharged so unobtrusively as to be scarcely perceptible. She did not pry, nor spy, nor hover distractedly over her charges.

As things were, she did not need to; but it was clever of Aunt Zeph, all the same, to have realized it.

For, to the casual eye, the four young people would certainly have appeared as two pairs of lovers.

This Sissy had to admit, even though she was sure that Ted's behaviour, ever since the first day, had been propriety itself. On their morning rides, when they were alone for several hours at a time, he never said anything he shouldn't. Indeed, he even seemed to avoid the north meadow and its hilltop, as if fearing that a return to the familiar scene might suggest the forbidden subject. Ted was, in fact, Sissy found to her surprise, an exceedingly tactful person. One would not have looked for tact in someone so simple and direct; perhaps it sprang straight from his affection, for Sissy knew instinctively he would not for worlds have distressed her. (See, for example, how easily he had accepted the Triggs' very peculiar domestic situation! Not once had he referred to the embarrassing fact that Papa and Mamma were not living together — quite unlike Aaron, who had been forever crying: 'But, Sissy, what do you think? But, Sissy, what will they do? But, Sissy, it's so unnatural!') Ted was a cheery companion withal, ready to laugh at anything or nothing. He teased her, too, once in a while — again unlike Aaron — with the kindly good humour of a devoted elder brother.

But he was not her brother. Sissy knew he didn't want to be; that under the surface, however manfully hidden, lay very different feelings. In the evenings under the larches he usually contrived to sit next her; at her place every night at dinner she found a small nosegay of flowers — roses or sweetpeas with her favourite mignonette. Sissy was all the more moved by these proofs of his sentiments because they were silent. She felt happy about Ted, and unhappy; proud, and ashamed; eager to put her emotions to the test, yet reluctant to confess they needed testing. . . . When she went up to bed she placed her posy in the vase with the doves on the high chest of drawers (where she had also placed Aaron's picture). Then she sat down and wrote her betrothed a short letter. There was not much to say, and Sissy had never cared about writing letters. But it was her duty. Besides, Aaron had written to *her* several times — *he* had not much to say either! Michigan was very wild, the nights were very cold, his work was going well, he hoped to see her soon, and Aaron remained affectionately hers. . . . Sissy kept his letters tied with pink ribbons under her pillow, but somehow she never cared to reread them.

After sealing her note she undressed, brushed out her long brown hair and braided it, standing on tiptoe to see herself in the looking-glass above the chest. Then she said her prayers, and blew out the candle, and jumped into bed to think over the events of the day. . . . Sometimes she smiled to herself in the dark, she did not know why; sometimes she cried a few tears, for some equally indefinite reason. Sometimes for a good many minutes she pondered the problem of Ted's future — wondering how he would get along in the West, fearing he would be lonely (who would mend his linen and see he had a clean handkerchief?), wishing he did not want to go and then, the next moment, that as long as he was going he would leave directly! If her conscience pricked her, she could salve it by insisting that, as long as nothing was *said,* there could be no sin. . . . Was this falling in love?

The case of Nancy and Wilfred was easier to judge — at least, Sissy found it easier. Nancy, of course, was a child; she knew nothing of life. Wilfred was her first admirer and, as such, naturally of absorbing interest. Sissy lamented in secret that her sister had not chosen someone more worthy. But there was no harm in Beau Morgan. His sighs, his smiles, his killing glances were all Nancy's merely because there was no one else to receive them. Any pretty girl, Sissy was convinced, would have done quite as well. Wilfred could not help flirting any more than Nancy, with her youth and her charm and her happy high spirits, could help enjoying being flirted with.

It was callow and trivial and a little bit silly. The worst of the affair, according to Sissy's perhaps unduly sensitive eye, was that Nancy and Wilfred at times seemed to be presenting a kind of comic caricature of her own relations with Ted. They made her feel guilty because they were so innocent. Nancy was not engaged. Wilfred had a right to admire her if he liked and she let him. . . . Oh, well! The acute stage would end soon enough, when they returned to the city. Wilfred wasn't the sort to confine his attentions to a single young lady, especially one who was *so* young and a family connection besides. Nancy, too, would meet other young men. At the end of his year in Chicago Wilfred would go home and, in all probability, the young people would never see each other again.

Mamma, Sissy felt positive, would not have approved of some of their conversations. She herself had been terribly shocked to discover, quite by accident, that Nancy had been told all about Miss Betty Blossom, of the Niblo's Garden troupe. Sissy considered that whole business too improper for words: Miss Blossom's existence should not have been mentioned in the hearing of a modest young girl! The meagre details she herself had been able to glean from what had passed between Uncle Charles and Aunt Betsy, she had not divulged to a soul. But apparently Wilfred was by no means so discreet. Nancy referred quite casually to the affair, as if it were of no consequence any more, but, if anything, rather redounded to their cousin's credit. . . . 'He says she had beautiful auburn hair, and her voice was almost as pretty as mine; but of course that was over a year ago — he was only twenty-one then, much too young to know any better! He says — oh, he says, if he should meet her right in the street, his heart wouldn't go pit-a-pat — she'd mean no more to him than the crossing-sweeper on the corner! He likes black hair best now.'

'Does he, indeed?' remarked Sissy tartly. 'And I suppose this time next year he'll prefer canary yellow.'

To this Nancy only shrieked with laughter and cried out that Sissy was a horrid tease to hector her so.

This revelation took place on Thursday, three days after their coming to Naperville.

On Friday Aunt Zeph appeared at lunch (as she called the midday meal that was dinner in Chicago) with a letter in her hand.

'You have received an invitation,' she said, 'all of you, to spend Sunday at your aunt Mrs. Walworth's in Geneva.'

'Oh,' exclaimed Nancy, making a face, 'must we go? I don't want to a bit: I hate it at Aunt Betsy's!'

'Nancy, how *can* you?' said Sissy at once; and then found, to her dismay, that *she* did not much want to go either.

'But you know very well,' Nancy insisted, 'how dull it will be. We're never allowed to roam about as we please. We'll have to sit in a row and stuff ourselves at dinner, and answer questions till Aunt Betsy can't think of anything more to badger us about. Besides, Uncle Caleb and Aunt Jane'll likely be there — they generally are, this time of year; it's much cheaper than going East to the Springs — *they'll* ask questions, too — and Aunt Jane gives such very wet kisses!'

'*Nancy!*' said Sissy once more, in her strongest tone of disapproval, while Ted and Wilfred shouted with laughter.

'It's true, though,' said Nancy, 'whether you admit it or not — they're as wet as can be! Anyhow, I don't want to leave Mrs. Amberley on our last day at the farm. 'Tisn't polite.'

Sissy looked inquiringly at their hostess. 'Surely Aunt Betsy has asked — '

Aunt Zeph assured them that she had — Mrs. Walworth's hospitality was genially proffered to all members of the Amberley household — 'Though I doubt very much, my dears, whether I shall be able to accept it. There are so many things for me to attend to here.'

'Then I shall stop with you, ma'am,' announced Papa. 'There's no love lost between Sister Walworth and me. But the children had better go. I don't want Mrs. Trigg to think I had kept them — '

'Nor do I,' said Aunt Zeph quickly. 'I am certain that Rhoda, at least, will agree with me, when she's read her aunt's note, that it will be wiser to say yes. Mrs. Walworth is everything that is cordial and kind, but I think I detect . . . that is, her feelings may have been a little hurt because you are stopping with me instead of with her.'

'Oh, but that's nonsense!' began Nancy. 'I mean, she doesn't care a mite, really. It just frets her because — '

'Dear Nancy,' Aunt Zeph interrupted her, 'I should never forgive myself if I allowed your politeness to me to cause you to neglect your duty to your family. And you need not regret your last day in Naperville because — I may tell them, Mr. Trigg, may I not? — I have persuaded your papa to alter his plans. He has just promised me that you will stay for another week.'

'Oh, Papa, *really?* How splendid! But what will Mamma say to that?'

'She'd say what I say,' replied Papa, 'if she could see your faces at this moment. I doubt if you realize yet how much good our visit's done you. I feel like a new man myself. I'm more grateful than words can express. Indeed, ma'am, I know not what recompense to offer — '

'Please,' said Aunt Zeph. 'It's my nephew and I should be grateful, not you. Then it's settled, I take it? — for I must write Mrs. Walworth an answer immediately — : the young people go to Geneva on Sunday.'

When Sunday came the situation was unchanged: the young people were still to go, whether they wanted to or not; and Papa and Aunt Zeph were to stay. (There was no doubt where their preferences lay!)

164

The two farms were so far apart that Aunt Betsy's prospective guests had to choose between church and dinner — or, rather, the choice was made for them by Aunt Zeph, who said easily that Ted could drive them to vespers in Naperville, later, in the cool of the evening. For it was again very hot, the hottest weather they had yet seen: the clouds were puffier than ever, with slate-blue centres, and the air was heavy with moisture that refused to come down as rain.

Sissy was in a quandary: never before in her life had she failed to go to church twice on Sunday. In the days preceding their visit she had speculated a good deal about Aunt Zeph's religion. She knew that Mamma had speculated, too, and had worried for fear she might be exposing her children to dangerous influences. They could have consulted Ted, but somehow neither had liked to: Ted, of course, was safely a Baptist; but that was because his father and uncle had been Baptists before him. Mamma and Sissy had steeled themselves to expect the worst — that Mrs. Amberley, like most of her unhappy race, would be a Romanist. Mamma had given her eldest daughter explicit instructions as to how she was to cope with this menace, should it arise. But what would her mother have said, could she have guessed the still more terrible truth?: Aunt Zeph was a heathen!

What else, after all, could you call it? When the carriage drove off to Geneva the two miscreants were left sitting under the larches, where they obviously intended to spend the entire morning. Aunt Zeph's thin little freckled face was paler than ever from the heat, but her hazel eyes sparkled; sparks gleamed, too, in her hair as the light filtering through the trees struck it. She leaned back in her chair, looking neat and elegant in her pretty white ruffled gown. In spite of all the things she had said she must do, her hands lay idle in her lap. Papa, at her feet on the grass, held a book in his: Sissy hoped none but herself had noticed that it was not the Bible, nor even Barnes's *Notes,* but a copy of *The Blithedale Romance.* He waved an amiable farewell, with a smile that included all six young people. Aunt Zeph also smiled, and kissed her hand, and called out: 'Amuse yourselves well, my children!'

But they did not. The excursion to Aunt Betsy's was doomed from the start; it was one of those parties, planned purely for pleasure, that seemed to please nobody. A cloud hung over the general spirits, quite as gloomily grey as the moist billows piling themselves upon one another aloft. The road was exceedingly dusty; Sissy silently regretted having worn her best bonnet, the one trimmed with roses. She was sorry, too, that they could not have driven Priscilla in the smart new red pony-cart; there were, of course, too many passengers for that; but Damon and Pythias, lumbering ahead of the surrey, made a solid rather than a stylish impression. . . . Ted, who was driving, appeared disinclined to talk. Loulie and Joshua had started to bicker over who was to 'own' May Lily's new calf, born the previous night — surely an academic question! Wilfred was troubled by the prospect of meeting his employer at dinner. It developed that he had secured a week's leave from the office on the plea of ill-health: he felt, and his cousins agreed with him, that Uncle Caleb might well conclude it had been granted on flimsy pretenses.

Nancy, alone of the six, was in her usual spirits; and with Nancy, of late, good humour had taken the unfortunate form of trying to be funny in public. All she needed to set her off was a masculine audience. She told, with great gusto, a deplorable tale about her 'conversion' — how, one night last winter, she'd been pushed to the altar at prayer meeting by Mamma and Mrs. Miles and persuaded to join the church, without realizing what she was doing until it was done.

Sissy would not laugh; she was frankly horrified; it was a relief to her when the surrey swung round a corner and came within sight of the broad, strongly flowing Fox River. On account of the drought the water was a little low and, it had to be confessed, more than a little smelly. Still the view was fair enough: the river, bending sharply between its tree-bordered banks; the high, round green hill at the bend; and on the summit of the hill, presiding over its gardens and meadows and wheatfields and cornfields, the red, boxlike buildings of the Walworth farm. Dutiful visitors were wont to remark, admiringly, that it was 'just like a picture.' Sissy, however, had always compared it mentally to a German toy village she and Nancy had played with as children. Aunt Betsy's brick house, in the centre of the compound, was as square and red as the barns; even the trees in front of it, a group of balloon-shaped maples planted in orderly rows, might have been carved out of wood.

But Aunt Betsy herself was far too big and too billowing to be

166

seen as a toy. As the surrey reached the top of the hill she hastened down the front steps with glad cries of welcome. . . . 'Such a pleasure, my dears . . . long way in this heat . . . must be exhausted . . . how do you do? how do you do? . . . Mr. Morgan, you honour us . . . Mr. Amberley, Seth'll take the horses . . . please come this way . . . Sissy, my dear, *what* have you done to your hair?'

As Nancy had foretold, Uncle Caleb and Aunt Jane were discovered on the front porch, which was screened from the sun by a luxuriant growth of Dutchman's Pipe. There were more screams, and a great deal of kissing. Everybody was glad to see everybody else. Uncle Caleb said 'Hum!' and 'Ha!' to Wilfred, and 'I hope you're quite well again, sir, ready to report for work tomorrow morning!' But he was too limp from the heat to be truly intimidating. Aunt Jane announced that she had had a stomach cramp last night, brought on by unwise indulgence in a raspberry sauce with her custard: she was feeling better today, though still rather queasy. Aunt Betsy, in spite of the temperature, was very well and very happy indeed with her party, regretting only that it could not have been *quite* complete. . . . 'We had hoped to see your papa and Mrs. Amberley, too. Mrs. Amberley wrote me a most polite answer to my letter, saying that she would have admired to come. Unfortunately, some farm business . . . Naturally, I can sympathize; I understand, none better, the cares of a country life. Still I should have thought once in a way . . . and a Sunday, too. . . . Perhaps she didn't feel she could leave Mr. Trigg. How is your father, Sissy? I hope quite recovered from the great fatigues of his journey. I must say I never . . . Your poor Mamma . . . not a word out of her. . . . Always said Julia was *weak* with him. . . . But there! This is no time . . . Come in! Come in out of the sun, everybody! Where will you be most comfortable — near the window, or away from it? Dinner'll be ready in just a few minutes. I told Maria to hold the fowls back till we knew you were here. If there's anything worse than dry chickens . . .'

By the time they were seated in Aunt Betsy's airless dining-room (all brown plush and black walnut, lace tidies and wax flowers under glass, with a large portrait of the late Uncle Walworth frowning resentfully from his place of honour over the sideboard), it was plain that the cloud depressing the younger members of the company likewise affected their elders. Not that they had not enough to say to one another. Oh, dear, no! They could talk a good deal about food — and they did. There was also a fairly brisk exchange of items of intelligence concerning The Family. Aunt Betsy had heard the Charles Bascombs had decided to have the new gas lights installed in their house. Uncle Caleb confirmed the rumour; he was able to tell to a penny how many dollars the undertaking would cost their brother. Aunt Jane added that Charles and Bertha were leaving next week for the White Mountains, to spend a month at the Profile House while the workmen were in possession at home. Imagine that! It was only two years since their last trip East! . . . One extravagance, rejoined her husband gloomily, fixing the gravy with a suspicious eye, almost inevitably led to another.

Nevertheless, the subject that really engrossed them could be approached only indirectly. That was Ted Amberley's fault. The children were an obstacle; but it was always possible to commune over their heads. It were wise, too, perhaps, to be careful in front of Wilfred; but he, if not of The Family, was at least allied with it. How, though, in the name of decency, would one ever be able to ask the questions one was burning to ask about Aunt Zeph — her house and her farm, her income, her style of living; above all, her relations with Jonathan Trigg — before the candid and serious eyes of Aunt Zeph's nephew by marriage?

Aunt Betsy, conversationally the most resourceful of the Bascombs, did manage to interrogate her nieces without seeming to do so. What a happy holiday they must be having, all by themselves in the depths of the country! She had been given to understand that Mrs. Amberley had no neighbours nearer than five miles away, and no servants except a wild Indian squaw with feathers in her hair, who talked no known language. . . . Oh, really? Marie-Claire did not wear feathers and spoke French like a native! How foolish some rumours were, to be sure! The Triggs must appreciate the privilege of sharing a real French home; Aunt Betsy believed French home life was beautiful. (Sissy, dear, was it true that each course was served separately at dinner? Mrs. Gaston, the wife of the new Baptist minister at Geneva, had once dined at the Amberleys' and had assured Aunt Betsy that the meal took two hours — even the peas made a solitary entrance!) What, however, she wondered, did they *do* all day, so far from town, without friends to drop in and be sociable?

Delicately but unmistakably, Aunt Betsy conveyed her conviction that, if her nieces were not dull, they should have been dull; if they were not dull, there could be just one reason why. Not hers Aunt Zeph's serene assurance that she could trust her charges. To Mrs. Walworth young men were inherently bent on mischief; young ladies frail and fatally prone to abet them; it was never safe to leave the two sexes together unchaperoned for more than a very few minutes.

Sissy's cheeks burned at the veiled innuendos (like pills wrapped in jelly), the purport of which was perfectly clear, even when, as now, her aunt appeared to be talking about Aaron Miles. . . . Dear Aaron! How they must miss him! Charles said it was wonderful what he'd accomplished up north. How often had Sissy heard from him since his departure? Really? Twice only? Well, but of course he must be terribly busy. And then maybe he'd heard reports — little birds flew so fast — that his bride-to-be was much occupied at the moment and had scant leisure to read or write letters. . . . 'Dear me! September will be here before we know it. It seems to me you'll almost have to start getting ready . . . Your Mamma was saying the other day . . . But of course I'd not be the one to suggest . . . old heads on young shoulders . . . responsibility . . . time for everything and everything in its time . . . Now who will have a second helping of chicken and vegetables?'

Sissy's gentle eyes looked rebellious and her cheeks burned still harder; she marvelled that Nancy's did not, when the guns were trained in *her* direction. Wilfred's obvious partiality for the second Miss Trigg could not escape notice. (Dear, dear! Some little curly heads would be sadly turned, one feared.) But Nancy only looked supremely indifferent; and she did not turn her head, she tossed it!

Towards the end of dinner Aunt Betsy, having exhausted her small shot on objects near at hand, could not resist aiming at the distant target. She hinted that it was no wonder Brother Trigg had not cared to come to Geneva. Why, after all, should he seek outside diversion, when he could solace himself with the society of his charming hostess? The French, she knew, the ladies especially, were quite fascinating. . . .

But here Uncle Caleb decided to call a halt. He cleared his throat loudly, pushed his chair back, and remarked: 'An excellent dinner,

Sister Betsy: my compliments to your cook! The gooseberry tart was very nice indeed, though it might have had just a *leetle* more shortening. What do you say, Jane, my love? Would it not have been better —'

Aunt Jane, already struggling in the throes of dyspepsia, shook her head wordlessly. Aunt Betsy flushed with annoyance and exclaimed: 'There, now, I knew it! I declare, it's too bad! I warned the girl to be careful — but you know what they are! Maria, do you hear what Mr. Bascomb's just said? He thought the tart wanted shortening. How often must I tell you —'

Sissy got up and left the room. She did not know why, but suddenly she felt she could not bear any more. Oh, what was the matter? Surely she loved her relatives as much as ever! *They* had not changed. Uncle Caleb and Aunt Jane were what they had always been. Even Aunt Betsy, despite her trying ways, was full of affection for them all. (The pills were so small, and there was so much jelly!) . . . Had she herself changed, then? Had exposure to another standard of life altered her own? Could less than a week at the Amberleys' have completely revolutionized her point of view? . . . It was as if she were looking at The Family through someone else's spectacles, so that they appeared very slightly out of focus . . . Or a new pair of eyes? Was *that* it? But whose? Not Ted's, anyhow: Ted, for all his integrity, was as uncritical of others as Loulie. . . . Aunt Zeph's, then? Or Papa's? (That *would* be a novelty! Sissy, heretofore, had regarded her father as having strayed from the ways of the Bascombs like a lost sheep: *they could not be wrong, so he had to be!*)

Somewhat shaken, she rejoined the party on the porch, where it was soon set in motion again by its indefatigable hostess. A tour of the farm was proposed: Aunt Betsy was proud, and with reason, of her flourishing acres. It was a pity that Mrs. Amberley had not come to be dazzled by her neighbour's superior situation. Failing that supreme satisfaction, it was well to make sure that Ted should be dazzled instead, so that he might carry the tale home to his aunt.

Uncle Caleb chose to join the expedition. Naturally, he had seen the farm already innumerable times. A fresh inspection, however, would provide opportunities for a frank appraisal of his sister's methods of agriculture. Uncle Caleb knew little of farming, but he knew enough to know that Aunt Betsy knew still less; he could criticize her cross-breeding and crop rotation to his heart's content. **Aunt** Betsy enjoyed answering back; she gave as good as she got and did not take his criticisms in bad part, secure in her certainty that it did not make much difference what either of them said, since all decisions were made by Brant, her able and hard-working superintendent, who took no one's advice.

Nancy and Wilfred voted to go, clearly suspecting there might be some matter for merriment here. Loulie and Joshua trailed along, too: Aunt Betsy's farm was not nearly so nice as Aunt Zeph's, but it was always amusing to look at animals, and after the long hours at table they were badly in want of exercise.

Ted, Sissy saw, glanced round to see if she were coming; but she shook her head, smiling, and said she would stay with Aunt Jane.

Sissy was everybody's favourite niece. She ran upstairs for the new medicine and a forgotten handkerchief; administered three digestive drops in a glass of water; searched for and found a small white paper fan that had been left on the parlour table; and finally subsided in a chair on the porch next her aunt's. It was queer: as she did these things she saw herself, just as she felt she had seen The Family, as never before. She was keenly aware of her own physical presence — the slim figure in fluffy white muslin, with the pretty flower-trimmed bonnet atop her brown curls; the round, rosy cheeks; the big, guileless blue eyes, so like Mamma's in colour, if not in expression. She heard her own voice, as if it were a stranger's, saying 'Yes, ma'am' and 'No, ma'am,' 'Is this it, ma'am?' and 'It's no trouble, ma'am!' (But oh, what a fraud she was! What a black-hearted hypocrite! What would Aunt Jane have said if she knew . . . ?)

It was hotter than ever on the porch. The air was clammily still; the clouds hung motionless as though painted on a stage backdrop; even the grasshoppers had stopped shrilling. The only sound came from the Dutchman's Pipe, where a wren hopped about unseen and sang its cheerful, bubbling, monotonous song. (Sissy, who had thought she loved birds, hated that wren.)

Aunt Jane lay back in her chair and fanned herself feebly. She seemed in no hurry to start a conversation, which relieved her companion, who had nerved herself in advance to parry questions by saying nothing that was not true, without admitting the whole truth. (Was not this, in itself, a heinous form of deception?)

As a matter of fact, it was Sissy who began by asking her aunt when she and Uncle Caleb had arrived at the farm and how long they intended to stop. Aunt Jane replied that they had come last night and she was to stay for a full six weeks. Betsy was kind enough to say she was no trouble; and really the heat in Chicago had been very trying. Uncle Caleb, of course, would be with them for week-ends only, though he hoped to be able to pass a whole fortnight in Geneva in August. He, too, was most anxious for his wife to remain in the country, even though it would mean solitude at the Tremont House for him.

'You see, my dear, how they insist on spoiling me,' said poor Aunt Jane. 'I feel real bad at deserting my post, for I know your uncle needs me. When I'm away he never can get the servants at the hotel to wait on him properly. . . . Why, last spring, when I was called East to my brother's funeral, his boiled eggs at breakfast were overcooked three mornings in succession! He's very good and don't complain, but I see how it is. If only I were a little stronger! . . . He's very firm, and Betsy, too. Between them both I feel quite torn and driven. He's going back tonight by the late train from Wheaton, though I begged him not to, till the weather's cooler. There's an important case coming up in court tomorrow — he thinks it his duty — and you know, with your uncle, when it's a question of duty . . . Could you hand me my shawl, dear? There on the peg it is, just behind your head. A suspicion of draught . . . Thank you so much. . . . Well, as I say, he's going tonight. I'd feel even worse about it than I do if I weren't sure he'd be seeing your mother. She most kindly asked him to supper, knowing that otherwise he'd be alone and how hard he finds it to get anything fit to eat by himself. Dear Julia, always so thoughtful of others! You're like her, my pet, very like. . . . You must think to send her a message by your uncle; she'll be thankful to hear how you are, especially since you're not going home as soon as you'd planned. Nancy told me at dinner you'd been invited to stop in Naperville for another week.'

Sissy murmured, she hoped not faintly, that it would be kind of Uncle Caleb to give their love to Mamma and tell her they were all, including Papa, quite well and happy, although they missed her. As

soon as she'd spoken she was sorry she'd mentioned her father's name
— she hadn't meant to — for it was certain to lead to trouble. She
blushed and looked away; but Aunt Jane, for once, did not seem eager
to seize the opportunity. Instead she leaned still farther back in her
chair, her eyes half shut, the fan slipping from her relaxed fingers. (The
wren sang more and more loudly.) And when she looked up again it
was to say, with unusual warmth: 'My dear, you are looking so well.
I said it to Betsy directly you came. I said: "I've never seen Sissy in
such spirits — and so pretty, too." You're a very pretty girl, Sissy.'

Sissy blushed still more — but cheerfully, this time — and laughed
and said that probably she looked well because she felt well. They led
a very healthy life at the Amberleys'.

Aunt Jane observed that that might be true, but health was not the
most important thing. 'I've been an invalid, or next door to one, half
my life, and so I know what I'm talking about. It's happiness that
counts.'

'I know it,' said Sissy pitifully, thinking of the graves of the three
little Calebs under the pines in the Hebron cemetery.

'I've had a lot to be thankful for,' continued Aunt Jane musingly, almost as if to herself. 'Health's been denied me, and the consolation
of children. I often think how different it might have been if even
one of my little sons had lived. . . . But there! Your uncle's never let
me see he minded. He's been devotion itself, all these years. Never a
wish not granted as soon as asked. I know how grateful I ought to be.
It's only . . . well . . . I've been thinking lately happiness is a queer
thing: there don't seem to be any way of making sure of it. But it's
not what you've got that gives it to you — I'm certain of that.'

'How do you mean, Aunt Jane?'

'I mean — when I was a girl I wanted to marry Ned Whitcomb.
He was just my age; we'd grown up together in Hebron. I can't remember a time . . . There wasn't anybody else for him, ever, nor for
me either. He was a good boy, too.'

'Oh,' said Sissy, 'but then, why didn't you marry him?'

'My people were Baptists, dear, as you know. And Ned's were not.
They weren't much of anything really, as I remember — Freethinkers,
I suppose you'd call them. And Ned was the same as his people, of
course. It made quite a scandal in those days. Ma and Pa would've died

if I'd even suggested . . . And now I can see they were probably right, though at the time . . . God's all-powerful, Sissy. We can't flout Him and expect Him to love us. Faithfulness in His service is the greatest duty that's laid upon human beings. I don't know how 'twould all have worked out if I . . . But of course it *couldn't* have been, dearie. There was nothing for Ned and me to do but tell each other good-bye, though it 'most killed us to do it. He married Sally Perkins, who was an orphan and hadn't any folks to bother about what she did. And they've lived together ever since, as contentedly as most married people do, I guess. After a while I plucked up my spirits, too, and took your Uncle Caleb — and I don't have to tell you how things have gone with us. It seems so long ago now. There's no sense in raking up such old stories, is there? I can't imagine why . . . It's only that today, when I saw you come in looking so pretty and gay, with your young man beside you . . . I wanted to say it still isn't too late . . . That is, I wasn't able myself . . . But there's a look on young faces sometimes . . . Dear me, Sissy, what's got into me? Now, I declare, if I haven't gone and dropped my fan!'

Sissy picked up the fan; then flung her arms round Aunt Jane and hugged her wildly.

The Spiritual Rappers

ALL THE LONG DUSTY WAY HOME from Geneva Sissy looked forward to seeing Aunt Zeph. At intervals throughout the disappointing day the vision of the serene little figure in frilly white, seated with folded hands under the larches, had risen before her refreshingly. It was, of course, absurd to expect to find her still where they had left her — Papa with the volume of Hawthorne at her feet. Hours had passed since then. Nevertheless, quite unreasonably, Sissy felt crestfallen when she saw that the lawn was deserted.

So was the house. Papa doubtless was dressing for dinner in his own quarters, but Aunt Zeph's room, too, was empty; and there were no sounds of life in the kitchen, where Marie-Claire should have been busy preparing the meal.

It was late; they would have to hurry. Sissy changed her clothes as fast as she could, then crossed the hall to help Loulie tie a refractory sash. The younger girls' room was at the back, overlooking the garden. As soon as Sissy came in she spied Aunt Zeph below walking amongst the flowers. Aunt Zeph was wearing the apple-green taffeta dress she had worn the first night of the Triggs' arrival. She was alone, moving deliberately along the path, pausing now and then to smell a rose or to consider, with her head to one side, a moon moth that hovered over a spray of Canterbury bells. It was so quiet that they heard the crisp rustle of silk on the gravel.

'Doesn't she look pretty?' said Nancy. 'I'm going to wave to her.'

'Yes,' said Sissy. 'So'm I. (Stay still, Loulie, for mercy's sake, how do you think I can make a nice bow . . .?)'

All three girls were standing in the window when they were startled — as Aunt Zeph was herself — by the sudden appearance of Marie-

175

Claire, who came running down the stubbly slopes of the north meadow, her skirts clutched high in one rigid bronze hand.

It was disturbing in itself to see Marie-Claire run: her movements as a rule were slow and premeditated. Now, however, she was in such a hurry to get to her mistress that she could not wait to go round by the gate, but scrambled down somehow over the stones of the retaining wall, without heeding Aunt Zeph's gently reproving *'Que fais-tu là, ma bonne?'*

She cried out at once: *'Ce maudit Lem, madame! Je vous ai toujours dit qu'il nous trahirait un jour!'*

Then came a flood of angry phrases, poured forth so fast, in such pell-mell confusion, that even Sissy, the French scholar of the family, was unable to follow her meaning. There was something about *'Ces chemineaux-là se cachaient tous les trois derrière la laiterie,'* which might have referred to the labourers who had been living that week on the farm to help with the harvest; then much that Sissy could not fathom at all; but the end, very dramatic, with a fiery sweep of both arms, was *'Quand j'arrivais au sommet de la colline je les ai vus qui me suivaient pas à pas, sans en avoir honte. Oh, madame, ils savent tout, et nous sommes perdues — perdues!'*

The whole was shouted in a hoarse, guttural voice, quite unlike the measured monosyllables that were all the Triggs had ever heard her utter. Aunt Zeph listened, frowning slightly, without trying to interrupt. She did not, Sissy was glad to see, appear to be much upset; she looked thoughtful rather than frightened; and when the speech was finished she lifted a warning finger to her lips and then shook her head.

'Voyons, ma bonne!' — Aunt Zeph's clear, cool tones were unaltered — *'Tranquillisez-vous! Il n'y a pas de danger. Nous saurons arranger la chose.'*

She put her arm round Marie-Claire, who was now sobbing loudly and brokenly, and led her into the house.

Nancy and Loulie gaped in amazement.

'My patience! What was fretting *her?*'

'I don't know, exactly,' replied Sissy. 'Lem's done something she doesn't like — she's angry with him.'

'*Lem!* He wouldn't harm a fly!'

'I know that,' said Sissy, no less puzzled than her sisters. 'I couldn't quite understand . . . We'd better pretend we didn't hear anything, though; I dare say we weren't meant to hear. Now mind — not a word out of either of you!'

In the library Aunt Zeph met her guests as calmly as if nothing untoward had happened. She apologized for dinner's being late — Marie-Claire had had an accident with her baking — and while they were waiting questioned them kindly about the excursion. . . . 'Oh, we had a good time, thank you so much, ma'am!' said Sissy; and Nancy and Loulie echoed their sister. As soon as Aunt Zeph saw that they did not care to pursue the subject she tactfully broke off inquiries; but Papa, who had been sitting hunched up in his chair, as he did sometimes when one of his perverse moods struck him, leaned forward and said with an impish grin: 'Come, now, children, this will never do! You must have a deal else to tell us. Did Sister Betsy seem glad to see you? How was she looking? Had she the grey poplin on, or the blue merino? Was she wearing her Cashmere shawl? Who else was there? What did she give you for dinner — roast pork with stuffing or fried chicken in cream gravy? I must say, I never did fancy Maria's way with a fowl — she means well enough, but the girl has no head! . . . Was there a pudding or tart for dessert? *What?* Children, you don't mean to tell me you *don't remember?* Sakes alive, what are young people coming to? When I was your age I could have recited the bill-of-fare for a month past, forwards or backwards, without a mistake. Really, my dears . . .'

Nancy and Loulie screamed with laughter. Sissy, who did not want to, could not help giggling. Aunt Zeph, not having met the original of Papa's wickedly lifelike imitation, was able — though she bit her lip — to look properly blank; and at that moment Marie-Claire appeared in the doorway to announce '*Madame est servie.*'

At dinner Papa scarcely spoke; he seemed to have retreated once more into himself and surveyed the company, not inimically, but as if from an immense distance. Having observed that Sissy and Nancy and the boys were also inclined to silence, Aunt Zeph concentrated on the children and was soon well launched in a discussion of the comparative merits of White Wyandottes and Buff Orpingtons and why Aunt Betsy's biggest black pig had a curly nose. . . .

Marie-Claire, who by this time had succeeded in mastering her nerves, waited on table efficiently. She did walk somewhat faster than usual, which caused her stiff white linen uniform to crackle alarmingly; and her eyes remained sparkling with temper. Also, from time to time, she made small inarticulate sounds deep down in her throat, which somehow suggested a cat preparing to spit.

After dinner they sat in the larch grove, just as they always did. The weather was worse than ever: thunder rumbled in the distance, and where the sunset should have been there appeared only an angry plum-coloured glow, like a bruise on the sky. Crickets and locusts were grating in the trees; it was so gloomy that Aunt Zeph called for a lamp, as she had some mending she wanted to finish.

Papa sought the darkest corner of the grove, where he took no part in the conversation. The young people, too, were still unnaturally quiet. There was, Sissy felt, for the first time since coming to Naperville, a kind of disharmony in the atmosphere. Was her own mood to blame? Or was it, perhaps, the result of a combination of petty trials — the heavy heat, Papa's glumness, the dull day in Geneva, even Marie-Claire's queer outburst before dinner?

Whatever the reason, Aunt Zeph must be held guiltless: she kept her flag bravely flying. As if aware of the general discord, she began to tell stories to amuse her guests. No one told stories better than Aunt Zeph. Sissy loved particularly to hear of the long ago days at the Château Valombre in the Alps of Savoy (which by this time she had identified completely in her mind with the painted castle on the vase in her bedroom). But tonight their hostess's mind reverted to a past less remote; she talked instead about her experience with Ted's Uncle Jim in the mining country, and the dangers they had run on the long, painful journey back from the camp on the Feather River. Mr. Amberley was by that time worn by fever, as gaunt as a skeleton; so ill that he was hardly able to walk. Yet he had insisted on being strapped to his saddle and riding each day till his sufferings compelled him to halt.

'The nights,' said Aunt Zeph, 'were really the worst. I had no one to talk to, for my poor husband would toss in delirium, half awake, half asleep. I'd keep the fire blazing to scare off wild beasts; but that only served, I knew it too well, to make our whereabouts clearer to the Indians or the bands of bad men that roamed through the woods, seeking whom they might plunder. I never dared let myself doze off for more than a very few minutes — even then, I had my loaded pistol lying in my lap. Mr. Amberley had taught me to shoot when we first took to the wilderness — and it was lucky I learned, as things turned out. But what with my fears for him, and my fatigue from lack of sleep, I don't know what would have become of me if it had not been for *you*, Mr. Trigg! How ashamed I was afterwards to think I nearly shot you by mistake, that first night when you came stalking out of the shadows into the circle of firelight!'

'Small wonder if you'd done so, ma'am,' said Papa gruffly. 'And better, too, perhaps, for all concerned.'

'For you did look so much like a brigand,' continued Aunt Zeph, paying no heed to this interruption, 'with your black curly hair and a month's growth of beard on your chin. But ah, after I'd got to know you, I was thankful to God, many and many a time, that you were there! . . . Your father, my dears, was kinder to me, for less reward, than anybody has been in all of my life. He helped me carry my husband to an abandoned cabin he knew of, and stayed with us there until Mr. Amberley was strong enough to travel again. No woman could have been a tenderer nurse: night after night we'd sit up together by the fire, talking or playing bézique. And then each would take a turn sleeping, while the other kept awake to watch. What was best of all was that I was not a lone woman any more, and the cutthroats knew it. They did not come near us till the last night before we reached Sutter's Fort — do you remember, Mr. Trigg? . . . I was happy because our troubles were nearly over; only a few more hours separated us from civilization. I'd made some soup out of venison; Mr. Amberley drank it and said he felt better, and that encouraged me, too. . . . Mr. Trigg had gone into the forest to fetch wood. I was sitting alone by the campfire, thinking how lucky we were, after all, when two dreadful-looking rough men rode up, dismounted from their horses, and asked if they might share our meal. What could I say? I was sure it was more than food they were after.

'They saw my pistol and knew I knew how to use it (for I told them it was I shot the deer); but they were careful to keep on opposite sides of the fire from each other, so that I could not have covered them both. Most of our gold was hidden away in our saddlebags, but I had quite a bit of dust left over that I'd stuffed inside the quills of some condor feathers — that was a trick I'd learned from a Mexican I met in San Francisco, before we went mining. I'd tied the feathers together — huge long things they were — to make what looked like a great fan. They were lying on the ground partly hidden under a blanket. I saw one of the thieves edging towards them, and realized I was lost; for who could shoot two ways at once? I was all-a-tremble, not having the least idea what to do. The man was just stretching out his hand, and I was praying to the Lord for guidance, when Mr. Trigg stepped out of the forest, just as he'd done the first night I met him, and said: "Good evening, gentlemen!"

'I saw he had the man next me covered, so I pointed at the other one, who was after my feathers. . . . "This is yours, ma'am, I think," said Mr. Trigg, as cool as you please. . . . He stooped and picked up the fan — never losing his aim with his pistol — and handed it me. "Rather outsize for a lady, but everything's larger than life in California, I'm told."

'Well, that was all. The thieves slunk away and never came back, though I can assure you we did not even try to sleep the rest of that night! And the next day we got to Sutter's Fort. But I shall always know I owe my fortune, and perhaps my life as well, to Mr. Jonathan Trigg.'

There was a short pause filled by the crickets and locusts, and by the rumbles of thunder, still safely far away. Then Nancy cried: 'Oh, Papa, you never told us that story!'

'Jolly for you, Mr. Trigg!' exclaimed Wilfred, with enthusiasm, if less than his usual elegance. 'Why, you were a hero!'

'Hero fiddlesticks!' said Papa, who seemed unaccountably cross. 'I wish you had let those old stories rest, ma'am. Now I'll have no peace till my girls have heard everything I did in the West.'

'Well,' Aunt Zeph observed, with her sidelong smile, 'one has always the right, I think, to edit one's reminiscences.'

She held the stocking she was mending up to the light, and Sissy saw, with a shock, that it was one of her father's.

'Oh, Papa,' she said, full of remorse, 'you never told me your stockings needed mending!'

'I saw no reason to bother you,' said Papa. 'I should not have bothered Mrs. Amberley either, but she found it herself when the linen

180

was washed. I am used to darning my own stockings; I could do it as well as not.'

'I am sure you could,' said Aunt Zeph gently, as though humouring a spoilt child. 'But it gives me pleasure; I always mend Theodore's things, you know.'

'Yes, but that's different!' persisted Sissy, more and more remorseful. 'Papa is *our* father. It's our duty — mine and Nancy's — to see that his linen's in order. Oh, please, ma'am, give the stocking to me! And are there any more? Because, if so — '

'There are no more,' replied Aunt Zeph. 'And this one is quite finished — see?'

She held it up once more, and then folded it and put it away in her basket. Something in the quiet domesticity of her attitude worried Sissy: it seemed as if Aunt Zeph had usurped Mamma's place — as if, somehow, Aunt Zeph *were* Mamma! (This was terrible! Did not Papa feel it, too? Was that why he was cross?)

Aunt Zeph, apparently unconscious of the feeling she had aroused, glanced round the small circle in the lamplight and said: 'How still it is! I believe the thunder's coming closer. It must soon rain. Are we to have no music tonight, before it is time to go in? . . . Well, you are right: one does not always feel in the mood for singing, nor for games either, I judge. I think, however,' said Aunt Zeph, sweeping the circle again with her bright, suddenly mischievous eyes, 'that perhaps it is a night for spirits.'

'My faith, ma'am,' said Papa, 'but you're bent on corrupting the family!'

Aunt Zeph laughed and explained that she did not mean *that* kind of spirits. . . . Sissy had known it at once. She realized, with a guilty thrill, that Aunt Zeph was referring to the supernatural world. The 'Spiritual Rappers' had lately become such a fad that editorials were published against them in the papers; Doctor Travers had roundly denounced them from the pulpit, only a few Sundays ago. Everybody said it was wrong, yet many people patronized the Rappers in secret: Sissy had even heard Aunt Betsy tell Mamma that she had half a mind to consult Mr. Whiting, the celebrated trance speaker, who had achieved some remarkable results. Through him Mrs. Leslie had talked to her uncle, dead these thirty years; and the Huntingtons were said to have communed with a daughter they'd lost in her infancy, who had given them much useful information about the duties and delights of the world to come.

Aunt Zeph declared lightly that she herself was more than a little skeptical as to the worth of her experiments. To her they were merely a parlour pastime, hardly more serious than a game of cards. She and Marie-Claire sometimes 'tipped tables' to beguile the long winter evenings. They were most successful in cold dry weather, when there was a good deal of electricity in the air. But the moment just before a hard thunderstorm was also a very favourable time. At any rate, it could do no harm to try.

Nancy and Wilfred sprang up, eager to begin. Ted remarked that he did not believe in the Rappers, but he was willing to be convinced. Even Sissy felt that it could not be so wrong as she had feared. If the manifestations were caused simply by animal magnetism and electrical currents, as Aunt Zeph seemed to think, they were stripped of their sinister glamour. . . . Only Papa refused to take part in the game.

'My dears,' said Papa, in response to his daughters' urging, 'I'm much too old for such nonsense. Run along and raise all the ghosts you like: *I'm* going to finish my cigar.'

The party adjourned to the library, where the first business was to clear the table, a small inlaid mahogany one that Sissy recognized directly, for Aunt Zeph had served currant wine from it the afternoon they'd arrived. Five chairs were arranged in a circle about the table.

'Put out the lights,' commanded Aunt Zeph.

She was so calm and matter-of-fact that Sissy's scruples were almost, if not quite, laid to rest. Ted blew out the candles on each side of the mantel and then quenched the big oil-lamp that stood in the window.

'Now sit down everyone. Place both hands on the table, all fingers touching the surface, all hands touching one another.'

It was very dark in the library. Nothing showed but three dim grey squares where the windows were. The lightning, playing constantly now along the horizon, was still too distant to mitigate the gloom. It was very quiet, too, except for the locusts, the muffled drum-rolls of thunder, and Nancy's occasional giggles.

Aunt Zeph was impatient with gigglers.

182

'You must concentrate as hard as you can,' she said. 'It's only a game, but even a game must be played quite seriously.'

Sissy, between her sister and Ted, tried her best to do as she was told. She felt Ted's breath on her shoulder, rising and falling; unconsciously her own breathing fell into a similar rhythm; and once, when she shifted her position a trifle, Nancy's curls brushed her cheek.

Nothing happened for what seemed like a very long time — though Sissy told herself it could not have been more than five minutes. Then — it was extraordinary! — the table really did move a little. At first she thought she had fancied it — but no! One corner rose into the air, rather tentatively, and then dropped down at once with a click, as if awed by its own boldness.

Nancy started to giggle once more.

'Silence!' said Aunt Zeph sharply. 'No one must interrupt. Keep your hands all together — do as I say!'

The same corner rose again, and again fell back into place. Then the whole table rose, very slowly and evenly, as though pulled by magnets.

This time Nancy gave a great gasp, but controlled herself immediately. Sissy's heart was pounding so hard that she thought they must all hear it.

'There we are!' said Aunt Zeph. 'Hands still together — don't anyone let go — drop it gently — *gently*, I say! Now we're ready to ask it some questions. One rap for "yes" — two raps for "no" — and the alphabet spelled out all the way from one for A to twenty-six for Z. Do you understand? . . . Spirits of the table, have you a message for us? . . . One rap — *yes!* . . . Is it for one of us here in this room? . . . Yes! . . . Can you tell us which one? . . . Yes! . . . Is it for me? . . . No! . . . For Rhoda? . . . No! . . . For Nancy? . . . Yes! A message for Nancy. Are you ready to give it to her? . . . Yes! Let's proceed, then. Count the raps carefully, everyone! One-two-three-four-five . . .'

It took a long time to spell out the message, and when they had the whole of it Sissy did not think it was particularly interesting:

> *Sing again, with your dear voice revealing*
> *A tone*
> *Of some world far from ours,*

> *Where music and moonlight and feeling*
> *Are one.*

'I don't see what it means, exactly,' said Wilfred.

But Nancy was delighted with her message.

'It means I'm meant to be a prima donna, of course,' she said, 'just as I've always told you. You see, the spirits know what they're talking about! I wonder who wrote the poetry.'

'Shelley, surely,' said Aunt Zeph. 'Isn't it from the poem *To Jane?* I thought it most appropriate for the songbird who's given us so many hours of pleasure.'

It seemed odd that Aunt Zeph should know the quotation so well, and that none of the others should ever have heard of it. That is, it was odd unless . . . The table began tapping impatiently once again; and when pressed to explain itself announced it had another message to convey, this time to Wilfred.

Wilfred's message was also in verse:

> *Six hours in sleep, in law's grave study six,*
> *Four spend in prayer, the rest on Nature fix.*

'Why,' said Nancy, 'that's on the sampler Aunt Jane worked for Uncle Caleb when they were first married: he keeps it framed on the wall of his dressing-room. I wonder how the spirits knew about it!'

'I guess it's fairly well known,' said Ted. 'I remember I saw it in the book of *Familiar Quotations* I gave Aunt Zeph last Christmas.'

'Couldn't I take two or three of the hours for prayer,' asked Wilfred, 'and add them to sleep? And what does "Nature" mean?'

'Eating your meals, I suppose,' said Nancy; 'there's nothing more natural than that!'

'Oh, I don't think so,' said Sissy. 'I think it means looking at flowers and scenery and things.'

'Oh, I say!' Sissy could picture the grimace Beau Morgan was making. 'Not eight hours in a row!'

'Hush!' Aunt Zeph's voice, thin but peremptory, was wafted from the end of the table. 'The spirits have another message.'

This one proved to be for Sissy, who thanked her stars that no one could see her face. The lines from *Ingomar the Barbarian* were familiar to her for the best of reasons: last Saint Valentine's Day she had received them scrawled on a card with a bouquet of roses, whose sender she'd never been able to determine:

> *Two souls with but a single thought,*
> *Two hearts that beat as one. . . .*

'Dear me!' said Aunt Zeph. 'How sentimental! Still, to be sure, quite correct for a young lady engaged to be married.'

Sissy felt Ted's hands quiver next hers. His voice, too, was not perfectly steady as he said: 'I'll spare you the trouble of asking whom the next message is for. Spirits of the table, whoever you may be, what have you to say to me?'

Now the table began to act very strangely. It seemed uncertain what to do; slid this way and that; started to spell several messages that either remained incomplete or relapsed into gibberish.

'Come, come,' said Aunt Zeph at last, as if admonishing an unruly child, 'this won't do! What are you trying to tell us?'

The table, apparently irritated, flashed back at once: 'I-have-nothing-to-tell-you.'

'Come, come — do you mean there's no message for Theodore, after all?'

With laconic finality the table replied: 'Theodore-has-already-had-his-message.'

'Confound it! That's not fair!' cried Ted. 'There's no pleasing the plaguey thing! I haven't had any message. I wonder what under the sun it means? Do you think — '

Then he choked and subsided abruptly, as the probable meaning dawned upon him. Sissy felt his fingers quiver again. She was as much embarrassed as he: Thank God for the dark!

'Well,' said Aunt Zeph regretfully, 'we may as well light the lamp now. Once the spirits turn sulky it's useless to try to coax anything more out of them.'

Her tone was still gaily prosaic; it was impossible to tell whether or not she thought the whole thing a joke.

Sissy shivered a little; it had seemed too convincing for comfort to her. Of course, she did not *really* believe . . . That would be silly and wicked as well. Still there was something . . . Those lines from *Ingomar* had been in her mind, off and on, all day.

'Light a candle, my dear,' Aunt Zeph told Ted.

As Ted rose to obey her he pressed Sissy's hand long and hard; she was so entirely taken by surprise that she failed either to return the pressure or to repudiate it by drawing her hand away. Then Marie-Claire appeared in the doorway with her lamp and the nightly *tisane*.

'*Je vous dérange, madame?*'

'*Au contraire,*' replied Aunt Zeph. '*Entre donc, ma chère.*'

There was a warning puff of wind, followed by a patter of rain in the leaves; and Papa stood on the threshold next to Marie-Claire.

'The storm's about to break. Have you finished communing with spirits, young people?'

'Oh, Papa,' cried Nancy, 'it was perfectly splendid! Do you know what my message was?'

'Yes, we've finished,' said Aunt Zeph. 'No, we've not. *I* know what we will do! We'll try for a message for *you*, Mr. Trigg—then you'll *have* to believe in our sincerity!'

'That you won't, ma'am,' said Papa, preparing to depart.

Aunt Zeph, however, jumped up and laid her hand on his arm so persuasively, made such a point of his joining their game—'for it's just a game, I assure you; we don't take it seriously'—that in common politeness he could do nothing but allow her to lead him to the table. ('He won't forgive her for this, though,' thought Sissy. 'Papa never forgives being made do what he don't like.')

'And Marie-Claire will help us,' exclaimed Aunt Zeph, who was suddenly very merry. 'That should convince you, my friend, if anything can; for she knows not a word of English. But like most of her people she has great spiritual powers. *Tu nous aideras, n'est-ce pas?*'

'*Volontiers, madame.*'

Marie-Claire sat down next her mistress, across from Papa, who was on Aunt Zeph's right. The others took their places as before, and Ted doused the lamp the maid had brought in.

It was clear at once that Aunt Zeph had not overestimated Marie-Claire's abilities. The table began acting much more promptly than before. It rose into the air almost immediately, slid back and forth under their fingers like a restless live thing, so fast and far that those

186

in the circle were constantly forced to push back their chairs to make room for its unpredictable swoops.

'Keep the circle firm!' said Aunt Zeph. 'Don't break it, whatever you do!'

Sissy began to be frightened. It seemed serious now. Marie-Claire made the difference; for her, it was plain, the thing was no game. She was breathing heavily, and moaning a little from time to time. The almost continual flashes of lightning showed her in glimpses sitting rigid in her chair, chin lifted, eyes staring straight ahead.

After some minutes of these agitating preliminaries Aunt Zeph ventured to ask whether the spirits had a message for Mr. Trigg.

The table rapped out a decisive yes.

'Of course!' said Papa. 'That was only to have been expected. I dare say I can even tell you —'

'Hush, Papa, you'll spoil things!' warned Nancy.

'And what, O spirits, is the message?'

The table flew busily about and produced a mysterious 'All-will-be-well-if-you-follow-your-orders.'

'Naturally,' said Papa. 'But *whose* orders?'

'A-well-wisher's,' replied the table promptly.

'Naturally,' said Papa again. 'But who is the well-wisher?'

That the table was not prepared to say.

'Coy,' said Papa. 'The feminine touch, surely?'

'Ask indirectly,' said Aunt Zeph. 'Is it a man who sends this message, or a woman?'

The table hesitated; then began tapping a great many times, obviously headed all the way to W. There was a bright flash of lightning, revealing the group once more: Marie-Claire, tall and motionless in her white dress; Papa leaning forward, a scornful smile curling his lips; Aunt Zeph between them, smiling, too, with a kind of cheerful inscrutability. . . . Then came a heavy crash of thunder, apparently just over their heads. Papa thrust the table from him and sprang to his feet, exclaiming impatiently: 'No, really, it's too much — damned if I'll stand it!'

Without another word he stamped off and out the front door, slamming it after him. Ted jumped up, too, and lighted the candles. Marie-Claire rose deliberately all-of-a-piece and started methodically shutting the windows. . . . It was high time, for the wind blew the curtains straight out like flags. . . . Sissy hurried to help her. Nancy and Wilfred ran out on the steps, where they could observe the storm's approach from the shelter of the carriage porch.

Aunt Zeph was left sitting at the table. She gave her shoulders a shake, as if to bring herself back to real life; the queer little smile was still there.

'It's come at last, hasn't it? And I must run down to the cow-barn for a minute. I'm not content with May Lily's condition, and Lem's had too little experience to be trusted.'

'Oh, mayn't I go with you?' asked Sissy.

Ted said: 'Let me go instead of you, Aunt Zeph. You shouldn't venture out in such weather.'

Aunt Zeph shook her head. 'No, my dears; what could you do? I shall be quite all right. It's only a step, you know, and I've my mackintosh and a stout umbrella. Besides, I shan't be alone; Marie-Claire will come with me. *Viens, ma bonne!*'

Sissy and Ted were alone in the library, in the flickering light of the candles. They looked at each other at last; they could not help it. The wind was howling, rain beat furiously against the glass, the thunder and lightning were more terrifying than ever. It was not the storm, however, Sissy feared. As Ted's arms closed round her she felt breathless with delight, but her happiness was clouded by a sense of pure dismay. Why had the spirits spoken only half the truth? 'Two souls with but a single thought'—Oh, yes! What, though, in Heaven's name were they to do when that thought was *deadly sin?*

The Letter

THE FOLLOWING DAY Sissy overslept. There had been reason enough for her doing so: the storm had continued to rage half the night, and until its fury abated there was little use in trying to sleep.

While she was undressing a knock had come at her door, and she had opened it upon two small round frightened faces. . . . 'Oh, Sis, we're scared!' . . . Loulie and Joshua sought refuge, wrapped in a quilt, on her bed; Sissy forgot her own fears temporarily in doing what she could to alleviate theirs. Presently Nancy also sued for admittance. She was not at all nervous, she said, but joined the party 'just for company's sake.'

It must have been past one o'clock before the wind and the rain, tired of blowing back and forth over their heads, disappeared finally on their way towards the lake. Sissy tucked the children safely in bed. As she opened the window in Nancy's and Loulie's room she thought for a moment she saw a light in the north meadow — a bobbing lantern somewhere far up on top of the hill. . . . Then again, after she had blown out her candle and got into bed herself, it seemed to her she heard a carriage drive out of the farmyard and splash through the mud on the Naperville road. The sound of hoofbeats was hard to mistake. Yet who, at this time of night . . . ?

Sissy was too sleepy to care. She was too sleepy even to worry about what had happened that evening in the library. When she had come upstairs she had supposed she would lie awake for hours, a prey to hot shame and remorse. But her eyelids were weighed down and shut of themselves, almost as promptly as if she had taken a potion . . . and the first thing she knew it was morning. The sun was streaming in a brilliant flood over the counterpane — which it never did at dawn — and just as she opened her eyes the clock in the hall struck ten.

Dismayed, Sissy jumped up and struggled into her clothes. Her face in the glass looked as rosy and rested as though her conscience had been perfectly clear. (How was that?) She flew downstairs, not giving herself time to be anxious about whom she might meet. . . . Ted, of course, would by now be safely off in the fields.

No one was about but Marie-Claire, who gave her her breakfast in stony silence. How queer it seemed to be sitting alone at the oval table, where a gay group was always assembled! Sissy was too much out of spirits to make experiments in schoolgirl's French. (Was it her fancy that there was something accusing in those black beady eyes?) She choked down her coffee and toast and then went outdoors in search of company. *Anybody* would do: what she wanted above all was not to be alone. . . .

It was a very fine day. The air had been washed clear by the rain, and the heat was quite gone. But the landscape looked beaten down by its ordeal: the lawn was littered with leaves and twigs and some big branches that had blown down during the night, and the longer grass in the orchard was full of little green apples. The foliage was still glistening wet; strangely black, the tree trunks appeared wet through, too. Robins hopped about hunting for worms, but they did not chirp: summer was just at the turn; the happy early time of blossoming and songs seemed suddenly over.

As Sissy stood forlorn on the front steps Lem drove Priscilla in the pony-cart up to the door and Aunt Zeph came out of the house, wearing her best shawl and a green feathered bonnet and carrying a sunshade.

'Good morning, my dear,' said Aunt Zeph, who looked tired and white, but whose smile was as kindly as ever. 'I hope you had a good rest. I gave orders not to have you disturbed. What a fearful storm we had! I ought to go on a tour of inspection with Lem, to see how much damage was done; but instead I am off to Naperville. There's to be a meeting of the landowners of the county at the Preëmption House that I dare not miss. You know, our farm's half in Naperville and half in Wheaton, and as the town officials are always squabbling with one another, we're kept in constant hot water. Would you like to come with me? The meeting will be dull, but it can't last long, and I'm afraid otherwise you'll be alone: the children all drove in to the station quite early, to take Wilfred to his train. Even your father went with them. My farmhands gave notice last night, unexpectedly, and Mr. Trigg very kindly offered to help Theodore look for others. We both appreciate it so much; Theodore is quite inexperienced and your father's judgement will be most valuable to him.'

'Oh!' said Sissy, who never could get used — though it pleased her enormously — to Aunt Zeph's unorthodox opinion of Papa. 'I'm sure he's happy to do what he can. We all are, Mrs. Amberley. You do so much for *us*. I mean — '

Tartuffe, barking loud and long, came bounding up the hill.

'Dear me!' said Aunt Zeph. 'It must be a pedlar; he'd never make so much fuss about someone he knows.'

She craned forward, peering nearsightedly with her big, brilliant eyes. Sissy shaded her eyes with her hand and spied, perhaps halfway between the round pond and the house, the figure of a woman. The woman was in black, with a bonnet and veil. She was still some distance away. Nor was she always within sight as she slowly followed the drive that wound up amongst the apple trees. But there was no doubt for a moment in Sissy's mind who it was.

As she ran to meet her mother she told herself, rather unreasonably, she had known all along that it would end like this.

Aunt Zeph dismissed Lem and the pony-cart — naturally, she would not think now of driving to Naperville, 'But pray do not let it distress you, madam; I'm only too pleased, Rhoda can tell you, to find an excuse for not going!' — and ushered her guest into what she called the *salon*.

This was the pretty room with the old marble clock and the flowered Aubusson rug: Sissy felt at once that their coming there marked the occasion as especially formal. Mamma, smiling but firm, refused all offers of refreshment. . . . No, thank you, ma'am — neither coffee nor tea nor wine. . . . Well, perhaps, just a glass of cold water. The walk from the station had been longer than she had expected.

'Rhoda, my dear . . . ?' said Aunt Zeph.

When Sissy came back with the water she found the two ladies seated on opposite sides of the fireplace engaged in a kind of ceremonious contest, to see who could be most polite to the other. It was really quite dreadful how polite they were! Aunt Zeph, of course, was never anything else; her manner, however, had acquired an extra

191

silken finish as she divided her attention graciously between Mamma
and a piece of embroidery she had been working at, Sissy knew, for
months. (Aunt Zeph, one felt, had no more natural taste for sewing
than for farming — she was successful at both through innate force of
character.)

But Mamma, too, was almost intolerably suave — and that in direct
contradiction to her customary plain-spoken ways. Glancing about her
with a slightly glazed eye, she remarked what a charming house they
were in. Aunt Zeph said it was too good of Mrs. Trigg to admire it.
Mamma then thanked Mrs. Amberley earnestly for giving her family
such a happy week in the country — she could tell, she asserted, from
Sissy's face how much good it must have done them; indeed, Brother
Caleb had reported last night that they were *all* looking splendidly.
Aunt Zeph civilly protested that the pleasure had been *hers;* she could
not overestimate the delight it had been to her to have the dear young
people in the house. And now that Mrs. Trigg had arrived to complete
the party, she could honestly claim her contentment to be unalloyed.
. . . 'Ah, but you should have let us know your plans in advance! It
is terrible that there was no one to meet you at the station — and
there might so easily have been. Mr. Trigg and my nephew drove
into Wheaton early this morning . . .'

Mamma protested, in her turn, that she had really wanted to walk.
And she had come on the spur of the moment; there would not have
been time to send word, even if she had wished to. That morning she
had waked with a strong feeling she needed a holiday. The air after
the storm was so clear and fresh; and it had been a very long time
since she had allowed herself a respite from housekeeping cares. So,
on an impulse, she had simply ordered a cab after breakfast, boarded
the first westbound train at the station — and here she was! Would
her hostess pardon her — that was all that was troubling Mamma — for
taking them entirely by surprise?

Ah, cried Aunt Zeph, but there was no question of pardons — it
was the most agreeable surprise in the world! . . . 'Madam, you must
believe me when I say we have wished for you a hundred times. Is
it not so, Rhoda? I call you to witness: have we not sighed, over and
over again . . . ? Since you are here at last, my dear friend, let me
dare hope you have come prepared to stay. We shall not be satisfied

with a short visit. Surely you will give us the rest of the week, especially as your husband and children have promised to do so? I am sorry only to see you've no luggage — but how stupid of me! Of course you could not have carried a bag from the station. Rhoda, my dear, find Lem, will you, please? and bid him not unharness Priscilla, after all; we shall drive into Wheaton presently to fetch your mamma's things.'

Mamma, still smiling, shook her head. Mrs. Amberley was too hospitable, too kind altogether. Unfortunately, she had no luggage at Wheaton or anywhere else; could not, much as she would like to, stop even one night; was in fact, though she disliked having to say so, here on a disagreeable errand. . . . 'I have come, ma'am, to take my family home.'

Aunt Zeph flung up her hands. Impossible! . . . But Mamma was as firm about that as she had been in declining refreshments. She regretted the necessity; she was more grateful to Mrs. Amberley than she could express in words; but there it was! The pleasantest times could not last forever. As a matter of fact, however, for Sissy another good time was about to begin. The Charles Bascombs were leaving to spend a month at the Profile House in the White Mountains, and they had asked their eldest niece to go with them. It would be the best thing for Sissy; she'd come back in September, rested and refreshed, for the wedding. Uncle Charles had taken their tickets for Friday, so there was no time to waste: they'd need the whole of this week to get ready.

Aunt Zeph understood. Naturally Rhoda must not lose such a wonderful opportunity. The White Mountains — how delightfully cool they sounded! But since Nancy and Loulie were not included in the invitation, might they not remain at the farm? . . . 'If you all go at once,' said Aunt Zeph, 'I shall feel as sadly bereft as Niobe herself.'

Mamma shook her head again. As she'd said before, the best of times must end. At the close of the week the children would still not be satisfied, but would beg for another week, and yet another. Thanks to the Amberleys, they had had their breath of fresh air — Mamma hoped that they were properly grateful for it and had not made too much trouble for everybody. Now, alas! it was *time to go*.

Sissy, seated with downcast eyes on her stool in front of the hearth, was painfully conscious, as the ladies went on lightly crossing their rapiers, of two overwhelming truths. One was, that Mamma *knew everything*. *How* she knew, was beyond Sissy's power to conjecture. What Uncle Caleb had been able to report — though no doubt he had made as much as he could of the story — would have been at most a mosaic of guesswork, glued together by strong natural Bascomb suspicions. But Sissy was as sure of the fact as if she had seen an accusation in writing — and that although Mamma had scarcely glanced at her daughter; had not even bothered to notice (perhaps the omission was significant) that she was doing her hair a new way. (The Aunts had oh'd and ah'd over that, yesterday, for a good half hour.) Armed with her knowledge, Mamma was coping with the situation brightly, efficiently, with as little fuss as possible. There had been no scene, and there would not be one, if she could help it.

The second truth was that Mamma was unique, irreplaceable. Aunt Zeph was not Mamma. The supposition was absurd. How could Sissy, even momentarily, have seen her so? Mamma was, as always, the centre of the universe, no less sure of her power because she made no effort to assert it. From the moment of her arrival she had resumed her old dominion. There she sat, pink-cheeked and blue-eyed, her soft hair, scarcely flecked with grey, more golden than ever under the severe black bonnet. There she sat, smiling and chatting decorously on a dozen indifferent subjects. And, without lifting a finger to bring it about, she suddenly produced a counter-revolution. All that had been topsy-turvy for Sissy righted itself once more. All that had seemed agitated became calm. Aunt Zeph, charming and appealing as she was, moved a little farther off, appeared strangely wraith-like and unconvincing. In the whole world only Mamma was real.

The feeling persisted at lunch, when the family met for the first time. (Mamma had not wanted to stay for a meal, but the next train to the city did not leave till late in the afternoon.) The party was, naturally enough, a melancholy one. Aunt Zeph seemed depressed at losing her young guests. Nancy and Loulie lamented their forced departure, though the former's cries sounded, to Sissy's ears, more noisy than earnest. (Would not Wilfred be awaiting her in Chicago?) Mamma, it appeared, in her preoccupation with larger issues, had forgotten about Wilfred; she was probably sorry now she had insisted on

194

the return of her younger daughters — but what was done was done: her code did not permit a change of decision, if it involved acknowledging a mistake.

Papa, to Sissy's astonishment, agreed with Mamma that the children had better go. He seemed, fortunately, to have got over his fit of temper; alone of the company he was in his usual spirits and had greeted his wife very pleasantly. . . . 'What a delightful surprise, my dear Julia!' . . . Nothing was said for some time about *his* plans. Mamma, of course, would rather have died than ask what they were. She simply bowed her head courteously when he announced that he meant to remain in Naperville for the present; and when he elaborated his excuses by stating he thought he was needed on the farm, she did not contradict him. She knew, she said, how hard it was to get labourers. Betsy was always complaining . . . Yes, Papa added, and still it was easier by a good deal for Sister Walworth, who could employ ten men steadily all the year round. Mrs. Amberley's farm was too small to warrant keeping more than a skeleton staff in winter; Lem was enough for her then. But now, with the grain standing ripe for harvest, it was irritating beyond words to be left without anyone. Papa and Ted had scoured the Wheaton neighbourhood all morning in vain; they were on the track of two fellows they had heard of in Warrenville and hoped to drive there this evening to see what could be done. Meanwhile, however, Papa did not feel like deserting his friends. It was not as though he were of any use in Chicago. He had no place there as yet, no work to return to. . . .

'That,' said Mamma, with a flash of temper, 'depends on you, Mr. Trigg.'

'It depends, Mrs. Trigg,' replied Papa imperturbably, 'on a good many things, some of which are not under our control — or are they?'

'We can't discuss that now,' said Mamma, compressing her lips and glancing askance at Aunt Zeph, who murmured uneasily that Mr. Trigg had done more than his share already. It appeared — did it not? — that it was her destiny to be rescued by him: having saved her life once in California, he had again arrived in the nick of time . . . 'But indeed,' said Aunt Zeph, 'what I should like above everything, as you know, is for *all* to stay!'

195

Mamma repeated bleakly that Mrs. Amberley was very kind, but they really must go — and they were back where they had started.

Sissy listened attentively to this not particularly agreeable discussion, concentrating in turn on each of the principals. She had to do this, for otherwise she could not have avoided a pair of eyes insistently seeking hers. All morning she had longed for Ted, and yet dreaded to see him. How were they to be friends again, with a guilty secret to share? Could she ever forgive him for kissing her? Could she forgive herself for returning his kiss? What was she to do, when the mere remembrance of it still had the power to make her blood race through her veins and her heart beat almost to the point of suffocation? (For she saw now what a kiss really meant: Aaron's prudent pecks on her cheek were not kisses at all!)

If Mamma had not come, Sissy did not know what she would have done. But she *had* come; the thought of her comforting presence sustained her daughter through the last difficult hours at the farm — that, and perhaps the fact that everything happened so quickly there was no time to think.

As soon as lunch was over the girls were sent upstairs to pack. Sissy declined Marie-Claire's unexpectedly amiable offers of help. She hurried through the painful process with her habitual neatness and despatch, so as to be able to lend a hand to Nancy, who, left to her own devices, would have rolled her best dresses into balls and crushed them haphazard into her trunk. Loulie, too, was in need of assistance; her labours were immensely complicated by the necessity of making room for a number of small keepsakes Mamma would have cast away as rubbish. There were dried flowers and grasses, a pine-cone or two, some birds' eggs and butterfly wings; worst of all, a lethargic but obstinate mud-turtle. Sissy had to persuade the child not to pack Pokey (as he was called) with her bonnets or in her purse, but to stow him instead in a square cardboard box with breathing holes punched in the lid. (Doubtless this particular treasure would soon be confiscated anyhow.)

All this took so long that when it was done it was time to go to the train.

Sissy plucked a rose from the vase with the doves and pinned it to her bodice. Then she ran downstairs to bid good-bye to Marie-Claire

in the kitchen and to Lem, holding the horses at the door. Papa —
who was not going with them, but would be off shortly to Warrenville instead — was waiting to fold her in his arms. As they kissed
each other Sissy could not help being struck by something very odd
in his expression: he was smiling, of course, as he always did at her,
but — could it be that she had somehow disappointed Papa? . . .

'I don't know what to say,' said Sissy, suddenly on the point of
tears, to Aunt Zeph. 'Dear Mrs. Amberley, it's all been so . . . I can't
thank you as I ought . . . '

'Then don't even try,' advised Aunt Zeph.

She leaned forward to press her lips gravely on each round bloom-
ing cheek. *'Au revoir, ma chère Sissy!'* (It was the first time she had
called her so.) 'I shall see you again before the great day. Good-bye,
Nancy; good-bye, Loulie!'

'Oh, good-bye!'

They were off down the hill, their last glimpse of Aunt Zeph the
white flutter of a handkerchief through the apple trees.

It was over.

Sissy kept saying it to herself all the way to Wheaton. She dared
not look at Ted, who, silent and grim, held the reins by her side. She
paid no heed to Nancy's chatter or to Loulie's unsubtle attempts to
keep Pokey out of sight under the seat. She was hardly conscious
even of her mother, who sat very straight in the middle of the back
bench of the surrey and made bright, detached remarks about the
scenery — purely from a sense of duty: Mamma detested scenery!

At Wheaton they discovered there was still some time to wait.
Ted took the ladies across the street to the hotel, but just outside the
door Mamma remembered she had something to say to the station-
master. . . . 'No, Ted, that's all right; I'll do it myself. Come, Nancy!'

As she marched off there shone, Sissy fancied, a gleam of com-
plicity in her mother's eye: she had meant all along, then, for the
lovers to have their last minutes together. . . .

The hotel was small and unpretentious. Spindly pillars supported
the sagging porch, on which stood a row of rocking-chairs. Only one
of the chairs was occupied, by a young farmer's wife who had a baby
on her lap. The baby wailed fretfully, in spite of her efforts to soothe

it. Ted impatiently led the way inside, where a drowsy clerk at the desk indicated the door to the parlour.

The parlour was small, also, and rather musty. It was furnished with a round, ugly black table and a set of chairs to match, upholstered in worn dark green plush. The walls were covered with brown paper of an indeterminate pattern, badly mildewed in spots; one huge heavily framed oil painting, the Falls of Niagara, dominated the scene. Although the afternoon was warm, all the windows were shut; a bluebottle fly buzzed up to the top of one of the panes, only to fall down and begin his maddening journey again and again.

'Oh,' said Sissy, dismayed, as she entered, 'how stuffy it is!'

Without answering, Ted flung open the windows one after another: the bluebottle fly escaped, but the baby's wails were heard more plainly than before. . . . Sissy seated herself on one of the green plush chairs. She wanted very much to say something, but she could not think what. Her mind felt dull and empty. Yet she would have to find words now, if ever: this might well be the last time in their lives she and Ted Amberley would be alone.

'Sit down, Ted,' was all she could manage at first; and Ted would not help her by sitting down. He went on striding the length of the parlour and back, then suddenly halted in front of her and burst out with the phrase she'd been repeating to herself — only he turned it into a question:

'So it's over, isn't it?' cried Ted savagely, in a hopeless attempt to conceal his soreness of heart.

Sissy said feebly — more to gain time than anything else —: 'I don't know what you mean.'

'You know right well what I mean! If it wasn't over, you'd not let your mother drag you back to Chicago.'

'Nobody's "dragging" me anywhere,' protested Sissy, trying to be dignified and telling herself that, whatever happened, she must not lose her temper.

'Oh, yes, they are!' said Ted. 'If they aren't, there's just one way you can prove it: tell your mother how things stand between us. Tell her the whole business from beginning to end! Or give *me* leave to do it instead. How would that do? I'll say you're engaged to Miles, but you realize now you can't possibly marry him.'

'But, Ted, I never said — you know I didn't —'

'What difference does it make what you said or didn't say? What do words mean anyhow? It all came clear to me last night. We love each other and we're going to belong to each other — a dozen mothers and a hundred Aaron Mileses can't stop us! Do you hear me? We'll be married before I go West. We're engaged to be married this minute. Either you speak to your mother, or I will! I've got you now, and I'm not going to lose you.'

'Oh,' said Sissy, 'take your hands off my shoulders — they hurt — and please, Ted, don't make so much noise! Someone'll hear you.'

'Hear me? Lord, I only wish they would! What the dickens is the use in trying to hide things?'

'I don't try to hide things.'

'Yes, you do — you know you do. On my soul, I swear I believe you'd be willing to go home and act as though nothing had happened. Caring for me, and knowing that I care for you, you'd go right ahead and marry a man you don't care for, just because you're afraid to speak up for our rights.'

'But, Ted,' said Sissy, 'what *are* our rights? I guess we haven't any. Oh, I'm so miserable! so terribly ashamed, when I think . . . It's my fault. At least, it's more my fault than yours. I should never have let things go so far. I'm engaged to Aaron — I've got to marry Aaron — and you'll forget me . . .'

'Nonsense! Can you look me in the eyes, Rhoda Trigg, and tell me you're in love with Aaron Miles? . . . No! You see you can't say it because you don't feel it. You don't love him at all. You never did. Now wouldn't I be a fool to let you go?'

'Ted, it's wrong — I've given my word — I can't go back on —'

'Bother your word! I've told you, words don't mean a thing. It's feeling that counts — the sort of feeling that's been between us since the first, though you've done your best to deny it. Listen! You speak to your mother — and right away, too! There's been too much time lost already. Why, do you know — oh, *damn* that baby!'

He slammed down the windows as hard as he could, as the child out on the porch, frightened by the sounds of dispute, raised its voice from a wail to a scream.

199

Sissy was frightened, also. She felt helpless to calm the scene she had provoked without meaning to. The fine, firm arguments she had hoped to produce in defence of her duty died away on her lips. With pale face and blazing eyes Ted stormed up and down the shabby little room, saying many times more what he had said already.

That was the worst of scenes. In a book or a play their dialogue would have had a beginning, a middle, an end. It would have come to a climax, which, trying though it might have been, Sissy felt she could have borne if she were sure that was *all* there was to it. In life it wasn't so simple: people wouldn't stop tormenting themselves. They said the same things again and again. Ted kept crying that he loved her and she loved him and they were going to get married in spite of all. He told her, fifty times over, either he'd speak to her mother or *she* must do so. And Sissy had nothing to offer except her foolish bleating refrain: 'I can't — you mustn't — it just isn't possible . . . '

At the end of ten minutes of constant talking nothing had been settled. Ted had boasted and blustered, but he had not produced a single concrete suggestion as to how his beloved was to make a promise to him without breaking her promise to Aaron. Sissy had pleaded and temporized, but she had not given him a definite answer; she wasn't in the least sure whether she'd said she would marry him or not. . . . Finally, out of sheer frustration, she began crying; and then Ted stopped his nervous pacing to and fro, lifted her chin to give her a kiss, and said: 'Darling, forgive me! I didn't mean to distress you. It's just that I love you so much I can't bear to lose you!'

Sissy cried even harder at that, and held his hand to her cheek — and the whole torturing cycle started over again.

It might have gone on for hours if Nancy had not rushed in to say that the train was coming and they had better hurry, for Mamma was getting worried.

On the platform Sissy gave Ted her hand. He pressed it hard and said: 'Don't forget what I've told you.' Sissy replied, 'I won't,' without thinking what she meant by it. Then the train came puffing into the station. The Triggs climbed aboard. Ted heaved up their boxes and bundles and stood out on the bare boards in the blinding sun, waving his hat while the engine pulled out. Sissy leaned through the window and waved, too, as long as he was in sight. When the train turned a corner she drew in her head and set her bonnet to rights, hoping that Mamma might not notice that she had been crying.

Mamma was sitting quietly in her seat, clutching her pocketbook and the tickets as she always did on a journey, as if she rather expected someone to try to take them away from her. Her head held high, she gazed straight ahead, smiling a little; but Sissy was not deceived by her smile. In her state of overwrought nerves she understood now what otherwise she would never have seen: Mamma was wretched because she had failed in her mission. And she had failed, in spite of apparent success, because deep in her heart — Sissy saw it only too clearly — Mamma had hoped all along that Papa would come home with them, too.

At the house Sissy found a letter from Aaron awaiting her. Even before she opened the envelope she felt it would be different from his other letters. Not that it was longer — Aaron was always too busy to write at length — but it was the first one she ever had had from him that contained a personal note. He had just returned from an exploring trip through the Gogebic Mountains, full of admiration for the wild, wonderful country he had seen.

. . . *It's so clean and new and untouched — miles upon miles of virgin forest, and here and there lakes as blue as the sky. And to think that, with all this beauty, the land is productive, too, or can be made so! No man can say what treasures of copper and iron, perhaps even gold, lie hidden in these hills. Personally, I believe your uncle is on the track of something bigger than even he knows, something that may well mean a fortune to him and his, a thousand times greater than the grain or the shipping business. I am more grateful than I can say to be allowed to play a part in it. And some day I want to bring you up here, to show you the things I've found.*

But now, dear girl, my thoughts are in the South with you. I trust you will forgive me for not having written more often. Believe me, it's not been wilful neglect. I think of you constantly, Sissy, with tender hope and affection. I look forward with all my heart to the re-

201

turn voyage next month, and to our union, which is to join our lives forever. May God bless and keep you till then, and make him worthy to be your true and loving husband who signs himself, with devotion,
                                        Your Aaron.

The Family

SISSY DECIDED, long afterwards, that everything might have been different if only Aaron had been able to come home and they had been married directly. He had still a good month's work to do at the mines, the same month Sissy was to spend in New Hampshire as the Charles Bascombs' guest. Of course, they could write to each other. They did correspond often after Sissy's return from Naperville, and their communications took on a perceptibly warmer tone. But Aaron never sent her another love letter: Sissy supposed she ought not to expect it; it was extraordinary enough that he should have been inspired even once to try to put his feelings on paper.

Meanwhile, however, she was left in the unenviable position of not being sure whom she was in love with and whether or not she were engaged to two men at the same time. She felt exceedingly guilty, and perfectly helpless to remedy matters. There was no one to whom she could turn for advice: whatever course of action she feebly considered seemed so dangerous that she ended by drifting along during the whole of the crucial week doing nothing at all.

In her state of nervous preoccupation she could not force herself to take more than a mechanical interest in the discussions concerning the wedding arrangements, which now got under way at full speed in the family circle. There were, it appeared, innumerable points at issue. First the date: Monday was too early, Saturday too late in the week; Friday was unlucky; most people's 'girls' were out on Thursday. It took Mamma and Aunt Bertha and the Uncles an hour of spirited debate before they finally fixed upon Wednesday the twenty-fourth of September as the one day predestined for their purpose.

Then the *time* of day: the Uncles preferred a morning ceremony at high noon, with breakfast to follow. Aunt Bertha had heard that afternoon weddings were beginning to be stylish in the East. Mamma herself had been married at night; the refreshments could then be much simpler. Aunt Betsy wrote from Geneva to present her views and Aunt Jane's; the latter was worried principally for fear an indigestible hot supper might be served. . . . Well, perhaps they could decide that later.

Uncle Charles was anxious to offer his sister the use of his house for whatever form of entertainment they chose. Mamma said she appreciated his generosity more than she could say, but *that* she could not agree to. Unpretentious though it was, she felt she wanted to welcome her friends in her own little home. Did not Sissy agree? . . . It seemed, continued Mamma, that they were already accepting a great deal in letting Aunt Bertha pay for the bridesmaids' dresses. . . . Aunt Bertha had set her heart on having both bridesmaids and ushers, as they did in the East. Provincial Chicago had never even heard of such a thing — but it was high time it began! Nancy and Minnie Miles were the logical choices for bridesmaids; the material for their dresses had been ordered from New York — blue silk with yellow trimmings for Minnie, corn-yellow with blue trimmings for Nancy; and if there were enough silk left over, Loulie had been promised the office of flower-girl, and a frock to fit her office.

Aunt Bertha would have liked to provide the wedding-gown also, but there again Mamma was firm: she favoured patronizing local tradesmen as much as possible and Potter Palmer was showing goods as handsome as you could hope to find anywhere. Mr. Palmer himself waited upon Mrs. and Miss Trigg when they went in to make their purchase; he snipped the yards of lovely shining stuff from the bolt, wrapped them with particular care, and handed the package across the counter with a beaming smile and his 'respectful compliments to the bride.'

Sissy somehow could not make herself believe she was really going to wear it.

On the last night before leaving, while she and her mother were packing her trunk, she made a belated attempt to confide her troubles. The attempt was blankly a failure: at the first hint of confession Mamma had drawn herself up and stated, very definitely, that she did not care to discuss what had or had not happened in Naperville. 'It's all past and done with. I blame myself, child, far more than I do you. I should have foreseen the danger, but I trusted foolishly in your father's judgement — or, if not in his, at least in Mrs. Amberley's. I'm afraid it is only too true, the French have no standards of conduct.'

And when Sissy protested that it had been no one's fault but her own — 'though indeed, Mamma, I didn't mean to do wrong! That's what worries me now — I want to do right by them *both!* There's Aaron, and Ted — what shall I say to Ted?' — Mamma folded her lips austerely and replied that it would not be necessary to say anything. 'Ted Amberley has no more to do with you than you've to do with him. You've given your word to Aaron Miles — *your word,* Sissy — that's as binding in God's sight as if you were married already. Where is your moral sense? Maybe I ought to ask Doctor Travers to speak to you. . . . Now don't let's say anything more about this most distressing subject, which certainly should never have come up between us. Will you take your green cashmere as well as the brown alpaca? Or do you think that makes too many warm dresses for the mountains in August?'

So Sissy had to go on suffering in secret. She cried a good deal at night in her room; ate so poorly that she lost several pounds, which was not unbecoming; and altogether fretted herself into a state of nerves that would have irritated her uncle and aunt very much, if they had not been just then peculiarly disposed to indulgence. No doubt the dear child was pining for Aaron. That was natural, in the circumstances, wasn't it?

Uncle Charles glanced fondly at Aunt Bertha and said he remembered only too well how dismal he'd felt in their own courting days, when his darling had quitted the Springs to go back to Albany. Aunt Bertha laughed and blushed and tossed her head, and vowed that *she,* on the contrary, had not missed him a particle. There'd been young men a-plenty at home to console her. 'Indeed, my good parents found it hard to believe I wasn't disposed to take Cordy van Tassel or Livingston Ransome — I'm sure they were quite as devoted and ten times as rich!' But she patted her husband's hand as she said it; and then Uncle Charles ordered a bottle of port for dinner: port was so strengthening, a glass with each meal would be sure to improve their dear Sissy's health.

Like many prosperous persons, Uncle Charles was at his best away from home. Even in Chicago he was less inclined to be pompous and boastful in other people's houses; and somehow the farther he got from the scene of his frenzied daily activities, the simpler he seemed — such boasting as he still did was for his city instead of himself. Uncle Charles had always been the most benevolent Bascomb. Outside of making money his one idea in life was to make everyone round him as 'cheerful' as possible. When they travelled, cheer for his entourage appeared to consist in engaging the best suite of rooms in the hotel and a private carriage and pair; ordering a great many good things to eat and drink; and arranging an endless series of parties for their acquaintances. He could not bear to be alone: he would rather have three guests for dinner than none, thirty than three, and (Sissy sometimes privately thought) three hundred than thirty. This he admitted frankly. Aunt Bertha, although she was not so frank, was almost equally sociable.

The trouble with the Profile House was that it was too quiet. Saratoga or Richfield would have suited them better. Aunt Bertha's doctor, however, had strongly advised mountain air for his patient's nerves; they had tried New Hampshire two years before with excellent results; and the Profile House, which had then been struggling through a hazardous first season, was beginning now to be thought fairly fashionable.

It was still slightly eccentric to prefer hills to springs or the seaside, but when they arrived the big, flimsy, wooden hotel in the woods was gratifyingly crowded, Aunt Bertha was pleased to note, entirely with Eastern people. For a day or two Uncle Charles was contented. But after a week of the monotonous *table d'hôte,* with long drives by day to various scenic points of view and the gayest diversion at night a tea-party in their scantily furnished sitting-room, it developed — not altogether to the surprise of either his wife or his niece — that 'business interests' in Concord demanded his instant attention. Bidding the ladies an affectionate farewell, and pressing into Aunt Bertha's palm a sum of money twice as large as she needed, he whirled away and was not seen again for a fortnight.

During the whole of their stay — which was lengthened, no one knew why, to six weeks — Uncle Charles appeared and disappeared spasmodically. One of his trips, later in the month, took him as far afield as Hebron: he reported on his return to Aunt Bertha that she would not have known the place. The hotel was dirty and badly run,

206

the *clientèle* undistinguished — 'Poor Pa! I'm glad he's not alive to see it.' It seemed, nevertheless, to afford Uncle Charles a certain melancholy satisfaction to brood on the ruin; one could not help feeling he would have been thoroughly annoyed to have to admit that anyone but a Bascomb could make a success of Chancellor Hall.

In the meantime Aunt Bertha had settled down, in spite of her bitter complaints at her abandonment, to a prosy, easy routine of naps and drives and meals, enlivened by the society of those guests whom she felt to be deserving of notice. The Boston element she rather condescended to as dowdy and dull. Two or three New York families, on the other hand, she made much of, leaning heavily, in her conversations with them, on her stylish connections in their city. (Wilfred's mother, Cousin Clara Morgan of Rhinebeck and Gramercy Park, came in handily here.) To Sissy Aunt Bertha lamented privately, after meeting Mrs. van der Grifft and Mrs. Cuyler, that she had not brought a real lady's maid. To be sure, apple-cheeked Delia, who dusted the parlours at home, was better than nobody. The New York matrons, however, had starched English Bartons and Partons; one breathlessly aristocratic family from Baltimore, of authentic Cavalier ancestry, were accompanied by a tripping little French soubrette in a flounced apron and an amazing cap with streamers.

On the whole, Sissy felt, her aunt's most durable consolations were supplied by some old acquaintances from Albany, a Mrs. Clark (*née* Douw) and the Misses Margaret and Angela Clark, long-nosed, pale-eyed ladies of a marked Dutch type. With them she could hash over endlessly local scandals both ancient and modern. They were also the recipients of numerous confidences concerning her 'exile' in Illinois.... 'A life sentence, that's what I call it!' Aunt Bertha declared, with a heart-breakingly gallant smile. 'My dears, you can't possibly picture how primitive conditions are in the West. We're quite deprived of all the amenities, indeed of some of the actual necessities of a civilized existence. The houses are most of them little better than hovels, and the streets are so muddy that one don't dare venture off the place without rubber boots — children are drowned in the slime every day!'

Although she did not actually mention them, Aunt Bertha managed to imply that Indians and buffaloes roamed the city freely and every man carried a pistol in his belt, prepared to shoot his rivals at the drop of a hat. Mrs. Clark and the Misses Clark, enormously impressed, clicked their tongues and turned up their light grey, almond-shaped eyes. . . . Sissy, recalling the comfortable mansion on Michigan Avenue and the busy, buoyant procession of the Charles Bascombs' days, bent her head over her embroidery and kept discreetly silent.

But in spite of her sharp tongue and her snobbery there was much good in Aunt Bertha. She seldom said a kind thing, but she never did an unkind one. As generous with her small inherited fortune as Uncle Charles was with the dollars he'd made, she was constantly making presents to Sissy — a flower-trimmed bonnet, French gloves and perfumes, a handsome guipure lace mantle she'd worn once or twice and found unflattering to her figure. She was much obliged to her niece for her company. Uncle Charles was obliged, too: he showered her with trinkets on returning from each of his journeys, and was as debonair and as solicitous of her comfort as only Uncle Charles could be.

But, ungrateful as she felt herself, Sissy was not happy. Although her problems had receded temporarily with her departure from Chicago, they crept back unerringly one by one, since she was unable to find anything to replace them. It was dull for her, too, at the Profile House. The days were all exactly the same; they seemed, with nothing to sharpen their outlines, like one oppressive, interminable day. She ate with Aunt Bertha and drove in the carriage with her, and went for walks in the forest while Aunt Bertha napped. . . . There were not many people of her age at the hotel, and her situation as an engaged young lady caused her to be eyed with respect by young men, and with envy by other young ladies, but to be avoided by both sexes. She was seldom asked to make up a set for croquet or to join the merry group round the fire in the hall after supper.

This was natural; Sissy had not expected it to be otherwise. But her enforced isolation gave her far too much time to brood. She recalled with aching regret the summer holiday, two years ago, when the family had been assembled in full force and she and Nancy and Loulie had romped the whole time, all carefree children together. How happy she had been then, without realizing it! How old she felt now, weighed down by her inner conviction of sin!

In her painful state of suspended animation the daily post was the sole dependable solace. Aaron's letters continued to arrive with moderate regularity; they were not especially nourishing, but it was reassuring to know that he *wanted* to write. . . . From Naperville Sissy heard nothing. There was no reason, of course, why she should hear from Aunt Zeph, but Papa's silence was wounding; and Ted's could mean only one thing. For several weeks Sissy looked daily for a letter from Ted. She longed for it and dreaded it, just as she'd longed and dreaded to see him, the morning after the storm. As time went by and it did not come she began to understand it never would: that was Ted's way of showing her the next move was hers. And she was unable to move!

Mamma wrote often and voluminously, confining herself to practical matters. It developed that she and Mr. Miles had found the ideal house for the young couple on Wabash Avenue, south of Jackson. Of course, it was very remote, really almost in the country — it was, in particular, inconveniently far from church —; but the neighbourhood was improving fast. More and more people seemed to be building out that way to escape the growing congestion in town. Mamma was sure Sissy and Aaron would be delighted with the house itself; it had three storeys and a basement of Athens marble, with one of the fashionable 'French' roofs. Best of all, it was so large that there would be room in it for the whole family. Mamma had long been dissatisfied with her old home. Her lease would be up in October, and on Uncle Caleb's advice she did not intend to renew it. The new house had a fine big bedroom on the second floor front for the bride and groom, and another at the back for Mamma. The girls would have ample space on the top floor with Susan. There was even a kind of closet that with a minimum of reconstruction might be made into a tolerable spare room for Aunt Betsy.

Naturally, Mamma meant to pay her share of the rent and the housekeeping expenses, so that she and her daughters would not be a burden. Was that not an admirable arrangement? Uncle Caleb highly approved; so did Mr. and Mrs. Miles, who were themselves looking for a residence in the same locality. The air was so good and there was so much room. It might even pay to keep a cow! . . . And now there was no need for Sissy to fear being separated from her family. They could continue together as always, with the simple addition to the circle of a beloved son. . . . Thus wrote Mamma, in her cramped, scratchy hand, dashed off, as Sissy well knew, at furious speed in the evening at Grandpa Bascomb's walnut desk with the worn leather top. Not a word was said of Papa's place in the 'admirable arrangement.' For all Sissy would have known, she might not have had a father.

It was Nancy who reported what little there was to tell about Jonathan Trigg. Nancy, with excellent intentions, was not a good correspondent; Sissy owed this particular letter, indirectly, to Wilfred Morgan, who, having taken 'rooms' in Pine Street, had bought a smart little phaeton and a dappled grey pony, and had then asked his young cousin to drive: they had stayed out too late and as a result Nancy was kept in for a week. In solitary confinement she took up her pen to complain of her lot — was it not a horrid shame? And just now, of all times, when Papa was back from Naperville. . . . He had arrived at the Lake House only the day before and come unannounced to call. Mamma had received him kindly; they seemed to be getting on splendidly together. Papa even talked that night of building a house of his own, out by the lake in the North Division, and of going into business for himself in Chicago (what kind of business had not been specified).

Three days later, Nancy wrote again to say the project was spoilt. Uncle Caleb had spoilt it. He had pressed Papa too hard — had insisted on trying to get him to promise to sell out his holdings in California and return to Bascomb and Company. Papa, not unnaturally, had resisted the pressure and wavered evasively, to Uncle Caleb's annoyance. And the very night after their argument a new complication had arisen: into the parlour where Mamma was entertaining the ladies of the Missionary Society at tea, Papa had burst without ceremony, holding in his arms a grubby two-year-old boy. The boy was Susan's nephew: Susan, unknown to them all, had a sister married to a teamster and living in a tumbledown cottage somewhere in Hardscrabble. The sister was ill of a fever; the teamster was an habitual drunkard; Papa had surprised the maid crying over her dishes and had at once rushed impulsively to the rescue. 'Here you are, ma'am!' he had shouted on his entrance to Mamma and her guests. 'If you're looking for objects of charity, why not begin at home?'

Mamma had been horrified, and so had the ladies of the Missionary Society. They had explained, as soon as they'd heard who little Tim was, that they could do nothing for him. As the child was a Catholic, he should have been taken to the Sisters of Mercy. Papa, however, refused to be sensible. He carried the boy to the Lake House and arranged for him to stay there with Susan until it was certain that Mrs. O'Flaherty was out of danger. Susan was speechless with gratitude — but Mamma and Uncle Caleb had both been furious. They had actually called at the hotel to expostulate, only to find Papa in his private sitting-room with the child . . . Papa, it was later reported, on his hands and knees with a paper cap on his head. Moreover, they had not been alone: the objectionable Jake Ralston was there, and his young lady friend with the sparkling earrings; also Mr. and Mrs. MacFarland from the theatre. The table was spread with sandwiches and cakes and littered with glasses. . . . Mamma believed they were drinking wine, though she had been too shocked to stay and make sure. . . . 'You see, my dear, *I'm* having a party, too!' Papa had cried. 'Won't you join us?' . . . But Mamma and Uncle Caleb had stamped off in a rage. And the next day Papa had gone back to Naperville, as suddenly and mysteriously as he'd come. Nothing, wrote Nancy, had been heard from him since.

Coming home in the train, the first week in September, Sissy could not help being reminded of her last homecoming a little over two months ago. Some things were the same: the rattling wooden railway carriage, with its lumpy plush benches; the basket lunches (Uncle Charles had provided the best the New York caterers could give them); the tiresome overnight stops at Pittsburgh and Toledo (which would soon no longer be necessary: they were talking of building cars with beds in them, so that one might continue one's travels while safely asleep — would not *that* be wonderful?). . . . Sissy was wearing the same grey travelling-dress and the little hat with plumes in which the graduate of the Utica Female Academy had returned to the bosom of her family.

But, in other ways, how much was changed forever, herself most of all!

The train was late; it was almost supper-time before it pulled wearily into the Lake Street Station. Sissy, following her aunt and her uncle and Delia out on the platform, felt unsure of herself and oddly deflated. Would Aaron be there to meet her? He had, she knew, come back from Michigan, but there had not been time since his return for them to communicate with each other. The station was crowded; there was a bustle of porters and passengers and simple sightseers, for the arrival of the Michigan Central from the East was still a novelty to Chicagoans. For a moment it seemed there was no one. Then she caught sight of a tall figure hurrying towards her — of a dark head held high, a welcoming smile — and Sissy ran straight into Aaron's arms.

She had never done, or thought of doing, such a thing before. She did not know what force impelled her; but that it was *right,* she felt immediately. It bridged the difficulties of meeting again after so long a separation; it was both an apology for the past and a promise for the future.

At the little white house Mamma and the girls were waiting to greet her. *They* had not changed, thank goodness! — or if there were some small differences to be noted, they had nothing to do with their attitude towards Sissy. Mamma seemed a trifle pale, Nancy was perhaps rather quieter than usual; but that was probably due to the heat; August, it seemed, had been terrible. . . .

Sissy was ushered into her own small room, the one prepared for her in June. No doubt now but that the bride, with less than three weeks to go before the wedding day, would need an apartment for herself, however tiny. The blue opaline jar on the dressing-table was filled with roses — how touching that was! Nancy announced she had bought them at the florist's in Cleaverville; Wilfred had driven her out that afternoon.

At mention of Wilfred's name Mamma looked severe. But it was no time for arguments. Sissy unpinned her bonnet before the glass and straightened her curls, while Mamma sat in the one armchair, Loulie crouched on a stool at her feet, and Nancy danced in and out between the hall and the bedroom. There was so much to say! Susan rang the supper-bell long before they had finished their questions and answers.

Aaron, of course, was staying to supper. Afterwards, as it was a Friday, he went with the Triggs to prayer meeting. Across the supper-table, and on their way to church, Sissy glanced shyly at her bridegroom, trying to make up her mind what had happened to him in Michigan. He was deeply tanned by the northern sun — but that was not it. Did he talk more readily than of old? He seemed willing, if

212

not eager, to tell his experiences; but Aaron would never be precisely a fluent conversationalist. Nor, though he might well be fonder of her than ever, could he say so, except with his eyes. It was not even that he had grown surer of himself: Aaron had always been sure. The difference was subtler; his manner was at once more modest and more mature. The priggish boy had turned into a man!

This conviction struck Sissy so forcibly that she was unable to forget it or to think consecutively about anything else. Her mind wandered wickedly while Doctor Travers was speaking, though she pulled herself up short several times; even Uncle Caleb's eloquence, never more imposing, could not hold her attention tonight. She was conscious only of a vague feeling of contentment at being back again amongst her own: the big, brown, dimly lighted church, smelling faintly of lamp-oil, was as familiar as her home; and so were the faces surrounding her. When they got up to sing—

> *'And are we, wretches, yet alive?*
> *And do we yet rebel?*
> *'Tis boundless, 'tis amazing love*
> *That bears us up from hell!'*

Aaron opened the hymnal and held it out for her to share with such a heart-warming smile that Sissy returned it before she realized what she was doing: try as she would, she could not feel oppressed by a sense of original sin. . . .

The next day being Saturday, a half-holiday at Bascomb and Company, Mamma had asked all four Mileses to dinner. Later, the two families combined on an excursion to show Sissy the marvels of the new house on Wabash Avenue.

Sissy was duly impressed. The building stood in a grove of elms, splendidly free, as it was one of only three in the block. It was rather narrow, all its lines forbiddingly perpendicular; but the flight of front steps was pronounced very 'dignified' and the iron curlicues on the high peaked roof had a breath-taking elegance. (Even Aunt Bertha, it was felt, would not be able to find fault with the roof.)

Led by Mamma and Mrs. Miles, Sissy walked upstairs and down; admired the fine woodwork, the gay flowered wallpapers, in the front and back parlours; gave her opinion, modestly but confidently, as to the best arrangement of their old furniture and what new furniture would be required. (The stove they had would do very well for the present — the piano could just be fitted between the front windows — and, yes, perhaps the oil painting of Chancellor Hall might look better in the long hall than the dining-room!) . . . All the while the top layer of her mind was dealing capably with these practical matters there stirred underneath a faint but increasing feeling of astonishment. Sissy had known for months that some day she would be Aaron Miles's wife. But until today, when she saw with her own eyes the chamber they were to occupy together, she had never really believed it.

As soon as the tour was over Mr. and Mrs. Miles and the Triggs went home, for it was a very warm day. But Aaron proposed to Sissy that they should walk a little farther, and Minnie, heedless of her mother's warning frowns and winks, insisted upon coming with them.

Shaded Wabash Avenue had been pleasant enough, but out in the open country, amongst the cow-pastures of Twelfth Street, the sun was glaringly hot. It had been autumn in New Hampshire, but in Chicago September was summer still, a fly-blown, airless month. The pastures looked brown and dry, the road was uncomfortably sandy — and Minnie *would* talk.

Sissy sometimes wondered whether she were as fond as she ought to be of her future sister-in-law. For Mr. and Mrs. Miles she cherished a deeply affectionate regard: even the fact of their being southern — and exceedingly southern indeed, in spite of twenty years in the Middle West — had erected no barrier between them. But poor, fidgety, self-conscious Minnie — who, having been born like her brother in Chicago, seemed as northern as anyone else — she had to tell herself firmly she cared for.

Minnie was especially talkative today. She babbled on tirelessly about the bridesmaids' dresses, and plans for the wedding trip, and various relatives who hoped to be able to come to town — Just imagine! Mr. Bascomb had promised to send them all passes to make the journey by railway: wasn't that generous? — till Sissy felt she could bear no more. Aaron was quiet and looked glummer and glummer; he, too, found Minnie hard to bear. At length, to distract him, Sissy broke in with questions about the new house: was not the neighbourhood extremely pleasant? With so few other buildings near-by,

214

they could count on sun the whole day through, couldn't they? And the kitchen and storerooms — well, of course, Sissy didn't expect a man to appreciate such conveniences . . .

'But I do, Sissy,' said Aaron suddenly, fixing his dark serious eyes full upon her. 'I do indeed. I am sure we ought to be very comfortable — we *shall* be, of course; there's no doubt of that. It's only that — well, I should have liked to have had more to say in the matter, shouldn't you? I should have liked to have chosen our home for ourselves, just you and I together, and nobody else. Oh, I know it wasn't possible, since both of us were away at the same time. I know how grateful we must be to your mother and my parents — that this is the very best arrangement for everybody. But sometimes I can't help wondering how it would have been . . . I mean, I hope we shan't have to stay there so terribly long, because I really feel a much smaller house would suit me better.'

Sissy was so greatly taken by surprise that it was several moments before she said: 'You mean, you'd rather not live with the family at all?'

'Yes,' replied Aaron; 'that's what I mean.'

Minnie tittered shrilly.

'My goodness me, Sissy'll think you don't like her folks!'

'Sissy will think nothing of the kind,' said Aaron, with his old firmness but a new dignity. 'She knows very well I'm almost as fond of her family as I am of my own. But you don't have to live with people in order to love them. No! As soon as ever I've got enough money together I'm going to buy a house for the two of us — see if I don't!'

On the way home they stopped to call on Uncle Charles and Aunt Bertha, who were discovered taking their ease on the high front porch under the white Doric pillars. Immobilized, as it were, by the heat, they sat enthroned, one on each side of the door, placidly surveying their Paradise Regained, the broad avenue, the flat blue lagoon with its little boats, and, in the distance, the heaving and glittering lake. Inside the spiky iron fence the grass was as green as if there had been no drought. The geraniums and begonias in the round flower beds looked as spruce as if Abel the gardener had just set them out, and even the leaves of the trees on the velvet lawn seemed to know better

215

than to wither like their less fortunate neighbours on the public domain.

Uncle Charles lolled in his chair, his checked waistcoat partly unbuttoned for comfort; Aunt Bertha sat erect and expressionless, in mulberry silk and a new lace cap overladen with ribbons. They both sprang to their feet when they saw the young people; it had been long enough since dinner for any company, even Minnie's, to be welcome. Uncle Charles was anxious, also, to display the wonderful new gaslights that had been installed during their absence. . . . 'My dears,' said Aunt Bertha, shrugging her shoulders, 'he plays with the jets as though they were toys! He's been turning them on and off all day — it's *his* fault that the house is as hot as a furnace!'

But she accompanied the party inside and watched with a satisfied smile while her husband flooded the great hall and the various parlours with the flaring, hissing flames. Sissy and the Mileses expressed their admiration; then Aunt Bertha suggested a return to the porch for some cold refreshments. Uncle Charles laid his hand on his niece's shoulder. . . . 'Child, I'd like a word with you.'

Sissy followed him into the Yellow Room and took the chair he motioned her to. Uncle Charles sat down in front of his big roll-top desk, with its rows of pigeonholes stuffed with mysterious papers; he leaned back and thrust his thumbs into his empty waistcoat buttonholes; then fiddled, one after the other, with his watch-chain, some glass paper-weights, and a long malachite letter-opener. The light filtering through the fringed damask curtains, which were drawn to keep out the glare, was the colour of butter. From the garden Joshua could be plainly heard shouting as he romped with his Shetland pony.

As her uncle, for once, seemed to hesitate to begin, Sissy ventured to say that she had not known her cousin had come home.

'Yes; oh, yes!' said Uncle Charles, as though thinking of something else. 'Young Amberley brought him back this morning; and I must say the boy's looking fine and seems immensely improved in every way. His summer on the farm's done him nothing but good. I'm disappointed in Amberley, though.'

'You are, sir? Why?'

'Why, he's not a man one can trust, I'm afraid. I'd engaged him last spring positively, you know, to tutor Joshua this winter. Now he tells

216

me, quite without warning, he can't take the job. His aunt needs him, he says; and anyhow, 'twouldn't be worth his while to come back, for he intends to go West after Christmas. All damned nonsense, of course — and most annoying for me, after I'd made my plans and was counting on him. He's a slippery, vacillating fellow, like his uncle before him.'

Sissy remarked, greatly daring, that, on the contrary, Ted's singleness of purpose seemed to her his salient trait — to which Uncle Charles testily retorted: 'Obstinacy, my dear; that's all it is; call the thing by its right name! What a different sort of chap your Aaron is! Now, I'm *delighted* with Aaron. Always knew there was good stuff in him; he's been an honest, intelligent worker from the start. What he needed was waking up! The trip to Michigan seems to have done the trick. He's alive now as he never was before. It's often so with a young man. Love does it for some — I suppose you women will claim it's the only incentive, and to some extent I agree with you — but a man must find the right work, too, and the right country to work in. . . . Aaron, you might say, is made for the iron business, and he knows it. You're a lucky girl, Sissy. Why, there's no limit to the possibilities up North! Aaron grasps 'em as clearly as someone twice his age; he's the very fellow I need to help realize . . . There's no limit, I guess, to *his* possibilities either. A fine young man, my dear, in every way, and, if I'm not mistaken, he'll give you a fine life.'

Sissy murmured conventionally that her uncle was very kind. . . . 'Not at all, not at all!' Uncle Charles interrupted. 'Anybody'd say what I've said. In fact, the whole family's agreed there's been a great change for the better in Aaron. Maybe I can sympathize with the boy a little more keenly because the same thing happened to me in my youth. The moment I struck Chicago I saw it was the town for me. Raw and undeveloped as it was, there was a life in the air, a feeling of opportunity waiting round the corner, I'd never found in the East. I'd not have believed it if I'd hadn't come and seen for myself. Why, when Brother Trigg first wrote and said . . . That reminds me, my dear' — Uncle Charles bestowed upon Sissy a designedly guileless look, which made it quite clear that only now was he reaching the object in view — 'have you heard anything since coming home from your — er — father?'

'Why, no, sir,' replied Sissy. 'But I've hardly had time to; we arrived only yesterday.'

'Well, that's true, of course; I'd forgotten that. But it's occurred to me . . . I had a talk with your mother this morning and found she had no idea of his plans. It seems — I don't know if you knew — that he did come into town for a day or two about a fortnight ago; gave Julia to understand he might go into business here on his own — though what business *he* could possibly . . . Well, that's neither here nor there. It's a great pity I wasn't here to handle the matter. Your Uncle Caleb tried to do his best. I've the highest respect for your Uncle Caleb's integrity, but he lacks what I call the diplomatic touch — you know what I mean — he don't know how to make things easy all round the way some of us . . . Well, anyhow, the upshot was that your father went back to Naperville to that . . . hm! hm! And nothing's been seen or heard of him since. Now, as I say, I was talking to your mother this morning . . . A remarkable woman your mother, my dear.'

'You don't need to tell *me* so,' said Sissy, smiling, to fill up the pause.

Uncle Charles took out an immense monogrammed white silk handkerchief and wiped his bald forehead, which was glistening with drops; he seemed, for the first time Sissy could remember, cruelly embarrassed. Finally he continued, though haltingly: 'She never complains or speaks of her troubles. Wild horses wouldn't drag it out of her, no matter how much she's had to go through at the hands of . . . But I know what she's suffering because she's so close to me. I could always read Julia like a book. I can tell as well as if she'd put it in words that she's worried half sick for fear your papa won't come to your wedding.'

'Oh,' cried Sissy, 'but he *must* come! What makes you think he won't?'

'Ah, my dear,' said Uncle Charles, solemnly shaking his head, 'it's not at all certain. There are depths of iniquity in the human heart . . . What I mean to say is, it would distress us all beyond measure if the worst were to happen. What would Doctor Travers think? What would our friends say? After all, the Bascombs stand for something in this community — and the Triggs, too, of course — It's *essential*, from our point of view, that the head of your family be here. Now, your

218

mother's not willing to write to him. Her pride forbids it, and I don't know as I blame her. Nor is she willing to delegate the authority to your Uncle Caleb or me, though we've both told her we stand ready to try whatever lies in our power. We can't go against her wishes. But *you* could write, Sissy — or, better still, you could go out to Naperville, see how things stand, and try to persuade your papa to his duty. I can't believe he's so far lost he'll refuse to hearken to an appeal to his higher nature. Tell him we make no demands, no conditions whatever. All we ask is his presence at the wedding and for about a week before the wedding, to attend such small gatherings as may take place at that time. God prosper your mission, my child; for if it should fail, I truly fear your poor mother's heart will break at last.'

September Afternoon

AFTER ALL, Sissy's trip to Naperville was easily arranged. She had not been many days in Chicago before she received a note from her father, welcoming her home: he had meant (said Papa) to write long ago, but, what with one thing or another . . . Now, however, with the wedding less than three weeks away, it could be postponed no longer. Mrs. Amberley, also, had asked him to write. She had hoped to be able to be at the wedding, but unfortunately her plans were uncertain; she wondered, therefore, if Sissy might spare the time to come out once more to the farm? If so, she had but to name the day and Papa would be at the station to meet her. (Nothing was said about Ted — was this perhaps Papa's way of telling his daughter she need have no fears on that score?)

Sissy was sure, after her talk with Uncle Charles, that it was her duty to go. Strangely enough, she rather looked forward to going; her one regret was the necessity of deceiving her mother. Never before had she told her a lie — yet in this case was it not inevitable? . . . Inwardly quaking, Sissy announced at the supper-table, a week after her return, that her schoolmate Eva Wilson, who lived in Cottage Hill, had asked her out to spend the day tomorrow (if tomorrow were fine). She had a friend named Eva, and the Wilsons did live in Cottage Hill; that much of her story was true; and luckily Mamma was far too busy these days to entertain her customary suspicions.

Tomorrow *was* fine. . . . When Sissy got out at Wheaton Papa was standing on the platform, as he had promised. He was wearing his red shirt and the black fitted breeches, and looked unusually well. No one else was in sight, and Papa said, almost as soon as he'd kissed his daughter, that Ted had had to drive that morning to the cattle fair in

Aurora; he might be gone two whole days; he had been very sorry to miss Sissy's visit; he'd sent her his love and would see her at the wedding, if not before.

All this Papa reported quietly, in a perfectly natural voice. Sissy said 'Oh!' because she did not know what else to say. Then Papa helped her into the pony-cart, chirruped to Toby (Ted had taken Priscilla), and they drove off on the familiar road to Naperville.

It was a beautiful day, at once mild and brilliant, such as the Middle West often provides in September as compensation for the long, hot summer lived through. There had not yet been a frost, so that it was autumn by courtesy: the sun shone brightly, the grass grew emerald green; even the few trees that had turned appeared to have done so from force of habit. In fact, if it had not been for the haze on the horizon and the wild aster and goldenrod along the roadside, Sissy might have fancied the calendar had not moved since her earlier visit.

Toby was lively this morning and took a good deal of managing, so for the first few minutes she and Papa could not talk very much. But they did not need to talk. They smiled at each other: how good it seemed to be together again! Sissy felt a strong surge of warmth and well-being, which she could not explain except as the result of their mutual affection. On looking at Papa more closely, however, she reversed her original verdict: he did *not* look well. Brown as a gypsy he always had been, but he was thinner than when they had parted in July, and there were numbers of little tired lines she did not recall having seen before, etched in the skin round his eyes.

Sissy was so happy that she very nearly forgot why she had come to Naperville; it was a shock when Papa said, without preamble: 'You know, my dear, that I am going back with you.'

She could not help starting — so, almost before it had begun, her mission was a success!

'I didn't know,' she said simply. 'Of course I'm very glad — we'll all be glad — we've missed you.'

'I'd have gone long ago,' Papa continued, 'but truly we have been very busy out here. The summer was so hot that the corn crop was bigger than we expected — it's only two days since we got the last of it stacked. I didn't feel I could leave, in fairness to the Amberleys, till that job was done. Then, too, my dear, I was waiting until you were

221

back. I did go to Chicago once while you were gone — perhaps you heard?'

Sissy nodded; and Papa shook his head ruefully.

'My dear,' he said, 'it was a dreadful mistake! I should have known better than to risk it without you. Between your Uncle Caleb's bellowings and that awful Missionary tea . . .'

'Little Tim,' said Sissy demurely, 'is getting on very well. Susan bade me be sure and tell you . . .'

'Bother little Tim!' exclaimed Papa. 'No, but seriously, child . . . I shall soon have to come to a decision. For months I've been putting it off. I just didn't know . . . I've had a queer feeling the choice wasn't mine to make — that somehow things would shape themselves in spite of me. But that's nonsense, really. It's up to me. If only . . . Well, we'll talk of this later.'

Papa sighed as he turned Toby's head between the brown wooden pineapple gateposts.

Sissy's heart began to beat faster. Although she had lived on the Amberley farm only a week, so much had happened to her there that she often felt that week bulked larger in her memory than all the rest of her life. How strange it was to see the corn cut and stacked that had tossed its streamers in the summer air, two short months ago! Some crows strutted impudently in the stubble, searching the ground for stray kernels of grain. On the pond in the hollow the ducks were still quacking and preening their feathers; as they climbed the hill through the orchard Sissy could see the reddening fruit and smell the warm, winy smell of apples fallen in the grass.

Tartuffe came bounding down the drive to meet them with a volley of barks — *that*, at least, was as it had been — and when Papa pulled Toby to a stop the front door flew open and a thin, small woman appeared on the threshold. Today Aunt Zeph was not wearing gingham and a sunbonnet; she was arrayed for the occasion in a white dress of some cool soft material sprinkled thickly with black polkadots, a dress exquisitely simple and rather handsome, too; for it was very much ruffled and the sleeves were quite short. In her hair she had thrust a single dark red carnation: although Aunt Zeph had flowers always about her, Sissy had never seen her wear one before.

This time she did not throw up her hands when she saw the car-

222

riage; instead she smiled her sad, slanting smile — which contrasted
so oddly with the bright hazel eyes that never looked sad — and said
gently: 'Our Sissy has come home.'

Sissy kissed her hostess on both cheeks and exclaimed, with enthusiasm, how good it was of Aunt Zeph to have invited her, and how
glad she was to be back, and how she felt now she had never been
away. But it was not true — she knew it even as she said it — : she
had been away for centuries and nothing was the same. The farm was
not home any more: had it ever really seemed so?

Aunt Zeph was surely not to blame. She was as kind as she could
be, as she had been from the first. Putting her arm round Sissy, she
drew her into the house, through the row of little drawing-rooms into
the library. Sissy noticed that a fire was burning in the grate and
that an immense bouquet of white and lavender asters stood in a jar
on the table they'd tipped.

At lunch the queer feeling of estrangement persisted. Marie-Claire
met her with a casual *'Bonjour, mademoiselle,'* as though they'd seen
each other only yesterday. But the oval board looked small for three;
Ted's empty place mocked them; and in spite of Aunt Zeph's affability the conversation seemed to be manufactured, instead of making
itself as formerly. They talked of farm business — Aunt Zeph was still
having trouble with labourers — and of Ted's absence, which she deplored. What a pity it was he had had to leave them, today of all
days! Aunt Zeph would have asked her guest to change the date, if
she had not realized that, for the latter, little time was now left.

Sissy was urged to tell her news, too. Aunt Zeph vowed she was
interested in everything, from Aaron's gift to his bride — a handsome
set of seed-pearls (necklace and earrings, pin and bracelet) from Tiffany's in New York — to the wedding-dress itself, which had been
made by Miss Tweedy, the seamstress, at Mrs. Carpenter's Fashionable
Dressmaking Establishment in Lake Street. (The bridesmaids' dresses
were being run up at home, to save money, by Mamma and Aunt
Jane.) The wedding journey would take them to Clinton, Iowa, and
then back again — because that was as far as the railroad went. Aunt
Zeph agreed pleasantly that, although short, the trip ought to be well
worth while.

Papa spoke little; only towards the end of the meal, when Sissy was

223

describing the new house on Wabash Avenue, did he rouse himself to declare the plan a mistake.

'Young married people ought not to live with their families,' said Papa, very flatly. 'Much less should their families want to live with *them*. It's absurd! It's uncivilized! Don't permit it, Sissy. Don't let your mother persuade you . . .'

It was in vain that Sissy pointed out the advantages — that the little white house was too small for them now — she would have hours every day by herself if she were deprived of Mamma's company — they all got on well together and would doubtless be perfectly happy. . . . Papa went on repeating, more and more angrily: 'It's a mistake, Sissy — don't do it, don't do it!' And when, unguardedly, she admitted that Aaron was of her father's opinion, there was a positive explosion: 'Of course he is, child! He's not the sensible, intelligent fellow I take him for if he's content to be tied to your mother's apronstrings. My dear, be warned in time. This can come to no good issue. It's absolutely ridiculous for the Bascombs to have their way. They're relentless! They're insatiable! They'll ruin your life if you don't watch out!'

Sissy, out of patience at last, cried: 'Well, after all, Papa, what else is there for Mamma to do? If you think so poorly of her solution, you might at least offer one of your own!' — And Aunt Zeph, who had remained aloof from the discussion, rose rather hurriedly with a murmur of 'If no one will have any more pudding . . .'

They had coffee outside under the larches — it was too cool now, Aunt Zeph said, to sit there in the evening — and then Sissy asked permission to go upstairs and see her old room. It was not until she was halfway down the hall that she remembered, with embarrassment, it was really Ted's room — he must have moved back directly she'd left — what would Mrs. Amberley think of her? . . . On the threshold she paused, hardly daring to enter.

Her sense of its owner's presence was more poignant than if he had actually been there, though it was hard to say why: Ted was an orderly person; his few belongings were most of them stowed out of sight. His comb and brushes lay on the dressing-table; an old corduroy jacket Sissy had often seen him wear hung over the back of a chair. And there was a scent of tobacco smoke, so slight that only a woman would have noticed it. Otherwise the room was just as she had left it . . .

yet stay: there *was* something missing, after all. Where was the vase with the doves and the oak leaves, and the little painted castle on its sharp-pointed hill? Had it been broken by accident? If not, Sissy could not imagine why it had been taken away. Mourning its loss rather foolishly — for she could not reasonably have supposed she was ever to see it again — she drifted across to the window and sat down for a minute in the chair where she had often sat before, to enjoy the view of the larch grove.

Papa and Aunt Zeph were still under the trees — Papa on the grass (he *never* sat in a chair if he could help it), hunched up in a characteristic pose with his hands clasped round his knees. His eyes were narrowed and concentrated on nothing that Sissy could see; but though she might not share his vision, she no longer made The Family's mistake of assuming it did not exist. Aunt Zeph lay back at her ease, her head slightly to one side (how vastly the red carnation in her hair became her!), her chin supported on one hand. She was looking at Papa. This was natural; they were talking to each other; and it was one of the lady's chief charms that she always gave her interlocutor her entire attention.

It was impossible to hear what they were saying: that, too, was as usual, for Aunt Zeph never raised her voice unnecessarily. Sissy had seen them thus a dozen times during her week at the farm; how many times more, in the weeks that had followed, must the tableau have been repeated! What was different now? What made her feel she was spying upon them — and yet unable to look away? . . .

Suddenly Sissy recoiled from the window, jumped to her feet, rushed from the room, downstairs, and out the door — not the front door leading to the lawn, but the back one, to gain which she had to push past the astonished Marie-Claire, washing dishes at the sink. Through the kitchen garden she stumbled — vaguely conscious of the proud giant dahlias, blazing scarlet and yellow and rose — and then up the hill, running blindly, saved from falling only because the grass was so short that her feet avoided the holes almost of themselves. As she ran she said to herself: 'Mrs. Amberley loves *Papa* — she *loves* him!'

For that was the discovery she had made from the window in Ted's room. *How* she had made it, she could not have told. Was it because she was seeing the pair for the first time after long absence? — or because they were sitting together for the *last* time (and knew it only too well!)? Whatever the means of their unmasking, there could be no doubt of the terrible fact. The picture admired as anonymous had been given a title — and what a title!

In the light of her disillusionment Sissy saw many things clearly that had been obscure: Aunt Betsy's hateful innuendos, Uncle Charles's troubled looks and halting confusion, Mamma's reticences and evasions — most of all, her air of defeat that day in the train going back to Chicago, when she had been worsted in undeclared battle with the woman who threatened her home. Oh, it was awful! incredible! How could it be? Husbands and wives ought to love each other, no matter what happened. Anything else was too dreadful to contemplate, too unnatural, like something in the novels Aunt Betsy kept on her bedside-table.

Sissy realized she had been sure all along, in spite of everything, that some day Mamma and Papa were going to come together again. She felt she hated Aunt Zeph, the intruder who had broken into their circle. That the circle had been broken already, long before her appearance, seemed beside the point. That perhaps Papa had never been hers, and in any case was leaving her now, mattered even less. All her sweetness and strength were without value, since she chose to put them to such base uses. She was a thief! a thief! . . .

For what seemed a long time Sissy wandered disconsolately about the north meadow, unable to focus her thoughts or to arrive at a plan of action. She felt she could not go back to the house. In her blank misery she was hardly aware of the beauty around her: the sun's declining rays more golden than ever, the distant haze all an opalescent blue, the woods on the hill splashed with brilliant colour — smoky-red and purple for the ashes, russet for the hickories, green for the oaks still unturned.

She sat for a while under one of the ash trees, her back propped against the trunk, while a squirrel scolded high above in the branches and the leaves fluttered down in a painted shower with each puff of breeze that blew. . . . What moved her at last was the certainty that, if she did not go down, they would come up to look for her. Straightening her bonnet as best she could, she smoothed her curls and

226

congratulated herself that there were no traces of tears to hide: she'd been really too angry to cry!

In her descent, skirting the wood, where walking was easier, it happened that she passed behind the old barn instead of in front, as in her walks and rides with Ted. The abandoned building had always both interested and repelled her. Now she noticed, with surprise, that it had a back door facing the wood as well as a front door facing the field. The back door, unlike the front, was neither locked nor barred. Yielding to a sudden impulse, she pushed it ajar and stepped in. . . .

At first she could see nothing, after the brightness outside. Like all barns, it seemed much bigger inside than out, an immense gloomy cavern filled with the smell of musty hay and the toneless twittering of sparrows. After a moment Sissy began to distinguish another sound — a kind of dry rustling unpleasantly near. Fearing snakes (though Ted had told her none were poisonous thereabouts), she shrank back; as she did so the rustling grew louder and, almost at her feet, a voice whispered: 'Is dat you, missy? Is it time? We'se ready whenever you wants us.'

Her eyes at length becoming accustomed to the darkness, she perceived that there were several men in the barn — or, rather, several people; two she identified as women — crouched on the floor amid bales of old hay. The reason she had not seen them before was that they were *black* — yes! Negroes all. It had been their glistening teeth, the rolling whites of their eyes, that had first shown her she was not alone. Some rude provisions had been made for their comfort; there was a row of straw beds in one corner and, in another, a rough plank table with the remains of a meal. (The coffee-pot was a large one Sissy had often seen Marie-Claire use.)

Sissy shrank back still farther; she was terribly frightened. The man who had spoken shuffled closer till he might almost have touched her, repeating anxiously: 'Is it time, missy? Is it time?'

'Time for *what?*' said Sissy; and, at that, one of the women hissed warningly from the shadows: 'Shush, Sam! 'Tain't no good — *she* not Missy Amberley!'

All the Negroes crept forward as far as they dared; and their leader, who Sissy now saw was an old man, nearly blind — his eyes did not shine like the others' — clutched her knees in an agony and cried out:

227

'Fo' de Lawd's sake, missy, don' tell on us! Whoever you are, go away and leave us be — but don' tell on us!' And the chorus behind him went on moaning: 'Don' tell on us, missy!'

Sissy understood at last. Gently withdrawing her skirts from the old man's desperate fingers, she said, in a soft voice: 'I won't tell, I promise. I'm not Mrs. Amberley, but I'm a friend of Mrs. Amberley's; and I wouldn't betray her for the world. *She'll* let you know when it's time. Now just you stay here and be quiet till it's dark. . . . '

She stepped out of the barn and shut the door after her.

It was amazing, when she got back to the house, to find that she had been gone, all told, something less than an hour.

Papa and Aunt Zeph were in the larch grove where she had left them. They had not, however, been there the whole time. Papa was wearing his dark city clothes; he'd finished his packing, he said. Aunt Zeph, meanwhile, had been busy picking a basket of grapes to send to Chicago. There they lay on a bed of silver-backed vine leaves, fragrant clusters of purple and green. A pitcher of grapejuice stood on the small rustic table under the trees.

Before her return Sissy had been wondering how on earth she could manage to face Aunt Zeph. According to Aunt Betsy's novels, of course, her duty was plain: she ought to have charged on the scene with a shriek of 'Vile creature!' or 'Traitress!', to be followed perhaps by a virtuous 'Father, you'd better come home with me.' But what actually happened was that Aunt Zeph smiled at Sissy (to be sure, she could not be expected to realize that her duplicity had been discovered) and handed her a glass of grapejuice. Then Sissy smiled back (for which there was no excuse!) and thanked her; before she knew it the impossible proved to be possible and they were chatting away quite as usual.

'You've been for a walk, child? How hot you look!' said the traitress. 'Sit down and rest; the train does not go for a long time yet. Will you give these grapes to your mother and tell her, please, that the dark ones are ready for jelly-making? I'll send more later when they're ripe enough for wine. I'd have liked you to take some apples, too, but your father thinks they're rather heavy to carry. Perhaps Theodore will be going in later in the week. . . . Where were you, my dear? In the wood? Ah, that's a glorious place, these days! I often

228

wish autumn might last forever. It's the best American season. And then how pleasant to be able to rest a little, after the strenuous work on the farm is over, and enjoy all this beauty with a clear conscience!'

'It's beautiful now,' said Papa; 'but what will you do when it's winter, the leaves are fallen, and the wind howls round the house like a soul in torment? There are no winds in the world so bitter and searching, I think, as those on our Midwestern prairies.'

Aunt Zeph made a little face.

'I know,' she said. 'I thought so, too, when first I came to Illinois. I saw nothing fine in the landscape all brown and grey and lifeless. After the snow had covered us up, and the frost sealed the windows so that I could sometimes not even look out, I would stamp my foot in anger and cry: *"Ce n'est pas mon pays! Ce n'est pas mon pays!"* But I don't know — I've grown used to it now — winter seems to me beautiful, also, in its way. Surely the trees are lovelier bare than ever they are in full leaf! And when the snow-blanket turns the colour of indigo at nightfall and the young moon rises above it through scraps of cloud in a soft blue sky — no summer sky's as tender as the winter sky can be — why, then, I feel I'd never call the birds and blossoms back.'

'Madame is a philosopher,' said Papa, with a half-mocking bow.

'Madame has had to be,' retorted Aunt Zeph, shrugging her shoulders. 'If it weren't for philosophy, she might often have come near to starving, my friend.'

'But aren't you afraid of the awful storms?' asked Sissy; 'and the wolves and the Indians? And won't you be lonesome for company after Ted has gone West?'

Aunt Zeph shook her head valiantly. 'Why should I be afraid? I've Lem and Tartuffe to guard me; besides, I've my pistol and still know how to use it! The storms *are* bad, but they're not to be feared by the self-sufficient; many's the time we've managed for a month without once going to market. There are no wolves left in this part of the country, and no Indians either, save for my good Marie-Claire. Of course, I shall miss Theodore very much — but then, I've never had him in winter. No — I shan't be lonesome and I *won't* be pitied! I'd not exchange my lot with any of you.'

'Upon my word, ma'am, I believe you!' said Papa. 'And this year at least you'll be able to keep the boy a little longer than usual, if he doesn't start out until after Christmas.'

'I feel, of course, that for his sake the sooner he goes the better,' said Aunt Zeph. 'He's waited so long for his great adventure, and looked forward to it so eagerly. Then, too, the bright new sights and scenes will help him to forget his disappointment.' She glanced at Sissy, not archly — Aunt Zeph was never arch — but with an unwonted softness in her jewel-like eyes. 'Ah, my dear, you did not think your papa and I were unaware of Theodore's little romance? I said nothing at the time — for what was there to say? Besides, I saw at once you were capable of handling your own affairs without interference. But now that it is over, may I thank you for your wisdom and your kindness to my poor boy? He feels now — it is natural he should — that the life of the heart has come to an end — before it is even begun!'

Sissy felt more deeply ashamed than she ever had since the day she was born. A heavy blush mantled her face and throat, and then receded, leaving her white and trembling.

'I wasn't wise! I wasn't kind!' she cried. 'If I had been, things never would've gone as far as they did. But truly, ma'am, I tried . . . I didn't know . . . I mean, I didn't mean . . . '

She halted, utterly unable to proceed. But Aunt Zeph's eyes were still soft. 'Don't be too sorry for him, child. It will only do him good. Theodore should be grateful to you. Indeed, I do not think I wish him to forget too soon. Next to the love of God — that's for the few — and the love of humanity — that's not for many either — a love like his, hopeless and stainless, is man's best teacher.'

There was a silence. Papa would not speak; Sissy *could* not. Aunt Zeph stretched out her hand and picked up the banjo that lay on the grass against her chair. Idly she struck a few chords; then, having found her key, she began without accompaniment to sing:

> *'Derrièr' chez mon père (vole, mon coeur, vole!),*
> *Derrièr' chez mon père y-a-t-un pommier doux. . . .*
> *Trois joli' princesses (vole, mon coeur, vole!),*
> *Trois joli' princesses sont couchées dessous. . . . '*

Sissy had never heard Aunt Zeph sing. It was as she herself had

230

said, she had no voice to speak of — the merest thread of sound, scarcely louder than the wind in the larches overhead. Nor did she try to express any emotion in her singing, though it was perhaps the more expressive for that. She sang with her head thrown back, her hazel eyes fixed upon nothing at all. . . .

> ' "*Ça*," *dit la première*, "*Je crois qu'il fait jour*." . . .
> "*Ça*," *dit la seconde*, "*J'entends le tambour*." . . .
> "*Ça*," *dit la troisième*, "*Ce sont nos amours*." . . .'

The tune was old and in a minor key, but not sad. The verse about the three princesses under the apple tree, and their lovers who went to war, was not especially sad either; yet there was in both words and music a feeling of resignation — so-it-was-and-so-it-had-to-be! — perfectly in accord with the mellow beauty of the dying autumn day.

> ' "*Ils vont à la guerre* (*vole, mon coeur, vole!*),
> "*Ils vont à la guerre combattre pour nous*" . . . .
> "*S'il gagne bataille* (*vole, mon coeur, vole!*),
> "*S'il gagne bataille, aura mes amours*'. . . .
> "*Qu'il perde ou qu'il gagne* (*vole, mon coeur, vole!*),
> "*Qu'il perde ou qu'il gagne, les aura toujours!*" '

Only with the last words of the third princess — '*Whether he win or lose, my love he'll have forever!*' — did the singer turn her head towards Papa. Her clear, bright gaze held no appeal, certainly nothing that could be construed as proprietorship: there was a bond acknowledged, that was all, a bond that would not sever. Sissy saw now, with a rush of remorse, that Aunt Zeph meant no harm — *her* love, also, was hopeless and stainless — out of all the ways in the world there were to love, that way, by a miracle, was the one she would have.

In the end they had to hurry to catch their train: Sissy had known they would. Papa had no sense of time, and Aunt Zeph, who saw so little company, naturally wanted to keep her guests as long as possible. At parting she had taken Sissy into her arms and given her, not a pair of sharp foreign pecks, but a warm, real, American kiss. She had given her, also, an oblong package neatly wrapped in white paper and tied with scarlet ribbons — her present to the bride — and Sissy had guessed at once what it was.

'It's the vase with the doves and the *château impossible*,' she said. 'Oh, Mrs. Amberley, that's too much!' And Aunt Zeph had smiled and said Sissy was very clever — but it was not at all too much; Theodore, too, wanted her to have it; they regretted only not being able to send it by post, but it was to be feared that the porcelain, so old and so fragile, might not survive the trip. . . . 'If the doves lost their tails,' said Aunt Zeph, 'what a pity!'

Sissy begged her to be sure to come to the wedding; and Aunt Zeph had smiled again and answered that she would by all means if she could . . . but one knew somehow that she wouldn't: this was *really* good-bye. . . .

In the train going back to the city Papa produced a book from his pocket, a small shabby volume called *Moby Dick* (what could it be?), and settled himself to read. Sissy was thankful to be quiet for a while, to restore her thoughts to order. It seemed that a great many important things had happened today . . . and yet, after all, what had she done? Reduced to the simplest statement of fact, she had looked through a window, opened a door, and heard an old song. Why did she feel, then, that she would never be the same again?

Of these three experiences, that which had perhaps touched her least nearly was the only one she could mention to her father. Presently, when she had grown tired of being silent, she stole a sidewise glance — for they were sharing a bench — to see if he were engrossed in his book; and, finding that he was not, she plucked up courage to begin: 'Papa, I've something to tell you. This afternoon when I was up on the hill I went into the old barn.'

Papa looked at her sharply, but not as if he were angry.

'I thought that was what you might be doing,' he said, 'when you were gone such a long time. Mrs. Amberley thought so, too. It makes no difference now, my dear, of course — but you must never speak of what you saw to anyone — not to Aaron or Nancy or even your mother.'

Sissy promised seriously that she would not. 'Papa,' she said then, 'those poor black people, I suppose they are slaves?'

'They *were* slaves,' Papa corrected her, 'before they escaped from their masters and ran away towards Canada and freedom. You've heard, I imagine, about the Underground Railroad — well, now you've seen a bit of it in action. The Amberley farm is one of the stations. Our friend has been engaged in this work almost ever since she came back from California — and a noble work it is. You can understand now — can't you? — why she chooses to live as she does, retired from the world, with no one to serve her but a half-daft lad and an Indian girl who can't speak any English. It's the only way she feels safe. If it were discovered what she was doing, the law would stop it at once — it would have to, though the sympathies of the people are all against slavery. You can understand, also, why she so seldom leaves home. Weeks, even months, sometimes go by undisturbed; but she never knows when the next band of fugitives will arrive.'

'Of course,' said Sissy, 'so many things are clear that seemed strange before. I see now why you wouldn't go to Aunt Betsy's that Sunday: it all fits in — the lights on the hill — the carriage driving away in the night — Marie-Claire's fit of temper with Lem . . . '

'That was all Lem's fault,' said Papa. 'Poor fellow! He let the cat out of the bag without meaning to. Once the hired hands knew what was afoot there was nothing to be done but bribe them to keep their mouths shut and get rid of them — and hurry the Negroes on to the next station a whole day earlier than we'd planned. It's a risky business — and so I've told our friend a hundred times — but Zéphirine Amberley is an obstinate woman. She feels herself dedicated — she cares so much, you see — she has such an overmastering passion for freedom in the abstract that she's willing to give up her own to help those poor wretches find theirs.'

There was a pause. Sissy was remembering how when she first came to Naperville she had marvelled that Aunt Zeph could so cheerfully accept her restricted existence; it had seemed that only a great mission would make such a sacrifice worth while. Yes, but then she had not known Aunt Zeph *had* a mission. Given the clue, it was easy to see that the mainspring of her life was the love of humanity of which Aunt Zeph herself had spoken as being 'not for many.' . . . 'Not for *me!*' thought Sissy, with a shiver, repelled in spite of herself by the spectacle of this cold, selfless nobility. She could not help being curious as to how it struck her father.

233

'I am glad I know,' she said, sighing. 'Yes, she *is* a wonderful woman. But, Papa, could *you* live like that? Is that your idea of the good life?'

She glanced at him almost timidly; perhaps she was daring too much. It was a great relief when Papa slammed *Moby Dick* shut on his knees with a vigorous 'Good God, no, child! I'd rather be dead! Oh, it was all right for a summer: I was at loose ends and Mrs. Amberley knew it — she's been amazingly kind. She helped me so much that I was glad in return to help her and Ted. But as for making a permanent career of self-immolation, no, thank you! I'm afraid I'm not chivalrous enough for that, my dear.'

'I'm glad,' said Sissy, feeling oddly comforted by this admission. But something in the situation still troubled her: 'You said you were helping Mrs. Amberley and *Ted* — did Ted know about the runaway slaves, too?'

'Why, yes,' replied Papa; 'he could hardly have been kept from knowing. His aunt was reluctant to involve him, but she needed him, also; besides, with her strict sense of honour, since the farm is half his, she'd not have felt it right to engage in such traffic without his approval.'

'He knew, then — he knew all the time — and he never said a word to me! Oh, I do think he might have trusted me, don't you?'

'It wasn't precisely a question of trust. The fewer persons who were in on it, the better for all concerned. Besides the Amberleys and myself, and their two servants, not a soul in the world had the slightest idea — not anybody anywhere, Sissy.'

'Yes, I realize that,' said Sissy, frowning because Papa did not see what she meant. 'But I wasn't "anybody"! Ted ought to have known . . . It makes me angry to be left out, not relied upon, kept in the dark. I don't like it at all! I like to be told things!'

Papa gave her a curious look.

'That sounds like your mother. But do you know, my dear . . . perhaps you're too young to have learned that the more one longs to be told, the less likely others are to tell. I say "too young," but that's something no Bascomb has grasped at any age.'

Sissy looked still more troubled.

'Oh, dear,' she said, 'how dreadful it sounds! I mustn't be like the rest of them in that. I mustn't let you think so. All the same, though, Ted *might* have seen . . . '

Then she stopped and began to laugh; and the rest of the way they sat quietly hand-in-hand, gazing out at the sweet evening light on the prairie.

It was not until they were driving home in a cab from the station that Sissy remembered she had no explanation prepared for her mother. She had said that morning she would probably not be home to supper, so that was all right: how, though, was she to explain her appearance in Papa's company after a day spent ostensibly with the Wilsons at Cottage Hill? Would it do to pretend they had met by accident in the train? . . . 'Not *too* convincing,' said Papa. 'But I can't think of anything better, can you? Let us hope my arrival may cause enough commotion — it usually does, I've observed — to cover any weaknesses in our story. Now for it, my dear!'

Having helped Sissy out and paid the driver, he strode in the blue autumn dusk up the path with a step so firm that Sissy was sure he felt as full of misgivings as she did herself.

The lights were all lighted in the little white house, and the door was opened, with suspicious speed, not by Susan, but by Mamma in person. Mamma did not say or do any of the things Sissy had imagined she might. She took no heed of her daughter, little more of her husband; but peered anxiously into the darkness, crying sharply: 'Where's Nancy?'

'Nancy?' said Sissy. 'I don't know, Mamma; where should she be?'

'I thought you might have found her somewhere.' Mamma passed her hand nervously over her hair and straightened her cap automatically. 'I sent her to the north side with a note to Mrs. Leslie — but that was over three hours ago. She should have got home before dark. We waited supper as long as we could. . . . Oh, I don't know what's got into the child lately! She seems to take a perverse delight in irritating and alarming me.'

'Don't worry, Mamma,' said Sissy soothingly. 'Most likely she stopped to see Uncle Caleb and Aunt Jane on her way home and they kept her to sup with them — or maybe she's with one of her school-mates. Whichever it is, I dare say she'll turn up any minute now.'

'Jane would know better than to do such a thing; she'd realize I'd be nervous. And none of Nancy's friends that I can recall live north of the river. No, dear, I'm afraid Wilfred's to blame. His rooms are in Pine Street, you know, and I doubt not the minx made a point of passing them on her return. Oh, I wish I knew what to do!'

In the midst of her lamentations Mamma suddenly remembered that Papa was back, unexpectedly, and that she had paid no attention to him. 'Jonathan — forgive me! I hardly can tell what I'm saying. You've come in from the country to stay, I hope? Will you have a bit of supper here? I kept things hot for the girls and I'm sure there's more than enough for you, if you can put up with roast-beef hash and muffins and a plain green salad. I'll get Susan to dish it up . . . '

'Thank you, Julia,' replied Papa. 'Yes, I've come back for good this time. I shall be glad to stay for supper, if it won't inconvenience you. And pray don't be too much upset by Nancy's pranks. The child is heedless by nature — you know whom you've to thank for it! I'll lay she'll appear before Sissy and I have finished our meal. But if she don't, I'll engage to find Her Ladyship for you. Chicago's not so large that she can manage to hide herself very long. I promise you I won't fail, my girl.'

Sissy had never heard him use that term of endearment. It seemed to please Mamma; she looked relieved in spite of herself. And Papa was right: Susan had scarcely brought in the hash before there was a sound of rapid steps on the porch and the front door burst open.

From her place at table Sissy could see her mother and Nancy in the hall. Wilfred kept a trifle behind his cousin, but Nancy stood full in the lamplight, her cheeks brilliantly pink, her eyes sparkling, as she tossed back her curls with an impatient gesture.

'Mamma, I'm so sorry,' she cried at once; 'I didn't mean to do it, truly! I meant to be back hours ago. Wilfred just happened — wasn't it queer? — to be calling on the Leslies when I got there. He said he'd take me home, but it was such a fine evening it seemed a pity to come in so soon. So we drove north for a while . . . '

'Dear Mrs. Trigg, it was my fault,' protested Wilfred, who looked much more embarrassed than his companion. 'I persuaded Cousin Nancy against her better judgement . . . '

'Her *what?*' Papa whispered to Sissy; but Nancy, of course, could not hear. 'In no time at all we were in Pine Grove,' she continued; 'and

236

we were both so terribly hungry—it was quite supper-time, you know, by then—that we stopped at the Lake View House. Oh, I do hope you don't mind! My watch wouldn't go and Wilfred forgot his, so we hadn't the least idea how late it was getting till it started to grow dark. Then of course we came back as fast as we could—I didn't even wait to finish my pudding! Oh, Mamma, don't be angry! We had so much fun, and nobody saw us that mattered, I'm sure—there wasn't a soul at the inn but the waiters—you know, there never is except on Saturday night.'

'It was all my fault,' Wilfred repeated. 'A thousand apologies, dear madam! But I do assure you Nancy's come to no harm; I even made her wear my jacket on the homeward journey, so that she mightn't catch cold. Please believe us . . .'

'I believe you,' said Mamma, in the voice like ice that Sissy most feared; 'but that's not the point. The point is—ah, but I'll not stop to argue with you now! You had better go, Wilfred, since you've supped already. I bid you good night.'

She shut the door firmly in the young man's face, cutting off his shamefaced attempts to renew his excuses. Then she turned to Nancy, who was waiting uneasily for her punishment. 'As for you, miss, get to bed as fast as you can—not a word!—I'll deal with *you* in the morning.'

Nancy shrugged her shoulders, but did not dare dispute her mother's command. She started slowly upstairs, dragging her feet sulkily like a spoilt child on purpose to annoy. All the pretty brightness had been wiped from her face.

Mamma came back to the dining-room. She must have known that Papa and Sissy could not help overhearing the scene, as the doors were open; but she did not refer to it; she went on quietly talking, as she had been doing before the truants' return, about preparations for the wedding.

Later, after Papa had left them for the night and Sissy, tired out by her recent emotions, had just got into bed and blown out the light, there was a tap on her door and Nancy, without waiting to be bidden, turned the knob and came in. She held a candle and was wearing her nightgown but not her nightcap; the dark curls tumbled unbound over her shoulders.

'Sissy, are you asleep?'

Sissy sat bolt upright. 'How could I be?' she said crossly. 'Child, what's the matter? Why aren't you in bed?'

Nancy set the candlestick on the dressing-table, away from the window, so that it would not blow in the wind, and then sat down at the foot of her sister's bed.

'Oh, Sis,' she cried, so much excited that she was barely able to keep her voice to a whisper, 'I *had* to see you! Guess what happened to-night — Wilfred and I are *engaged!*'

Sissy stared, quite unable to speak.

'What makes you look at me like that?' Nancy, obviously uncomfortable, jumped up again and began drifting about the room, fiddling with the articles on the washstand and the roses in the blue opaline jar. 'We've got a right to get engaged as much as you and Aaron have, I reckon. Wilfred's been in love with me for months. He liked me right away, you know, the very first night at Aunt Bertha's, but of course I never thought . . . I've known for a long time, though, he cared for me — since we were in Naperville — but I wouldn't let him speak before because — oh, because I just wouldn't! It was so much fun to tease the poor thing and keep him guessing. But tonight he looked so miserable I didn't have the heart to go on. He said he couldn't stand it any more: if I didn't give him some hope, why, he'd throw up the law and go back to New York, no matter what his family thought. I couldn't let *that* happen, now could I? So I told him I was fond of him, and he kissed my hand right in front of the waiter, and gave me his ring to wear — see, it's a topaz; *I* think it's quite pretty! — but he don't like it; he's going to get me a diamond from Tiffany's. . . . Aren't you surprised, Sis? Do say you're surprised! Of course, I can't tell anyone yet till I've talked to Mamma and Wilfred's written to his people; but we're really engaged and we're going to be married. And I shall live in New York City, and have a big house and a great many servants, and Wilfred says I can sing all day, if I like. He says — oh, he says he'll build me a private theatre, if I decide I want one. Isn't it wonderful, dear?'

Of all the shocks she had sustained that day, Sissy felt this must be the worst.

'Nancy,' she began, 'poor child — poor, silly child — I don't know

238

what to say! You must be out of your mind! How can you be thinking of marriage at your age? You know right well, no matter how the Morgans feel, Mamma'll be furious. She'll keep you locked up for a week maybe, or feed you on bread and water, or . . . she may even whip you! Why, you're only a baby!'

'I like that!' Nancy's eyes flashed angrily. 'I'm sixteen and three quarters, and I look a lot older, I know I do — why, Wilfred said himself when first he met me he thought I must be nineteen. Besides, sixteen is plenty old enough to get married. You're just jealous because you hadn't guessed what was going on, and it'll make *your* old wedding look like nothing at all. Who'd take a slowpoke like Aaron if they could get anyone better? I s'pose it don't matter to you because you've never really been in love. Don't you wish you could change places with me? Don't you, Sis? Don't you?'

Half laughing, half crying, Nancy darted towards the bed and leaned forward to bring her face, rosy with triumph, nearer and nearer her sister.

Sissy slapped her.

The Party

DURING THE FOLLOWING FORTNIGHT the problem of Nancy and Wilfred engaged the attention of The Family almost to the exclusion of everything else. Preparations for the wedding went duly forward, but were no longer of paramount interest; even Papa's return from the country, which ordinarily would have provoked an explosion, passed well-nigh unnoticed.

It seemed to Sissy that Mamma spent most of her time closeted with relatives, either singly or in groups. Aunt Jane and Aunt Bertha came to dine every day — unless Mamma were dining with them — ; Aunt Betsy hastened in from Geneva, on the plea that she'd shopping to do; the house was full from morning till night of tense, talkative knots of elders that dissolved, with suspicious suddenness, as soon as a young Trigg appeared. From the beginning it was agreed that Wilfred was chiefly to blame. He was a man, and by some years the elder; of course, he should have known better ... When, however, he was called to task by Uncle Caleb his demeanour was surprisingly manly. With disarming frankness he admitted the charges preferred against him, declared he was deeply in love with his cousin and determined to marry her; he was willing, moreover — since he realized Nancy's youth — to wait several years, if need be, to achieve his object.

Nancy's behaviour was less satisfactory. She turned sulky when scolded and saucy when reasoned with, while the torrent of complaint and exhortation streamed past her unheeded. . . . 'A pert, self-willed minx,' pronounced Aunt Bertha. Aunt Jane shook her head gloomily and said she feared the child lacked a *heart*. Aunt Betsy, bridling, added that it was easy to see where she got her stubborn nature. . . . None of the Aunts seemed to think Mamma could be in any way accountable for the catastrophe. That was odd, Sissy could not help thinking; for Nan-

240

cy was her mother's daughter no less than her father's; Mamma, in fact, had brought her up almost unaided: since Sissy's docility was always laid at her door, why not Nancy's perverseness?

After some days of indecision, and frequent consultations by letter with the Morgans in New York—who wrote appalled at the threatened disaster, and not a little inclined to reproach their dear Bertha for her want of foresight (which was plainly unfair, as Aunt Bertha had been in New Hampshire during the whole of the critical period)—it was decided to remove one of the culprits. Wilfred could not go without abandoning his work in Uncle Caleb's office (just, Uncle Caleb averred, beginning to show gratifying results); therefore, Nancy *must*. Uncle Charles generously offered to defray the expense of a finishing school: if Julia thought it would answer the purpose, he would be glad to send a second niece to the Utica Female Academy. Anna Turnham, Aunt Bertha's sister, was coming to Chicago for the wedding; Nancy could very well go back with her and either remain as the Turnhams' guest (as Sissy had done) or become a parlour boarder at Miss Crandall's select establishment.

Everyone said, with relief, that it was 'just the thing.' Mamma shed tears of gratitude; Nancy seemed acquiescent, outwardly at least; only Aunt Betsy dared hint, with her customary acidity, that perhaps dear Mrs. Turnham might not be an altogether unexceptionable chaperon —had it not been while under her wing that Sissy had met and become involved with 'that peculiar young man who lived on a farm in the wilderness with a French aunt and a mad Indian maid'? (But it was felt Aunt Betsy was going too far; the Uncles told her to mind her own business—let bygones be bygones—besides, look at Sissy *now!*)

As for Papa, no one asked his opinion, and he submitted none on his own initiative. Truth to tell, since returning to the city he had been seen hardly more often than if he were still in Naperville—which proved, of course, once more the utter incapacity and insensibility of Jonathan Trigg.

Matters stood thus, and it lacked but a week to the twenty-fourth of September, when something happened so extraordinary, so far-reaching in its effects, that all previous topics appeared stale and pale by comparison. Sissy was awakened one morning by an insistent drumming on the headboard of her bed. This was strange: could the house be on fire? These days she was a privileged person; in consideration of the ordeal ahead and her prospective increase in dignity she was not made to keep regular hours, but could, if she liked, sleep half the morning away. She opened her eyes now, rather indignantly, upon Loulie, who was teetering on her toes with an impatience as unaccountable as it was unusual.

'Oh, Sis, wake up! Wake up, do — please, Sis! There's a strange man and woman in the parlour with Mamma.'

Sissy yawned, not yet properly awake. 'Well, what if there is? Mamma'll attend to them, I suppose. Who let them in?'

'I did,' replied Loulie, still hopping up and down in her excitement like a ponderous puppy. 'There wasn't anyone else to — Susan's gone to market, Mamma was in the kitchen, and I couldn't find Nancy anywhere. Yes, I know my face is dirty — I've been playing in the park with Joshua — I just got in when I heard somebody at the door. But, Sissy dear, wait till you hear: that man and that woman, they said they was our uncle and aunt!'

'Impossible!' cried Sissy. 'How could they be?'

'Well, I don't know — that's what they said. The man looks a lot like Uncle Charles and Uncle Caleb — but kind of different, too. He's not bald and he's got a beard. He told me his name, but I can't remember it — 'twas something funny I couldn't pronounce. The woman said she was our Aunt Sophie. She's *awful* funny-looking, Sis — dark and fat and smells real strong of flowers. I think she meant to kiss me, but I ran away to call Mamma. Mamma came as fast as she could, and when she saw who it was she threw her arms round the man's neck. "Sal!" she said. "Sal!" That wasn't what *he* told me, though. And then she started in to cry and laugh all at once, and Uncle Sal laughed, too, but he didn't cry at all. And then Mamma told me to come upstairs and fetch you and Nancy, and she took Uncle Sal and Aunt Sophie into the parlour and shut the door, and they all began to scream, and I guess they're in there yet.'

'Well, I never!' Nancy drifted in from the hall to survey the pink and breathless Loulie with amusement. 'I always thought the child could talk if it wanted to. Go on, Loulie, tell us some more!'

'That's all the more there is,' retorted Loulie. 'But, Sis, how can we have an aunt and uncle we never even heard of before?'

'How many Bascombs are there?' Nancy wondered. 'There's Uncle Caleb and Uncle Charles, and Aunt Betsy — and Mamma, of course — and then the ones that didn't live — Aunt-Flo-and-Aunt-Fan, the twins, they died of scarlet fever when they were babies — and poor little Uncle William, who was drowned fishing for hornpouts in Queechy Lake at seventeen. We used to play in the cemetery sometimes when we were children, and I can just remember seeing their gravestones under the pines next to Grandma Bascomb and the three little Calebs.'

'Well,' said Sissy, 'of course there was Uncle Salathiel, too. He's not buried with the rest because he didn't die at home. He was the one between Mamma and Aunt Betsy, you know. He got into some kind of trouble after he left school — I don't recollect what it was — I guess maybe I never knew. It must have been bad, though, for he was sent away and he never came back. Uncle Salathiel . . . that *might* be Sal. . . . I asked Mamma about him, once when I found his name in the family Bible; and Mamma looked very sad and said he'd been wicked but his sins were all forgiven, man proposes but God disposes, and I must never ask about him any more, and 'specially never mention his name to the Uncles, because they'd been kind and noble and it wasn't their fault. Loulie, I wonder . . . but he's dead; he *must* be dead, mustn't he? Mamma as good as told me he was.'

'He *isn't* dead,' said Loulie indignantly. 'He's downstairs now. You go look for yourselves and you'll see.'

'And Aunt Sophie is his wife, I suppose,' said Nancy languidly (Nancy had lately made rather a point of languor). 'Dear me, it's like something in a book, isn't it? Hurry up and get dressed, Sis, and we'll go down together. I expect Mamma don't intend to keep 'em under lock and key *all* day.'

As soon as Sissy saw him she knew that, book or no book, the man standing in front of the parlour fireplace must be their Uncle Salathiel. He bore a strong resemblance to both his brothers, although, as Loulie had reported, he had a full beard and a mane of straw-coloured hair as well, which he had a trick of tossing back with one hand as he talked. He was taller than Uncle Charles or Uncle Caleb, and in spite of being five years the former's, and nearly ten years the latter's, junior, he looked older than either, his ruddy face crisscrossed by a network of wrinkles.

'Are these your girls, Sister Julia?' he inquired as his nieces trooped in rosy with confusion. (His voice was a Bascomb voice, but seemed softer and more slurring than The Family's brisk Yankee accents.) 'I declare they do you and Brother Trigg credit — they're a row of young beauties!'

'This is your Uncle Salathiel, children,' said Mamma, whose eyes were suspiciously bright. 'A wonderful thing has happened. We all thought he was dead. I still can't believe . . .'

'Never was healthier in my life, ma'am, I do assure you!' cried Uncle Sal jovially. 'A kiss apiece, my dears — I think you owe me that, since I've come all the way from New Orleans to see you. And now you must meet your Aunt Sophie.'

The lady on the sofa beside Mamma smiled broadly and held out a hand sparkling with diamonds and rubies. She was very stout and very, very dark, darker even than Papa. It was a different kind of darkness, Sissy decided — not burnt into the pigment, but somehow exuded from within; her blood, one felt, must be of richer hue than the fair-skinned Bascombs'. Her hair was jet-black, quite straight, heavy and lustreless as wool; she had tanbark-brown eyes and full red lips that parted to reveal completely two rows of dazzling white teeth. Her voice was low and liquid; the words slipped out almost reluctantly in an accent even softer and more slurring than Uncle Sal's.

'How do you do, young ladies?' said Aunt Sophie. 'Perhaps you will honour me also?'

She did not rise — being apparently too tightly encased in purple velvet to attempt it — but opened wide her arms, which movement caused her fringed mauve silk mantle to slip off one plump shoulder. As this happened a tiny monkey with a long curling tail sprang out from under the folds of the mantle and sat grinning and chattering in its mistress's lap. The monkey was dressed in purple velvet, too; it wore a small cap adorned by a plume that was an exact copy in miniature of Aunt Sophie's.

Mamma eyed the monkey with marked distaste, heroically making no comment; but Loulie gave a scream of delight and Aunt Sophie, pleased by her interest, smiled more broadly than ever.

244

'You must meet my Coco,' she said, 'then you will know all the family.'

'Not *all*,' Uncle Sal corrected her. 'You forget the children, beloved. Did you know, girls — but I'm forgetting, of course you *couldn't* know — that you have four new cousins at the Sherman House waiting to make your acquaintance? Julia and Caleb and Sophie and Baby Baptiste: they're a bit younger than you; Julia, our eldest, is scarce nine; yet I venture to say you'll find them tolerable company. I'd have brought them along, but I did not want to alarm your dear mother with too many new relatives at one blow, so to speak. Julia, I know you're a busy woman. I feel we owe you apologies for taking you thus by surprise with a morning call. After debating all possible alternatives it seemed wisest to do it this way. I could not bear to announce my arrival to my own sister on cold, unfeeling paper! But this time we're come merely to make our bow. As you know, we are lodged in your neighbourhood — in very passable quarters, too — and we should take it kind of you to be willing to try potluck with us there — shall we say tonight, if you have no other engagement? Sophie, my love, we are free tonight?'

Aunt Sophie added her persuasions, in a creamy contralto, to those of her husband; but Mamma shook her head decidedly. They were the strangers — this was *her* city — nothing would do but that Uncle Sal and Aunt Sophie should dine with the Triggs. 'I'm sorry only I can't ask you today. The morning's half gone already; there wouldn't be time to prepare a fitting meal. Besides, my Susan's no head — she's a good cook, but quite useless in an emergency. But come tomorrow, Sal, at half after one, you and — Sister Sophie, and as many of the children as you think would enjoy it. I'll engage to get Caleb and Charles and their wives, and Betsy, too — it's most fortunate she's just in from the country to stop till after the wedding — and we'll make it a gala reunion.'

Uncle Sal and his wife were delighted to accept Sister Julia's invitation. Baby Baptiste was still in the cradle, and little Sophie, it seemed, had just got to the teething stage and was too fractious to be presentable; but they could be left at the hotel in charge of their nurse and Aunt Sophie's reliable maid. The rest of the family would be on the Triggs' doorstep at the appointed hour with all the pleasure in life.

Uncle Sal then kissed Mamma and his three nieces again, pinching Sissy's cheek with a roguish 'Is this the little bride? She favours you, Julia — as fair as roses in June, 'pon my honour!' Aunt Sophie tucked Coco back under her mantle — as she did so Sissy saw that his red leather collar was attached to his mistress's wrist by a chain of gold links — got to her feet by a supreme effort of will, and sailed across the parlour, tinkling and jingling her numerous bangles and necklaces. She did not kiss Mamma, but dropped her a splendid curtsy instead and swept out on a strong wave of jasmine, smiling and bland to the last. Uncle Sal looked back and waved his hat as they let themselves out the gate. Sissy watched them enter a hackney coach that had evidently been waiting during the whole of their visit — though the Sherman House was hardly three blocks away —; the cabman cracked his whip, the horses trotted off — the Salathiel Bascombs disappeared.

The door had barely closed on their exit before Mamma clapped her hands smartly together and cried: 'Sissy, run as fast as you can to your Uncle Caleb's office and tell him I want to see him immediately. Nancy, do you do the same with your Uncle Charles.' (In spite of her mounting excitement Mamma was still able to recollect where Wilfred worked.) 'Aunt Betsy's out shopping in Lake Street; you might look into one or two stores on your way back from Bascomb and Company; but don't waste too much time — I presume she'll be in presently. Explain to your uncles what's happened, children, and why it's important that they should come right away if they can. Merciful Heavens! My head's in such a whirl that I scarce know where I'm at!'

Sissy had already started to put on her bonnet without comment; but Nancy, though not loath to be the bearer of interesting tidings, hung back a little and was perverse enough to inquire: 'But *why*, Mamma? Why is it so important? Your dinner-party won't be till tomorrow, will it?'

Mamma stamped her foot. 'Do as you're told, child, and don't stop to argue. My patience! Can't you see that between now and then we've got to decide What to Do about Uncle Salathiel?'

For the first time since the day Grandpa Bascomb died Sissy and

Nancy saw the Uncles at the house in State Street during business hours. Both left their desks with all possible speed, pausing long enough only to despatch messengers to inform their wives of the news. Aunt Jane and Aunt Bertha dropped everything and hastened to join the parley; as they entered the gate they encountered Aunt Betsy, her arms full of bargains from Palmer's and Ross and Foster's. . . .

The meeting lasted the rest of the morning; recessed during the dinner hour on Susan's account — poor Susan! flurried at having on such short notice to feed four extra guests according to Bascomb standards of adequacy — ; continued the whole of the afternoon; recessed again for supper; and wound up late in the evening, after the Uncles had had an opportunity of paying a call at the Sherman House and reporting their findings to the women.

Loulie was told firmly to 'go and play somewhere about, dear.' Aunt Betsy, who for some reason had taken the Wilfred affair harder than anybody, betrayed a desire to exclude Nancy as well; but Mamma asserted that her two elder daughters were old enough to be told the truth — they'd hear it sooner or later anyhow.

To Sissy's surprise the truth in this instance was different from anything she had been told before. It appeared that The Family had known all along that Uncle Sal was alive; they had said he was dead — 'Dead to *us,* dears,' explained Aunt Jane lugubriously — merely to avoid embarrassing questions. Uncle Sal was the Bascomb black sheep. He had never, said Uncle Charles vigorously, been worth a tinker's damn; and Uncle Caleb, though frowning at his brother's choice of phrase, sombrely agreed with him. Grandpa Bascomb had been wonderfully patient with the young wastrel; Uncle Caleb and Uncle Charles, as they became men enough to share the family responsibilities, had also helped him out of pickles again and again. Finally, when Uncle Sal was eighteen, thinking that he might do better away from home, they had got him a job in a bank in Pittsfield. . . . Six months later a large sum of money was missed; Uncle Sal was accused of the theft; though he loudly maintained his innocence, he could not prove it, and would undoubtedly have gone to jail if his brothers had not scraped up enough money between them to cover the deficiency.

After that, they had given Salathiel his coach fare to Boston and told him tersely to get out and stay out — he could look for no further rescuing actions from them.

That had been over twenty years ago. . . .

So much for the past. Uncle Sal did not at present, quite understandably, care to refer to it more than he had to; nor had he yet, although plied with assiduous questions, gone into really satisfying detail concerning his subsequent adventures. All that was certain was that he was now, amazingly, a very wealthy man — richer by far than Uncle Caleb, and as rich at least as Uncle Charles. How he had got his start, was not quite clear, but he had been for some years one of the leading cotton brokers in the South. . . . 'No, Betsy, *not* a planter. He don't grow the stuff; he just buys it for resale from those that do.' . . . Apparently Sal's Yankee sharpness had found just the field that best suited it. He had a town house in Saint Charles Street, a country estate some ten miles from New Orleans, a sailing yacht, and a stable of trotters. He seemed to know intimately, at any rate in a business way, most of the leading men of the community; he was talking of running as state senator at the next elections.

Aunt Jane could not help wondering whether all this prosperity could be real. Sal had always had a vivid imagination, source of most of his troubles in youth: might he not be drawing a long bow to impress his brothers? Perhaps the racing stable and the yacht — nay, even the house in Saint Charles Street and the cotton business — had no existence outside of their owner's mind?

Uncle Charles observed that the point was well taken. He would himself have been inclined to doubt the whole story if it had not been for the evening call at the Sherman House. There was no discrediting the actual evidence of their eyes. Sal and his wife were snugly ensconced in the presidential suite; half of one floor seemed to be at their disposal. Their train included a maid and a valet, a nurse and a tutor (all blacks, to be sure, but the last); their children were ostentatiously well dressed; while as for Aunt Sophie, who had made a belated appearance in a scarlet satin gown with some kind of arrangement of plumes on her head, she had been blazing with jewels from top to toe.

Mamma regretted that their new sister-in-law was so fond of ornament; she had been wearing a most unnecessary number of diamonds that morning. The monkey Coco was a deplorable possession; it was likewise unfortunate for Mrs. Salathiel Bascomb that she was addicted to such heavy perfumes. . . . Aunt Jane thought perhaps in the South things were different. Did not the Creoles . . .? 'But *is* she a Creole?' asked Aunt Betsy. 'And if she is, don't it mean she must be also . . . you know what I mean?'

Aunt Bertha said briskly that that did not follow. All Creoles were dark, but it was no sign that there was the slightest admixture of . . . In fact, it was well known that the aristocratic families of New Orleans dated back to the early eighteenth century and were of the purest French or Castilian origin.

'Sophie sounds French to me,' said Aunt Bertha. 'And why should she call the baby Baptiste if she's not? Do you be sure, Julia, the next time you see her, to enquire what her maiden name was — I'll wager she comes of fine old *émigré* stock.'

After hours of exhausting debate Uncle Caleb, as foreman of the jury, seemed to sum up the feelings of all by saying: 'Brother and sisters, what's done can't be undone. Sal was always a reckless fellow, ornery, ungrateful, sadly lacking in grace. But I dare say he's paid for his past transgressions — if not, he'll be made to answer for them in the Hereafter. That's for Our Father above to judge. On the other hand, it has apparently pleased Heaven to allot our erring brother a measure of material affluence here below. Naturally, this should have no weight in influencing our decision. I, for my part, had far rather have found him in sackcloth and ashes, mourning his sins with a contrite heart. But Sal has succeeded — there's no denying it — and no man can succeed without the Lord's help. It occurs to me, therefore, that we are justified in holding his worldly success a token of spiritual salvation. Moreover, I take it that his seeking us out, the brothers and sisters he so cruelly wronged in his youth, for the purpose of making amends, is evidence of a change for the better in that wild and undisciplined nature. And finally, what in these circumstances would Pa have wished us to do? Brother Charles — Julia, Bertha, Betsy, and my own Jane — can you doubt for a moment what his advice to us would be? . . . *I say unto you, that likewise joy shall be in heaven over one sinner that repenteth, more than over ninety and nine just persons that need no repentance.*'

Uncle Charles, deeply moved, wrung his brother's hand. Aunt Jane gave a little sob — for Uncle Caleb always spoke so beautifully. And Mamma, her face suffused with happy tears, brought the conclave to a close by crying enthusiastically: 'Then I'll expect you *all* to dinner tomorrow!'

During the next few days there took place a good many dinners, for naturally, once the die had been cast, all The Family wanted to entertain Uncle Sal and Aunt Sophie. The Caleb Bascombs ordered a stately repast at the Tremont House, for which their best Crown Derby was got out of storage: Uncle Caleb kept telling his guests that the rib roast he served had cost twelve cents a pound — was that not an outrage? The Charles Bascombs were 'at home' in the mansion on Michigan Avenue at an evening reception; Uncle Charles likewise gave a businessmen's breakfast at the Washington Coffee House (such as once he'd offered Papa); while Aunt Bertha, whose enthusiasm for her new sister-in-law was only faintly diminished by the discovery that Aunt Sophie's parents had been named Leblanc (which did not somehow suggest a feudal aristocracy), asked her circle of ladies to tea. The Sunday was spent agreeably at Aunt Betsy's farm in Geneva.

On the Monday before the wedding the Salathiel Bascombs entertained in their turn at a supper-party in their suite at the Sherman, with, it was generally agreed afterwards, gratifying good taste. The meal was lavish, but not too lavish; Aunt Sophie wore plain black velvet and a judicious selection of gems; and Uncle Sal very quickly recovered from his initial mistake of having wine bottles set on the table by explaining that his wife had been told by her doctor to drink a glass of claret or port with each meal. The children, who did not come to supper on this occasion, but trooped in afterwards to shake hands, were shyly well-mannered, though all, like their mother, seemed disconcertingly dark. ('Not a true Bascomb in the lot,' Uncle Charles pronounced later.)

Uncle Sal and Aunt Sophie proved themselves as unaffectedly kindly and cordial hosts as they had been guests. They made no secret of their pleasure at having been so sympathetically received; there was nothing they did not offer their relatives in return. The whole family was pressed to visit New Orleans during next winter's carnival. It would, Uncle Sal was sure, be a delightful experience for them all, but particularly for his nieces — Mardi Gras was very gay for young people — Sissy was promised a ball every night; Nancy, as many operas as she cared to hear; Loulie, an unlimited supply of pralines and *petits fours*.

What was perhaps most surprising in people so forthright and simple was their delicate comprehension of others' difficulties. Their attitude towards Papa, for instance . . . Sissy had known from the first that The Family had dreaded having to confess the facts about her father and mother. Since Brother Trigg was in town again, he could not be ignored. In fact, it was highly desirable, as Uncle Charles had pointed out, that he appear at as many functions as possible, 'for the look of the thing.' But how did things look when he and his wife neither arrived nor left any social gathering together? What must Salathiel and Sophie, amiable and tolerant as they were, make of that?

It was a wonderful relief to find that they made nothing at all. They accepted the unacceptable, overlooked the ambiguous, with an indulgence so easy as to suggest to the sensitive mind that, in the past, much might have been pardoned them.

On the night after Uncle Sal's supper, which was also the night before the wedding, the series of festivities was to come to its climax with an assembly at the Lake View House in Pine Grove. The Lake View House, scene of Nancy's and Wilfred's unauthorized tryst, had, ever since its opening two years before, been a popular place of resort for Chicago young people. It was just far enough out of town to provide a goal for a drive, and though the house itself was unpretentious — a rambling, three-storeyed white wooden structure surrounded by a picket fence — it was roomy and cheerful and the grounds, sloping down in the back to the sandy lake shore, had a rather untidy charm.

During the brief days of their courtship Sissy and Aaron had often driven up with a crowd of their friends, taking a fiddler along, to enjoy an impromptu dance and a supper of scalloped oysters and chicken salad. The spot had happy associations for them both, and when Uncle Charles and Aunt Bertha — in lieu of the wedding reception itself, which Mamma still obstinately claimed as her right — asked their favourite niece what kind of party she would like them to give, she had not hesitated for an instant. Uncle Caleb, of course, disapproved; but for once Mamma did not listen to him. If Sissy wanted a dance, a dance she should have — all the more definitely because it seemed probable that soon she might never be able to dance again. The church had lately frowned on the pastime; Doctor Travers had preached several sermons on the licentious character of the waltz and the redowa; and two young matrons of Sissy's acquaintance had been summoned before the Board of Deacons and told they would have to choose between God and their worldly pleasures.

So a dance and a supper it was to be — or, rather, a supper and a dance, the normal sequence being reversed in deference to Aunt Jane, who wished to go home early without missing the collation.

The evening arrived, crisp, dark blue, and windless, with the prospect of a moon later on, quite ideal for the purpose. Sissy, who had driven out early with her uncle and aunt to superintend final preparations, glanced round the big, brightly lighted dining-room surprised to see what a numerous company was seated at the long trestle-table. The list of supper guests had been limited to the family: one could not say 'families,' for North Carolina was so remote and train connections so uncertain that, in spite of Uncle Charles's offer of railway passes, none of the Mileses had been able to come, with the exception of Mr. Miles's brother, a quiet, inconspicuous little banker from Cairo in downstate Illinois, who had managed to combine pleasure with his semiannual business trip to Chicago. Of Aunt Bertha's relations, too, only the Turnhams had, understandably, cared to make the long journey West. (Aunt Betsy had been pleased to ascertain, on their arrival, that dear Anna still had russety hair and front teeth like a rabbit, although the pug dog companion of years gone by at the Springs was naturally no longer in evidence.)

The Clan Bascomb was present in full force: Grandpa Bascomb's five living children, with their husbands and wives — Uncles Charles and Salathiel rosy and jolly, Uncle Caleb rosy and just a touch glum; Mamma and the Aunts fine in their new silk winter gowns — Mamma's black moiré with a cantilla lace fichu the happiest foil to Aunt Jane's violet, Aunt Betsy's grey, and Aunt Bertha's puce brocade and Spanish blond shawl. Aunt Sophie, of course, was more spectacular in vermilion satin sewn over with brilliants; she wore a long chain of pearls round her swarthy throat and another shorter one — though the pearls in it were equally large — wound through the dusky loops of her hair. (Coco, the monkey, had luckily been left at home.)

There were also numerous cousins, some of whom Sissy had not seen for years: the George Bascombs and their children from Beloit, the Ezra Bascombs and theirs from Springfield; old Cousin Ethan Bascomb and his daughter Selina from Stephentown, the last of the name left in the East, who were known to the Trigg girls as the 'Maple Sugar Bascombs' on account of their annual offering from the ancestral groves in the Taconic Valley. But the star of the occasion was Aunt Zilphah McCracken, Grandpa Bascomb's sole surviving sister, from Goodrich Hollow near Hebron. Aunt Zilphah was so old that no one now living could tell when she had been born. Grandpa, who she seemed to think had been cut off in his youth, had been her little brother; he had been nearly eighty at the time of his death, seven years ago. But Aunt Zilphah had been a grown woman during the Revolutionary Wars; she had danced with several of Washington's officers, and even talked with reminiscent familiarity of the Father of his Country himself. She was tiny and dried-up, but exceedingly lively, with twinkling black-marble eyes sunk deep in her skull, an amazing mobcap of a style unseen for generations, and an ear-trumpet, which she flourished energetically, but which apparently did little good, as her high, cracked 'What say?' pierced the cheerful tumult continually.

The ancestress sat, as befitted her age and position, upon Uncle Charles's right. She took something of everything that was passed her, ate everything she took, contradicted her host's opinions, and seemed to be under the impression that the Lake View House was the Charles Bascombs' own home; for Sissy heard her shrill out malevolently as they found their places: 'Land's sake, Charlie, what under the canopy do you want with a dining-room the size of this? I ha'n't set down in such a barn since your Pa sold Chancellor Hall!'

Sissy, on Uncle Charles's left, felt as if in a dream. The whole last week had glided by with mysterious swiftness; nothing that had happened in it appeared to have been quite real. Even now, with Aaron beside her, it was hard to grasp that these exciting preliminaries were taking place because she was going to be married tomorrow. Dazed as she was, however, she was conscious of a strong sense of solidarity with The Family. These were her own people: from old Aunt Zilphah to Cousin George's youngest boy, little Danny Bascomb, who was so small that he had had to sit on a book to get his chin above the table, she loved them and trusted them and wanted them always about her. It made one feel so safe, so reassuringly cared for, to have the clan back of one, didn't it? Sissy had a warm, comfortable glow at her heart as she thought of them all, such as she felt sometimes when she repeated her favourite psalm: *My cup runneth over: surely goodness and mercy shall follow me all the days of my life. . . .*

In the midst of her reverie her eyes straying down the table encountered Papa. Sissy had seen little of her father lately, and then only in crowds; they had not been alone together since the trip back from Naperville. She had not even had time to think very much about him; she had been too busy to think about anybody. But now quite suddenly, with a pang of distress, she saw him as never before.

His place tonight, between Aunt Jane and Mrs. Ezra Bascomb, if not conspicuous, was sufficiently honourable. Nobody, Sissy was sure, was bothering him, or had dared to do so since his return from the country on the new tentative terms. Yet somehow it seemed his defences were down. As he sat there gazing straight ahead, crumbling a fragment of bread in his long, nervous fingers, and making, for once, not the slightest attempt to engage either of his partners, he looked more unhappy than Sissy had ever seen him — not sulky, as sometimes; not perverse, as too often; but simply oppressed by intolerable loneliness.

This, his look seemed to say, was a Bascomb festival, in which he had no part. He was a stranger here, and always would be one. Not even Aunt Sophie, bland and begemmed as a heathen idol, appeared so utterly alien as poor Papa. . . . That, of course, one saw now, was because Aunt Sophie did not care a pin whether she were alien or not — while Papa cared supremely. For the first time Sissy understood how terribly much he cared — that the difference between him and his wife's people was quite as tragic to him as to Mamma.

Just then, as though feeling the force of her sympathy flowing towards him, Papa lifted his head and caught his daughter's glance. Raising his glass — in recognition of the festive nature of the occasion a mild claret cup had been served — he toasted her with a smile so tender and understanding that tears welled up unbidden in Sissy's eyes.

She was saved the necessity of explaining her feelings to Aaron by

Uncle Charles, who, flushed and beaming, got to his feet to propose the bride's health.

Uncle Charles was in his most expansive mood tonight. There was nothing he enjoyed more heartily than playing host to as many people as possible, and the fact that these people were all relations, or as good as relations, set the final seal on the quality of his pleasure. He overflowed with kindliness for and pride in The Family. They were all Bascombs together. It was good to be a Bascomb. Of course, some were better than others: Uncle Charles felt he might justifiably be pardoned a reference here to his late father, Captain Caleb of Chancellor Hall, who had perhaps represented, if allowance be made for a son's partiality, the quintessential characteristics of the race. In that connection Uncle Charles was reminded of an anecdote, which some of his guests were undoubtedly already familiar with, concerning Pa's childhood in the Berkshire Hills and illustrating the hazards of life in the wilderness and how sometimes the destiny of a whole family hung on so slender a thread as a baby's voice. . . . There followed the Indian Story, told at great length, with its customary conclusion: 'And do you know, if that baby had cried, my brothers and sisters and I should not be here now!'

After another long digression, during which he recited the principal events of his father's career, the speaker reverted to the main topic by declaring that, in his opinion, next best to being a Bascomb was being married to a Bascomb: this, then, with a suitable compliment to Sissy, became the theme of his discourse, addressed in some sort to Aaron, as a candidate for admission to the tribe.

The Bascombs, said Uncle Charles, were excellent citizens. Their history in this country dated back more than two centuries to the time when the original pioneer had arrived in New England, shortly after the landing of the *Mayflower*. Before that, less naturally was known of their activities; but doubtless they'd been excellent citizens of old England as well. In America it was a matter of record that they had done their full share, chopping their trees, tilling their acres, raising their families, becoming more and more numerous and thriving as they gradually spread westward over the continent. Honest men were the Bascombs, sober, God-fearing, industrious; there were no cranks and no wasters among them; they made good farmers, good merchants, good lawyers, good doctors, now and then good ministers of the Gospel (though Uncle Charles could not help feeling that their temperaments were more suited to the active than the contemplative life). The women they married were worthy of them in every way, helpmates in the true sense of the word — good daughters, good wives, good mothers, good church members all. . . . There was something in the Bascomb nature that made for domesticity — they married early, and often, if need were . . . Fortunately, in these days of enlightened medical knowledge, wives appeared more durable than in the past; Pa, for example, with his plentiful progeny, had required but one. . . . Yes, healthy, happy, hearty homes were the Bascomb rule — had been from the beginning, were now, and always would be, the Lord permitting. . . .

At this point Sissy began to feel slightly uncomfortable. Of course, Uncle Charles must be right on the whole; still she could not help remembering poor, ailing Aunt Jane and the three little Calebs, Aunt Betsy's late childless marriage and early bereavement, Uncle Sal's sulphurous past. Above all, thought Sissy, how could her uncle forget, with the principals there before him, the wretched estrangement of Papa and Mamma? Did he not see these things? Did he never stop to think that the world might not be quite so safe and well ordered as he liked to believe it? . . . Apparently not; for he went on cheerfully to wind up the personal part of his address, welcoming Aaron into The Family with a few appropriate words of commendation and encouragement . . . 'This fine young man . . . meritorious achievements . . . great possibilities . . . tender romance . . . sacred bonds . . . United they stand, facing the dawn in our new western home, where the Bascombs have staked their claim to a glorious future. . . .'

Insensibly Uncle Charles passed from the bridal pair to his favourite subject, Chicago's greatness and the part he and his had played in its early development and would, he trusted, continue to play as time rolled on. Facts and figures poured forth in an inexhaustible stream, the city's growth inescapably linked with that of The Family, till it seemed hard to tell whether Joliet or Grandpa Bascomb had discovered the Chicago River, and if the marvellously rapid increase in population were not somehow a by-product of Bascomb and Company. Chicago, concluded Uncle Charles, would inevitably be the biggest city in America. Why, some authorities even predicted that one day it might number a million souls! As their home town rose to the top of the heap, so would the Bascombs rise with it. To tell the truth, they hadn't done too badly already. Perhaps it might interest his relatives — here he exchanged a look of interrogation down the length of the table with Aunt Bertha, who nodded her stately approval — to examine the sketches of the new house he and his wife intended to build next spring in the North Division. The matter, it seemed, had been kept secret up to now, till the purchase of the land had gone through and the architect's plans been drawn up and officially approved. Uncle Charles had received the elevations from the builder Van Osdel — a most talented fellow, by the way — just in time to have them mounted to fetch along tonight as a special treat for his guests. If they would be good enough to pass the pictures from hand to hand all the way round the table . . . The front elevation . . . the rear elevation . . . the side elevation . . . the stables . . . the dairy . . . a view of the projected summerhouse from the garden gate . . .

After supper, while the room was being cleared for dancing, the small children and some of the elder ladies, Mamma and Aunt Jane amongst them, went home. Uncle Charles suggested that perhaps they would not mind taking old Mrs. McCracken back to her hotel, but when approached Aunt Zilphah refused to leave. 'No, indeedy! I'm goin' to stay and watch the young folks steppin'!' . . . As the sets were formed for the quadrille she began to cackle excitedly, and during the figures, in spite of Aunt Bertha's efforts to calm her, she kept tapping her foot in time to the music and yelling out 'Hi-my-rinktum' and 'Hoop-de-do,' much to the embarrassment of the staider sections of the company. Fortunately, not long afterwards she was discovered asleep in her corner, with her cap tilted over one eye and her ear-trumpet cast on the floor, and was sent home semi-conscious in one of the Bascomb carriages with Cousin Ethan and his daughter Selina.

Sissy caught sight of Ted Amberley's red head almost as soon as he entered the room. A number of the Trigg girls' young friends had been asked to come in after supper to swell the ranks of the dancers; Ted had evidently been among these; with Minnie Miles as his partner he was dancing in one of the sets farthest from the bride and groom. They met for the first time in the grand chain, when there was no chance to do more than smile and nod a greeting; and as soon as the quadrille was over the music changed to a waltz and Sissy, her fluffy pink organdy skirts taking the air, whirled off in Aaron's arms. Now and then during the evening she had a glimpse of her friend; he was doing his duty manfully — or perhaps more than his duty; for he laughed and chatted quite unconstrainedly with his partners.

Sissy was glad of that; there was no reason, was there, why Ted should not enjoy himself as much as he wanted to? She felt full of the kindliest feelings for the young man. She was not angry with him any more; she was not even angry with herself for what she now thought of as her ridiculous behaviour at the farm; all that had happened between them appeared misty and far away and totally unimportant. Surely, then, since her sentiments were both blameless and cordial, Ted's ought to be the same. Why could they not approach each other without confusion, and talk and laugh together as Ted seemed able to do with every girl at the Lake View House except herself? Yes — every one! Really, when she came to think of it, it was rather insulting to be so markedly ignored at her very own party. The longer she surveyed the situation, the more it annoyed her. Ted Amberley had no right to act so — none whatever! It was perfectly infuriating to be treated as if she simply did not exist. Sissy's face grew more and more flushed, her eyes larger and brighter, her laugh tinkled almost incessantly, as she observed the devoted air (which could not possibly be genuine) with which the miscreant bent over that ugly little Mary Wheelwright.

During the interval between dances she turned to Wilfred, her partner for the moment, and said crossly — she was surprised to hear how sharp her voice sounded — : 'I hadn't any idea that Ted was coming tonight.'

'Oh, hadn't you?' said Wilfred, finding a chair for his cousin with the gallant good manners that were instinctive with him (for he and Sissy had never really been friends). 'Come to think of it, though, it was rather a last-minute decision. He arrived in Chicago this morning to spend the night at my rooms, so I went over at once to Cousin Bertha's to ask permission to bring him. You've not seen him lately, I suppose?'

'No,' said Sissy, still more crossly; 'and as far as I can make out it

258

doesn't make any difference to him whether he sees *me* or not. He's not been near me all evening.'

Wilfred gave her an appraising look through his thick blond eyelashes.

'Oh, well, my dear, you're such a belle it's not easy to get a word with you, much less a dance. But I dare say he'll come round before long, don't you know. I've the next dance with my dear little Nancy — shall I tell Ted before joining her that you're expecting him?'

'I wish you would,' said Sissy, waving her fan very fast, though it was not at all hot. 'I wish you'd say I think he's behaving horridly — that I can't understand — that he ought to be downright ashamed of himself . . .'

The music began to play.

'May I have the pleasure, Miss Trigg?'

Ted Amberley was bowing before her.

Sissy bit her lip. She was engaged for this number to her cousin George Bascomb, Junior, whom she could see starting towards her from the opposite corner of the room. She rose and stood for a moment uncertain what to do. Ted held out his arms; without knowing how it happened she was in them, and they moved off to the prancing strains of the *Twinkling Star Polka*.

When they reached the doorway they danced through it into the hall; then Sissy picked up her shawl she'd left on a chair, flung it about her shoulders, gave Ted her hand, and together they passed down the steps out into the cool silence of the garden.

A few couples, it seemed, had already discovered this refuge and were strolling amongst the yellowing poplars and black scraggy pine trees that dotted the lawn leading down to the lake. Wilfred and his partner were among them — Nancy's high giggle was clearly audible somewhere in the shrubbery — but there was no use in worrying about Nancy: the child would soon be snatched out of harm's way; in less than a week she was to leave for Utica with the Turnhams.

Along the shore a full moon was rising out of the water. There was enough breeze to ruffle the surface to beaten silver; little waves lapped softly on the sand; in the distance the lights of the night boat to Milwaukee sparkled brightly, its dark shape plain to see against the sky.

Up to this, neither Sissy nor Ted had spoken a word beyond the merest greeting; but now suddenly both began to talk. They seemed to have a good deal to say to each other, but the things they said were not in the least what Sissy had hoped or expected they would be.

In fact, in no time at all they were in the midst of a quarrel.

Sissy did not know what was the matter with her. Her voice did not rise; she heard herself saying, in a reproachful wail, almost as though it were someone else talking: 'Why didn't you write? What was I to think all those weeks in New Hampshire? You might at least have given some thought to my feelings. Oh, it was selfish of you! I don't see how you could have forgotten so easily . . .'

And Ted, hoarse and angry, muttered back at her: 'It was your fault, not mine — it was your place to write! You know I told you you'd have to act. I waited and waited — but never a word! No, Sissy, *you're* to blame for what's happened — you didn't care for me as I cared for you!'

The more they said the more there was to say. Sometimes they spoke at the same time, not even troubling to answer each other. Their voices remained low and complaining; they paced back and forth on the beach, Sissy's gloved hand on Ted's arm. From somewhere very far away came the squeak of the fiddle and the rhythmic pound of feet, more remote even than the boat to Milwaukee or the great rising disk of the moon. . . . Most of the strolling couples had gone back into the house. One or two of them had ventured down as far as the waterfront, but when they saw the place was pre-empted they'd walked away again. In the midst of her bitter upbraidings Sissy had paused to resent the wiry quality of Mary Wheelwright's laugh.

It seemed a long time — though it could not really have been more than a few minutes — before they got through saying the hard, unkind things they'd apparently, unknown to themselves, been storing up in their minds for weeks. They stopped speaking at the same moment, as suddenly as they had begun, and stared at each other in dismay, while the waves went on sighing and the boat ploughed its path across the silver platter of Lake Michigan. . . .

Sissy neither knew nor cared what happened after that, until she was shocked back into a sense of reality by a rustling noise amongst the pines and the poplars. Feeling horribly guilty, she struggled away

260

from Ted's grasp; her heart was pounding; the blood sang in her ears.
. . . 'Oh, Ted! Oh, Aaron!' (If it should be Aaron . . .!)

But the man who walked out of the shrubbery into the circle of
moonlight, and stood surveying them calmly, was Papa.

Papa's Story

from Ted's face, her head bent, he could hear song in her ears.
"Oh, Ted. Oh, Ann!" they cried together...
But the man who walked out of the shrubbery into the circle of moonlight, and stood surveying them calmly, was Papa.

Mᴀʏ DEAR (said Papa), have you the key? . . . I see the lamp's still on (your mother's always thoughtful) and there's a fire in the grate. We'll poke it up a bit — so! . . . Sit down, child; are you cold? . . . That's well. I think, though, you'd best drink a thimbleful of brandy; it's a long drive down from Pine Grove. . . . I've my flask with me, as it happens. . . . Don't try to say anything yet. There's no need for you to be nervous. No one could have possibly seen you — and I told Brother Charles I'd take you home myself, if he'd a carriage to spare. . . . I said you were tired and had a headache and we thought it wiser to slip off without disturbing anybody. He understood; after all, it's quite natural, in the circumstances. . . .

There, my dear, do you feel better now? . . . The fire's burning well. Let us sit here together on the sofa and watch it. I'm going to stay a few minutes with you. It's not late, barely half-past eleven; but I hope your mother don't hear us. I saw a light in her window as we came in. Poor Julia! She looked worn-out tonight. . . . No, don't try to talk — let *me* do the talking! You said the other day — d'you remember? — that you liked to be 'told things.' Well, that's what I'm going to do now. If I never break silence again, for once in your life you'll hear the truth from me.

First of all, let's get this straight: you couldn't help what happened in the garden with Ted. Ted couldn't help it either. I know that as well as if I'd been in his place. This was bound to come, sooner or later. Of course, you tried to fight your feelings; you even ran away when all else failed to stop them; but what was the use? You *can't* stop that sort of thing. It's good, Sissy; it's the best thing that can be between a man and a woman. The trouble is, we can't command it. Without it, nothing else is worth much; but by itself, without the rest,

262

'tisn't worth much either. I ought to know: that's how it's been with your mother and me. We weren't ever happy together, and we couldn't be happy apart.

I've thought about it a great deal since coming home from California. I thought about it before, too. It was always there, like a wound in my side; but some days the pain hurt worse than others. Lately, though, I can't seem to get it out of my head. I've worried and wondered, asking myself why everything had to be as it's been and if there wasn't some way I could mend what we'd spoilt — but I don't know — it's a problem without a solution, I reckon.

It first came down on me good and hard last spring when I went to Hebron. . . . Oh, yes; I was there; didn't I tell you? That was the one thing I wanted to do when I got back from the West. I was ill in Boston after I landed — I told you that, though, didn't I? 'Twas only a cold I caught on the voyage — we had bad storms all the way north from Hatteras, and I suppose I wasn't used to such weather after so many years in a warmer climate; for I couldn't seem to fight it. It turned to inflammation of the lungs and I came as near dying as I expect I ever shall till my time's come. While I lay ill I thought continually of your mother and you girls. I felt I couldn't go without seeing you again and trying to make up for having failed you. And the queer part is, I was sure I could do it; I believed I knew the one word that would set all right. Of course, it was just the fever made me think so, for when it left me the word was gone, too.

Well, anyhow, as soon as I was fit to travel I took the stagecoach to Pittsfield, and after I'd rested there for a day or two — for I was still pretty weak — I started out to walk home. I wanted to walk all the way; it seemed vastly important then, though I can't tell now why. It was a kind of pilgrimage to the past — perhaps that was it.

I had to go fairly slowly, but on the whole I got on better than I'd feared. When I reached the top of Hebron Mountain and came over the crest where the view opens out down the valley, it struck me as never before. It was a beautiful afternoon in early May. Maybe you've not forgotten that it rains a lot in the Berkshires and the Taconics in spring, but when it's fine there's nothing to beat it. And, according to my notion, no scenery in the world equals the Hebron Valley, with its fine, cold, rushing streams and its maples and elms that seem to grow taller and thicker than trees elsewhere. The woods were just budding that day into a mist of new leaves; but what touched me most were the pastures and fields with their hedges round 'em, sweet and green to the top of the slopes right across from the road where I stood.

I stopped for a while to admire the view, and then I began to realize I'd walked enough for one day. It was getting on towards evening anyhow, so I turned down the hill to the Shaker settlement and begged them to lodge me for the night. I'd never cared much for the Shakers — cold, dismal folk they seemed to me — and I wasn't best pleased, in the old days, when your mother would drive over there with you and Nancy to see her great friend, Sister Deborah. I used to think your mother had too much of the Shaker in her make-up as it was: she'd have taken to the life only too easily — bright and busy from dawn till dark, with plenty of praying and no time for emotions. Even the houses she lives in — have you noticed? — have the regular Shaker smell — waxy-clean and soapy, as if they were scrubbed every day. But I've got to admit the Brothers and Sisters treated me well. They fed me and warmed me, bade me stay with them for as long as I cared to, and never asked a single question as to where I had come from or what I meant to do, though Sister Deborah was still there and she and some of the others must have remembered me perfectly. In the end I spent near a week on the farm, walking to and from Hebron village every day. Living so, I could do what I'd planned, without getting involved with old friends and acquaintances.

One person I *did* want to see, Sissy, was my mother — your Grandmother Trigg — but I found she'd died the year before: all I could do was lay a wreath on her grave. I shouldn't have been surprised at that; she was well past eighty when she went; but somehow I'd always counted on finding her waiting for me — it never occurred to me Mamma *could* die. Do you remember your Grandmother Trigg? . . . I'm glad you do. She was a fine woman and she was fond of you children, though she didn't get many chances to show it. When you were small I used to take you to see her in her little house on the Stephentown road, but your mother didn't like it any more than I liked her trips to the Shakers. I recall once Mamma gave you a batch of gingerbread cookies to take home with you — you couldn't have been more than three or four then — but Julia and Sister Betsy said they were too

264

rich and took them away, and you cried for an hour. Your poor grandmother! . . . Ah, well, it's all over with now. . . .

As I say, I spent almost a week in the valley. It'd been eleven years since I'd left Hebron, but places like that don't change very fast: I was able to find all the old landmarks — the Hall and the school and the various houses we'd had. The first thing I did was to go to the church at the foot of the hill where the two brooks meet, because that was where I met your mother. . . . It was the summer I was thirteen, so she couldn't have been more than nine, could she? Mamma and I had just moved to Hebron from Stephentown after my father's death. He was the doctor for all that part of the country, you know, and a good one, I've always been told. But he wasn't strong and the work was too hard; he was still young when he died, not much over forty. Mamma was poor; about all she had left was the cottage you remember, that had been in her family for years; so we had no choice but to go live in it. . . .

I was lonely at first. I missed the children I'd known at school; the five miles to Stephentown might as well've been five hundred, for all I could see of my playmates. I had no brothers, and my sisters were much older than I — they'd married and gone before we left Stephentown. . . . The first Sunday in our new home we went to church, and there I saw the Bascombs. You couldn't have avoided them very long in those days, there were so many of 'em, and Captain Bascomb, of course, was the big man in Hebron — he owned the Hall, and most of the stores in the village, and acres of land in the valley besides. They filed into their pew in a body: first your grandfather and your grandmother — he so proud and fierce (or so I thought) in a black suit and a high white stock such as gentlemen used to wear (he stuck to the mode till the day of his death); your grandmother sweet and smiling in her fine fringed mantle and feathered bonnet. Then came the children: Caleb, who was fifteen years old; Charles, maybe ten or eleven; Julia and Sal and Betsy, and, last of all, poor little Will, who was drowned not so long afterwards. Julia was in white with a white lace bonnet and her long yellow hair hanging down her back; it shone like gold where the sun through the window struck it. I thought I'd never seen such a pretty little girl. She was then very much what she is today — motherly with the little ones, and interested in everything and

265

everybody; it seemed to take a great effort of will on her part to keep her still in her seat. I saw her look at me and then nudge Betsy (a chubby little trot of four); and during the sermon, which was intolerably long and dreary — you may think Doctor Travers talks too much sometimes, but in those days an hour to an hour and a half was the rule — they both glanced across the aisle and smiled. After the service was over Mrs. Bascomb spoke to Mamma, whom she'd known by sight for years, and we children were introduced to one another.

I suppose it was expected Charles and I would be friends — and so we were, after a fashion; but we were too unlike to be really intimate. He and Caleb were well grown for their ages, and good at games; I was small and rather clumsy, mostly for lack of training. In the beginning Julia often came to my rescue; she'd berate her big brothers for laughing at me when I'd dropped a ball or done something equally stupid. I can see her yet, flying at them like a fury and hammering with her little fists on their chests as she cried: 'Nay, you *must* not make sport of Jonathan — he's doing the best he *can!*' 'Twas mainly to please her I learned to do better; for myself I never could see why games were important. But it amazes me now to look at my brothers-in-law and note how flabby they've grown, while I can still ask well-nigh what I will of my muscles. (That's no credit to me, however — it's the life I've had to lead, whether I would or no.)

Well, in spite of my awkward ways, the Bascombs were pleasant enough so that it wasn't long before I spent about as much time at their house as at my own. Julia, of course, was the great attraction for me. In summer we used to go berrying, and nutting in the fall. I reckon there isn't a copse or a stream or a meadow for miles around we haven't explored together. I'd hurry into Hebron as soon as I could after midday dinner; she'd be waiting for me, always in the same place; there was a big mossy rock under a willow tree across from her house, which you remember was the first one in town as you come in on the Stephentown pike. Every day in fine weather I'd find her on the rock; she wore a sunbonnet over her curls; it was a pink one, that first summer. . . . I don't recollect what we talked about — perhaps we didn't talk much — children can feel friendly without it, can't they? . . .

We were a good deal together in winter, too. I'd wait for her outside the school door, to carry her books home; then we'd get out the bobsled and go sliding back down the same way we'd come, past the Hall and the schoolhouse to the very floor of the valley. You can't have forgotten that slide, my dear; not so many years later it was your turn to try it. . . . And there were good times at the Bascombs' house. We'd parch corn in the evenings, and fry apples, and tell stories by the fire. The place always seemed to be full of young folks, and your grandmother was never so pleased as to see it so; she often looked as though, if it hadn't been for your grandfather, she'd have liked to join in our frolics herself. I can't help being sorry you didn't know your Grandmother Bascomb. You're very like her, Sissy — has no one told you? — much more than you are like your mother, though you've Julia's eyes and colouring, and your grandmother was dark. She was a gentle soul, with not a thought in the world apart from her husband and children. If they were contented, why, then, so was she — and I think you'll follow in her footsteps there.

Well, a year or two passed in this way, and then Julia was sent to school in Schenectady. I went away, too, on a scholarship I won at the Pittsfield Academy. Poor Mamma! She was so proud of me. It makes me feel bad to think it's really the only thing I ever did in my life that she *could* be proud of. Summers I helped pay for my schooling by working round the Hall during the season, at any odd jobs they would give me. I hadn't much leisure for play, and Julia was gone a good deal of the time, visiting her mother's people in Berlin or the McCracken cousins in Goodrich Hollow. However it happened — and it was no design on our parts — we scarcely saw each other till that winter's day, more than nine years after our first meeting, when I took her driving over the mountain. . . . But it seems to me I've already told you about that drive. . . . Yes, I thought I had.

I fell in love with your mother that night, once and forever. She was the little Julia Bascomb I'd always been fond of — but somehow she was someone quite different, too — or perhaps I saw her through different eyes. They weren't eyes blinded by love, though — I can testify to that! That's a queer thing about falling in love: while you're doing it you can see the other person just the way they are, faults and all, maybe even more clearly than if you didn't love them. Julia'd always been positive and managing in her ways: she knew what she wanted, and what she wanted *had* to be right: if the other children didn't defer to her wishes, she couldn't get on with them at all. Well, that side of her nature had developed even more strongly as she grew up. She was a headstrong young creature at eighteen, if ever I saw one.

I don't know how it happened, really — for I was as far from her ideal in character as she was from mine — but she fell in love with me almost as soon as I did with her — and in less than a fortnight we were engaged.

That was a hard time for both of us, Sissy. It ought to have been the best time in our lives, but it wasn't — there's no use in pretending. Your grandfather was violently opposed to the match. He thought that *his* daughter ought to do better — I was a nobody! The Triggs were as well born as the Bascombs, as far as that goes — and that's not saying much: we're all of good English burgher stock — honest, respectable, nothing more. But Julia was rich, or would be one day; while a poor country doctor had little to leave to his children. In spite of the education I'd managed to get there wasn't much I could do in a village like Hebron. I hadn't had the money to go to medical school like my father, or to try the law as Caleb was doing — and neither of those professions attracted me anyhow. I was a moody young fellow with a taste for music (your mother and I always sang in the choir) and literature. I spent half my spare time in the Hebron free library; good books were my passion; I soon began collecting them whether I could afford it or not. I'd rather have been a writer than anything else I can think of. I still want to write, you know, Sissy. It seems to me that perhaps . . . even now . . . I liked public speaking, too. We young men had a debating society in those days, and I always took part, especially when a political topic was foremost. The Bascombs were Democrats, so I was a Whig — not that I cared very much, one way or the other, but I was perverse enough to be pleased to take the opposite side.

As you can imagine, those tastes and talents were pretty well useless twenty-odd years ago, as they would be today, in remote up-country New York. I had to think of some means of supporting my mother and myself, and at the same time put by a bit towards my marriage with Julia. There was nothing for it but to ask my future father-in-law for a job. I clerked at his supply store winters, and worked at the Hall summers, making myself useful any way I could. The work wasn't dull, exactly, but the pay was small — I started at ten dollars a week — and there didn't seem to be any future in it. Your grand-father made it quite plain he didn't think much of my abilities and put up with them only because Julia had had the bad taste to fall in love with me.

Often I'd get so discouraged I'd feel like running away and getting Julia to run with me. I tried to persuade her to it more than once — and then she'd say I didn't love her enough to be willing to wait for her — we'd break out into the bitterest quarrels over nothing at all. It seems to me now we were quarrelling most of those three years be-fore we married. That ought to have warned us, perhaps, against taking the step, but it didn't — we were as madly in love the whole of that time as a young man and young woman could be. That's the pity of it. Julia was forever in tears and a temper, and I was as sulky and ob-stinate as a savage — a sore trial to her and my mother and everyone else, I make no doubt.

Things went better for a while after we were married. My work wasn't any more interesting, but it paid more; and at least we had a home of our own and could be together as we wanted to be. We lived just down the road from the Bascombs in that little white house with the pillars in front facing the post-office. To my mind, it's the prettiest house in Hebron, though it's not too well arranged inside — we had the ground floor only; the postmaster had the apartment upstairs — and there's almost no garden. On my walks last spring I used to stare and stare at that house, remembering how happy we were in it. You were born there, Sissy, and so was your brother Bart, who didn't live to be two (he was named for my father, Bartholomew Trigg). Then your Grandmother Bascomb was taken sick and died quite suddenly of some fever the doctors couldn't name and didn't understand how to treat. And, after that, your mother insisted on giving up our home and moving back with her father and Betsy. I did all I could to per-suade her against it, but it was no use.

We were never really happy again. At any rate, *I* wasn't; perhaps I shouldn't speak for your mother, for her contentment springs from sources other than mine. I used to wonder, though, what she could have thought of her plea that Father Bascomb needed us, that he'd be desperately lonely if we didn't come home, when I saw what a houseful there was from year's end to year's end. Sal was gone by then, and of course poor Will, too; but your Aunt Betsy was there, and so were Caleb and Jane; and Charles and Bertha spent more than half their time with us, though they had a house of their own in Albany. Then there were cousins — George and Ezra Bascomb and their wives — one couple or the other pretty constantly boarders — and the McCracken branch forever coming over from Goodrich Hollow. 'Twas nothing for us to sit down at table twenty strong.

Your mother loved it, naturally; she was in her element and ran things to suit herself. And Father Bascomb was delighted to have her back under his wing; he took a kind of petty satisfaction, too, in thinking he'd got the best of me and outwitted my desire to be free. You remember your grandfather, Sissy, I'm sure; but probably you think of him more as he was towards the end of his life, when he was broken in health and didn't care much what became of him. But let me tell you when I first knew him, and for years after that, he was a mighty mean man. He'd been too successful too young and he thought he was smarter than anybody in Columbia County. Sometimes I think he was a combination of the worst qualities in his children: he had Charles's vanity, Caleb's sanctimonious ways, your mother's hot temper — and, with it all, he was a busybody like Betsy. He had to meddle with everybody who came near him and everything they did, whether or not it concerned him.

In summer he was kept pretty well occupied over at the Hall. The Hall was his big interest in life. He'd made it himself, you might say: the springs had been known for thirty years before Father Bascomb bought them, but he was the one who built up the business till Hebron was about the most fashionable watering-place in the country. I couldn't help asking myself what he thought of that kind of life and the people who led it — he was a shrewd old Yankee, but prim and straitlaced as they come. I figure he rather despised his patrons as fools, though he liked the money they spent well enough. At any rate, he kept himself and his family as far as possible from any contact with the cure-seekers at Chancellor Hall.

I had to be at the hotel a certain amount, though my work was mostly down at the store. I used often to marvel at what it must be like to be free to come and go as one wanted, when I saw those rich men and women in their stylish clothes from New York and Philadelphia and the South. (Some even came from foreign parts as well.) They'd arrive in late spring like a flock of chattering, bright-coloured birds, pause awhile to refresh themselves in the country seclusion, and then flutter off again, Heaven knew where. . . . I'd take you up with me to the Hall once in a while, when you were big enough to walk. Do you remember it at all, I wonder? . . . Yes? Then maybe you haven't forgotten how the cooks in the great kitchen, Alphonse and his helpers, would make much of you; they'd always give you a cake or a sweetmeat if your mother weren't by to forbid it. What you liked best, though, was to promenade through the upstairs corridors with the housekeeper, old Mrs. Twitchett, when the ladies' maids were carrying their mistresses' fine gowns out to air — the swish of the perfumed silks was something you never tired of. Once I let you ride on the back of Black Prince, the huge stallion your grandfather kept to help haul the coaches up the steep hill to the Hall door. You loved that, too. I walked beside him to catch you, if need be; but you weren't afraid; you laughed and clapped your hands to see how high you'd got in the world. Then Father Bascomb came stamping out of his office in a towering rage and put a stop to *that*.

On the whole, though, near as we were to that gaiety, we might have lived on another planet for all we saw of it. And when the cold weather came everyone left, the Hall was shut up, and Hebron settled down to its long winter nap. The winters were the worst, Sissy. They're bad enough, Lord knows, in Chicago; but here on the plains there's always the hope of a change. It snows, or it doesn't — and in between storms it's often quite mild. But up in the hills we always knew when the snow came in November it came to stay. It folded down like a mantle over everything — blotting out houses and roads and fields — so that all that was left was the soft, sparkling whiteness. At first it looked beautiful, but after a while — ah, God, how I hated it! 'Twas a common occurrence for the village to be cut off for weeks from the outside world, and there'd be days at a time we'd hardly dare venture out of the house. Father Bascomb killed a cow and a pig at the beginning of every winter, and salted them down; chickens, of course, were plenty; and we'd all the preserved fruits and vegetables your mother and Betsy put up in the summers. So there was no danger of starvation — it was something else than food I went hungry for then.

Our life revolved round the kitchen. It was the only room in the house that could be kept decently warm, so we made it our winter parlour and sat there every day — all together, eternally together. I hadn't much excuse to get away, for work would be slack at the store then, and Father Bascomb preferred to have me at home, to go over accounts and be scolded for blunders. I can see us now, Sissy, as plain as though 'twere yesterday, sitting about that low, brown-raftered room — terribly stuffy it was, and as hot as fire from the coals in the stove. It was dark, too, once the sun started setting behind the hills; we made our own tallow candles, you know, and Father Bascomb kept strict account of them — if more had been used at the end of the week than he thought fitting, there was the devil to pay. Of course, *he* had two of 'em just for himself, to read the Pittsfield papers by — he took the *Argus* and the *Register,* conned them from first word to last, and wouldn't allow anyone to touch either one till he was through with both — though like as not he'd fall into a doze halfway along in his task. (He wore a black skull-cap with a tassel on top to ward off the cold; when he slept his head nodded and the tassel would tickle his nose till he woke — but he'd never let Julia cut it off.)

Your mother and aunts would be sewing, most likely — quilting a dress for one of the children — by that time Nancy'd been born, and your poor Aunt Jane always had hopes. . . . Caleb and Charles'd come in after a while, stamping the snow off their feet. Your grandfather'd rouse up to listen to them — he never bothered to stay awake for *me* — but they always had something of interest to tell him about this smart trick they'd played in their business, or that lucky turn. Presently Betsy would join the party; perhaps she'd bring in some butternuts or a plate of corn to parch, and she nearly always had some of her girl cousins visiting her — silly, giggly creatures they were, as like Betsy as so many plump, dough-faced dolls. Then they'd all go on talking for hours, just as though they'd never seen one another before. I used to lay wagers with myself that they would talk themselves out some day — but they never seemed to. They *enjoyed* one another so much. That was what most impressed me. And allowing for little differences in temperament here and there, they were so much alike in

272

their ways. They thought the same thoughts about money and business and food and clothes and people and God. It seemed, though, to give them untold pleasure to say what they thought — even if nobody disagreed with them — over and over again.

Once in a way there'd be a break in the routine. There was the year the stables burnt at the Hall, or the time the old minister died and the new minister came. And one fall the Anti-Renters rode over from Albany and frightened everybody almost to death with their hideous masks and their Indian war-whoops. (I sat up all night with you children then.) But on the whole in the four years I lived with your grandfather there wasn't a break in the deadly monotony. Lord! It was terrible. . . . I sat there day after day and night after night, trying to shut my ears to the babble and concentrate on my book (the Bascombs didn't read books), saying never a word except to your mother, unless I were directly addressed. I knew they thought me a churlish fool, but I couldn't help it. Father Bascomb had despised me from the first, and the others took their cue from him. They weren't unkind by design, you know; often they didn't know when they'd hurt me. But your mother knew; it must have been hard on her. . . . I'd think of that and then I'd try to do better, for her sake; but Caleb would make some scornful remark, or Father Bascomb'd tread on my toes — and I'd be worse than ever. I was an obstinate fellow, and wretched enough to be willing to snatch at any straw to make my escape.

You know how I did it at last. When Charles bought that shipping company on the lakes it seemed like a sign from Heaven. He'd been dissatisfied, too, for some time; he was too smart a man to remain in Hebron; even Albany couldn't contain him. It was a wonderful stroke of luck for me that he wasn't able to go West when he wanted to. Caleb didn't know about anything outside of his own law business, so there was nothing to do but take a chance on me. I doubt not Charles thought he was taking a terrible risk — if he'd felt the company had any particular future, I suppose he'd never have sent me. As it was, he spent hours impressing instructions upon me: when I left for Chicago I had a portfolio of letters telling me what to do and whom to see and how to go about everything, though Charles had never been there and was as ignorant as I of conditions in Illinois. But I was too wild with joy at getting away to be depressed by his officious ways. I was sorry to leave your mother, of course — she was still nursing little Louise and it didn't seem wise for her to attempt the trip — but, aside from that, I judge there couldn't have been a happier man in all York State, that hot August day twelve years ago, than your father.

I was thirty-six years old and had never been out of my native state before, except just over the line to Pittsfield — not often even out of my native valley — ; so you can imagine what an adventure it seemed to me. I felt a load slide from my shoulders the minute I boarded the stagecoach to Albany, and once I'd struck the prairies I was a new man. It was all fresh and free and unspoilt. I didn't mind the rawness and roughness — Chicago wasn't much more than a village then. . . . Perhaps you remember a little what it was like, for you saw it the next year. There weren't above ten or twelve thousand people here; it was a frontier settlement and it looked it — crude and unfinished, a huddle of little wood houses along the river, the muddy streets full of horses and oxen and wagons and — pioneers, I guess you would call 'em. Men had come from all over the country to make their fortunes — and they made 'em sure enough, some pretty quickly, too. You felt it was a town with nine-tenths of its history in the future. Anything was possible in Chicago.

I liked it from the first. I got on all right with my work — there wasn't much could be done, really, till Charles was able to come out himself, but go over the accounts and see that the men in charge of the office did what they were paid to do. I missed my wife and children terribly; a Clark Street boarding-house was cold comfort at night, and a year's a long time to be lonely. Still, on the whole, it was a happy year for me. Before it was done I wrote to your mother to tell her I wanted to live in Chicago. Charles was disposed to give me employment; it seemed the one chance I might ever have to shake off my shackles; I couldn't but think that, if only I got my family clean away from the Bascombs, we might be a lot better off. . . . Your mother was willing, she said. It would be a wrench for her, but she saw my point — and when I went back to Hebron I knew it wouldn't be for long.

You know what happened then, Sissy. I hadn't been home twenty-four hours before Julia told me the whole family was moving. As ill luck would have it, 'twas just then Father Bascomb had a good offer to buy the Hall; he'd grown pretty old since his wife's death and the work was really too much for him; besides, he claimed he couldn't face being parted from his favourite daughter at the end of his life. If he came, Betsy would have to come, too. Charles and Bertha, it seemed, had been thinking of going West for some time; and of course Caleb and Jane couldn't bear to be the only ones left behind.

So, by thunder! there was an end to my hopes. I was to get out of prison right enough, but my jailers were all coming with me. Once I found that out the whole thing was ruined. I went through with my plans, of course, but I took no more joy in them.

It was a shock to Sissy when Papa stopped talking. The big centre log in the fireplace had suddenly fallen in two, releasing a flight of sparks up the chimney. Papa rose to replenish the wood; then he laid his hand on her shoulder. . . . 'Are you tired, my dear? Is it time you were abed? Shall I have done with my nonsense?'

Sissy shook her head.

'Oh, no, Papa — please go on! I want to hear everything. I'm not tired at all.'

Papa smiled.

'Well, if you're not, I am, a little. I'll pause for another sip of this brandy. It's fine mellow stuff; that French fellow in Clark Street has cases of it in his cellar. Will you have some more?'

Sissy shook her head a second time. She did not like to confess she had never tried brandy before; it had brought her to a comfortable glow, but she had no further need of it.

Papa filled his glass and raised it to his lips, but did not seem in a hurry to drink it. Instead he came back to the sofa and resumed his seat by Sissy, cupping the glass in his hands and turning it gently to warm the contents. The fire was crackling now, the new log having quickly caught alight. Papa began staring at it again, as he had been doing all the time he'd been telling his story. It was as if he *had* to hold his eyes there in order to tell it. Sissy, however, looked straight at Papa.

You remember our trip, don't you? (Papa continued.) . . . Somehow the part that's most vivid to me is the week we spent on the Erie Canal. I can see the boat now — it was white with green trimmings — and you and Nancy playing about on the deck, wearing the checked calico sunbonnets your mother had made you. Julia held the baby most of the time — she was terrified for fear that plump roly-poly would slip overboard — but you two elder girls were all over the place, making friends with everyone from the captain down. Your grandfather was up on deck, too — for it was mortal stuffy below in the cabin — smoking his pipe and staring at the scenery, which is fair enough at midsummer in that part of New York. It was strange to see him idle. He'd sit in one position for hours, not talking at all, gazing backward, always backward, as if he were trying to look at his old life. I never looked back myself; it seemed to me the one thing *not* to do. I strained my eyes ahead, hoping to catch a glimpse of some brightness in our future. . . .

Well, we got to Chicago eventually, as you know, and settled down in the grey stone house by the river. From here on I expect you'll be able to call to mind most of the story yourself, for you were seven years old when we moved and a bright child for your age. I've noticed, though, Sissy, that you're not one to dwell on the past. I've scarcely ever heard you mention those times; you're content to live in the present and face each day as it comes — and maybe you're none the worse off for that.

It must have been a complete change for you, after living all your short life up to then in a little hill village remote from the world; but it didn't take you long to get used to things. It didn't take any of The Family long except Father Bascomb. Your grandfather never cared for Chicago; he was too old and too broken in health to adapt himself to new conditions. The next few years he was gradually failing; when he actually died it didn't seem sad, even to his children who loved him, for the best of him had already been buried in Hebron. . . . But my brothers-in-law took to the place as ducks take to water. They'd been there hardly a week before Caleb had found a law partner and hung out his shingle: in less than a month Charles had Bascomb and Company organized and going full steam ahead — he knew every man in town worth knowing and was talking already of running for alderman and starting the Board of Trade. They took hold of the church as well; we'd had letters to the minister from our minister at home. . . . Charles got himself elected treasurer right away, and Caleb was put on the Board of Deacons, and they've run things between them pretty much ever since.

Mind you, my dear, I'm not criticizing your uncles. I admire their spirit of enterprise; I always have. Men like the Bascombs are the salt of the earth, I suppose. They're right and they know it. Sometimes it seems they're able to make things be as they want them to be through the sheer force of their belief in themselves. They tell the world something is so — they convince themselves first, then others — and before you know it, by God! it *is* so, in the face of all reason and probability. I've no quarrel with them for that. Where your uncles and I part company is over *my* place in their scheme. They've simply no use for my kind of person. They've no use for anyone who can't think as they think and won't live as they live. It took me a very few weeks in the office of Bascomb and Company, after Charles's arrival, to realize I'd made a fearful mistake. It was worse even than working for your grandfather. Charles thought I was a cipher, a fool — and because he thought so I *was* so. He didn't bother to get angry with me; I could have stood it better if he had. I was given only the most trivial tasks to perform, but truly I understood why: I wasn't capable of anything more while his easy, contemptuous eye was upon me.

I'd have looked for a job with some other firm if I could have thought of something I was fit to do — but what had I been trained for? I wasn't so young any more, and I hadn't been able to save enough through the years to go into business for myself: it took all I earned to keep my family and send a bit home each month for my mother's support besides. I'd have liked to have tried to write — but how could I have lodged you and fed you while I tried? It was a bad time for me, Sissy. . . . I had Charles's disdain to bear all day, and at night and on holidays the same old crowded community life I'd hoped to escape forever. Sister Betsy lived with us permanently; she was beginning to be afraid she was going to be an old maid and her temper was very uncertain; she was the same Paulina Pry then that she's always been. Father Bascomb was with us most of the time, too. He was supposed to divide the year amongst his three children with houses, but Julia made him more comfortable than his daughters-in-law and he liked her best — I won't say 'loved' of that selfish old man. And, of course, Caleb and Charles and their wives were continually coming to see us — unless we were going to see them.

All in all, I was more miserable then than ever I'd been in my life.

I just didn't know what to do. I felt caught in a trap. At first I thought I might go back to Hebron, but we'd cut our ties — there was really nothing to go back to. . . . I used to take long walks by myself in all kinds of weather — along the lake shore or over the windy prairie — trying to think things out, so I could make up my mind how to act. But what finally gave me my great idea was something I saw in my own back yard. . . . I remember your mentioning once this summer how you and Nancy, as children, used to see travellers camped in the empty field next our house on the river — how you watched them tether their beasts and build fires by the wagons and cook supper there in the open, on their way to the western plains. . . . Ah, my dear, I wonder if you know how often *I* used to watch them, too! Night after night I'd stand at the fence, staring at the flames flickering in the dusk, and trying to understand why it was that those poor wretches looked so cheerful, in spite of the discomforts they were enduring and the dangers they must have known lay ahead.

I can hardly say how it happened, but one day it came to me — not as a new idea, but as if it were something I'd known all about for weeks — : *I* wanted to travel on, too. I felt I'd had the right idea in going West — the trouble was, I hadn't gone far enough. For those campers Chicago wasn't the goal; it was just a stepping-stone on the way to it; and so it ought to have been for me.

It was just then we left the house on the river (because your mother thought it was damp for your grandfather) and took this place instead. There was a bit of carpentering to be done before we could move in, and Eben Jenkins was the man I engaged for the job. . . . It didn't take long for us to find out what was in each other's minds; he had the same overmastering desire that I had, only he'd nursed it a lot longer and was nearer its realization; for, though he was poor, he was single — whatever he made he could save towards the journey.

Well, we talked and talked. . . . I wasn't alone on my walks any more — and soon enough your mother got wind of what was up. I hadn't meant to keep it a secret; only there didn't seem to be any use in mentioning it till we saw our way clear. . . . Poor Julia was terribly upset. She was perfectly happy here; she didn't see why I couldn't be, too.

I tried to explain how I felt, but she just couldn't understand. That's always been what ailed our marriage: we love each other, we feel the right things in our hearts — but when it comes to thinking we're miles asunder. She can't see life through my eyes any more than I can through hers.

Of course, she said at once she couldn't leave your grandfather; that settled it for her. I'd feared as much; but it was plain by then the old man was failing and wouldn't last another winter. If cholera hadn't carried him off, something else would have. . . . After he was gone I broached the subject again. It seemed to me now was the time to go. Julia had inherited something from Father Bascomb, so we were in easier circumstances. And Betsy was still unmarried; she'd have been glad to take charge of you children. Besides, Eben was wild to be off — he was going anyhow — all that held him back was his wanting me to join him, less for the bit of money I could contribute than for the sake of my company.

It was a risk, I know — but I thought it worth taking. Lots of men took their wives to California. Neither of us was old yet, and we were both as strong as could be. That was what drove me mad, Sissy — to feel all that life surging inside me, and to have no outlet for it. . . .

But Julia wouldn't say yes. I used every argument I could think of to persuade her. We quarrelled more in those weeks after your grandfather's death than we had since the days of our engagement, long ago. Caleb and Charles were in on it, too — of course, Julia got them to help her — it seemed we were bickering, bickering all day and half the night, without getting anywhere.

The end came quite suddenly in April. It was raining hard, I remember — it was one of those dreary spring days we have so often in Chicago, with a cold wind off the lake — the trees looked black and their leaves wouldn't bud and the sidewalks were slimy and crawling with earthworms. I came in from the office early that evening to find Julia on the sofa, just where we are sitting now. The fire was burning briskly like this one, with a sound like a fluttering flag — your mother's fires always burn so. . . . She was alone, for a wonder, making a cloak for one of you children. I've never seen her sit idle, have you? . . .

She looked up as I came in, with a blue glint in her eyes that meant trouble; and we were at it again in no time. We'd gone over the ground so often before — yet somehow we couldn't stop. Finally I said to her: 'Then you're sure you won't go? That nothing I can say or do will make you change your mind? You won't go, though you know it means the world to me — that it's perhaps the last chance we'll ever have to be happy together?'

'No, I won't go,' said your mother. 'That's flat and that's final. 'Twouldn't be right to leave the girls — besides, I'm quite contented as I am. But since *you're* not, Jonathan, why shouldn't you go West without me? You say you'll die if you don't go — very well, *go!* I'll not stop you. You may as well do it as stay here as you are, dragging around half alive, no good to yourself or anybody else. If Charles weren't my brother, I wonder how long he'd keep you at Bascomb and Company? Oh, I could die with shame when I think . . .'

She stopped talking then for a minute and bit off her thread with a snap. Your mother had never assailed me directly before. Though I couldn't help knowing I'd been a disappointment to her, she hadn't said so; in our family disputes she always took my part loyally. But I suppose she'd had too much to bear; her nerves snapped then as well as the thread. She flung me a glance full of scorn as she cried: 'My brothers were right about you from the first. You've been a failure at everything you ever tried to do — why should I believe 'twill be different now? Do what you will, Jonathan — what you *must* (if you'd rather put it that way) — but for Heaven's sake leave me and my children in peace!'

That was the end for us, really. I've never forgotten those words. . . . Oh, she was sorry as soon as she'd said them. She tried to make it up to me afterwards — we spent the night crying and kissing and telling each other we loved each other. But it was over just the same, and we both knew it. When I left for Independence to join Eben Jenkins I wasn't sure I'd ever see my family again. I didn't even trust myself to say good-bye to you children: on account of the cholera you'd been sent to the country with your Aunt Jane, who was mortally afraid of infection; and I thought it best not to disturb you. . . . Sissy, you know the rest of the story. You mustn't think I forgot you all those years I was away in the West. My heart ached with loneliness — time and again I longed to send for my wife and my daughters — but always when it came to the point I'd recall the look in your mother's eyes as she begged me to leave you in peace. It wasn't till I was well established in Sacramento that I felt I could safely come back and fetch you — and you saw how much good that did me. Maybe the Bascombs *are* right — but hang it! that doesn't make *me* wrong, does it? My way of life suits me as well as their way suits them — why can't they admit it instead of pretending my way's just no way at all?

I don't want to stay here and fall back into the treadmill — and, what's more, I *won't* do it, no matter what happens. . . .

Now, Sissy, I am sure you see why I've told you all this. You've a problem to face in your marriage, just as I had. I've nothing to say against Aaron — I know as well as you do he's a fine young man. But what chance have you to be happy with him, unless your family is willing to let you alone to work things out for yourselves? And they *won't* be willing. I solemnly swear to you, they'll wreck your life as they wrecked mine — with the best of intentions, of course. You know already what I think of the plan of your mother and sisters to move in with you after the wedding, so I shan't have to repeat it. How much liberty do you fancy you'll have under those circumstances? Why, Brother Caleb himself told me tonight that you weren't to leave on your honeymoon till the day after the ceremony — you're to spend the first night of your married life here in this house, because, forsooth! he don't think it 'proper' for you to be in such great haste to quit it.

Sissy! Sissy! Can't you see where such submission will lead you? Open your eyes, child, before it's too late!

Now all this wouldn't matter so much if you were truly in love with young Miles. But I can't feel you are; I doubt if *you* feel it either. You accepted him because you're both young and good-looking — 'twas time you were married — and he was there next door, the first man who ever wanted you in that way. I don't say you're not fond of him — I presume you are — or that you won't make him an excellent wife. You'd make *any* man an excellent wife, my dear — you're a pattern of the domestic virtues, like the grandmother whose name you bear. . . . But it's Ted Amberley you care for, isn't it? From the first I've seen he had the power to move you, struggle against it as you would. I hoped in the summer you'd see for yourself what a great mistake you were making and would right it while yet there was time to do so easily. After you went away from Naperville I abandoned that hope. I've been in two minds ever since as to whether to bring it up

281

again; but now, after what's happened tonight, I *must* speak, for it's still not too late, is it, Sissy?

With Ted, you see, you'll have a chance for freedom, such a chance as won't come twice to you. I know you don't care for the life he's chosen, but, however things go, at least it *will* be life, not a deadly tedious imitation. . . .

I'm so sure of your choice that I've already made my plans to help you. . . . I've grown much attached to Ted — I believe in his future — and you know how I feel about you, my darling. . . . I've never called you so before, have I? But that's what you are. Mrs. Amberley was quite right when she guessed you meant more to me than my other children. Parents ought not to have favourites — but how can I help it? I've always loved you. You are my eldest; you were born in our first home where your mother and I were happy. Nancy may look like me, but all the same she's more of a Bascomb than you. Your likeness to them is a surface thing; you're capable of loving without recking the cost — that's something none of The Family could ever understand. . . .

My dear, listen carefully: this is what I can do for you, if you want me to, mind — only if you want me to! . . . Tomorrow I'm going to drive you to church — but we needn't stop at the church — we can go straight on to the station, where Ted will meet us. Then by train to Naperville, where you can be married. (It's the county seat, you know, and I'm your father, your legal guardian, so there'll be no trouble about that.) Afterwards you young people can stay at the farm until Ted is ready to go West. I'll engage to make your peace with your family. They'll be terribly angry, of course — but what can they do? In the end they'll have to forgive you. . . . Yes, it *will* be hard on Aaron — but surely it's better to do this than find out too late you've made a mistake and ruined three lives instead of damaging one temporarily. . . . How will you manage for money? Ah, my dear, that's where *I* come in! I dare say you've wondered before this why I've given you no wedding present. It's not that I haven't meant to, only that I've been waiting to see what you most needed. . . . And now I think I know. . . . I told you the other day I'd written to Sacramento to try to dispose of my interests; only this week I heard the deal has gone through. They weren't worth a powerful lot of money, but I

282

have realized three thousand dollars — and those three thousand dollars are yours, my dear, and Ted's, with your father's blessing. It's not a great fortune by any means, but 'twill be enough to tide you over till Ted can get established somewhere. I know that, for I've been through the same experience myself. . . .

No, I shan't need the money. . . . No, I don't want to go back. California is finished for me — it was finished the minute I saw your mother wasn't willing to try it. . . . Not another word, child — you're tired out — I know it — Off to bed with you! Rest as well as you can and think over all I've told you. There'll be plenty of time in the morning to tell me what you decide. . . . We'll leave the fire as it is, shan't we? — the lamp burning and the door on the latch, for our night-owl Nancy's not home yet. . . . Come, my dear, I am going upstairs with you. I see there's still a light in your mother's room and, late as it is, I must talk to her. . . . What's to become of *me?* Ah, Sissy, that I can't answer. My fate's not in my own hands as yours is. It depends on another; so it has done for more years than I care to count. . . . Pray for me, child, as I'll pray for you. May God in His Infinite Wisdom and Mercy show us each the right path to follow. . . .

Papa did not knock: slowly, almost fearfully, but as if moved by a strong inner compulsion, he turned the handle of Mamma's door.

The Wedding

NEXT MORNING the stir of excitement concerning the wedding was eclipsed momentarily by the appearance of Papa at the breakfast-table. However, once the first shock was over it seemed perfectly natural to find him, clad in dressing-gown and slippers, in his accustomed place: after all, it had been his *not* being there that had upset the whole summer. Mamma even took it so much for granted that she did not refer to it, but poured out her husband's coffee with the children's quite as a matter of course. . . . Mamma, though, did not look triumphant (as Sissy felt would have been her right); her face was white and drawn and she complained of a headache, as always when the wind blew from the southwest. (Oh, those prairie gales! It was unseasonably warm again, but there was hope that the breeze might calm down before night.)

While they still lingered at table there was a knock at the door and Aunt Betsy bustled in to discuss details of the forthcoming feast. Aunt Betsy, much to her chagrin, had been forced this week to move to the Tremont, where she was stopping with the Caleb Bascombs: her room at the Triggs' would be needed for Sissy and Aaron. Nevertheless, it was impossible for her to stay away from the principal theatre of activity; she 'dropped in on Julia' early and late, and her visits were seldom unrewarded by material for gossip — Sissy's latest wedding present, Nancy's current impertinence; at the very least, if all else failed, some winter fashion note gleaned from omniscient Miss Tweedy, the seamstress.

This morning, of course, the plum was toothsome indeed. Aunt Betsy's eyes were popping: it cost her obviously an almost superhuman effort to refrain from commenting on Brother Trigg's return to the fold. At any rate, Sissy reflected, Papa's action had had one beneficent result, since their caller, instead of lingering as was her custom, could hardly choke down a belated cup of coffee fast enough before scuttling away to retail the fascinating news that there was nothing to the business with that outlandish Frenchwoman. . . . 'Jonathan's been spending the night at Julia's and I miss my guess if he's not come home to stay.' . . .

After breakfast Papa dressed himself in a suit Mamma found for him in the ancient store of habiliments she had stowed in the spare-room cupboard. Before going out he approached Sissy, who was standing unhappily in the hall; no question was asked, but it was only too easy to interpret the inquiring look he gave her. In reply she could do nothing but shake her head foolishly and beg for a further reprieve. . . . 'Not yet, Papa. I haven't had time . . .'

Her voice died away; it sounded absurd; she hated herself for her irresolution. But Papa, who understood everything without need of words, nodded as if satisfied, kissed her affectionately, and departed, saying that he would see her later.

'I shall be busy all day today,' said Papa. 'I've business myself to attend to, you know.'

Sissy could imagine what it might be. . . . With a moan she pressed her hands to her temples. Surely Mamma's head was not aching so hard as her own! . . . 'I must think — I must think!' . . . But what if one were not able to think? Besides, thought in this case had been powerless to guide her. She had lain awake half the night reviewing Papa's story from beginning to end and debating the course she ought to pursue, without coming any closer to a decision than she had been before. Papa had really not helped. He had done nothing more than state the problem — that was something, but not enough. How could she choose between Aaron and Ted? Whomever she took, would there not be inevitable bitterness, perhaps lifelong regret? What was right? What was wrong? . . . When at length towards morning she had fallen into troubled slumber it had been with the earnest prayer on her lips that the Lord might answer the question while she slept — that she might wake in the morning resolved to do her duty, and sure what her duty should be. . . . 'If not,' thought poor Sissy, 'then it were better I never woke at all!'

But the Lord had refused to answer her prayer. Her wedding day was here; the hours were passing only too quickly; soon it would be time for her to put on the shining white dress and the long tulle veil already laid on her bed like an armful of glistening cobwebs . . . and she still didn't know . . . Oh, God, what to do?

Her usually brilliant colour had deserted her; she was so nervous that she was unable to eat; she started to faint whenever she tried to stand up. There was nothing for it but to stay in her room until she succeeded in gaining control of herself.

Fortunately, in the circumstances, her behaviour could attract no unfavourable comment. In fact, Mamma and the Aunts seemed to think it most becoming in a bride. As the day wore on they hovered about her devotedly, suggesting various remedies — *eau de cologne* on her forehead; hot mustard baths for her feet; sal volatile; brandy cocktail; beef, iron, and wine. . . . Finally Aunt Jane fluttered down to the kitchen to brew her niece a cup of tansy tea so nasty that, rather than drink it, Sissy sat up and declared she felt better.

Having said so, she found she had spoken the truth without knowing it. Late in the afternoon, though still pale, she had recovered her forces sufficiently to trip downstairs to receive old Aunt Zilphah Mc-Cracken and Cousin Selina, who had come to inspect the wedding presents.

With pardonable pride Sissy ushered her visitors to the upper hall, where her treasures were passed in review: a velvet-bound, gold-embossed Bible from Mr. and Mrs. Miles; a handsome set of china from Mamma and the girls; the Caleb Bascombs' linen; the Charles Bascombs' flat silver; a gilded and faintly funereal urn from Aunt Betsy. . . . Uncle Sal's and Aunt Sophie's gold-mesh chatelaine bag was so thickly encrusted with emeralds and diamonds that Cousin Selina — a flat-chested spinster with a sallow face and incipient beard — croaked her quavering disapproval. But Aunt Zilphah, who had been raised in a more robust era, paying small heed to the lavish array, cocked her head to one side like an inquisitive hen, rolled her terrible old eyes, and cackled: 'I'll wager the child ha'n't no taste for such trophies today — she's busy dreaming of her handsome bridegroom and the joy that he'll bring her — hey, my poppet?' Thereupon she exploded into a shrill volley of most unseemly mirth.

As soon as the old ladies were gone it was time for Sissy to dress.

This was a momentous operation, entailing the attendance of Mamma, Aunt Jane, and Aunt Betsy, who stood stiffly about, not daring to sit for fear of crushing their festal brocades, while Miss Tweedy assumed command. The plump little seamstress had pervaded the house all day like an uneasy spirit, pleading through a mouth full of pins for a final fitting, 'just in case, my dear, that there bodice don't sit as intended it should.' Now at last her word was supreme: none of the ladies breathed as the gleaming lengths of silk were clasped round Sissy's slim waist, the airy tulle cloud pressed into place with the crown of orange blossoms Mamma had been holding in readiness. . . . There stood the bride — Sissy still, yet Sissy no longer — a veiled, mysterious figure. . . . No one spoke for a minute; then Miss Tweedy flung up her hands in admiration of her own handiwork and exclaimed: 'There you are, ma'am — not a hairsbreadth out, is it? I declare if I didn't calculate exactly right! Turn around, miss, and look at yourself in the glass — elegant, ain't it, dear?'

Loulie in her flower girl's costume came running to report that the carriages were drawing up at the door. Uncle Charles, it appeared, had sent the barouche and the landau for the bride's own family; while the great char-à-banc, unused since Grandpa Bascomb's funeral, had been put into commission again to accommodate the rest of the party.

Sissy, however, was to drive to church alone with her father in a brougham hired especially for the occasion. Papa had made the request himself at breakfast, quite casually, but with such tender warmth in his voice that Mamma had not known how to refuse him.

No one had seen Papa since early morning. From time to time Sissy had speculated as to where he might be. When the hour arrived to dress for the wedding and he had still not come back, she began to ask herself anxiously whether perhaps, in spite of his promises, he had not flown for good. . . . Later she realized that of course he would have had to dress at the hotel, where his trunks were.

She walked downstairs very slowly, with a train of relations behind her — 'Mind the newel-post, dear — watch out for your skirt! — the bottom step's not solid, remember!' — to find her father waiting in the hall below. As he looked up, brushed and glossy and dapper in his fine frock coat, Sissy had an odd feeling that *he* must be her bridegroom — it seemed somehow as if she were going to marry Papa! How absurd that was!

'I've come for my girl,' said Jonathan Trigg.

The babble of the relatives burst forth again: 'Here's your cloak — take care not to rumple your veil — Don't drive fast, Mr. Trigg, whatever you do . . .'

Just as Sissy was leaving Nancy ran out of the parlour to embrace her sister. Looking radiantly pretty in her corn-coloured silk, she smiled and blushed as she cried: 'The last kiss, Sis — the very last, you know, before . . .' Then, suddenly, she choked and could say no more, while the bright brown eyes filled with tears. . . . Long after most of the events of her wedding day had faded in her memory Sissy could recall at will that sob and the warm, impulsive kiss.

The wind had fallen, as Mamma had hoped; only the tops of the elm trees rustled dryly overhead. It was a dark, starless night, strangely mild for so late in the year. Papa handed Sissy into the brougham and then followed her, after saying to the driver, in his peculiarly distinct tones: 'The First Baptist Church, if you please.'

Inside he turned to his daughter and added: 'That's right, isn't it, my dear? Or have I made a mistake? If so, it is easily rectified.'

The brougham smelled strongly of leather and horses, as all hired vehicles did. (Uncle Charles's carriages, on the other hand, thought Sissy inconsequently, were stuffy with fumes of the camphor used to discourage moths.) They clip-clopped deliberately towards the corner. Half a short block south on State Street, and three long blocks west on Washington . . . three blocks and a half to decide one's whole life. . . .

Papa's eyes were shining in the dark.

'Well, Sissy?' he said.

Sissy flung him a desperate look. In spite of the heat she felt chilled through: the words she spoke seemed not to be chosen, but to force their way out of her mouth of their own volition.

'Oh, Papa, I can't — I *can't* go through with it! It's too late. Think of poor Aaron — Doctor Travers — the people waiting in church — our wedding journey all arranged — the house on Wabash Avenue! How could I do such a terrible thing? And the supper, Papa — have

288

you forgotten that? There's a whole ham and a turkey, you know — who would eat it if I . . . if I . . .?'

Papa chuckled grimly. 'Yes, I imagine it might be wasted. That would be awful, Sissy, wouldn't it?'

'And then,' said Sissy, still shivering, 'and then, Papa, what if Ted and I didn't love each other enough to make up for the rest? You see, we really don't know each other very well, do we? What if things didn't go smoothly with us in California? We've no assurance of that, have we, Papa?'

'No,' replied Papa slowly. 'No; we've no assurance of that.'

He said nothing more; neither did Sissy for a minute. The carriage creaked round the corner into Washington Street; there was very little traffic at night in this part of town.

'But that's not all,' Sissy continued, finding it easier to explain than she had feared. 'There's The Family, too: how can I bear to disappoint them? How could I live without their approval? They love me and believe in me, and I love them — I can't help it — I know I'm not brave enough to face the future cut off from all contact with what's been my whole life. I *need* The Family, Papa, just as much as they need me. Oh, I *wish* it didn't mean failing you and Ted! I wish I could do what *everyone* wants! But I can't — there's no way — someone *has* to be left out!'

'That's true,' said Papa, very quietly — Sissy was astonished to see how little fuss he was making — ; 'someone has to be left out, of course. I was a fool to imagine for even a moment that it might be the Bascombs. . . . Then everything's settled, I take it? Don't worry, child; it'll all be all right.'

The brougham stopped in front of the church. Before the cabman had time to climb down from the box Papa sprang out and helped his daughter alight. Overwrought as she was, Sissy noticed with surprise that there was a crowd assembled round the steps, a crowd not of people she knew. How queer that strangers should care to stand there for hours in the dark, just to catch a glimpse of Sissy Trigg on her way to be married at the first church wedding in Chicago!

Smiling a little uncertainly, she laid her gloved hand on Papa's arm and mounted the steps to where Aaron was waiting.

Sissy had been Mrs. Aaron Miles for almost two hours. The party was nearly over: the candles were burning low on the deserted supper-table; the ham had been slashed to the bone; scarce enough turkey was left to make one of Susan's savoury hashes for breakfast. A row of champagne bottles, empty to the last drop, stood on the sideboard: these had been Uncle Charles's contribution, and for once Uncle Caleb had bowed with good grace to his brother's wishes. The speeches had all been made. Greatly to Sissy's surprise, Papa had delivered the sprightliest of the lot. . . . Papa was as gay tonight as he had been morose the night before. True, he had eaten next to nothing; but his laugh rang out merrily again and again, and his compliments to the bride and groom had seemed as sincere as they were neatly turned.

Listening to them, Sissy had wondered whether she might have imagined the events of the last twenty-four hours. As she looked at Aaron beside her — a new Aaron, handsome and glowing with happiness — she asked herself how she could ever have considered an alternative to their union. (Had Papa *really* meant . . .? No, of course not — it must have been a bad dream!) The awful chill she had felt on the way to church was quite gone: now she was smiling and rosy, lapped in warm waves of calm reassurance. She was not even nervous about the ordeal ahead. Sissy had only the vaguest ideas about marriage. Mamma and the Aunts, to be sure, had lately been full of strange smiles, resigned looks, and dark hints concerning a husband's requirements, a wife's obligations; but they were all equally vague; and Sissy could not suppose that *Aaron* would want her to do anything she'd not be glad to do. . . .

It was Mamma, actually, who appeared nervous. Ever since they had quitted the supper-room she'd been glancing obliquely at the clock on the parlour mantel: was it to be marvelled at that her restlessness at length communicated itself to her guests? . . . It was high time in any case for some of them to be abed. Old Aunt Zilphah had been nodding unnoticed in her corner for the last quarter of an hour. The younger children were yawning and fractious as they were assembled by their parents and adjured to 'bid good night to Cousin Julia and thank her for a very pleasant evening.'

Sissy was just taking leave of her father- and mother-in-law, and promising Mrs. Miles — whose long, lean face was suffused with tender emotion — that she and Aaron would run over for a minute tomorrow before catching the train to Iowa, when she found her mother at her elbow.

'Child, have you seen Nancy anywhere?'

'Nancy? Why, no — where should she be?'

'I've not laid eyes on her since the bride's cake was cut,' said Mamma, with a worried frown. 'I sent her upstairs to fetch a handkerchief; it seems to me she didn't come back, but I was too busy to heed, for 'twas just then little Danny upset his plate of ice-cream all over Grandma Bascomb's best tablecloth. And after that we left the dining-room and people started to leave. . . . Wilfred's gone, too, I think.'

'Oh, Mamma, don't fret! I dare say they're out on the porch; it's a very warm night. Have you looked for them there?'

'No — but I will.'

Still frowning, Mamma slipped away from the crowd of departing guests. When she returned, several minutes later, the parlour had been emptied of all save the immediate family — that is, Aaron, the Triggs, and the Uncles and Aunts.

'Have you found her?' asked Sissy.

'I have not! She's not on the premises — that I could swear to — and neither is Wilfred.'

'Are you looking for Nancy?' Aunt Bertha rustled up in her prune-brown taffeta-and-lace to join the group round the fireplace. 'I'm almost sure I saw her with her cousin Wilfred in the garden, just a few minutes ago. Poor young creatures! I suppose all this must have been most upsetting to them.'

'Well, she's not in the garden now,' said Mamma. 'Oh, dear, I can't think *where* . . .'

'My dear Julia, I beg you not to be alarmed,' Uncle Charles interposed soothingly. 'Doubtless young Will has taken his lady-love for a drive: wasn't that his phaeton outside the door as we came back from church? I'm positive 'twas his grey pony tied to the hitching-post. Youth will be careless, you know . . .'

'Yes, Charles — but at this time of night — it's mad! Besides, Nancy knows very well I've forbidden her —'

'Ah, I'm afraid there's a great want of discipline here!' Uncle Caleb wagged his head, mournfully smug. 'If Nancy had been *my* daughter, after the first disobedience she'd have been whipped soundly and put to bed for a week. Julia's been lax — now she must face the consequences.'

'Caleb, you don't really think anything's wrong, do you?' cried Aunt Jane, turning pale.

'What *could* be wrong —' Uncle Sal was beginning impatiently, when Aunt Betsy, the one Bascomb not in the room, stalked in from the hall with an air of barely suppressed triumph.

'Nancy,' said Aunt Betsy, 'has disappeared!'

'Sister Betsy, we know it.' Uncle Charles was still smiling and imperturbable. 'But I can't suppose she's gone very far, or that she won't be back in a very few minutes.'

'In my opinion,' Aunt Betsy continued, 'she's never coming back at all. Her clothes have disappeared, too. The cupboard upstairs in the Red Room is perfectly bare, except for Loulie's things. Now what do you make of *that?*'

Mamma wailed aloud in distress; then all The Family began talking at once, as they usually did in a crisis — exclaiming, explaining, telling one another over and over (a), that they'd always known something would happen to Nancy, or (b), that they couldn't imagine anything *had.* The hubbub persisted for several minutes, while Aaron stared, Papa stroked his moustache, and Aunt Sophie, in one of the Shaker rocking-chairs that creaked alarmingly under her weight, looked inscrutable as she fanned herself slowly with a sandalwood fan. . . . What stopped it, at least temporarily, was a squeal from Loulie that succeeded at last in piercing the din. She followed this squeal with another, and then clapped one hand to her mouth in a gesture of unstudied dismay.

'Land's sake, what's got into the child?' exclaimed Aunt Jane. 'Is she having a fit?'

'Too much wedding-cake, I make no doubt,' crushingly commented Aunt Betsy, who was annoyed at being interrupted in the midst of her flow of eloquence. 'She's allowed to indulge her gluttonous instincts entirely too often, it seems to me. We can hardly suppose that *Loulie* has particulars to impart concerning her sister's whereabouts.'

Sissy felt that, for once, Aunt Betsy was probably right. Loulie, however, having captured the centre of the stage, seemed in no haste to relinquish it. She went on shrieking in a gradual decrescendo as her breath declined, but desisted only when her mother told her sharply she'd be smacked if she didn't. By this time she had contrived to produce from the pocket of her blue-and-yellow silk dress a much-crumpled scrap of paper.

'Nancy gave it me,' explained Loulie, in a loud, expressionless voice. 'She gave it me this evening while we were dressing, and bade me give it to Mamma after the wedding was over and all the folks were gone. She said to be *sure* to keep it hidden till then. . . . If I did what she told me, I was to have all the pennies in her savings-bank to buy pickled limes. . . .'

Mamma snatched the paper, unfolded it, read the first line, and then collapsed, moaning.

'*My dear Mamma: By the time you receive this, Wilfred and I will be married . . .*'

The tumult burst forth afresh: 'Oh, my dear! . . . Oh, I hadn't the *least* idea! . . . Married, for pity's sake! . . . Well, all I can say is, I'd never've believed 'em capable . . . The wicked, wicked girl! . . . Good God in Heaven, Julia, the chit can't do that to *us!* I'll comb every hotel in town, every railway station . . . Just the same, I can't help feeling there must be *some mistake* . . .' (This, of course, was Aunt Bertha, slightly on the defensive, since Wilfred was *her* cousin.)

The hot little parlour fairly hummed with irascible voices. Sissy, bewildered, crept into a corner with Aaron and gave him her hand for comfort. She was as much amazed as anyone else, though she could not see what good it did to get angry. . . . She glanced from one flushed, contorted Bascomb countenance to another, wondering how best she might calm them; then at Loulie, half pleased, half frightened at the unexampled effect of her news; from her to Aunt Sophie, whose face was darkening ominously as she fanned herself faster and faster; finally at Papa. . . . It was on Papa that her eyes rested longest. He appeared to be surveying the scene with something less than his usual detachment; actually he was laughing a little, as if the spectacle of The Family's confusion rather amused him. As she noticed this a horrible suspicion jumped into Sissy's mind: was Papa perhaps responsible for the disaster? If he had been willing to help one daughter elope, why not another as well? It seemed only too likely. . . . Sissy shuddered at the thought, trying to guess how long it would be before it occurred to the Uncles and Aunts.

More than once he showed signs of being on the point of speech; and Sissy did not know whether she wanted to hear him, or if what he was about to say might be so awful that silence were best.

But it was not Papa who prevailed at last. . . . Aunt Sophie, who for some time had been betraying symptoms of heavy displeasure, rose to her feet: her huge yet somehow shapely figure, swathed in tropical reds and purples, was so impressive in itself that she did not need to open her mouth to command general attention. All The Family stopped talking at once — even Uncle Caleb, the most vocal of the lot, ceased his bellowings of 'The Bascombs have been disgraced! No Bascomb ever before . . .,' etcetera, in order to gaze with startled surprise at his sister-in-law.

'Bascomb!' cried Aunt Sophie. *'Bascomb!* I am sick to death of the sound of the word. What else have I heard for the last week? 'Tis Bascomb here and Bascomb there: is it such a wonderful thing, then, to be a Bascomb?'

More terrible even than her words was her voice; once so liquid and lazy, it had risen to a kind of snarling scream; it sounded foreign, too, but in a manner Sissy had never experienced — and it was as revealingly common as the New Orleans gutter from which doubtless she'd sprung. . . . 'My faith! Let me never — but *never!* — be forced to look on your faces again! That is all I ask. Ah, how I envy the little Nancy! *She* at least has been clever enough to get where she need be bothered no more. What an insupportable family! One thing I must say before I go: I wish that the Indians had massacred the lot of you — you, and you, and you, and your fathers and mothers and grandfathers and grandmothers, too! *Nom de Dieu!* If only that *sacré* baby you're always talking about *had* cried . . .! Bah! I tell you, bah! Come, Salathiel!'

Crushing the sandalwood fan she was carrying till the sticks snapped in two, she flung the fragments into the fireplace and heaved herself across the room. Her husband, with a shamefaced air — at least, Aunt Betsy said afterwards it had been shamefaced — followed her. The

294

door opened, then shut — and that was the end of Uncle Sal and Aunt Sophie.

There was a pause — not that The Family had no more to say, but merely because Aunt Sophie's revolt had been so sudden and violent that no one knew quite how to take it. Papa, who was smoking, walked up to the fireplace and flicked the ashes from his cigar into the grate. (Mamma never liked to have them left about the room.) Then he shrugged his shoulders and remarked, with the same dry chuckle Sissy had heard him give in the brougham: 'So Sister Sophie's veneer has cracked at last! I've been wondering how long it would take for that to happen. Well, upon my word, I don't know as I'd have said it myself, but it seems to me Mrs. Salathiel has put the situation in the traditional nutshell.'

There was another pause, more sinister than the first: then, with one accord, the Bascombs turned upon Papa. Here at last was a scapegoat on whom to unleash their full fury. Nancy had unaccountably slipped through their fingers; Aunt Sophie was too belated and, obviously, too impermanent an addition to The Family to be taken quite seriously (though what she had done was of course unforgivable and would be, so to speak, simply filed away for future reference). But Brother Trigg was at hand; as the runaway's father the fellow should for once be made to explain himself. Why, damme, sir, 'twas more than likely he had abetted this disgraceful elopement, if indeed he hadn't engineered the whole business himself! . . . Uncle Caleb was sputtering with rage. Uncle Charles kept shouting that Jonathan had better make a clean breast of the matter before it was too late — that is, if he knew what was good for him. Aunt Jane dissolved into tears, murmuring something incoherent about 'a sad want of principle.' Aunt Bertha wished it distinctly understood that *she* had no part in her brother-in-law's nefarious schemes. Aunt Betsy, who'd turned a deep crimson to match her gown, declared with vigour that the thing to do was to send for the police at once — *they'd* make Brother Trigg tell what he knew! . . . 'We've been patient too long, for Julia's sake!' cried Aunt Betsy passionately. 'But even Julia must see now what kind of a man she married.'

Meanwhile, the object of all this abuse stood still in front of the fire, facing the circle of his accusers. He had thrown away his cigar;

his pose, his head thrown back, arms folded, legs wide apart, made Sissy remember the day of his return, when for the first time he'd been called to account by The Family. He did not seem to be particularly upset; he did not even look at the Aunts and the Uncles; his eyes sought Mamma on the sofa, sitting silent and tear-stained, the picture of woe between her two brothers. (This, also, was as it had been, that Sunday in June.) Neither did he appear to be in a particular hurry to attempt a defence. Perhaps from long experience he realized that it was wiser to hold his tongue till the storm had spent itself naturally. His slight smile — of the mirthless, mechanical variety so often his favourite device — remained fixed on his features. Patiently he waited until the noise began to abate. Only then did he lift one hand and start forward a step or two.

'Now, then,' said Papa — his quiet, precise tones a sharp contrast to the preceding uproar — 'if you've quite finished, my good people, may I be permitted to say a few words?'

That, of course, started the Bascombs off once more. They *weren't* his good people . . . was ever such impudence? . . . how dared he imply he'd not have every chance to clear himself? . . .

Papa waited again, smiling more broadly now. Then he said: 'Perhaps, dear brothers and sisters, you have forgotten, in the heat of the moment, in your very natural excitement over this sudden disclosure, that it's really none of your business. You may be sufficiently interested — indeed, I know that you are — to make all manner of suggestions. I welcome them all; I take it very kind of you, for I'm sure you mean them kindly; but the final decision must, of course, rest with Julia and me. We are Nancy's parents. I think you tend to overlook the fact that I'm the child's father, her legal guardian — though Lord knows there've been times in the past when I've seemed to overlook it myself!

'First of all, let's make this clear: I have nothing to do with Nancy's and Wilfred's elopement — nothing whatever — d'ye understand? I'm quite as much surprised by the news as any of you. In a way I don't blame you for thinking I might be responsible. I confess I did entertain hopes for another of my children . . . I dare say you may have suspected . . . but why speak of them now? Sissy has made her own choice, I doubt not a wise one; I wish her very happy in her new life.

'Our present business is with Nancy alone. Like the rest of you, I

296

have had only a few minutes to reconcile myself to the thought that the little girl is also a bride. Like you, I was shocked at first by the very idea; but the more closely I examine it, the more easily do I find myself disposed to accept what's inevitable. We speak of Nancy, we are accustomed to think of her, as a child; but she's no child — she's a woman grown — and she's demonstrated plainly that she's a woman who knows her own mind. Is sixteen so young, after all? My mother was married at fifteen, and at Nancy's age was a mother herself. If I'm not mistaken, your parents, also, were joined when Mother Bascomb was still some months short of her seventeenth birthday. And those two good women lived none the less happy and fruitful lives.... True, Nancy will miss a year or so's schooling — but what's a woman's schooling amount to? No offence to the sex, but their most important instruction is not to be learned in a young ladies' seminary.

'You *can*, I suppose, if you care to, make an attempt to find the children, and drag them back if you find them. I dare say, even if it were too late and they were already married, the bond could be annulled, as the bride's under age. But what advantage think you to gain by that? . . . If you have taken the trouble to read Nancy's note to the end, you will see that their plans are to travel by railroad at once to New York, where they intend to throw themselves on the mercy of Wilfred's parents. Is not this the best that could be hoped for in the circumstances? Will not a telegram to Mr. and Mrs. Morgan at Gramercy Park be more to the point than frenzied last-minute efforts to set the young people's schemes at naught?

'Besides, if you can bring yourselves to look at the matter dispassionately, I feel you must come to the same conclusion as I have — that our Nancy has really done better for herself than we might have expected. Indeed, I am somewhat surprised that you need *me* to point this out — for Beau Morgan's always been more to your taste than mine. At worst, though, there's not much can be urged against him, beyond a certain hotheadedness and a frivolity natural to his years and station. Young Wilfred's well-born, good-looking, of suitable age, and exceedingly rich: can you deny these are solid advantages? Moreover, he's in some sense an ally already through his Cousin Bertha — is it not to shame her to repudiate the connection? Surely the Morgans, of all possible people, are the most sortable to your purpose! They are —

are they not? — a kind of Bascomb *in excelsis* — as rich as Charles, as pious as Caleb, as fashionable as the lot of you put together. I am certain, once they've sustained the first shock, that they'll make Wilfred's wife most heartily welcome.

'Now if, in spite of what I've said, Mrs. Trigg feels it her duty to intervene, I'll raise no objection. Let her reflect well and then act as her conscience dictates. (You will do so, my dear, will you not?) But as for the rest of you, I conjure, nay, I *command* you, as you value your lives, *to keep out and stay out!* Do you understand? By God! I hope you do, for I mean every word.

'I'm leaving you now, since there's nothing more for me to do here. I've intended for some time to tell you, but my plans were not definite till tonight. They depended a good deal on others: if Julia were willing to come with me — and I tell you frankly I've done my damnedest to persuade her — I should not be in so great a hurry. Or if Sissy had needed my help . . . but there's no use in mentioning that. My wife and children are happier without me; I see that plainly. I don't mean to settle in Chicago, and since I don't, the sooner I go the better — do you agree? I've *wanted* to settle, God knows. I've lingered on from week to week, hoping that somehow in spite of all . . . But I've failed and I know it — failed miserably. I can't get on with you Bascombs any better than you can get on with me. It's been so from the beginning, hasn't it? You despise the ideals I live for as cordially as I despise yours. Why not admit it? We can, you know, without hating one another.

'I've a cabin aboard the *Queen of the West*, sailing at midnight for Buffalo. I engaged it this morning when it seemed likely I'd not be needed much longer. Julia, my darling, I took leave of you last night, but it's not too late for you to change your mind. If you will come, the offer stands. I'll be at the Lake House till half an hour before sailing time; the ship leaves from the State Street dock. I can't promise you an easy life — I never could — only the wayfarer's crust and a heart full of devotion. But assuming you're still of your old way of thinking — brothers and sisters, you'll permit me, I hope, a moment alone with my wife?'

Papa held out his hand. Mamma, her eyes shining tragically blue through her tears, rose from the sofa and gave him hers: together they passed from the parlour into the hall, then through the front door to the dark porch outside. . . . Sissy held her breath. How romantic it would be if they never came back! — if they just walked off into the night and sailed away in the *Queen of the West!* . . . But in a very few minutes the door that had been shut opened once more; and if Mamma did not return, it was not because she had run away with Papa, but simply because she was crying so hard that she could not bear to face The Family. Holding her handkerchief to her eyes, she hurried up-stairs — poor Mamma! — and did not reappear.

Papa, however, came back directly to say good-bye. This took a long time. The imminence of his departure seemed to have revived dormant affections: Brother Trigg had never been so popular since the first day of his arrival from California. The Bascombs clustered about him, exclaiming, expostulating, entreating, lamenting. . . . Papa was very kind, but very, very firm. He kissed Sissy and Loulie tenderly; embraced Aaron as his son; shook hands politely with the Uncles and Aunts, asserting he hoped they'd continue to prosper, and, yes, of course he'd write — perhaps, if he succeeded in establishing himself in the East, it would soon be *his* turn to invite them all to visit. . . . Oh, he had plenty of money for the trip . . . Brother Charles mustn't think he would lack for anything . . . 'No, don't worry about me; there's no need. . . . Comfort poor Julia, that's all I ask. . . . Now God bless you, I must really be going. . . .'

At the door Sissy clung to her father for one last agonized kiss. (What an end this was to her wedding-day!) Her heart felt as if it were melting; she did not even try to wipe away the drops that rained down her cheeks. For she could not help knowing this parting was final: whatever befell him in future, they had seen the last of Papa.

The End

ABOUT NINE O'CLOCK on the evening of Wednesday the twenty-fourth of September the row of loungers in the reception hall of the Lake House were startled by the precipitate arrival of a young man. Hatless and breathless, he almost ran up the short flight of steps from the street; swept the prospect with a piercing glance; then, obviously disappointed in his search, strode across to the desk, where an elderly clerk dozed behind ledgers. Disappointment awaited him there as well; the elderly clerk shook his head; whereupon the young man, with an impatient gesture, turned away and began furiously pacing the length of the room.

He was a very tall young man, with a mane of dark red hair and curious light green eyes, which blazed like a cat's in his pale, anxious face. His looks, however, were less remarkable than his actions: as time passed these betrayed a state of mind not far from frenzy. Tired of his pacing, he tried this chair and that, only to jump up again directly. At regular intervals he consulted his watch, and flung a tormented look at the obstinately empty entrance. . . . Finally, as if he could no longer bear the suspense unaided, he stamped into the dining-room and ordered a whiskey from the grizzled Negro, who, in default of customers, had been amusing himself killing flies, with immense deliberation, on the tall mirror behind the bar.

Tossing down the drink, the young man called for another; disposed of that, too; paid for them both; and returned to the hall to resume his travels.

The loungers, who sat smoking and spitting and swapping stories in the east window — purely from habit, as it was far too dark for a view of the lake — began to be irritated by the stranger's behaviour. What was he doing here, anyhow? The dinner hour was long past; he could not have come from a train, for he had no luggage. It had been years since anything of the sort had occurred at the Lake House. That was one of the main reasons they had made it their meeting-ground: a man could relax in such soothing surroundings, safe from the hustle-bustle of those big showy places on the other side of the river. Life had long ago passed the Lake House by, and its patrons were content to have it so. They were resentful at being reminded that there was a world outside these humdrum walls where appointments were kept, business transacted, fortunes made and lost, hearts gladdened or grieved by a word quickly spoken. . . . But even their resentment was a sluggish emotion; they soon forgot the red-headed, wild-eyed young man so completely that few of them troubled to notice when his feverish vigil came to an end.

The door to the street opened abruptly to admit another man — as short as the first one was tall, as dark as he was pale, as mature as he was unformed, as carefully and expensively dressed as the youth was negligent in his appearance.

'Good Lord, sir!' cried Ted Amberley. 'I thought you were never coming! I waited at the station as long as I could, till there weren't any more trains and they shut the place up for the night. Then I came here to look for you — I didn't know what else to do. I — I suppose by this time she's — married?'

'Damned if she's not!' said Jonathan Trigg. 'I'm sorry, my boy — I did my best for you — but my best wasn't good enough: the cards were stacked against us from the beginning.'

Ted's face, which had flamed suddenly on receipt of the news, now became paler than before.

'I hadn't much hope, sir, myself. What had I to offer compared to Miles? And it was really too late, you know; I suppose Rhoda felt she couldn't go back on her word. It was a mad idea of ours, surely . . .'

'Mad indeed,' Jonathan assented. 'But you'd have been perfectly satisfied, wouldn't you, if it had succeeded, as mad plans sometimes do? Not *all* the Triggs are averse from elopements. It's too bad, young Ted, you didn't set your cap for my *second* daughter: what will you say when I tell you that Sissy's and Aaron's has not been the only wedding in the family tonight? Nancy, my friend, has done unsupported what

301

Sissy, with all our urging, would not—Nancy's run off with Beau Morgan!'

Ted listened to Jonathan's story in utter amazement. He had had no suspicion of what was brewing, although stopping at Wilfred's rooms; his host had said never a word. To be sure, he had started to pack that morning after breakfast, but he'd explained he was leaving on a short holiday to visit his people. . . . 'How was I to guess he meant to take a wife with him? Lord, sir, it doesn't seem possible! That little minx Nancy! Why, I waltzed with her only last night—and she didn't breathe a syllable about her plans—she kept telling me how much she was going to miss Sissy while the bride and groom were away on their wedding journey! Confound it! Aren't women . . .?'

'Yes,' sighed Jonathan; 'I'm afraid they are.'

'Good old Wilfred! I wish him all the luck in the world. He don't need it, though; he's always got what he wanted. What wouldn't I give to stand in his shoes! Well, there's no use repining . . . If I'd known what had happened, of course I'd have realized what was keeping you. I'm surprised you were able to get here at all.'

'I had to,' said Jonathan, glancing at the round clock over the desk and comparing the reading with that on his watch. 'I leave by boat for Buffalo in less than an hour.'

Ted clutched his brow.

'Sissy married—Nancy run off with Will—you sailing for Buffalo —I guess I'm just not smart enough to understand it all.'

'I don't blame you,' said Jonathan sympathetically. 'I'm not sure I quite understand, myself. I tell you what let's do: there's half an hour yet before I need leave the hotel and I may as well get a bite to eat here. I had no stomach for Julia's baked meats, as you may imagine. Perhaps you'll join me, old fellow—that is, if you've not supped already?'

Ted shook his head vehemently.

'Food would choke me, sir, I'm afraid. But I'll gladly sit with you while you eat.'

Jonathan smiled.

'Oh, I shan't order a four-course dinner! There wouldn't be time to eat it, even if the kitchen could produce such a thing at this hour, which I very much doubt. My desires are restrained; they don't at the moment comprehend more than a glass of beer and a bit of cheese. That much, I hope, I'll be able to induce you to share with me. I think you'll find, once you've broken your fast, it will be easier to take a reasonable view of the business. Philosophy and an empty belly don't sort well together.'

In the vast deserted dining-room over their supper — served, with smouldering indignation, by the grizzled Negro, who must certainly have supposed his duties discharged for the night — the men grew confidential. Ted soon discovered that his companion was right: he *had* been terribly hungry, without knowing it; after he had eaten a little and drunk some beer he had no trouble entering imaginatively into the practical and sentimental difficulties of Jonathan Trigg. He understood everything, except the compelling reasons for the latter's departure.

'I hate to see you go, sir,' he said earnestly. 'Why should you leave the field to the Bascombs? It's like admitting defeat.'

'It *is* defeat,' said Jonathan. 'I wish with all my heart it weren't — but there's no good in trying to blind myself. The Bascombs have always beaten me; they always will beat people like me. I'd stick it out, no matter how hard it was, if there were some chance of a change — but there's not. In a week, a month, a year, ten years, they'd be the same and so should I. Don't think I'm not angry or rebellious! I am. God! What wouldn't I have given tonight, when I saw my poor Julia sitting as she's always sat, with Caleb on one side and Charles on the other — betwixt "Sacred and Profane Love," as it were — to snatch her up and carry her off where she'd never set eyes on the pair of 'em again! But what'd be the use? She can't live without them and she *can* live, very well, without me. That's what it comes down to in the end, doesn't it?'

He pushed back his plate, produced a cigar and lighted it as deliberately as if he had the whole evening before him.

'Where will you go, then?' asked Ted, still deeply concerned about his friend's future. 'How will you manage, now that you've cut your home ties for good?'

Jonathan calmly watched the smoke curl its way up towards the high-raftered ceiling as he made answer.

'I'll manage well enough. I rather think I'll go first to New York;

303

there's more doing there in circles that interest me than anywhere else in America. I've had a fancy for years to try my hand seriously at journalism, you know; that's what I should have done as a young man, if the way had been clear. When I was in California I met a number of newspaper men: I've a pocket full of addresses they gave me — friends of my friends who'll be able to furnish the information I need. And Jake Ralston has offered me letters, too. Then some day I may take ship for Europe — I've never been to Europe; I've always wanted to go. Oh, there are plenty of things to do before I'm old! . . . Maybe you'll think it strange of me to talk so, at eight and forty, with my hair greying fast; but I can't help feeling I've a deal of living to get through yet before I die.'

'But won't you be lonely?'

'Lonely? To be sure — but when have I ever been anything else? I'd have liked a son to go shares with, a companion to take on my travels. What could I do, though, with three little daughters?'

'Two of them married.'

'And two of them married,' agreed Jonathan, with a twitch of the muscles round his strongly marked mouth. 'Good Heavens! Now that's enough about *me*. Let's talk of *your* plans instead. They're shaping up well, I trust? You've got the letters of introduction I sent you?'

'Yes, indeed, sir — and I can't thank you enough for — '

'Pshaw! The favour's not worth mentioning. I think your aunt told me you'd engaged passage from New Orleans to Nicaragua, and so up the west coast by boat. I'm very glad you've decided to do it that way. The voyage round the Horn's altogether too long, and the overland route's still no Sunday School picnic, though they say it's nothing now to what it was in my day. When do you leave, boy?'

'I've my ticket for New Year's Day. I'd have liked to go sooner, especially now that — well, you know what I mean . . . But I don't see how it's to be done. I'm afraid Aunt Zeph'll be hard enough pressed, as it is, to let me have the money by Christmas. I hate like the devil to touch it, even though it is partly mine.'

'I know . . . I know . . . I'd feel the same. Perhaps there's something can be done about that. I've intended to say this before, but I've not had a chance: those three thousand dollars I planned to give Sissy for her wedding present — 'twas as much for you as for her I meant it — ;

and now she won't need it at all; as Aaron's wife she'll have more of a fortune than any young woman should spend. So the money's still yours, Ted, every penny. With that much in your pocket you ought to be able —'

'Sir, you're too good, but I can't take it. I've no right. Why should ,you stake me to my trip? Why should you give me what you've made yourself? — what you realized by the sale of your very own business?'

Jonathan laughed.

'Nonsense, boy! The money's none of mine. You've a far better claim to it than I. That tale of the sale of the bookshop was invented, quite simply, for Sissy's benefit. I thought it would look better so; that she'd have less hesitation in accepting so much than if I told her the truth.'

'But what *is* the truth?' cried Ted, in bewilderment. 'I still don't see —'

'The truth,' said Jonathan, speaking dryly and rapidly as he beckoned the barman to bring him his bill, 'is that I haven't yet sold my business. I mean to sell it; I shall never return to California; I have written my partners to that effect. The letter was posted on the first day of September. . . . Sissy knows when it left, for I told her. I should not expect to find a profound knowledge of the geography of the North American continent in a graduate of the Utica Female Academy, but I must say a young man who's spent four years at Hamilton College ought to know how long it takes a letter to travel from Chicago to Sacramento. . . .

'Those three thousand dollars belong to your aunt, Zéphirine Amberley. They represent exactly one-third of the stake your Uncle Jim gave his life to secure. His widow has kept the sum apart and intact all these years, because she felt it should be mine — that it was the part I'd earned by helping her save the whole. Naturally, I don't approve of her attitude. It seems to me reckless, uncalled-for, foolishly quixotic. So I told her the first time she broached the subject; so I have continued to tell her ever since. Your aunt is a stubborn woman, Ted. (I need hardly point that out to you, need I?) She's been after me all summer to get me to change my mind. There's no argument so flimsy, no means so specious, she hasn't resorted to in her resolve to get the best of my scruples. (Remember the "Spiritual Rappers"?) But *I* can be stubborn, too. I'd never have come round to her way of thinking if I hadn't seen it might pave the way for your happiness with Sissy. . . . That can't be now; but the money can still be useful to you. Be reasonable, boy. Take it, if you like, as a gift from your uncle — *he* made it, anyhow. It's yours, with his blessing and mine. You *can't* refuse us. As a matter of fact, the bank draft's already in the post on its way to you. . . . Now, my lad, I hate to hurry, but the *Queen* sails at twelve, and though my packing's quite done, it's not always easy to find a cab late at night on this side of the river. Are you coming with me? Good! Then let's be off together.'

The *Queen of the West* lay in the river at the head of State Street, twinkling with lights, the one bright spot in the sullen September night. One of Uncle Charles's newest additions to his fleet, she was a huge paddle-wheeler with two smokestacks, a topheavy deckhouse, and, within, a wilderness of brass fittings (including several score strategically placed spittoons) and gloomily handsome black-walnut paneling. The dock below swarmed with prospective passengers, and friends who had come to see them off. There were Irish porters, sweating and cursing as they heaved an unending stream of boxes and trunks aboard; bearded men with top-hats and canes; bonneted women with bundles; plaintive children clinging to their mothers; casual Negroes enjoying the spectacle . . . all the usual sights and sounds of sailing time. As Ted and Jonathan trod the gangplank a puff of breeze brought them the fishy warm-weather smell of Lake Michigan.

It did not take the latter long to see his meagre luggage bestowed in his modest cabin well underneath the black-walnut level. It was fearfully close inside, and would be so till the ship had left port: the two men returned to the deck. . . . Up and down they paced, up and down, as silent now as they had been talkative before. It was queer: they had had so much to say to each other. . . .

After a little Ted muttered half to himself, it seemed: 'I wish you weren't going alone, Mr. Trigg! Shall I come with you? I can, you know, if you like. It wouldn't be hard to arrange. . . . I don't think the boat's full.'

Jonathan shook his head.

'Then why shouldn't you come with *me*? Good Lord, it'd be twice as much fun if you were along! Why need you go East at all? Or, if you must go, why not take ship from New York next month and plan to meet me in San Francisco? I don't see why it's not perfectly possible . . . '

But Jonathan still demurred.

'I'm through with the West. I don't know why . . . No, that's not true: I do know. It's a young man's land and I'm no longer young. Besides, I might want to write about it some day, and you can't write about the place where you are — it's in the mind's eye only that all becomes clear. I've sometimes thought I'd like to try to get my own story down on paper. I've no son to tell it for me . . . but perhaps my grandson will . . . or *his* son . . . Or if it's never told, why, that's no matter either.'

The *Queen* was getting up steam; the warning bell had begun to ring; black against black, smoke poured from her funnels up into the dingy sky.

Ted felt almost desperate.

'We'll keep in touch, anyway,' he urged, still trying to pierce the other's armour. (So much composure, such treasures of resignation, seemed almost inhuman.) 'You'll write to me, sir?'

'How can I — when you've no address? I'll have none myself for some time to come. But,' added Jonathan, as he saw Ted's face fall, 'there's no reason why we can't both write to your aunt, is there? Of course, I'll be anxious to hear how you fare; she must needs be our means of communication until we're both settled. If I'm not mistaken, she'll like that: we can always count on Zéphirine Amberley.'

'Yes,' said Ted, 'I guess that's true.'

Most of the visitors had left the ship as they approached the gang-plank once more. Jonathan laid his hand on Ted's shoulder. . . . 'Now, then, you'd better go . . .'

'Oh,' cried Ted, his eyelids suddenly stinging, 'I can't *bear* to leave you like this, Mr. Trigg! What have you left? . . . No money, no job, no wife, no children . . . not *anything*, really . . .'

Jonathan smiled, very gravely.

'I've one thing no one can take, Ted.'

'Your freedom, you mean? Of course; I'd forgotten. Still after all —'

'No; I didn't mean freedom — though that's been mine, too, ever

307

since I left home with the gold-miners. But there's something more important — something I've never had before — something without which nothing else matters.'

'And that is — ?' began Ted, partly understanding.

Jonathan smiled again, this time more cheerfully.

'Peace of mind, son,' he said.

The young man and the middle-aged one clasped hands. Then Ted strode off, not daring to look over his shoulder. The gangplank was lowered; the whistle blew an overpowering blast; slowly and clumsily the *Queen of the West* pushed off from shore into the murky main stream of the river.

Ted stood on the dock, his eyelids stinging worse than ever, waving his hand as long as the ship remained within view. Even after he had lost sight of the straight little figure in the dark coat by the railing, he knew that Jonathan was still there, gazing back towards the lights of the city; gazing with deep affection, with aching regret, but also with the serenity of spirit that came from the conviction that all had happened as no doubt it was meant to happen from the beginning.

When he could no longer distinguish anything moving against the black curtain of the sky, Ted turned to go.

THE END